TWISTED TREE

BOOKS BY KENT MEYERS

The Work of Wolves

The Witness of Combines

The River Warren

Light in the Crossing: Stories

Twisted Tree

Twisted Tree

◆

Kent Meyers

HOUGHTON MIFFLIN HARCOURT

BOSTON / NEW YORK

2009

www.hmhbooks.com

Library of Congress Cataloging-in-Publication Data
Meyers, Kent.
Twisted tree / Kent Meyers.
p. cm.
ISBN 978-0-15-101389-0
1. Missing persons — Fiction. 2. Loss (Psychology) — Fiction.
3. City and town life — South Dakota — Fiction. 4. South Dakota —
Fiction. 5. Psychological fiction. I. Title.
PS3563.E93T85 2009
813'.54 — dc22   2009013288

Book design by Brian Moore

Printed in the United States of America

DOC 10 9 8 7 6 5 4 3 2 1

Portions of this book have appeared, in different forms, in *Quarterly West,* the *South
Dakota Review,* the *Georgia Review,* the *Southern Review,* and on StoryQuarterly.com.

Lines from W. B. Yeats reprinted with the permission of Scribner, a Division
of Simon & Schuster, Inc., from *The Collected Works of W. B. Yeats, Volume I: The
Poems,* Revised, edited by Richard J. Finneran. Copyright © 1933 by The Macmillan
Company. Copyright renewed © 1961 by Bertha Georgie Yeats. All rights reserved.

To Zindie *and* Derek *and* Lauren *and* Jordan

A lonely ghost the ghost is
That to God shall come.

—W. B. YEATS

TWISTED TREE

Joseph Valen arrived in the area that would become Wright County in the 1880's, though the exact date is unknown to this historian. He is generally accepted as being the first white settler, other than traders or soldiers, to claim land in the county and build a house on it. While others streamed to the Black Hills for gold, Joseph Valen saw his future in the land. It is to him, and men and women like him, that we owe our present lifestyle.

—BEATRICE CONWAY, *A Wright County History*
(Lone Tree, SD: Brokenwing Press, 1999), 38.

"We believe it's the same man. Both victims were female, extremely thin. And the broken bones. We're checking missing persons files. We think there may be others."

—CAPTAIN XAVIER HERNANDEZ,
Spokane Police Department, "Is There an I-90 Killer?"
Spokane Plain Dealer, August 3, 2003, A2.

Chosen

THE FASTER HE DRIVES, the thinner the freeway's painted lines become. He thinks, *If I went fast enough I could reduce them to threads.* In science fiction movies, he loves that moment before warp when even the stars thin to streaks and disappear. Insects had swarmed around him, obese with light, when he filled the Continental with gas above the Missouri River at Chamberlain. Now, as he accelerates down the ramp, they streak like meteors out of the night and fatten against his windshield. He floors the accelerator, the car downshifts, he feels his weight pushed back against the seat. But when the speedometer reaches seventy-seven miles an hour, he pokes the cruise control and sinks into the anonymity of ordinary traffic, barely breaking the law.

His headlights dilute to a broth in the borrow pit, speeding through dry grass and brittle weeds. When he reaches the broad lake of the dammed river, they disappear into the emptiness. He imagines a man in a boat in the blackness seeing his headlights pass on the bridge: his hand in the water, a dark spread of ripples. Then his tires quit booming, he's off the bridge, passing Oacoma and the painted, oversize cement buffalo at Al's Oasis. A mosquito whines in his ear. He lets the sound rise in pitch, hears it stop, waits for the piercing of his earlobe. Then, knowing the insect is trapped by its gorging, he lifts his hand and without hurry crushes it. He holds his palm near the dashboard: the smear of blood blackened by the green light, the crooked, hairlike legs and skewed, transparent wings. He fumbles in his back pocket for a Kleenex, daintily wipes his palm, and thinks of his Rapid City Ana.

He finds his Anas everywhere (their name a sigh, wind in a leafless tree), but his Missoula Ana was the best, and ever since he's dreamed of them in bookstores — their dark eyes gazing out of skulls under stringy hair, their polite, shy offers of help, and colored titles on thin spines flickering as he follows them, the barest elegance of light. It reminded him (when he followed his Missoula Ana) of the smears of color on his fingertips when as a child he caught butterflies, such patient, almost breathless stalking, all of summer suspended waiting for his finger and thumb to close and clasp, and then the faraway, membranous struggle, the feeble legs disjointed in the air. When he rolled his thumb and finger together the tissue wings turned to colored dust. He dropped the crippled things, watched their stick legs pump mechanically as they crawled away. Up and down the legs went stupidly over the grass, dragging the shreds of wings. They were very small. He rubbed the dust stains on his fingers off onto his pants, then wiped his pants with his palms and his palms on the grass until he didn't know whether the stain was gone or had permeated everything.

The Missoula Ana's fingers moved in her brittle hair as she turned to him with a book in her hand like an offering. He began the small talk, he has to draw them out, they are so focused on their devastating god. But he knows so much about them — it might be roses, origami, running, in Missoula it was cuckoo clocks, their delicate knocking and exquisite gears, their little ticks so brief they have no beginning and no end. He spoke of these things to the Missoula Ana and held the book, she enthralled by his interest in her interest, thinking it chance, and all of it behind shelves where no one watched, with the smell of ink and paper and coffee.

It was the best, but he won't repeat a bookstore. He refuses to be controlled, even by himself. He won't make things that predictable. There is no shortage of Anas. He will find them waitressing, even, transparent as the steam off the plates they carry. He imagines their fragile arms breaking under the weight of ceramic, carrots, mashed potatoes. He likes to stop them—*Excuse me, Miss*—and as they turn to him lift a forkful of potatoes to his mouth and pretend he can't talk, holding them mesmerized, with his fork describing little circles in the air. They watch him chew and swallow. They feel superior, proud, removed. But he knows them: birds who will come to his hand cocking their shy heads, tripping over their frail legs.

When he reaches Rapid City, he pays cash for a motel. The next morning he visits a pawnshop. Outside on the sidewalk, he touches the door, bows his head, breathes deeply, then pulls it open. The proprietor, leaning over a glassed-in counter under which hundreds of rings glitter, stares at him. He tells him he's a collector of western memorabilia, he's looking for anything to do with ranches or rodeo. The proprietor grunts. People don't bring in old branding irons, he says. You want to see that kind of thing, drive out to Wall Drug.

Rodeo, he repeats. How about rodeo stuff?

The proprietor spreads his hands in a gesture of helplessness. But he can see it: the man remembers. Has he sold it already? No—it's here, he doesn't want to sell. But why would he care? For a moment the world wobbles. Then he sees the proprietor's eyes cut to the wall.

I'll take a look around, he says.

And sure enough, he finds it concealed behind a couple of dusty golf bags, hanging on a low pegboard hook. He holds it up: a gaudy belt buckle with the words FIRST PLACE, BARRELS engraved in a pretense of silver. He traces the words with his fingers, then takes the buckle to the counter.

It's perfect, he says. Just what I'm looking for. He pays the asking price, then requests a receipt, to rub in the victory of finding it against the proprietor's will. Before getting into his car, he opens his fingers and lets the wind blow the receipt away.

That afternoon he drives to the Rushmore Mall. In the store where he knows she works, he spots her, her hair cut short, her blouse as loosely hung from the slats of her shoulders as those, draped on wire hangers, that she stands among. From a distance he watches. It had been so hard to tease her out. He'd sensed her lurking, a virgin Ana, unadmitted, and tapped in questions.

When he first discovered the pro-Ana sites, he loved how they talked of protecting their Anas against the world. He heard Paul, Jeremiah, the Desert Fathers: the thorns of the flesh. He understood. He began to wander a wilderness between transcendence and shame, a prophet in a land of thistles and honey, where Ana spoke in the wind. Sacrifice as passion, saints risen up on denial. He understood. He understood it all: the more they controlled their flesh and sculpted their bodies, the more the irreducible bones emerged to shame them. Bones cannot be thinned or changed. Bones only become (he knows) more brittle: mandible, clavicle; radius, ulna; tibia, fibula; femur, humerus — liquid, chanting names for things so breakable. And, best of all, the scapulas rising under the skin, creating mounds of light, havens of shadow.

He moves through the racks of clothes, brushing the fabric, the hair on his arms erect with electricity, and as she retreats, swan-like, before him, he feels immense, swollen, towering, the flowing dresses banks of clouds. Then she recovers and steps toward him on thin ankles (he can see her tarsi shaped beneath her socks) and stops him in his tracks. He imagines the anvil bone in her foot, her bare weight over it. He becomes aware of his belt's indentation in his sweaty flesh.

Can I help you? she asks.

The first spoken words. A sacred moment. It devastates him. Amazes and charms. He doesn't answer, holding the words' shape, texture, intonation, pitch. He will hang them in his memory, preserve them there forever.

To this Ana he was Mary, though he's been Emily and Josephine and Edwina. The avatars shape themselves out of conversation, seeded and entwined in the Anas' individual needs, until they emerge fully formed, revealed. He loves them. They surprise him. They are the Anas' avatars as much as they are his. Edwina was elvish, otherworldly, an Ana alien and exotic, but Mary is calm and quiet, Mary has maintained her Ana for years, becoming wise and imperturbable, a guide to show the possible. He'd given Mary a few gray hairs. He'd given her some wrinkles. But kept her beautiful. Made her glow. He loves the manipulation, the freedom to present a face that isn't, and then harden it into truth — the great divide of Enter, the veil of Send, the judgment seat of Save. In residential areas he finds home networks unsecured, and he has programs that bounce messages to a dozen different nodes in random order. While he sits, fingers moving, in midnight calm behind the Continental's darkened glass, within the shadow of protective trees, he imagines the words pulsing through their electronic darkness, banging off the rails of the Internet before dropping into his screen, the softest, pocketed light before his eyes.

It took Mary four months to turn this Ana. She had a friend named Laura Morrison she wouldn't let go of. It was always, *But Laura says,* to everything Mary advocated. He had to keep ends in mind, project wisdom, stay poetic. He had to show the Ana what she didn't even know herself: awe at who she was, interior seas,

5

horizons beyond which *Which* is. *What* is. *Who*. Turn and turn: inward toward largeness, smaller and smaller toward infinity, the dark core lightening, growing. Through, through, through. And then the revelation, the turning inside out, the opening up: the *Is* of Ana, the *Am*.

What does Laura know of Ana? Mary wrote. *Oh, Hayley Jo, don't you see? You're becoming someone else through Ana. Someone new. Of course Laura's hurt. She doesn't understand. But you can't allow yourself to be held back, not by your body or your friends. You're going inward, to a place you feel already. Don't you? Don't you feel it already?*

He felt the words wrapping the Ana up like arms, moving over and through her. The boundaries of his own body dissolved, lost shape. He sent. Finally Laura was defeated. The Ana deleted all references to Laura on her profiles. Like blown flour. Gone. And when she confirmed by giving up the rodeo belt (*You have to,* Mary wrote. *Your old life has passed away*), that night he ate a good meal, toasted himself with a bottle of wine, told the waitress he was meeting an old friend the next day (he fingered the wineglass, looked at the waitress's bland, incurious face, imagined its change if he told her who he was), and put himself on I-90 again, the green-and-white signs for all those noplace, puffed-up towns rising out of the distance like something pulled on a conveyor belt, and falling behind him: Rochester, Albert Lea, Blue Earth, Jackson, Worthington, Windom, Luverne, Sioux Falls, Mitchell, Kimball, Chamberlain (of the meteoric insects), Presho, Vivian, Draper, Murdo, Frontier Village (with its skeletal silhouette of a leashed dinosaur, and the bony man who leads it), Okaton (abandoned, eaten away), Kadoka (somewhere beyond it Twisted Tree, his Ana's hometown, and Wounded Knee beyond that, where Hotchkiss barrels had turned, he's read about it, no place too small for greatness, the machine gun first used against civilians, the precursor of Ludlow, Jallianwalla Bagh, Izalco, Guernica, Babi Yar, No Gun Ri, My Lai, Tlatelolco, Tiananmen, all contained, all imag-

6

ined, at tiny Wounded Knee), and then Wall (another dinosaur), Wasta, New Underwood, Box Elder, Rapid City.

Yes.

He savors his own first spoken word to her, how his breath goes out to speak it, how it connects them, how her eyes shift slightly when it strikes her ear.

Yes, he repeats. I could use your help. My daughter's birthday is this week. She's about your age. Your height. And—

He raises his hands, getting the uncertainty right, the little bit of helplessness. He stares at the clothes surrounding him; he could be lost at sea.

What do young women wear these days? He sighs.

She almost smiles, and together they move into the racks, lifting dresses, conjecturing whether or not the nonexistent daughter who connects them would like certain styles. He mentions that he owns a small ranch near Newell (how useful the Net is: he speaks of dry streambeds there, particular hills), and then he mentions horses.

My daughter's been riding since she was this tall, he says. First thing I told her when she got on a horse was, *Watch the ears.* Horses'll telegraph their movements with their ears.

This is it: the rush, the flow, the sinking in. He could be a hundred people, a thousand. Sometimes he feels he's not even making it up. It's who he is. There is no bifurcation. It's like splitting yourself and not knowing which you is you. Amoeba—no: shape shifter, god. Tongues of flame, the *Metamorphoses.*

That's so *true,* the girl says.

She goes still. It's like in Missoula when he spoke of the interior workings of cuckoo clocks, how time ratchets woodenly within them, and the Missoula Ana was his. You can open their pasts like envelopes and unfold them like letters. A horse's ears: the smallest thing, telling her what she'd told Mary. She forgets the sundress she's been showing him. It's limp in front of her. He imagines buy-

7

ing it and, when everything is over, discarding it in some small-town park. He takes the dress from her, noticing how her fingers open to release it, her nails reflecting small half-moons of light like tired pearls. He feels its bare weight in his hands as it floats toward him, its hem delayed, until it clings around his knees.

Do you ride? he asks.

I used to.

You enjoy it?

She nods.

Why'd you stop?

Put it behind you, Mary had said. It's like stalking an animal, being right next to it, and it doesn't know you're there, or like playing poker and having an unbeatable hand, but no one knows. He can hardly bear the tension.

The bones of her shoulders move beneath her blouse.

I moved, she says. My bathroom's too small.

Huh?

To keep a horse in. Makes it hard to shower.

It's so unexpected, he laughs. But he's devastated, too, he never expected her to respond that way, and he thinks of that dopey *Huh?* and feels like he's losing control.

Well, he says, trying to regain it. Horses do need space. Awful thing, a horse penned up.

Yeah.

All that muscle. That flesh? Beautiful animals.

He wants to keep her teetering way down underneath. He moves on, letting the statement rest with her. He lifts the dress and says, I think this'll do. Can't ride in it, but hey.

Then, as he sees the dress's hem ripple, his conspiring mind sweeps him away. Later he will indulge disgust: *You fat fool, control yourself. When are you going to learn? You're so goddamn stupid.* But in this moment, with the dress filling his eyes, he thinks again of discarding it and forgets where he is, imagining it dew-drenched and

8

found by a man walking a dog, a Labrador, yes, shining in its blackness, man and dog standing over this dress which he's abandoned:
shining black dog, shining wet dress, shining grass, and the man so
pale with longing he's two-dimensional, imagining the girl whose
body filled this gauzy thing. He looks up, that man does, thinking
of the lover the girl removed the dress for, how they'd lain on this
grass in darkness, moon silvering her skin (shadows between the
ribs) and the grass imprinting her with vegetative, random lines.
Then other stories cascade (so many worlds contained) into the
man's imagined mind: a rape, or an innocuous falling out of a bag
as she hummingly rode a bicycle home from shopping. The man
shakes his head to cast away desire, and only the dog, sniffing the
dress, knows no body ever filled it. (His, his, his: man and dog who
don't exist and the girl who doubly doesn't, and what they know
and don't, all his.) The man walks on, disturbed, tugged zigzag,
arm extended, looking into the trees lining the park, now imagining himself a savior — finding the girl, offering his coat, covering
her: her gratitude. He glances back at the dress once more. The
dog sniffs an empty candy bar wrapper.

They are beautiful.

He barely catches what the Ana is saying, his eyes swim to find
her, the store swirls, waves of color coalesce into shapes. Is she
wistful? Philosophical? What? He's furious at the man with the
dog. The hypocrite! Pretending he wants to help that girl! He
fights for control, trying to recapture the conversation they'd been
having. He stares at the cowboy boots on his feet to keep the Ana
from seeing his face. Finally he remembers who he is and what
they were talking about.

When he looks back up, the Ana seems to have faded into the
racks of dresses, her face a mannequin's, still and dreaming. He
ticks off the possibilities of what she might be thinking, like he
used to do in grade school before a test. With each tick he feels his
control of things solidify: the ranch she left to come here and the

creek — Red Medicine — that borders it; her barrel racing; fishing with the neighbor boy; her father, the buffalo rancher. *My father's so into those buffalo,* she told Mary. *OK, fine. I mean, if that's his thing. But he hardly even thinks of anything else.* ☹ ☹ *Like he's going to save the world by raising buffalo? lol You bet!*

His mind contains so much.

Speaking of cooped up, he says, I've been driving all day. And this place — he nods roundly at the store — gives me claustrophobia.

Memorial Park's close. You could take a walk there, maybe.

Perfect — her suggesting it on her own. He looks at her quizzically, and she hurries on, as if she's paid to advertise the park's attractions: The Berlin Wall's there. Part of it. It's nice. The park I mean. The wall, it's just cement and stuff.

The Berlin Wall? he asks.

The words slip out. He can't stop them. He'd just got everything back together. And then, something he doesn't know. His stomach churns. He'd like just once to get it perfect.

But he corrects himself. Wait, he says. My wife and I were there a few years back. Didn't know that stuff was the Berlin Wall. Looked like a bunch of rubble. Figured it was art.

Brilliant. It's like riding a bicycle on top of a garden wall, charging ahead faster and more dangerously because it's safer than slowing down.

Well, she says, that's what it was.

Don't need to see that again, he says. You know, though, I wouldn't mind going back to Dinosaur Park. Took my daughter there, long time ago. Back when she was —

He pauses, reminiscent.

She loved those dinosaurs, he says.

The Ana brushes her forehead with a finger, tucks a strand of hair behind an ear, though it's cut too short to stay there and falls back along her temple. He prides himself on noticing. All the little signals.

We used to go up there, she says. Our neighbors had a boy my age. The triceratops was our favorite. We'd pretend we were riding it.

My daughter loved the triceratops. But you know what she really liked? This big tree up there. Big roots like fingers. She'd sit in them and pretend it was a great big hand holding her.

I sat in those roots, too!

She's told Mary about it. Too much coincidence should raise suspicion, but it doesn't work that way. People will insist on meaning—in falling stars, rolls of dice, any kind of randomness. It makes so much possible. She lets her arms drop to her sides: open, easy, waiting. He goes on.

Yeah? I guess kids are all the same. She was like a thistle seed. I'd look at her and think she could blow away. Had to keep myself from holding on to her.

And then it's not the daughter he's made up he's seeing, small and healthy and streaked with dirt, but this Ana, pre-Ana, a child held by tree roots, he's the one watching her, protecting her. Contempt, cool as lemonade and almost as delicious, bubbles in him, for the father who didn't watch as carefully as he would have.

Her face is as narrow as the light on the edge of a splinter, and almost as stressed. She's remembering herself, he knows it, a little girl clinging to a running, three-horned beast. There are names for winds, the Mistral, the Harmattan, the Haboob, the Chinook, the Barber, the Diablo, and the hand has opened and she's being blown about.

Now she's grown and gone, he says. And I can't even remember how to find the place.

It's wistful, sad, and she wants so much to help. A man could spread happiness just by going through the world asking directions. She becomes animated: Go two, no, three blocks. Anyway, it's called Skyline Drive. There are signs, with brontosauruses on them.

But he mixes left with right, then north with east, until he confuses even her, and she stops and looks around for someone else who might describe the route. He shakes his head and holds up his hands, his heart a falling leaf cut out of tin inside his chest.

It's OK, he says. I appreciate your help. But you've got work to do.

But she stays with him. It's happened: she needs him to find the tree, and his memory of his daughter.

It's not that hard, she says. Really. How about this — go back —

But he shakes his head, waves the sundress in surrender.

I'm sure it's easy as pie if you were raised here, he says.

I wasn't raised here.

No? Where'd you grow up?

Twisted Tree.

Twisted Tree? Really? I know a rancher from there. Name of Mattingly.

Richard Mattingly?

That's him. Met him at a stock show a few years ago. Good guy.

Wow. His son, Clay — he's the one — when we went to Dinosaur Park.

How easily coincidence adds up to normalcy. If he just doesn't push it now, if he just lets her arrive.

Crazy, he says. But you know, I better go. I'm taking all your time. Don't want to get you in trouble with your supervisor.

He knows how much she hates her supervisor, Reva is her name, and *Reva's the Wicked Witch, I swear she times you if you go to the bathroom. And the clothes. If you hang them up and they're not perfect, you'd think the world just ended.* ☹

I don't care what my supervisor thinks, she says.

The knot. The strands. Threads of her life he's coiled. He lets her tighten it, lets her pull the loops.

Still, I better go, he says. Just follow the brontosauruses, huh?

He waits, giving her time. It's easier when they think of it themselves.

You know what? she says. I'm off in fifteen minutes. I could just, you know, *show* you how to get there.

One way or another, he'll find a way. He's waited outside apartments in the dark. But it's so much more exciting when it's this, when everything he knows, even the time of day, matters. They're dancing. Approach and retreat, step forward, back. He's made her pleased with her own generosity, and he swings gently on it, they're moving together, even their breathing (he imagines) mirroring the other's.

That's kind of you, he says. But it's not necessary.

But I'd like to see it again. Now that I've thought of it.

He lifts the sundress, contemplative, doubtful, finally gives in. Fifteen minutes, huh? Well, why not? My wife wants me to pick up a few kitchen things. I suppose I could do that and meet you. Out that door? I'm driving a big blue Continental. I can bring you back here or drop you off wherever, after.

She hesitates. He picks it up so smoothly it's not even a missed beat.

Or you can drive yourself, and I can follow. I've got to come back this way, anyway, but —

He holds it all, balancing embarrassment and ease, chagrin and acceptance. Then silence, not turning away, letting the moment lie trembling between them.

I guess it doesn't matter.

She smiles an apology — that she'd thought to mistrust him.

You're sure? he says. Because either way —

He knows it will reassure her. She nods and smiles to say that everything is fine.

OK, then. I'll see you in a bit.

As soon as he's out of earshot, he releases a blast of sulfurous gas, an immense relief. He glances around, then turns down an aisle stacked high with men's jeans. He'd like to keep the sundress, have her wear it, then post a photo of it somewhere, part of the scatter of things that form the history and archaeology of all he is, if others could trace the connections. But it's too risky. Begone, begone. He won't be tempted. Reverently, he folds the sundress, then parts a stack of jeans and places the dress under them, tucking it in.

His car has turned into a furnace. He'd like to open the doors and stand outside while it cools down, but someone might remember him, so he gets in and shuts the door. Sweat pops from his pores. It gathers, runs, crawls around under his clothes, flylike, ticklike. He tries to distract himself by watching shoppers come and go, but it doesn't help. He could start the car and run the air conditioner, but instead he lets himself slide into disgust at his body, how it excretes and exudes, until he's in a haze of discomfort and rage, the stiff boots pinching his toes. When the girl appears in the door of the store, he doesn't move. She glances around, and he thinks she sees the Continental, but her gaze goes right past it.

He bangs the heel of his hand so hard against the steering wheel he bruises it. He slams his head against the backrest. Then he opens his door and stands. He doesn't call or wave, just waits for her to see him and sinks back inside and watches her slip between the parked cars, so thin she never even turns her hips.

His anger dissipates. He looks at himself in the rearview, fixes a strand of hair snaking onto his forehead, then reaches down to touch the knife tucked beside the seat. The Rochester Ana came out to say she'd changed her mind. He hates revealing himself before he's ready. It ruins the sense of the avatar awakening in him, to the real world. He had to press the knife against the Rochester Ana's neck. It was stupid, she could have screamed, but he was furious. Change her mind? After all he'd done for her?

The Rapid City Ana, still several cars away, meets his eyes

through the windshield and smiles tiredly. He releases his grip on the knife, overwhelmed by sorrow. Mayan priests lifting hearts on the tops of pyramids, Hawaiian priests lifting bodies over their crater, Catholic priests lifting cups of blood: it's always been the lonely work of blood and adoration, and Ana is no different.

His mother used to tell him he had to learn to sacrifice. He'd pretend to give up sweets during Lent but hide candy bars under his bed and smuggle the empty wrappers out inside his schoolbooks. He'd release them to the wind, then lick chocolate stains off the pages, leaving dull brown smudges. During Stations of the Cross, he'd feel his weight riding Christ's shoulders: a man stripped of flesh with a fat boy riding him. His was the sinful weight Christ bore up the hill, that crumpled His knees, drove Him to the dust. Still, he went on eating, smuggling, lying — triumphant and wracked with guilt.

Then one day he saw Karen Carpenter on TV. Ethereal, glowing, she didn't look strong enough to hold the microphone, yet when she began to sing, he felt weakened by her power. He stared at that skeletal body from which came the most mournful and resonant voice he'd ever heard, and his loins, biblically, stirred. He followed her every appearance after that, watched her fade, and he sensed some great thing happening, a public martyring, a thin and ascetic saint like those he was never able to imitate. When he came upon the pro-Ana websites he had his revelation. He was chosen, called. He saw what no one else could see: Ana as a force, a god, universal; televisions as stained-glass windows transmitting Ana's image, and women in supermarket checkout lines Her communicants shuffling past Her iconography on the covers of magazines. He knew Ana triumphant, militant, evangelical, in Her endless resurrections, which he saw everywhere, emaciated and lovely as Christ, taunting him with their superior female wills.

The girl opens the passenger door and slides into the car and puts her seat belt on. Such an endearing little act of faith and inconsistency, saving herself from randomness while killing herself more slowly. It arouses him.

Where to? he asks.

Go there. She lifts her finger into the light banging through the windshield: the translucent nail, the turgid knuckles. He takes the road curving around the mall, and she settles into the seat. At the stoplight she tells him to go left.

Now just keep going straight, she says.

But at the freeway entrance he swings the car onto the ramp, going east, the centrifugal force pushing her away from him, against the door. Her hand rises to the dash, he feels her eyes wide on him, he floors the accelerator to gain speed quickly.

No, she says, more confused than alarmed. You were supposed to stay on Haines.

Oh. I thought you meant — His larynx is a dry reed in the desert of his throat.

Take the next exit. LaCrosse.

He doesn't even slow for it.

They all react differently. The Bozeman Ana turned around in the seat to watch the road she wanted to be on recede behind her. The Spokane Ana hit him around the shoulders and head until he swerved and frightened her. The Missoula Ana — his lovely bookstore Ana — pled repetitively and sweetly, like the cuckoo clocks she loved, *Please*please, *Please*please. His Rapid City Ana looks down at her hands. That's all she does; she twists her fingers in her lap, doesn't protest, just twists her fingers and finally asks: Where are you taking me?

It excites him, her submission. Where you want to go, Hayley Jo, he says. Where you've always wanted to go.

Home?

It's so plaintive and innocent it pierces him.

Yes, he says. I'm taking you home.

A semitrailer passes, crowding the centerline. He grips the steering wheel, he hates the feeling of the slipstream pulling at the car, the feeling of a force he can't control. Then, at the edge of his vision, he sees her mouth open, her face turn to him.

How do you know my name? she asks, awestruck.

You know me, Hayjay.

Name and nickname both, and still she doesn't recognize him. They never do. His mother used to wrap her arms around him in church when he grew restless, as if she were merely holding him, then pinch him on his stomach where people couldn't see, and whisper in his ear to pay attention, God was right here, right now. He learned to stand still and pretend nothing was happening. When he got ready for bed he'd see the black marks spotting his soft, white flesh, like deformed, obverse stars, none of them constellated, forming no pattern at all.

But now he's so much wiser. His mother felt God's presence only because God was, after all, invisible. If God had actually appeared before his mother—a ball of light, a beggar—she wouldn't have recognized Him. Faith is stupid: God would lose believers if He showed Himself. Proof would ruin Him. The Anas are the same. They believe in Mary only when she's words, dots of glowing light. When she appears in the flesh, they don't believe her. And when they do believe—and they always, finally, do—she's no longer Mary, they won't let her be.

The trick and lie of faith: it's never joy and welcome when the Anas realize who he is, never happiness that here at last is their friend. They see his pudgy hands, the hair growing from his knuckles, his double chin and balding head, they smell his vinegar smell. And they turn away. He lets his anger swell.

We're good friends, he says. Don't you know?

The silence hangs in the car as Box Elder rushes past, a collection of trailer houses. When he first saw the name on the map he thought of bugs, and now he thinks it looks like a nest. A sound of thunder startles him, the car shakes, he panics, thinking lug nuts have loosened. Then he sees a shape filling the air — a B-1 bomber from the air force base passing over him. Involuntarily he steers away from it onto the shoulder, then recovers and cranes his neck, staring upward through the windshield. The plane appears again, in the right-hand window, and arcs away, an avenging angel out of Revelation. Then it's only a needle, a glint, then lost in some mission in the sky, and he finds the road again, and the girl beside him, her hands still in her lap. Her makeup is too thick, to hide the acne her starvation causes. He gazes tenderly at her. That human need to present a face to the world — it makes him want to take her in his arms. He loves her for her wish to be only herself, her perfect self, cut off from desire and need — a BuddhaAna, a ChristiAna — having a relationship with Ana and Ana only, to become independent, boundless, nirvanic, sculpted down to the mantric *I*, immortal, invisible (except for the bones), inaccessible, angelic (if it weren't for the bones), soaring.

The irreducible bones and the breath that on its own partakes of the world. One can slow the breath but can't stop it. Not even the Anas can do that. Except for the true martyrs, the gnostics, the Carpenters. The others, in spite of their faith and their superior airs, which cause them to avert their eyes from him, need a priest.

Don't you know who I am? he asks.

The girl is sitting almost demurely as the Continental hurtles over the plains that begin immediately past the air base. She shakes her head. Her dry-grass hair scrapes against her collar.

I've never met you, she says. She watches the ball of her thumb rub her knee. In a weak, little-girl voice she won't let become a plea, she asks: Are you really taking me home?

Yes. I'm taking you home.

You're going to kill me. Aren't you? You're the I-90 Killer.

His breath catches. None of them has ever said it like that. They've pled, screamed, cried, fought — but none has ever simply named it. All the time Mary spent talking to her, and still he had no idea she was capable of abandoning illusion like this. It's as if he's breathing blood when he answers, his tongue thick, his saliva paste.

I've come to help you. To give you what you want.

I don't want—

She can't finish. He's a little disappointed.

It's what Ana wants, he says, his voice hardening. You want what Ana wants.

Her hand rises to her mouth. Her eyes stare at him over her knuckles, wide as the eyes of plastic dolls that open, flicking, when you pick them up, that ingenious weight that closes the eyes when the doll lies down for its plastic sleep and opens them, such gravity, to its plastic waking, eyes perennially surprised like ever-budding flowers clicking open, clicking shut. When he was young he ripped the head off one of those dolls once. He was trying to hold it at an angle where the eyes would be half-open, he wanted to see that sleepy look, but the balance was too fine, the mere trembling of his hands enough to throw the eyes all the way open or shut. He tore the head off the doll and flung it at the wall, twirling, eyes opening and shutting, ceiling wall floor ceiling strobing until the head hit the Sheetrock with a *thwack*. She's staring at him with those eyes, her hand covering her mouth.

Hello, Hayley Jo, he says. He lets his voice rise into a high and tender female register. It's so good to finally meet you.

She shakes her head, her hand still lifted.

But Mary is—Mary is—

He knows what she's going to say: *Mary is a woman.*

Mary is my friend.

He's a spinning top batted by a cat. He gapes, paralyzed by the anticipated answer, now meaningless. A single word, and everything veers and skews. He wanted to hear her say it: *a woman.* It's ridiculous—*my friend*—as if friendship can't be faked. Why can't anything ever be the way he wants it? He wants to pound the dashboard, stomp his feet, and breathes deeply to gain control.

Ana is your strength, he drones. Your true self. You ran with Ana, miles and miles. Did Laura stay with you? She didn't. She couldn't keep up. If Laura wants you to end your relationship with Ana, it's because she's jealous, she's not your friend. Remember?

He's quoting Mary, the long, persistent arguments over Laura. He'd come away from the keyboard exhausted, as if emerging from an overdose of drugs. Dazed, enraged, hardly able to see, he'd go to a Dairy Queen and eat ice cream on a stick, peeling off the chocolate layer with his teeth, sucking the soft interior, conjuring Laura in his mind, inventing arguments. A snapping sound would rouse him, and he'd see that he'd broken the stick, a serrated piece in each of his hands. He'd peer at the other diners, hoping he hadn't been cursing aloud his Ana's pathetic loyalty and that little witch who inspired it.

Mary's words get through to her. He sees it in her eyes. He shifts in the seat.

And you finally dumped Laura, he goes on. For Ana.

He doesn't want to put her down — she is his Ana after all — but he swells a little. Is it too much to ask that she recognize his victory?

When she says nothing, he continues, a little sulky: You are Ana. Ana is you. You even sold your rodeo buckle for Ana.

He expects her to be awestruck with recognition. Instead she says: But your daughter.

He crumbles. The Continental drifts over the centerline. Her words are hammer blows shattering the world he's been creating, pulverizing Mary, and he feels himself exposed and writhing. How does she know? He raises his right elbow as if to fend her off.

Then he realizes what she means: the daughter he mentioned in the store, not *his* daughter, but the-man-he-made-up's daughter, the man he's already abandoned.

You dumb bitch! he cries.

He can't help himself and pounds the steering wheel, forgetting his hand is bruised, and then rubs it on his thigh to ease the hurt. Finally he's OK again. Everything's OK.

I'm sorry, he says. I don't want us to be fighting. I don't have a daughter. I made her up.

Saying it, he thinks maybe she'll be impressed, but she says: You were lying? About it all? The triceratops? The tree? You just *lied* about it all?

Later he will realize he should have laughed. But the accusation is so deep, so intended, that he recoils, pressing against the door.

I wasn't lying. I was pretending. It's OK to pretend.

She doesn't respond. He pulls himself erect, but her silence bothers him. Their relationship shouldn't be like this.

Just like a woman, Mary, huh? he says. Betrays you the first chance she gets.

He barks harshly. But she doesn't even smile.

Why? she asks.

He relaxes. They all ask that question. He stares at the faint teapot shape of the oil light, like a genie's lantern, barely visible under the dashboard's glass. Then he says:

Because you want it, Hayjay. Because you need my help.

I don't want —

He's patient. He says nothing.

You won't, she says.

Why do you think that?

He could show her the clippings in the trunk, the rodeo buckle. But that's for later.

We're *friends,* she says.

And I'm helping you. Like a friend should.

She shakes her head.

No, she says. No. You've got a *soul.*

Every time he thinks he has the conversation on track, she

comes up with something that derails him. He lifts his hand from the steering wheel, and for just a moment they're both convinced he's going to backhand her across the face. She shrinks against the door, so small she looks like she's folding into herself, like some magic origami bird that, just when it achieves its birdness, with one more fold will disappear entirely.

He gets control of his hand, forces it to grip the steering wheel.

Godgodgodgodgod, he chants. I knew a woman prayed all the time and never saw God. And then she died.

He snaps his fingers, but the effect isn't as dramatic as he wants, barely audible, absorbed by road noises and moving air. And because it isn't dramatic enough to snap the memory into cynical show, he remembers his mother in her coffin, how small she looked, swallowed by taffeta, a doll-like thing sinking away from him forever. If he holds on to the memory, he knows the face will sink further and further into the whiteness, smaller and smaller: a dot, a period, a point, a nothing.

Terrified, he shouts at the girl: If God wanted to save you, He'd zap the person starving you! But that'd be *you!* Don't you get it? Ana plays the God game better than God does.

It chases the memory away, leaves him blank and exhausted, but when he looks back at the road again, there's a highway patrol car parked in a turnout ahead. He almost commands her to duck down. But the patrolman might notice. No one even knows she's gone, there's nothing unusual about them, he growls at her not to wave or make a show, and they go by. Cops are so stupid. All the postings he's left on the Net, all the clues he's dropped, and they don't put it together. And here he is, the most wanted man on the freeway, and the idiot in that car only cares about his speed. And she—that was her chance to save herself, and she didn't take it. She just sat there. She obeyed.

They drop down the long hill to the Cheyenne River—thin,

slow water, the land crumpling into it, creased and broken. He drives, he doesn't know how far, sunk in gloom, then sees an exit. He takes it, alert again, checking for police and making sure all the doors are locked before running the stop sign at the end of the ramp and swaying onto the crossroad, looking at the girl triumphantly. But she doesn't seem to have even thought of jumping from the car, she's just staring into her lap, unimpressed. Sullen again, he checks his gas gauge. He'd filled up in Rapid City, and there's enough. He drives until he finds a gravel road, and as the car sways over it, he imagines piloting a boat. When he was young, he built model ships and wanted to sail around the world, wanted to see the ocean phosphoresce at night, and glowing fish rise out of it.

He forces himself back to reality and reaches across the Ana and opens the glove compartment. Candy bars are neatly stacked inside it. He takes one out and removes the wrapper, holding the steering wheel with his knees. He nods.

Help yourself, he says.

She shakes her head. Exactly! She clings to Ana. Her little, superior, condescending shake. Actions speak louder than words.

He crumples the candy wrapper, rolls down his window, throws it out. It disappears in the dust behind him. He rolls the window up.

Do you think I'm fat? he asks.

She won't turn to him. What do you mean? she asks.

It's not a hard question, Hayjay. Look at me. Do you think I'm fat?

That skeletal face looking at him, the bones so clear beneath the skin. He knows she's going to lie, he feels vulnerable and powerful, excited and debased. She grasps her bony elbows with her thin fingers and hugs herself. He reaches over to turn the air conditioner down.

No, she says in a timid voice.

I'm not fat? he asks again.

You're OK.

How about you, Hayley Jo? Are you fat?

When she doesn't answer, he nods.

You sure you don't want a candy bar? I got Mars. Snickers. Milky Ways?

She's turned away from him again. He sees the back of her head shake, her narrow shoulders hunched, the blades sharp under her blouse. He reaches over, shuts the glove compartment, returns both hands to the wheel.

So, he says. That's it, then.

They never deny Ana and take the food. He always gives them the chance — to be unfaithful. To save themselves. But they never do. They're more faithful than Peter ever was.

You remember when you used to fish? he asks. You and that boy, Clay?

She shivers, hugs herself tighter, refuses to acknowledge him. And only a few weeks ago she wanted to tell Mary everything.

You never said why you stopped. Why did you stop fishing, Hayjay?

The effect of the question startles him. It's as if she enters a new realm of silence, some reserve. She scrunches against the door, her head shaking. She's protecting something.

He grips the wheel, delighted. What has she hidden, even from Mary? What is he about to discover? What happened — between her and that boy? — that she hasn't ever told?

Why did you stop fishing, Hayjay?

Her hair is so short and thin he can see her scalp beneath it.

Hayjay? he says gently. You can tell me.

The road ahead and dust behind, and a single bird of some sort hanging in the air in the distance, and my God, what desolate land. Road and dust and miles, stones spitting up from the tires, he's probably putting nicks in the car's paint, the world just chips away and chips away.

He feels her going further and further into herself. If he presses too hard right now he may never bring her back. Nevertheless, he can't resist. He opens his mouth to tell her there's no reason they shouldn't talk, but she suddenly speaks:

Don't use my name.

You prefer Hayley Jo? he asks.

Don't call me anything.

He wants to chant *Hayjay, Hayley Jo, Hayjay, Hayley Jo* a dozen times. But he can't. Her command somehow somehow somehow tamps it down. He lapses finally into silence, the cloud of sullenness he's been fighting overwhelming him.

When he's a woman the Anas talk so freely, they trust him with their secrets, all their dreams and fears, even the littlest ones, the fragments and shards that, put together, make up the puzzle of their lives. On top of the televisions in the motel rooms where he stays, next to the framed pictures of Karen Carpenter and his mother, he arranges the framed collages for each Ana — photographs, and the obituaries that talk of how much they'll be missed, and news accounts that refer to the I-90 Killer and statements from the cops who claim they'll catch him. In the stories contained in those clippings he and the Anas will be together forever. It's something he's creating. A legacy. He sleeps with Karen and his mother and the Anas gazing at him, and when he wakes in the middle of the night, with the faint light of anonymous towns leaking through the windows, he sees them, without his glasses on, like watchful monuments.

He has all these worlds, and all of them so partial and so full. It's up to him to decide when a world is finished. He contains and holds them, and he has so many, it's a precious thing, a charge. This Ana's world isn't full yet, there is some thing she hasn't said, to Mary or to anyone. She'll tell him. He wants her to know he'll remember everything, he'll carry it inside him so it will never fade. He has in his mind the whole town of Twisted Tree with its streets and windows and eyes, and its people passing each other, bearing lives that no one else knows. Everyone has a life that no one else knows. He's just better at it, that's why he was chosen, a dozen tongues of flame on him alone. He'd like to ask her to draw a map for him, to help him remember, a memento mori from her hand. But she wouldn't do it. He doesn't need a map, of course. He has it all laid out. With the Internet he could go to Twisted Tree and find her house, it's on Red Medicine Creek Road, and the Mattinglys just south, and Shane Valen just south of there, and the Morrisons, Laura's parents, are a few miles north. He could identify the patterns, he's sure he could, he loves the thought of details clicking into place, turning into revelation as he locates their geography.

He has it all. All the little pieces. Except, he thinks, for one. He doesn't know what it is, but he felt it almost emerging that moment ago — a thing she hasn't told anyone. When she tells him, he'll make her life whole and faultless. She's so withdrawn, so curled up. Why can't they understand? It's not the living of their lives that matters but what he makes of them.

He gathers those lives and holds them, then he scatters them back out: little pieces on the Web, fragments that someone scrupulous and sensitive and smart enough could put together. Not just art, but lives, whole and eternal, unfading as the Web itself. Alexander Stoughton is doing something no one has ever done.

His mirrors are filled with dust. He'd be afraid to brake, if there were a truck barreling along inside that cloud, it would run right over them. In front of them, as the sun sets behind, darkness is rising. It will overtake them, and eventually he'll stop. But not just yet. He needs to enjoy the moment, that's what he needs to do, stay in the moment, they're together after all these months, this Ana and him and Mary, all three of them.

When he stops and the car goes quiet as a confessional and the red light of the evening shines through the dust cloud around them and they're completely alone together, she'll tell him more, the final things he needs, until he knows her life is complete: perhaps the name of her horse or the number of sequins on her blouse when she rode in the high lights of the rodeo, or the reason she stopped fishing, little things and littler, or maybe bigger, until he knows her better and more intimately than anyone ever has. Ana Glorious, rising.

She would have looked so perfect in that sundress — those big eyes in that taut and birdlike face. It's too bad he has to be so careful. But people don't like the truth. They like Ana glossy, full of light. Bones are the truth. Bones are as thin as it's possible to go. As final. The bony, stretched arms of Christ. The soldiers broke His bones. They counted them.

Running Errands

I'VE BEEN A CHECKER at Donaldson's Foods over ten years now. I talk with customers about the weather while passing groceries through the scanner: Cheerios or Toasted Os, Salems or Marlboros, Coke or Pepsi, fish or meat, margarine or butter. I can name the preferences of every family in Twisted Tree — who chooses vanilla over chocolate ice cream, who's daring enough for butter brickle. I can read resignation in the mac and cheese, desperation in the spices. When Lorraine Lipking first complained that she had to drive to Rapid City, to an oriental foods store there, to find star anise, I almost told her, *Well, Lorraine, there's an air base there. Those airmen marry Korean women. It makes sense. But you live in Twisted Tree.* But I looked up and saw her eyes, like damp brown stone, and kept my comments to myself. Rumors soon confirmed my premonition — Bill was having an affair with a woman he'd met at a golf tournament. Chinese cooking can't compete with that. Even in grade school Bill Lipking was too good for anyone but himself, so no one but Lorraine was much surprised. But you have to feel bad for her.

It should have been a routine checkout: Marge Germaine with her Oreos and chocolate chip ice cream, her SnoBalls for midnights when she can't sleep. Orville died a few years ago of a coronary I knew was coming, all that pork sausage and butter she bought while complaining constantly about him. Now she misses what she never had—wakes alone at night, sees herself in the dark light of the mirror, longs to be thinner, consoles herself with Hostess, and in the mornings, resolved, stirs NutraSweet into her coffee.

I was sweeping her second pack of Oreos through the scanner when she said: Well, Elise, I suppose you're going back to Central America now they've had elections.

My fingers twitched. The package crinkled audibly. The red scanning lights for a moment stayed wrapped around my hand. Then I moved the cookies through, and the scanner beeped its confirmation.

What are you talking about? I asked.

The last thing I wanted to do was bring up the past, especially with Marge. She'd made sure to offer me advice back then—stopped me on the church steps, drew me aside, simpering. I recalled too easily her false concern, her pursed lips, her pseudo-anxious look.

Elise? she had asked. What you're doing? Do you think it's wise?

I feel God is calling me, I told her.

God's call? Marge had laughed, raucous as a crow. People in their little after-church groups looked at us.

In Twisted Tree? Marge went on. Now *that's* long distance, Elise.

Now here she was again.

You sell the paper, she said. Don't you read it? Where you were's a democracy now. You could visit again. See the results of your work down there.

I beeped her SnoBalls through the lights.

Right, I said. I'll take the next plane out of Twisted Tree.

• • •

The second evening I was there I heard a soft, intermittent tap on the door of my adobe hut. I thought it was one of the big insects I'd seen, fluttering its wings against the wood. But when I opened the door, prepared to bat it away, a dark-skinned man stood there. He held his hat down near his side, and he said, You are Elise.

It was as if he were telling me my secret name. Then he said: Welcome, Elise. I am Roberto. Is there anything you need?

Need? I said. I thought —

I almost finished, *I came to give you what you need,* but his confidence stopped me.

I just got here, I said. I don't know what I need.

His smile was a string of pearls sagging behind a screen, suddenly tightened — that bright and astonishing.

Of course, he said. All is too new.

His English was so perfect it sounded like speech mixed in crystal jars and measured out in doses.

When you do know what you need, you must ask me. It is how I help.

I found it after my shift ended — two inches of print in the *Rapid City Journal.* I sat inside my car, in sun hot enough to set the paper ablaze, and thought: *No more squads of killer boys or machine-gunned villages.* Audrey Damish drifted past my windshield: granola, yogurt, tofu. With no husband or children, she can eat guided only by her own obsessions. Until she retired she taught high school science in Lone Tree and now is at loose ends, spending a lot of time tending her father's grave. The major event in her life may have been witnessing Hayley Jo Zimmerman's birth, and she never tells that story anymore. When she checks out she takes her glasses off and holds them to her open mouth, as if she's going to devour the lenses, some brittle hunger or magic act. But she merely moistens them with her breath, then wipes them clean, gazing about with an owly look before she returns them to her face. Her mother's at an assisted-care in Lone Tree. *She's still sharp,* Audrey tells me. *For ninety-two, she's still sharp.* That's the extent of our conversation. I'm tempted to sneak a candy bar into her bag someday when she has her glasses off, to see what might shake loose. She's not exactly a Shane Valen, who never even entered the store, but she's at the fringes, living almost beyond my reading. I fluttered my fingers at her through the windshield, but she ignored me, her eyes on something else.

I turned to the tiny headline again. I thought of the highway running south, out of the state and into Nebraska, across the Platte River down into Kansas, and then other roads, other states, into Mexico. Jonathan, my sixteen-year-old, had a baseball game that evening. By the time he reached the plate, I could be halfway through Nebraska. Balls punching white holes in the sky—holes I wouldn't see. Instead, the sound of tires, and all-night gas stations, and coffee, and whatever was beyond Kansas before me in the dawn.

The sound of crumpling brought me back. My fingers had devoured the page. My hand was stained with ink, as if the heat inside the car had melted news and flesh together. The whole world wax, the Easter candle melting, the Alpha and Omega. I recalled my mother's voice when I returned: *You've got to talk to someone. Whatever happened down there, talk to someone.*

Over and behind the abandoned bowling alley I could see the Catholic church steeple, freshly painted: volunteer work last summer, potato chips and bratwurst and baked beans on picnic tables set up in the shade, to which the men descended, to speak about wind shaking the ladders and how they couldn't look at moving clouds, the cross on top of the steeple sweeping vertiginously backwards. Under that steeple, I knew, Father Obermann waited inside the confessional, doing his duty whether anyone came or not.

No one knows he smokes. He never does in public. But occasionally, when he's been unable to get to Rapid for a while, he'll buy a carton of Lucky Strikes at the store, wandering around with them hidden under cereal boxes in his cart, until no one else is checking out. You'd think it was pornography. He'll make small jokes to let me know I'm part of the conspiracy, which I've always honored. He's such a devoted, pious man, and the vice so minor, I wonder why he bothers to hide it at all.

I drove to the church and parked. I squinted at its white façade, almost too bright to look at. I thought of the cool interior, which would not have changed in twenty years: the blond wood pews, the worn wood kneelers, the mournful wooden Christ.

While my classmates talked of boys and clothes, I admired St. Teresa of Avila and dreamed of acquiring the stigmata. My final year of high school I told my parents I was going to be a lay missioner. I'd already talked to the former priest, Father Caleb, saved my money, prepared. My mother was aghast, her face white and spare as snow drifting over rooftops. She turned her back, her spine showing through her dress like rosary beads of bone.

Don? she said. Will you say something?

My father sopped gravy from his plate with bread. A missionary? he finally said. Can't say I'm for it. But we been raising her Catholic, Erica. Never thought it'd haunt us.

So I went, neither blessed nor cursed, to teach English under the stern gaze of Sister Xavier, the mission's founder and director, in a tiny village I thought cut off from the world.

The first time I saw an army truck appear there, everyone in the village seemed connected by threads which the truck's grille grabbed, turning faces toward it. Men in olive green stood in the truck, cradling rifles as mothers cradle infants. Dust rose from the slowly turning tires, smearing drying clothes. I taught classes outdoors. I followed the children's gazes as the truck moved toward us. Then I shook myself, thinking it mere distraction.

Back to lessons, I said. Eyes on the board.

I swept the eraser over my chalked words. The board teetered on its wobbly stand. I reached for it as it fell away from me like a large, stiff wing. And there behind it was the truck, full of soldiers. And me with my arm out as if to beckon them.

They were boys in soldier uniforms, all staring at me. I felt as if I glowed there, an icon, unattainable as the saints in paintings: their passionate bodies, their eyes on God. The sun warmed my hair. I was probably the first white woman in that village whose body wasn't neutered by a habit and whose hair wasn't covered with a veil. I wasn't prepared for any of it—not the trucks or the boys' eyes or my body's reaction.

Roberto had become my confidant. He was a few years older, without Sister Xavier's seriousness. I asked him about the trucks but couldn't say what was troubling me: all those eyes seeing me and how it made me feel.

They come sometimes, Elise, Roberto said. They do not trouble the mission. It is not something to concern you.

But it is, I said. This is my life.

His dark face, shadowed under his hat, looked at the barren mountains. I felt I'd said something inappropriate. But he remained polite, restrained. If it hadn't been for his hat brim magnifying the movement, I wouldn't have known he shook his head.

He looked at me and said, very gently: This is *my* life, Elise.

I was hurt. I wanted him to know what I'd felt when all those young men stared at me. I wanted him to admit for me what I couldn't admit myself. We stood there awkwardly. He looked at the mountains again, the distant men gripping the earth with bare toes to keep from falling out of their steep fields as their hoes rose and fell. Then he met my eyes again.

The fighting has not reached us here, he said. So you—

He stopped. I thought he might say more. Instead, he turned his palm upward, swept it slowly in a circle, showing me the pale sky, the adobe village. A small green parrot flew past, swooping on pointed wings as if to say: *Even the birds fly differently here.*

Then Roberto turned his hand to himself, and with his index finger circled his dark face to frame it for me and then — such lovely, elegant gestures — he stretched his palm out to my face: my pale skin, my golden hair. He knew.

But what he said was: How could it be your life?

For years Sophie Lawrence has insisted on taking her invalid stepfather with her when she shops, even in the worst weather. She buys more salt than anyone I know, and great amounts of Lipton tea, and at least once a month suggests that we import a genuine Chinese brand. In winter she parks her stepfather's wheelchair next to the road salt and snow shovels near the doors. Every time someone enters, the poor man shivers. It seems an odd negligence for a woman this town considers a saint.

But people's business is their own. When Hayley Jo Zimmerman was about fifteen, she came in one day on an errand for her mother. She laid the groceries down the way a priest might lay a Host in a communicant's palm. One by one she placed her few things gingerly on the belt, then stepped away from them, a tiny half step within the confines of the aisle. She had an air of reverence and distance. I saw myself when I was her age — that sense of martyrdom and purity, of watching others' needs, convinced I needed nothing. I had the sense she was disclaiming the entire store — all its brands and choices, their profusion and anarchy, carving out who she was by negation and denial.

And I knew. She wasn't yet so thin she couldn't hide it. She was even beautiful in a crystalline, breakable way. But I knew. I thought to myself, *Girl, you've got a secret.* Before she quit barrel racing she'd been, not plump, but almost — a vital look, full of health. As I swept her groceries through the light, I saw she'd cut her hair. And her breath, even across the belt, even way back then, contained the stink of willful dying.

When I told her the total, she fumbled in her purse, then

34

dropped money on the belt as if discarding it. I picked up the wrinkled bills, stretched them across the edge of the cash drawer, laid them neatly inside, knocked the clip down. I held her change out until she raised her arm, then counted it slowly into her hand. Deliberately, I touched her palm. People sometimes wince when I do that, so I'm skillful at exchanging money without touch. But I wanted to go further with her, grasp her wrist, and speak to her.

But the moment I pressed the last coin against her skin she closed her fingers and snaked her hand away, leaving my arm hanging in the air. She hurried from the store, her running shoes squeaking on the tile, the plastic bag noisy against her knee.

An hour after Marge Germaine left, with her questions and her HoHos, Hayley Jo's mother, Kris, pushed her cart up to my belt. She used to cook and bake, buying nothing but fresh ingredients, but since her daughter's death her carts contain nothing but frozen pizzas and processed cheese and meats. She and Stanley used to love to tell of Hayley Jo's birth: they were on their way to the hospital in Lone Tree, but she wouldn't wait, so they stopped on the shoulder of the road and by God had a baby. Stanley joked that getting a new back seat for the car was cheaper than doctors' bills, and maybe they'd do it that way again. Kris would swat him, and they were both completely proud.

As I closed my shift, counting the till, I kept seeing Kris lifting her paltry groceries from the cart and dropping them on the belt, not looking at them or me but at the floor. I thought how easily, that time, I could have grasped Hayley Jo's hand, or called Kris and spoken my suspicions. But one hates to be a Marge Germaine. After Kris left, Sophie Lawrence had been in, and we'd had a strange conversation about the possibility of saintliness. Remembering it, I shuddered. Then Sister Xavier's face flashed before my mind, her mouth moving in prayer, her forehead's skin twisted like the clouds within a hurricane around a hollow eye.

• • •

The children were innocent spies, ubiquitous. But Roberto's command of English was astonishing. If I wanted to talk to him alone, I could say *igneous mass,* and he would know I meant the big rock outside the village. *Place of pedagogy* was the school supply shed. I became careful not to teach the children certain words. *Conifers and deciduous* was a grove of trees still standing in that all-but-barren landscape where everything else had been cut for firewood — a virgin place where the native small green parrots appeared out of green shadows and disappeared back into them.

For Roberto and me, language became a game. We learned to speak of anything with the children crowding around, sharing laughter at their puzzled faces. I didn't realize that nothing is more intimate than a private language. It creates its own world. Even now if someone says *deciduous* I slip back to a place real and illusory, rich and barren, that was and never was.

We were always short of chalk. Sister Mary Beth ground it into the board in long swoops of letters that were never fully erased, ghosts of former lessons when I taught. I took to hiding chalk from her. When I needed more, I asked Roberto. It was easier than asking Sister Xavier, who would fret about waste and then make the chalk communal.

Chalk again, Elise? Roberto made his voice stern, imitating Sister Xavier. He pulled his face into a frown. You must use fewer letters.

I burst out laughing. He'd taught me that sternness could be laughed at.

He maintained the imitation: I counted the broken chalk last night. Considering how many letters you were allowed this week, there were fewer pieces than there should have been. Now, Elise, what do you have to tell me? Have you been writing larger than you should?

He flourished his arm, his finger and thumb together in an exaggerated imitation of writing on a board, his hips swaying, his whole body engaged.

I confess, I said, pretending seriousness. No more extra tails on my letters.

But I couldn't maintain it and laughed again.

You know what I'd really like? I said. Not chalk at all. I'd like a purple ribbon for my hair. Something different than this.

I pulled the red ribbon that held my hair out sideways so we could look at it together.

The laughter in Roberto's eyes changed to something else.

A ribbon, Elise? he said quietly.

I'm tired of this same old red, I said.

For your hair.

Of course for my hair. What else would I use it for?

It was, I thought, the smallest thing. But he lifted his eyes to mine, and my laughter ended.

Oh, Roberto, I said. I'm not really asking. If you can't find one, it's all right.

But I *was* asking, and you cannot take an asking back. Especially when it's a personal gift you're asking for, even if completely frivolous and barely intimate.

No, Elise, he said gravely. It would not be all right. I could never forgive myself.

He disappeared from the village. He was always off on errands. Five days later he found me in the storage shed where I was putting things away. He must have waited for the children to leave and for me to go inside. My back was to the door when I heard his voice.

Your ribbon, Elise.

I started, turned. The clean light outside created his dark shape.

Roberto, I said. You're back. Come in. I can't see your face.

He moved into the room, his hand outstretched. A ribbon dangled from it.

Was it hard to find? I asked.

I hope it is purple enough.

In the light coming through the door, it was the prettiest pale lavender.

It is. More than. Was it hard to find?

I wanted to know where he'd gone, what he'd done, to get it: the narrow streets of the city, the old women selling cloth, their speckled, rummaging hands. I wanted to know it all: the words he'd used to describe what he was looking for, the colors he'd rejected, a dozen ribbons dangling from a fist, his finger pointing to one, the chickens squawking in a cage nearby, the huddled rabbits, a donkey walking by. I didn't want to accept the ribbon until I did know. But he merely shrugged and kept his arm extended. I played at waiting—cocked my head, pouted—but then, unable to resist, took the ribbon from his fingers. I untied the red strip from my hair and handed it to him, then gathered my hair in both hands, elbows high, and turned the lavender ribbon around it. Then I stopped and stood completely still.

Roberto? I whispered.

He made a gesture toward me. I thought he would touch my face. My cheek burned. But he checked the gesture.

How could it be hard, Elise? he asked.

He brought the red ribbon to his lips and pressed it briefly. Barely grazed it. Let it be accidental. If I chose to see it so.

The most dangerous secrets hang like spider webs in the structure of things. We inhale them in our sleep and pretend ignorance of breathing. Otherwise we couldn't sleep at all. And the little, private secrets we so treasure? The ones we box and fondle? They're nothing at all.

I sat in a pew, hearing Father Obermann's hoarse breathing be-

hind his door. There used to be booklets in the pews, sins cata-
logued. They were no longer available, but everything else matched
my memories.

Angela Morrison — fresh fruits and vegetables, or TV dinners, on
a mysterious, irregular cycle — entered and knelt behind me. She
was beautiful and black-haired and aloof when she first came here
from Sioux Falls. Everyone thought she would abandon Brock, but
somehow he managed to hold on to her as she aged into her present, elegant, streaked-gray state. She and I have little in common. I
hadn't been inside a church in twenty years, and she was once the
church's secretary, involved in everything. Though she quit soon
after Father Caleb left the priesthood and Father Obermann, with
his Jesuit sensibility, arrived, she maintained the rituals.

I motioned for her to go ahead of me. She clunked her kneeler
up and rose. I saw how her shoulders slumped: her daughter was
Hayley Jo Zimmerman's best friend. Faint, unintelligible murmurs
came from behind the doors. Then she came out to say her penance. For the past month she'd been in a TV dinner, bloody mary
phase. When I saw the resolve on her face, I had a revelation: tomorrow she'd buy fresh fruit and vegetables again. I hadn't known this
sacrament was the fulcrum upon which the change was balanced.

I can't help but notice. Even if I shut my eyes, I'd feel the lives I
scan: a blind and voiceless oracle. It's why I love baseball. Even if
the ball is hit, there is a mystery. You can't be sure how it will be
handled or how fast the runner is. It may be only white holes fleet-
ing in the sky. But it makes me catch my breath, not knowing.

I opened my compact, gazed into my eyes, devoid of any prophet's flaming, then snapped the case shut, rose.

The words I'd memorized when I was young were there.

Twenty years is a long time, Father Obermann said. Welcome
back.

I didn't expect such kindness. Thank you, I responded.

I heard you out there. I wondered if you'd come in.

It isn't easy.

No.

Take all the time you need, he said. The demand, you notice, is not high.

His humor disarmed me, let me speak.

When I was young, I said, I fell in love with someone. And let him fall in love with me. I think I wanted to escape myself. Or my own dreams for myself.

I stopped. I'd never thought of it that way. Yet in this small box designed for telling secrets, what I said seemed ordinary. Perhaps that's confession's real purpose — to make sin banal. Or grace banal. I don't know which.

Is that your sin? What you waited twenty years to tell?

I heard it in his voice: that he recognized what I was saying, a thing he'd heard before.

No, I said. Not the love. Or the letting love. Or what we did together.

Was he married?

It isn't any of that.

We must admit our sins if we're to be forgiven. By God or by ourselves.

What I had to tell him wasn't ordinary. He just expected it to be. But he was a good man. I tried again.

I tried to be someone I wasn't, I said. Then I was offered the chance to be that person. And didn't have the courage for it.

I'm sorry, but how can it be wrong to refuse to be someone you're not?

He was too willing to forgive me. Too willing to find a way to categorize what I'd done so that he could forgive.

I cared about ribbons, I said. When killing was going on.

I said it cruelly. How could he make sense of it? And when he didn't, I said: This isn't working, Father. I'm sorry. I have to go.

• • •

When I was a child my parents took me to a cave called Wonderland in the Black Hills. We walked down narrowing corridors, the earth closing in, all that weight of rock so close. Then suddenly, behind a narrow opening, space ballooned, its distance receding to darkness — a silent, private, underground cathedral. It was like that with Roberto — a ballooning into secrecy big enough to more than fill a life. I hadn't known such secrecy was possible, full of space, stalagmited with guilt and honeycombed with revelation. Or so I thought.

One night I woke with a hand on my mouth, pressed so hard I cut my lips against my teeth and tasted blood. I thrashed, made gurgling noises. Sleep wouldn't let me go. Then clay walls took shape, a face bending over me. His lips brushed my ear.

It is all right, Elise.

His fingers lifted off my lips.

Roberto! I whispered. You shouldn't be here. If Sister Xavier —

Yet I was overjoyed. I raised my arms and pulled him down, and without a word he removed his clothes, and mine, giving me no language by which to name refusal. In the silence and dark, with tropical insects swaying in the mountain night, we made wordless love.

Then he said: I must go, Elise.

I know.

I knew nothing: I kept him dangerous moments longer. From across the village someone was singing. I wanted to lie with Roberto and listen, as if that song were meant for us.

I'm so glad you came, I whispered.

He rolled off the narrow bed and knelt for a moment, his face over mine, before his eyes hardened, a resolve coming to them which should have frightened me. Instead, I basked in it, believing it was directed toward the two of us together. I watched him put his clothes on in the dark. Then he was gone. I'd never felt so glorious, so jubilant. Even holy. Or so frightened. This — now — had to

41

be my life. I'd betrayed all others. The things Roberto had pointed out, distinguishing our lives, no longer mattered. His life was mine. Mine, his.

I fell asleep and woke to army trucks carrying young boys holding rifles, and a screaming commander whose language was a babble. Except for the name, *Roberto*. I threw on my clothes, which were scattered on the floor. I knocked the dust off them. Even then I thought my secret mattered.

His name rose from the current of foreign curses like the music of a songbird among crows. In all that spewing language, it was the single word I understood. We were prodded, lined up like livestock. We moved in a cloud of dust lit by sun behind the mountains yet. Then we were made rigid in an uneven, ragged line, while the soldiers formed another, straighter line facing us. Between the lines the colonel strode.

People bowed their necks as he screamed into their faces. They shrugged, mumbled, shook their heads. He came down the line and then was standing in front of me, treating me no differently from the others. I thought my skin color, nationality, connection to the church, would set me outside these bizarre events. But I was implicated with the rest and was stunned by it. I stared at him, his mustached mouth forming words too fast for me to follow, spittle shining at the corners. Again I heard him say *Roberto*.

I had an insane thought—that the colonel was trying to force from me my own betrayal. That he cared what happened in my bedroom, that somehow it was connected to whatever else he was after. I feared I'd be exposed. That's how lost I was. How ignorant—and safe.

Roberto? I said.

But before I could find the Spanish to say anything more, to lie or tell the truth, deny or claim my actions, a voice said: Señor.

Sister Xavier stepped out of the line as if its force had never really held her, she had merely reconciled herself to it for a while. She shed the line like clothes and walked between the villagers and soldiers, a naked act. All eyes watched her. The young men lifted their rifles but had no idea what to do. Sister Xavier ignored them all. We were horrified, ashamed, and awed. Silence grew out of her footsteps like a vast, fragile structure. She walked to the colonel and said in Spanish, slowly enough for me to understand: The man you want is gone.

She pulled the colonel's eyes to hers, and his demands, screamed at her now, came too fast for me to follow. But her replies were slow and calm, and I realized she was speaking to the colonel but also to me. She never let her eyes drift to mine. Her discipline was perfect. But I sensed I was meant to understand her words and something inside them, too.

Because last night he told me he was leaving, she said.

My breath caught. Last night.

The colonel screamed gibberish again, and Sister Xavier replied in slow, perfect Spanish: He said that if he stayed, the mission was in danger. I didn't know what he meant precisely, but I was certainly not so foolish as to ask, or to find out where he planned to go.

This old nun, who I thought worried only about chalk and bookkeeping, was admitting to this dangerous man that she knew everything — except what she chose not to. If she pretended complete innocence the colonel would be insulted. Instead, she let him see she knew his world and knew that she was part of it — even let him see she opposed him in it. But then she winked. She invited him to see things from her perspective: ignorance as chosen and innocence as strategic, not as a state of being.

She was like a magician letting an audience in on the machinations behind a trick, confident that even then they'll be fooled and take delight in knowing that delight can have such tawdry, cheating bases. She held her innocence out to the colonel as a thing maintained and crafted. She was cynical and innocent both—a condition I would have thought impossible.

It was brazen and unbelievable. I was still trying to comprehend my own abandonment, yet I knew something much larger was taking place, and I struggled with what Sister Xavier was trying to say to me. The colonel screamed again. Sweat rolled off his forehead, down his cheeks, even his neck. Sister Xavier shrugged.

I may be lying, she said. That's true. But don't insult my intelligence, Colonel. Don't you think I know what not to know?

He stared at her, halted, no response within his repertoire. Then he pulled his pistol from its holster.

Even then she faced him down.

Do you really want to shoot an American nun? she asked. Especially one who really does know nothing?

He raised the pistol. He didn't care if she was American. Didn't care she was a nun.

But she'd said those things knowing he didn't care. In the game she was playing, they had to be said. She had to affect what was, in actuality, my innocence—had to make him think she was naive and proud enough to believe her habit and nationality and sex protected her.

When the pistol touched her forehead, her lips began to move, saying prayers inaudible to anyone but herself and God. I think—I believe—these were the sole authentic words she spoke, her true self expressed. But even this may have been part of the web of lies and almost-lies, knowns and not-knowns, she spun around the colonel, just so he'd believe a single thing: that she'd chosen her ignorance, and that because it was chosen it had to be genuine.

Around us there was a silence no one ever wants to hear. I could have spoken then. I'd finally found the Spanish words by which to claim Roberto—and thereby claim the life that hours ago I believed I'd taken on.

A parrot squawked, a young boy's pet, turning circles on a string.

The barrel dimpled Sister's skin.

I was silent.

The colonel pressed the barrel even deeper and twisted, and her skin whorled around that empty eye like satellite photographs of hurricanes. But her expression didn't change, and her prayers continued as if the colonel had become insignificant, his world beneath her notice now.

If you're lying, you old American whore —

He turned the pistol one more cruel quarter-turn. Her skin tightened even more, her whole face distorted. He looked at his accomplishment. Then suddenly he tipped the barrel down and strode away, shouting orders. The boys, who had been standing still, rifles ready through it all, suddenly came alive. They were just boys. They climbed into the trucks, some of them laughing, sharing cigarettes. Others slouched, clearly disappointed. One caught my eye as a truck went by. He had a cigarette half lifted to his mouth. His hand paused in midair, and suddenly he winked, kissed the air, and grinned.

Sister came to my side. She adjusted her veil with trembling hands.

What an unpleasant man, she said.

She tucked loose strands of hair, surprisingly dark, under the veil. I couldn't look at the angry red circle, like a blank eye, on her forehead.

Sister? I faltered.

It would be best if you returned home.

Please.

For safety's sake.

But you're staying? The mission?

Her hand took mine. It was cool. I was aware how much it wasn't his.

I don't mean your safety, she said. Roberto is a courier for the guerrillas. We shall pray the army doesn't find him.

Jealousy overwhelmed me. I thought I'd made him my life — and I didn't even know him. What he showed me was pretense: chalk and ribbons. To her he'd shown the rest.

A courier? I managed. He told you?

I was close to tears, fighting to shore up my own secret, but sensing how small it was.

But even that secrecy was a lie I'd told myself. Sister Xavier squeezed my hand, and her voice was firm but not unkind.

Let's be clear, she said. That colonel has lined men and women and children up. Whole villages. He has machine-gunned them. When Roberto was sixteen he returned from a visit to another village to find his family dead.

She squeezed my hand again, then let it go. I stood alone. I had no claim to any world.

I will protect this mission, she said, very gently. And Roberto. By whatever means. That includes removing his temptations to return.

I believed I'd see her brains blown against the wall behind her — and merely braced myself for it. He didn't pull the trigger. But I *knew* he would. My ignorance and my dreams had brought me to a point where I had no useful knowledge, even for saving a life, and no voice to speak a word of mere distraction. I'm not sure if what really happened redeems what could have happened. Perhaps it does. But sometimes I'll have dreams in which the trigger is pulled, and Sister Xavier's skull deforms and opens at the back like a broken, vomiting mouth. I'm standing in front of her and look down and see a pistol in my hand. I can hardly bear to hear Jonathan, fascinated with science fiction, speak of how, with every decision we make, another universe blooms into being in which the opposite decision takes effect. I fear my dreams may be emissions from that other world.

I didn't want to know Roberto's life. I only thought I did. I wanted a pleasant market, his only errand a lavender ribbon, and caged, waiting chickens the only jarring note. In spite of all my guilt, I believed in and wanted innocence. And it left me without act or speech or courage.

All for the best? Perhaps. Sister Xavier, surely a saint if I've ever known one, would tell me to forgive myself, and I have, if cheering my son's home run, and caring about where the ball is going, constitutes forgiveness. But I should have spoken to Hayley Jo Zimmerman. I have a voice here. I have a language. I should have grasped her hand before the last coin went into it, before the bills, before the quarters, even. Right away, while counting the pennies up. Grasped her hand and told her there is no hiding. Is there another universe where she's alive right now because another version of me squeezed her hand and spoke? This is my world. I can't be innocent here.

A Real Nice Girl

HE SITS IN THAT wheelchair, staring out the living room window, a goldfish in a sealed bowl suspended in the ocean. His right arm hangs like a limp flag at his side. He has words. He just can't speak them. They're like moths inside his head, batting against the screen his synapses have become. I pick them up after they've beaten themselves ragged, hold them in my hands: silky, barely fluttering. I breathe my own voice into them. My voice, his voice, myhis voice — if there is a difference, he can't tell me. Unless I give the words.

In the room where I write, a single prism hangs, a reminder of my mother's banal cheerfulness. It sends meandering light, color weak as the tea I drink, along the walls, stretching and bending into corners. I hear him out there, by his window, breathing. The right side of his face is beyond mind or nerves — as if a balloon could be half-inflated and half-not: the left side taut, expressive, the right sagging in misshapen pouches. He drools. In the light from the window the wetness shines on his chin — a slug track in morn-

48

ing sun on wilted lettuce leaves. I come out of my writing room, take a Kleenex from my pocket, and walk across the living room. I start at his chin and wipe up to the corner of his mouth. His skin pushes like putty away from my hands while his whiskers, gray as dirty snowflakes, catch on the Kleenex. I drop it in the waste-basket I've placed near him, then push his head erect, as if it were a crooked lamp.

You're not very levelheaded today, I say.

It's a joke he used to tell about Norwegians when I was just a girl: *How do you tell a levelheaded Norwegian? The snoose-juice runs out both sides of his mouth at once.* He told it whenever he had friends around. They always laughed. If I was there — silent as a plant, all eyes and ears — he'd catch my eye and nudge the air in my direction with a beer bottle.

Even before the stroke he never spoke, except with borrowed words. It's as if he's decayed into a full realization of who he always was. Within a year after my mother married him, he wouldn't lift his eyes from the television when she spoke to him. She never wondered why. He grunted — as if his voice box had a crack and he forced a little sound through it. Now he can't even grunt. Justice may be blind, but in this case it's also mute.

When I was young and the three of us lived here together, only the house had a voice, the squeal of its hinges the only protest. As if it had seen enough. Houses must grow weary of what they know. Sometimes I imagine them speaking among themselves, a deep bass register, like elephants, below our range of hearing. It would be a different story from anything Bea Conway's put into her rah-rah county history.

I've read how the young men of certain African tribes endure circumcision as teenagers. A bloody affair. They stand in public while older men with flint knives approach. The anthropologists say it aids the young men's memories. They learn the stories of the tribe and then are mutilated: sacrifice and fulfillment, something given for what is taken, words for flesh and blood, all tied up in sex. They never forget the stories.

He always turned the radio on. Just loud enough to hide the other sounds. As if my mother would ever have investigated. A little square radio by my bed, a Pandora's box of loveliness: *I've seen fire and I've seen rain. A peaceful, easy feeling. The clouds of Michelangelo.* Lovely phrases. Words I've never forgotten.

Do those boys, I wonder, late in life, feel satisfaction watching the old men die?

Until I was thirty-two I'd never held his gaze. *Never* — a word that chants all by itself. Its own echo. *Nevernever.* No wonder Poe loved it. I'd never looked into his eyes until that day he grabbed my wrist. I must have imagined if I didn't look into his eyes he couldn't see me. As if seeing was the fault — the crime, the sin. But the absence of my eyes on his never blinded him. He still sees as well as ever. Assesses weakness as well as ever. But he can no longer move toward what he sees, take it, make it his.

The only reason I'd agreed to help my mother was because I thought he'd die. Would tip his head further and further to the side until one day it pulled his whole body down. Oh, my mother's hips were bad, and she hobbled in her duties to him, grimaced when I visited, made small mutters of pain which she pretended to hide from me while making sure I heard them. Martyrs are artists of control, and my mother was a da Vinci. But I'd grown up seeing the brush strokes. It wasn't her martyring but his dying that made me agree to help her. I thought he was winding his life inside himself, coiling it around a tightening spool there: a fishing line snapping, that high, dissonant twang, the weight of too much life, a tiny question mark disappearing with a snick inside a reel.

When he was healthy I refused to visit. Ten years of absence. Only when I heard of the stroke did I return — a morbid fascination. My heart was in my throat when I knocked. But he was helpless. Still, I circled him. I stayed far from the reach of his arms and refused to touch him, though I knew my mother wanted me to — a sign that all was forgotten: wiped clean, erased.

Then, on one of my visits, I was about to step into the living room when I heard a sound like a shy, reclusive train whooshing and panting. Ignorant of my eyes, he was trying to move his wheelchair by himself. He gasped, and sweat beaded on his brow, and his left arm pumped up and down, up and down, the elbow pointing to the ceiling, then straightening, pointing and straightening, his large hand gripping the wheel, throwing it forward with a hideous frenzy. His fingers flew open as if they had spring catches in them, then clamped down again. And the result of all this effort was the right wheel staying put while the left one followed its own track compressed into the carpet, around and around and around. His head flailed on its neck, drool ran down his cheek. Like a burned-out lighthouse, its blank lens wobbling.

I watched until he dribbled to a stop, his eyes once more watching out the window, the acrid light out there. Then words went from my lips before I even formed them.

That didn't get you far.

His head jerked as if the wheelchair were electrified.

Keep that up, I said, we'll have to buy a new carpet.

The back of his head, with its neat barber cut above the flaccid neck skin, went still as a fly sensing the swatter. That's all. I told my mother I'd take a leave-of-absence from my job to come down and stay with her.

Ohnononono, Sophie, she protested. You can't quit your job. People depend on you.

This although she'd just let out a small cry, like a squeezed cat, to be sure I knew how much her knees hurt when she rose from her chair to get another cup of coffee.

I rolled my eyes. Paint laid on canvas. My job — I sat behind a desk at a personnel office and pushed forms at people. I spent years studying literature and psychology, hoping to find an explanation for myself, then concealed the degrees in order to get a job that would prove I didn't amount to much. I took some satisfaction in knowing what I was doing, but my mother bragged to friends how her Sophie was helping people. Convincing herself my life had turned out well.

But your hips, I said.

Oh. That—she shooed the air—I manage.

The house's rafters creaked. She let me argue until I'd committed myself—then closed the door: Well, I guess I could use your help. But only if you're sure. Because your job, you know. And I do manage. I don't get around like I used to, but—

I let her talk. Let her show her art to an empty room. I only cared about his dying.

Instead, she died first. Abandoned me once more to him, yet managed to be blameless. I had the feeling cancer hadn't found her, she'd found it. Gone seeking, plucked it from the air of the house, the history in its rooms, then pretended ignorance when she found her stomach swelling, complained querulously of back pain and of gaining weight—and only when she was past all cure did she go to the doctor, who told her of the tumor heavy as a child pressing against her spine.

A tumor? I cried when she told me. Can't they cut it out?

She misinterpreted my despair, pretended to be strong for me: It's too far gone, Sophie.

It was too familiar—that shaking of the head, that oh-well-what's-to-be-done? The boy who cried wolf, the martyr who sighed sorry. Her eyes teared up. I couldn't stand to have my sympathy elicited, even by a dying mother. I walked into the kitchen, snapped on a burner, put water in the teakettle, and listened to the bubbles hiss.

Five weeks later she died, and there I was, alone with him. I thought to sell the house, let the money disappear into a nursing home, and walk away. But for a few days I had to do my mother's duties. Either that or let him sit in his own stink and starve — which would raise suspicions. So I did what I had to until I could arrange to abandon him.

It's hard to think a body can be half-destroyed. If he'd had to move by halves to where he wanted to go, like Hercules chasing the tortoise, and then found his joints locked, his muscles para-lyzed — or if, when he tried to talk, he'd been able to speak the nouns and prepositions but not the articles and verbs, or the con-sonants but not the vowels — then I would have remembered the halfwayness of his body, that good left side. He wouldn't have sur-prised me then. But a face that sags on one side and has all its nerves and expressions on the other isn't seen in halves. The sag-ging part seeps into the healthy part. I saw a full face, stricken, not two half-faces, one diseased, the other good.

So he surprised me. I was retrieving a glass of water from the TV tray off which he ate his meals when suddenly his left arm shot out faster than I could see, and his hand closed around my wrist. His strength was astonishing, and it wasn't even his domi-nant arm. My bone hurt. Water sloshed over the lip of the glass and wet my wrist and the back of his hand. I almost cried out, but I clamped my throat down on the words: habit returned.

Out of his ruined face he stared at me. And I forgot the long discipline of my eyes. I looked directly into his. The first time in years. In years and years. One would have thought his stroke was infectious, that it had passed through his body into mine, cutting off my brain's connection to my limbs. I was a little girl again. The present had folded itself into the past, and there she stood, my ear-lier self.

Sometimes in summer I'll watch the nighthawks flying. They sweep low, in random, graceful flocks, each bird branding its individual pathway through the evening air, wings flicking like the off-beats of a song, as if it is the bird that is the counterpoint to birds, the bird that shows other birds an opposite way to fly that exists between the beats of normal flying. And there are times when I catch a single nighthawk's wing beat, when the bird is tipped at just the right angle so that the orange horizon turns the white wing bars orange, too, and the wing is arched in the upper blue, and the moment, the flicking, offbeat wing, expands to become forever, an opposite time caught out of time, so that it never ends.

It was that kind of neverness and everness—except that it was ugly. *Ugly:* surely the first word in any language, a grunt of dismay that the world could be so wrong and so surprising all at once. An *ugh* made into an adjective: an ugh-ly thing, an ugh-ly moment, an ugh-ly grip upon one's wrist.

Then it all broke down. Because I looked into his eyes for the first time in years—and what I saw was dust. Can eyes be dusty? They were. He was trying to speak. His throat worked, saliva collected at the corners of his mouth, his tongue moved in his skull, and his grip on my wrist was the kind of bright, illuminating pain that made me understand the crazed, redemptive light in the eyes of martyred saints in paintings—but also why a trapped animal would chew its own leg off. But beyond it all, above it, underneath it, was the dust: the lid of his right eye sagging like a fold of chicken skin, and behind that lid his brown-maroonish pupil. Like a piece of leather torn from the dusty cover of an old, unread book.

His yellow smell filtered up to me. His breath puffed from his moving mouth, warm and stale. The saliva gathered, pooled, crept over his lip like a thin, shy animal sneaking from a humid cave. His grip tightened even more, and his tongue strained randomly between his teeth, but he didn't speak. Of course he didn't speak. That dusty eye was pleading for something the way dust pleads—mute, plaintive—but it was nothing but dust, a dried-up, tiny-rivered, going-nowhere eye. The frizzy-haired girl relaxed her fist inside my throat. In this house, where only the floor joists had ever spoken, where only the timbers and hinges had ever complained, I could speak. Silence had at last caught up with him. He'd promoted it, and now it had taken him. Grown, like cancer, into and around him. But left me free.

Thirty-two years old, and my voice had finally been returned. A fairy tale. Well, they're vicious stories, fairy tales. I didn't struggle. I reached down with my other hand to the TV tray and felt for the napkin there, not letting my eyes leave his. I lifted the napkin, dabbed water off the back of my caught hand. The water on his wrist I left.

There, I said. You've gone and made a spill.

He shook his head as if by centrifugal force he could dislodge the words from his brain and fling them from his mouth. I feared the drool would spray, but it clung to his jaw. I could almost see the words. Are words that are formed, but never spoken, words? Or are they like Bishop Berkeley's silent tree? Was he trying to assert himself? Or was his urgency of a different kind — to ask forgiveness, maybe? I watched the words almost form on his tongue and realized they were mine. Whatever I said they were, they were. Or if I refused them, I negated them entirely: they never were, had never been.

His throat convulsed, his dusty eyes protruded, his mouth opened and wetly closed. His grip tightened into a cruel telegraph trying to imprint a message through my skin. I didn't struggle. I had two good hands. I could have thrown water into his face, slapped him. Numerous things. What use? I had my voice. And his. I pictured the words inside his mind collapsing wing-on-wing, syllable-on-syllable, phoneme-on-phoneme in dusty, twitching heaps.

I know just how you feel, I said.

I paused to see what he understood. Dust devils twisted in his pupils.

We can stand like this until your grip gives out, I said.

I held the napkin out to him. We both knew he couldn't take it. I watched the water roll down his wrist, between the hairs on his forearm, slow as a stalking summer fly. The glass in my hand magnified sunlight in a round, shaking ring across the walls and floor. It bent around corners. A shadow of light.

He let go. Turned his face away. Rubbed his arm on his pants to dry it. I stood a moment more, then turned, the glass by my side. I moved within a shimmering ring of light that wrapped itself around me tighter and tighter as I withdrew from the window until it disappeared — as though my body were its source and had pulled it back inside.

When I first came back, my mother had prepared my childhood bedroom for me. She displayed it with a flourish, done up in pinks and pastel blues, and frills. I was supposed to remark how wonderful it was, how much effort she'd put into it, and her hips bad, arthritis in her joints. But as far as I was concerned, it was all just evidence: she'd always known, and was now giving me the childhood I'd never had, without acknowledging anything.

Wonderful, Mom, I said. But I'll sleep in the basement.

Her face fell. I picked up my luggage and walked from the room. As I did, I brushed against the doorknob, and the hinges squealed like a hurt animal. The sound pinned me. Then I remembered the present: daylight, the adult body I stood in. I forced myself to step into the hall. On the other side of the doorway, I turned. My mother stood in the center of my old bedroom, disappointment stretching her face.

How can you live with that noise? I asked.

But I'd rejected her pinks and blues, and she was impervious to the question.

I guess I just ignore it, she said.

I guess you do.

I turned away and carried my luggage down the steep basement steps. I was the only one in the house who could navigate them. Halfway down, I realized: He was a carpenter. Surely he knew how to stop a squealing hinge. He hadn't cared. Had he wanted her to know, to prove she wouldn't do anything? Or worse, did he imagine her awake? Was that part of it?

The next time I went past that bedroom, I steeled myself, then pulled the door shut. I heard my mother in the kitchen stop moving. The house itself quit breathing. Then things resumed. After that we pretended the locked room didn't exist. A fairy-tale room.

But when he grabbed my wrist, and I saw the words floating in all their dusty disintegration behind his eyes, I began to see how life carves patterns in its offbeat randomness. Reversals balance out sometimes. What had been taken from me was being given back. I stepped into my mother's shoes completely. I brought him meals, took him to the bathroom, endured it all, showered and dressed him, wheeled him into the sunlight to let stray dogs sniff and growl at him and neighbors chirp their greetings. I did everything but talk to him.

From the door of the living room I watched him watch the world. I saw what he saw, and I saw him seeing it. I was the fly on the wall, buzzing with old lyrics, unforgotten, a reservoir he'd given me. So many words. Then one afternoon I saw him watching two high school boys in pickups riding up and down the street, smoking their tires and sticking their heads out the windows to call and laugh and grin at the girls who sat beside them. One of the girls had long hair that swirled in the pickup's wind and obscured her boyfriend's vision.

I saw his head move to follow her as she went by. I didn't even know I was speaking his words until I heard them in the room:

Love to get that little bitch where she couldn't get away.

It was so real. Like ventriloquism: as if the words came from where he sat. His good hand curled around the wheelchair's arm the way a touched caterpillar curls, and little creases appeared on the back of his neck as he stiffened. The pickups reached the end of the block and continued on, and we were staring at a world unmoving. Then, in my own voice, I said:

Too bad for you. A baby could get away from you.

I turned on my heel in that brilliant, new-made silence. *Even the house,* I thought. *Even the house's voice is mine.*

I went to the bedroom my mother had turned into a lie and opened the door and took down everything she'd put up: the pink curtains and bedspread with their matching lace, the glass angels hanging from the ceiling, praising on their strings, the rainbow stickers on the windows casting plastic light in arcs across the floor. I piled it all on the floor. Then I got in the car and went to the grocery store for cardboard boxes. Elise Thompson, who checks groceries there, so slowly she could be memorizing them, asked what I was doing with the boxes.

Putting things in boxes, I told her.

Oh. I thought maybe you were moving.

I'm not, I said.

I put everything—sheets and curtains and suffocated angels— into the boxes and taped them shut. I stacked them in a corner. Then I struggled with the mattress and box spring, dragged them across the floor, got them upright inside the closet, shut the closet doors, and taped them shut, too, gray seams of duct tape like bandages running floor to ceiling. I took the bed frame apart, hauled the pieces down the basement steps, then returned to the almost-barren room: walls, and a window with a rollup shade, a little desk and a chair, the boxes in the corner, and a single prism I'd left to spread thin, roving light. An anchorite's cell.

Only one thing left: I pried the pins from the hinges of the door, then set the door inside the room against the wall. Like everything else, it had always been a lie: lie of frills, lie of lace, lie of locks and latches.

I made tea. The first cup I cooled and iced and took to him sugared, with a straw. I set it on his TV tray next to his good hand. I kept my fingers on the glass, my wrist within his reach.

Tea, I said.

And for him: I don't want tea.

It was delicious, saying his words, my wooden puppet, for him.

You're welcome anyway, I said.

He stared at me, his smirchy eyes astonished and afraid. I returned to the kitchen, heated the water again, put the bag in my cup, poured the boiling water over it, stood dipping. Chinese connoisseurs use tea leaves again and again, until only the faintest flavor remains, an echo of taste receding, like something barely recalled from a dream. I set the bag on the counter, went to the emptied room with the cup, sat at the little desk there. In its varnished surface I saw the wavery reflection of myself in a world of wood. I set the cup down, arranged a piece of paper, uncapped a pen.

All afternoon I wrote. I sipped tea, using the same bag over and over, the flavor becoming, if I really paid attention, more delicate each time, though it was only Lipton. The prism circled on its string, the rectangle of light revolved, the house's rafters creaked, the windows watched. Time disappeared. The tea weakened with the weakening light until I may have only imagined its flavor, making it up as it touched my tongue. When darkness was complete outside, the cup empty for the final time, I rose and pulled the shade, then returned to duty, making supper, shaking extra salt in, setting it before him. I had him tell me it was far too salty, then told him if he didn't like it, he could cook his meals himself.

• • •

Once he stuck his finger in his ear.

I said, for him: How's that for irony? I'm a one-armed man with two good ears.

He took his finger out.

He can't leave, can't call for help. I'm free to take him among his former friends. They tell me how wonderful I am. I demur, of course. But what would he say if he could protest? That I've stolen his voice? I've given it back. If I interpret wrongly, who will judge the error? I would have to speak the protest for him — therefore interpret it first. But if the protest stems from my interpretation, what meaning can the protest have? The convolutions amaze, delight. And what if what is spoken is always truer than what isn't, even if it's false? I get lost in logic and what-ifs.

Whatif, whatif, whatif. It looks like an Arabic word, desert, palm trees, an oasis surrounded by dunes. One might say: *In the middle of the desert, I came upon a whatif. And squatting by that whatif was an ifnot.* What would an *ifnot* be? I can see it running away on all fours, monkeyish, but I don't know what it is. *Whatitis, whatitis.* Whatwhatwhat is a *whatitis?*

Across the street two of Marge Germaine's nephews are shingling her roof. I hate the sound of hammers. Marge waddles out occasionally, then turns and calls, inviting her nephews in for cake or ice cream. They shrug, look at each other, wondering how much of their fat aunt's time to waste, then untie their nail aprons and descend. He's been watching the slow progress of the shingles up the decking. He used to spend all day on roofs, barebacked, then every evening return home smelling of pine and galvanized nails, asphalt and roofing felt. It never left his skin.

I wheel him outside. Marge, calling to her nephews, turns. She lifts her hand and waves.

Good morning, Sophie, she calls. Good morning —

She never says his name. She seems to think that being voiceless requires being nameless. I reply for both of us.

Good morning, Marge. Good morning —

Marge turns back to her nephews. I call to them for him: How's the work going?

The older one, his nail pouch hanging from his fingers, the hammer dangling from its hook, shrugs and looks at me, though I'm not really the one who asked.

It's coming along, he says.

He drops the pouch. The hammer thuds on the roof — a hammerthud on the roof, a hammer thudontheroof. A hammer, the dawn, the roof. Or, with the second syllable accented and the *th's* softened, a kind of dinosaur. *A wet world, full of ferns, the Hammer Thudontheroof's knobbed head swinging stiffly on a long, thin neck.* A scientist finding its bones in the Badlands is filled with wonder and elation.

Sophie! Sophie!

My name, faint then growing stronger, a reverse echo. They're staring at me — the nephews looking down, Marge's fat face quivering. For a swimming moment the past almost takes me. He used to stand like that, looking down at me, when my mother forced me to go with her when she visited his work sites.

Yes?

Did you hear? In the news this morning. They found another body. Near Bozeman.

I clear my mind. The Zimmerman girl.

I don't watch the news, I say.

They think she was dead a long time. One of the first ones. But they just found her body now. Death isn't good enough for that man.

Someday, I say, we'll learn to resurrect people. Then we can execute the deserving ones three or four times.

Marge doesn't know what to make of this.

They could have a smorgasbord, I say. Like a church dinner. First the needle, then the firing squad, then hanging, the electric chair. Maybe even the guillotine. Juries could pick and choose, various combinations.

Well, she says. Even that wouldn't be enough.

There's stoning, too. And crucifixion. They're traditional. And if we wanted exotic, in India they used to have elephants step on criminals' heads.

She should never have gone to Rapid.

What's going to Rapid got to do with it? Eddie Little Feather was killed right here.

The poor man who killed Eddie wasn't trying to. It was Eddie's own fault.

Her sincerity defeats me.

I've got to buy groceries, I say, and jerk the handles of the wheelchair, spinning it. His head flops to the side, as if it could flop right off and tumble to the street. He gains control and sits upright again. I let him call back to the nephews.

That roof's coming along nicely. I'd help you with it if I could.

I knew her.

It's the older nephew. His words stop me. I turn back around and squint into the sun at where he stands, almost invisible in the brightness.

Hayley Jo, he says. We went out. When we were younger. For just a little while.

His voice breaks. He doesn't look old enough to have a younger. He walks slowly down the roof, descending into its shadow, and stops with his boots almost in the rain gutter. Then he squats down and when he drops completely into the roof's shadow, I remember: he was the pickup driver with the girl's hair in his face. That was her, then: the one I let him call a —

I push us away. The wheels are whooshing over the sidewalk with their sticky, tapey sound, when the nephew's voice comes down to me again:

She was real nice.

I'm sorry, I say. I'm sorry.

I don't want to say it twice, but it's out before I can stop myself. But maybe no one hears. I'm out of breath, and it comes out quiet, and maybe no one hears.

I slow down, collect myself, try to recall whether I was running. I don't think so. If people saw, they would call it walking fast. Exercise—because I spend so much time indoors. I wipe the sweat from my forehead with a Kleenex. I park him outside the grocery store in the sun.

There you are, I say. I'll get a few things and be back.

He stares into the empty street.

Bitch, he says. You could at least park my sorry ass inside where it's air-conditioned.

He uses the word even on me. So there.

Now, now, I say. The fresh air will do you good.

I get the things I need: groceries, a new notebook, some pens, a box of tea. I need less and less of it. I can taste the flavor in a bag dipped half-a-dozen times. The other day I was sure I tasted it after the eighth cup—a few molecules passing across my tongue, Marco Polo and spice and yellow dust, the Great Wall mortared by bones.

I'm putting the tea on the belt when I think: raped her, stabbed her, broke her bones. That's what they say the murderer did. It's always put in that order. But why? Do they know? Or do they know only what happened, but not the order? The grammar, the inflections. Even with the ugliest things we hope for the right order. We need it to be correct. Because any other order would. *Anyother-would.*

63

Are you all right?

Elise Thompson, the checker who asked what I was doing with the boxes, is looking at me. She left town for a while, did some missionary work, returned. Now she stands behind a rubber belt all day, staring at bar codes. She must go home seeing stripes in everything, the horses in the pastures turned to zebras, the streets immense piano keyboards, everyone in town a referee.

Of course I'm all right.

She nods. She picks up a can of tomato soup and sets it in the plastic bag hanging between its hooks. She pauses, her hand still in the bag. For a moment I feel this thread of commonality. We both returned.

But then she says: It's got to be tough.

Tough? I ask.

She tilts her head toward where he's sitting in the sun. She must know he's there. Does she peek out the window at people coming in, then scurry to her place behind the checkout?

Taking care of him, she says. Especially the way —

I stare at her.

He's your stepfather, she says, placing things in the bag just so.

He raised me. I'm who I am because of him.

Yes, she says. I suppose you are.

She looks at me as if I'm supposed to respond to such banality. Then she says: There are nursing homes. No one would think anything if — you could get on with your life.

This is my life.

Her face breaks up, startled, the way still water breaks when a gust of wind hits it. As if her face momentarily isn't there anymore, it's just reflecting points and waves. Then she collects it again, looks down at her hands resting on the belt.

My mother thinks you're a saint, she says.

She waits — as if she'd just offered me an invitation or a gift. I stare at her until her hands begin to move again. She beeps a box of tea through the scanner, then stops again, looking down at the Lipton Man, his gnomish face, the little *S* of steam rising from his china cup—his millionth cup, or hundred-millionth.

She's clearly thinking of saying something more. I snatch the box from her and reach across the counter. I hide the Lipton Man in the white darkness of the plastic bag, where she can't read his eyes.

I don't believe in saints, I say.

I'm not sure I do either, she replies.

I snatch the bag off the wire prongs and leave, feeling her eyes on me, stripes imprinted on my back.

I hang the bag on the handles of the wheelchair and march him home, waving twice to every driver who waves to us, though he has one good arm and could, if he wanted to, wave for himself.

I help him into bed as always, pull the covers up around his shoulders.

Good night, I say. I guess you won't be getting up till morning.

He waits a moment before saying, as he always does, Well, if I do, I've got a hand to take advantage of it.

A little joke. I smile, polite.

I turn out the lights. Usually I sleep when he does, but the house is too noisy tonight, an agitation of lumber, an organ of rooms. I get out of bed. For a while I stand before the picture window in the dark. Marge Germaine's nephew squats at the edge of the roof in the starlight, a gargoyle of sorrow. A car turns the corner at the end of the block, and the passing lights dissolve him. The houses rumble like elephants, the whole town chorusing. I stand in the hallway outside the door to my old room. I haven't been in it after dark since I returned. There's breathing inside it, low music, the sound of weight settling on a mattress.

No. There's not. I go to the kitchen to boil water. The first cup I pour down the drain. The second I take with me. I stand outside the doorway, holding it. The tea shakes rhythmically with my furious heart. I listen to the room, then step into it. In the dark the lines of tape on the closets look like seams, as if the house is about to burst or heal.

I turn the desk lamp on and sit. I have to write the combinations out:

> *Rape, kill, break.*
> *Rape, break, kill.*
> *Kill, rape, break.*
> *Kill, break, rape.*
> *Break, rape, kill.*
> *Break, kill, rape.*

They're not the same. Not anything like. I study them, repeat them slowly, imagining each act, how it changes with the order. Meaning changes. Awfulness. Everything.

But I can't concentrate. I lose track of the meanings. Then it's just the words themselves, and me alone with them. *Breakkillrape* is the loveliest to pronounce, almost music: the name of a bright fish in a clear lagoon, or a wind that bends palm trees over a certain kind of surf. You'd speed it up if it were language. I try it out: *As he cast his net he heard the breakkillrape sigh through the palms.* Or, *Underneath the clear water, a tiny breakkillrape darted over the coral.*

The fish, I think, not the wind.

I taste tea residual on my tongue. The prism catches a moment of light from the lamp, and on the wall a suggestion of color passes. I move my pen on the paper, but it's dried up and makes no mark.

Me, I write with it. I touch the invisible word but can't feel it either.

Him, I write, pressing harder, feeling again for the word. I think of them together: *Mehim.*

Then I think: *Himme.*

66

And suddenly I don't know. Have I made him me? What if I've made me him?

What if? What if?

It's terrifying. The house resounds, the town pounds and stamps and whispers. Himme? Mehim? I write them both, pressing so hard the dried-up pen grinds in the fibers of the wood, but even then I can't feel the words. I press even harder, and the tip of the pen bends. It feels like it melts away in my hand, into the paper, gone. And then the words, if so they are, just circle in my mind, a chant: *Mehim himme mehim himme mehim himme mehim.*

Losing to Win

THE SMELL OF ASPHALT and the stars rolling. The moon approaching, doubling. Breeding itself. A moonclone. Oh, man. And that rumbling. His ear pressed against the pavement, Eddie Little Feather feels more than hears it. Like it could shake apart his skull.

Was a time Lowell Bresnan saw mountains where no mountains were. Where no mountains ever been. He tried to tell Lorena about it, sitting on the edge of his bed at the Gold Star Inn in Lone Tree, South Dakota, still shaking, but he knew Lorena would be standing with one elbow on the microwave and her forehead in her hand and the phone in the other, her hair falling over her face, watching Abbie through it and wondering what kind of story he was telling this time, listening beyond his words for other breathing or a muffled giggle, listening so hard she couldn't hear what he was saying, listening right past his words to what wasn't there. Still, he tried: how his headlights had gone into the night and plucked mountains from the eastern seaboard, mossy, treegrown mountains. Plucked them from over the horizon and set them down in the middle of the highway. Except they were moving.

Headlights'll do that to you, you stare into them long enough. Make you forget distance and perspective. So you can believe for a moment the whole damn continent has sucked itself together, and the Appalachians've just slid to the middle of South Dakota, and you're going to climb up into them, engine grunting like a hog, toward the stars. And then, sweet Jesus Christ, it was buffalo, their humps in his headlights. It was like he'd driven the rig right into the past, or time had leaked through a crack in itself, and the next thing he'd see was Indians on horses, chasing. But Lorena wasn't hearing any of it, he could see her shaking her head until the microwave cart moved on the vinyl he'd installed the last time he had two weeks without a haul. He finally stopped talking, and when she said, *Lowell, I just* — and then didn't say any more, he looked at the dirty motel carpet and his white socks lumpy on his feet and whispered: I damn near died, Lorena. You imagine hitting buffalo at sixty-five? Even in a rig? You imagine?

But he knows she won't. Imagine it. Won't. How mountains came and went. How the past appeared, no mirage or apparition. And there he was, roaring at it. Sixty-five. A hundred yards. Loaded down.

The earth rumbling: Eddie lifts his ear away from it and gazes at the moons. Stars lie above him like marbles. As if he could reach out, take one of those moons off the horizon, and hold it between his thumb and finger like a steelie and knock the stars beyond the rim of sky. When he was a kid, he was ruler of the dust. Chief of the chalk circle. He squatted so low, taking aim, that the circle stretched into an oval, and the marbles loomed like monuments within it. He could smell the chalk. He smells it now, dusty and alkaline, through the smell of bile.

He feels like a glove turned inside-out. That's it. That's just how he feels — inside-out. He always lost his left-hand gloves, and his grandmother would turn his right-hand ones inside-out. Her fingers pecked like a bird, and the gloves bunched tight inside themselves, the fingers hard, cloth knots that relented and turned soft again. He'd wear the gloves out the door, the seams all frayed and cottony. But he'd take them off before he got to school. They couldn't afford new gloves, and it was his fault for losing the left-hand ones. He'd take them off to touch things, pick things up — and then forget. So he wore the inside-out gloves without complaint, until he was gone from his grandmother's sight, then stuffed them into his jacket pocket so no one else would see. The tips of his fingers went numb. He had to press his pencil into the paper just to feel it in his hand. Press so hard he'd rip the paper, and the letters he was struggling to make would be swallowed up, as if by an opening mouth.

Lowell stood on the brakes. He felt the load in the back shift, then worse — that first, faint judder that would become a jackknife. At sixty-five. Might as well strap on explosives. He remembered later, after hanging up the phone, as he stared at the cigarette burn in the motel carpet, a burn like a brown, wounded mouth, how he'd had this vision of the entire rig sliding around like a big clock hand and scraping the buffalo right off the face of the earth, and everything exploding, metal and meat and cargo. And he a part of it. Just more chunks. When they came to sort it out, they wouldn't know him from buffalo, and Lorena would walk through that scene, arms crossed, trying to pick out what was him, and shake her head at the impossibility.

He'd let off the brakes to prevent the jackknife. The buffalo seemed to be sliding sideways toward him on black, reflective ice, skating in a dream of speed and night, their humps like mountains receding behind each other and their horns a black glisten in the headlights. Wind and doom. Then his hands wrenched the wheel toward a slim redemption.

The roar is a racket now, shaking Eddie's head apart. *Racketa racketa racketa.* Like machine-gun fire. Like he's a Marine. Oh, man, would that make his grandmother proud. But those double moons. Maybe he's been abducted by aliens. He laughs. Wouldn't that be something? The stars lurch in the sky. Asphalt and dust. He's crouching, his nose almost touching the chalk circle. Glowing cat's-eyes lie scattered within it. The steelie squirts from his cocked thumb and smashes into two of them. They explode away from each other, and both roll out of the circle. The steelie stops like an obedient dog. Eddie raises his eyes. The cat's-eyes' owner scowls. But he picks them up, holds them out. Eddie lifts his palm to receive them.

At marbles, it didn't matter that when he tried to read, the letters twisted like black branches in a storm and turned themselves inside-out or that the paper ripped when he wrote. It was all pressed away by the touch of fingers against his palm and the warmed weight of glass there, the bright, encased helixes. He always said *Thank you.* He always said *Good game.*

He'd learned to crouch through life, to slip like a shy animal, a mink or fox, to where he was told to sit or stand. He kept his head down. Watched his feet. Hid his turned-around gloves in his pocket. But he couldn't control his grin when he was embarrassed or afraid. *Do you think it's funny to rip your paper? I've told you to write with your right hand. Maybe you'll think it's funny to stand with your nose against the chalkboard.* So he rose from his desk still grinning, feeling all those eyes on him, watching his feet pass over the lines of the wooden floor, dirt packed between the slats. He pressed his nose against the chalkboard. He tried to be invisible.

One day one of the white kids brought a bag of marbles to

school. The game was an instant sensation, white kids and Indian kids crouching together under the sky. Fathers found old marbles and gave them to their sons, who brought them to school in little mesh sacks. Boys held them up, examining the nicks in the glass and the bright purplings and greenings of light. Each scratch was a code, the key to a story of conquest. The marbles made *scritching* sounds, like contented shore birds in flocks, when pushed against each other in the bags.

Eddie listened. He had no marbles. No scratches to be felt with a fingernail or angled to the light. He wouldn't ask his grandmother to spend money on marbles, and without them he couldn't enter the game or conversation. He watched how his classmates cocked their thumbs, how the shooters careened, how the cat's-eyes scattered. With his hand under his desk as the teacher droned, he practiced the movement, hunched down — watching his thumb flick from his finger invisibly fast. His thumb would be crooked-then-straight, and nothing in between.

Then one afternoon, as he meandered home, he spotted an old bearing race in the Canada thistle and leafy spurge outside the DST Machine Shop. He knelt and pried it up. Dirt clung to it. Fingers of grass clutched it. It smelled of rust and old oil and green stain, like his father's pickup before he'd gone away. Eddie reached through the strands of grass and touched one of the bearings. It wiggled. He pushed it harder, but it wouldn't come out of the race. He looked at the door of the machine shop.

He stood in the rhomboid of light, the race hanging from his fingers. The mechanic turned from his engine.

You need something?

Eddie stared at a grease spot in the cement. It looked like a horse trying to run.

The mechanic, holding his ratchet, rubbed the side of his nose with the back of his wrist. His hand put a dark stain in the blond fuzz on his face. He nodded at the bearing race.

You want that there piece a junk, go ahead. Ain't worth nothing to me.

The marbles, Eddie said. He held the grass-laced thing up, cupped in his hand, a mechanical nest with hard, perfect eggs.

Marbles?

I can't get em out. The steelies. I tried, but—

The white man dropped his ratchet onto the bench and grinned. Shit! he said. Bring that sonofabitch over here.

He took the race from Eddie and gazed down at it reverently.

Those'd make a helluva shooter, huh? he said.

Eddie nodded.

Well, let's get them sonsabitches out.

He banged the race down on a metal table. Eddie watched the marvel of a cutting torch—the flint spark, the snap of the flame, the lazy, orange sheet of the acetylene turning hard and blue as steel itself when the oxygen pushed into it, the grass shriveling and blackening before the flame even reached it, and then the metal brightening, glowing—and finally the extra blast of oxygen that turned the flame into a claw that pried the race apart, spraying sparks. A steelie, freed, clunked onto the cement floor. Eddie bent for it.

No! Kid!

The white man's voice paralyzed him. He stared at the floor, grinning.

Sorry, kid. I ain't mad at you. It's, that bastard's hot as hell. Wait till I'm done.

The mechanic cut the rest of the bearings out, then picked them off the floor with pliers, held them in a tank of dirty water, then dried them with a terry cloth as carefully as if they were china. One-by-one he laid them in Eddie's palm—steelies tinged blue as tiny skies, one-inch round and deliciously heavy.

Jesus, the mechanic said. You got yourself a gold mine there. Wisht I'd a thought a that when I was a kid.

The next day Eddie brought two of the steelies to school in his pocket. They pressed against his leg when he walked. At recess he stood over the hunched players, rolling the steelies between his fingers.

I'm in, he finally managed.

Faces swiveled, squinting. Bill Lipking sneered.

You gotta have marbles to challenge, Little Brain.

Eddie withdrew his hand from his pocket, held it out, opened his fingers.

Trade one've these for five cat's-eyes.

Wow. Look't em. Where'd you get em? A chorus of voices.

Eddie closed his fist. Anybody? he asked.

It turned into an auction. He ended up with eight cat's-eyes, from Bill Lipking himself, who recognized in the steelies a threat and knew enough to buy it out. Eddie lost his eight new marbles, but the next day came to school with another steelie. As the mechanic had said, a gold mine. By the time he'd traded his fourth steelie, he owned the game. His thumb wrapped itself backwards around a marble so naturally it seemed an extension of his eyes.

The girls came to the games, jump ropes coiled, to coo over the kneeling boys. Eddie's pockets began to bulge. One day his grandmother's eyes widened when he walked out the door.

Takoja, she said. Are you all right?

Sure, Grandma, I'm fine.

You're not hurting — down there? She jutted her lips at his crotch.

He shook his head.

What do you have in your pockets, then?

He hesitated, then brought up a gleaming fistful of cat's-eyes. His grandmother stared.

You didn't steal those?

He was dismayed.

No. I won em.

I'm sorry, *takoja*. Why are you carrying them in your pockets?
Got nothing else.

She looked out the window. He realized he'd hurt her.

I like em in my pockets, he said.

You could get a hole.

She disappeared into the lean-to at the back of the kitchen and returned with a canning jar. Eddie could read the word *Ball* on it. The word seemed made of light, all those reflecting edges and angles. She tilted the jar for him, and he rolled the marbles into it. They filled it half-up — a silent new world, brooding on its own splendor, the marbles' gleamings magnified by the etched and curving glass.

He kept the jar on the flat shelf at the top of his wooden desk, next to the groove where his pencil stubs lay, and where some ancient student named Rodney Valen had immortalized, with a jack-knifed heart and arrow, his love for Cassie Janisch. Eddie's prowess at the game had affected even the teacher. She never asked him to remove the jar. It was like a trophy in the drab room. No one, boy or girl, would pick it up to look at it without asking his permission. One day when the teacher was out of the room, Bill Lipking, from his seat two rows over, said: Hey, Little Brain, what's with the jar? You canning those marbles? You and your granny eat em?

Bill looked around triumphantly but was met with silence. Then Sophie Lawrence, who sat at the front of the room and never said anything, not even when she was called on, spoke. She stared down, her nose inches from the top of her desk, but her voice filled the whole room:

If you don't like them in that jar, Bill, win them away from him.

The class tittered. Bill slunk down in his desk, red rising up his neck. Sophie met Eddie's eyes, then bowed her head to her desk again.

The jar changed time. If Eddie gazed into it and followed the helixes, the way the curved lines, extended in his mind, connected to other lines and curves, until the blues and reds and yellows and greens blurred into a glowing pudding of light — then the clock hands suddenly jumped, and the bell would be ringing for recess.

But he didn't understand the change on the playground when he ran a streak of three games against Bill Lipking. He'd beaten Bill before, but never three times in a row, and never so convincingly. As the second game progressed, excitement grew within the circle of boys, and Wows and Jesuses, and Holy shits erupted when Eddie knocked Bill's final marble from the ring, while a half-dozen of his own remained, placid as posts, within. The third time the girls formed a standing circle behind the kneeling boys, but the atmosphere had changed. Bill hardly got to play. After his first miss a groan went up, and then silence as Eddie leaned into the asphalt, his nose touching, the steelie a perfect, miniature egg in the nest of his knuckles. Then it flashed, and cracked so hard against one of Bill's marbles a tiny shard of glass glittered over the heads of the girls, and Bill's marble wobbled from the ring, lines of sunlight crazed within it. Eddie was so intent he didn't notice the collective sigh or the slumping shoulders or even, as the game progressed and the outcome became apparent, the girls wandering off in pairs.

He looked up, as if waking, from the ring emptied of all marbles but his own, at a ragged circle of somber faces. He held out his hand, but Bill glared at it, refusing the ritual of picking his marbles up and placing them in the victor's palm. Sophie was the only girl still watching. She stood to the side, a clear space between herself and the boys. Her hair hung straight down around her ears and forehead, and she looked at the ground when she spoke:

You've got to, Bill. It's only fair.

But power had shifted in Bill's favor. This is bullshit, he said, and walked away. The remaining boys grunted to their feet and followed. Eddie felt the weightlessness of his hand. He'd wanted to feel Bill's fingers placing the marbles there. He crawled to where his winnings lay scattered, but it was like picking up dull stones. Sophie squatted down and helped him, but he felt no comfort in her companionship, and when she held out the marbles she'd gathered he nodded at the Ball jar instead of taking them. When he picked the jar up he had to balance it carefully to keep the heaped marbles from rolling out. The fractured one he put on top. It was like a world of stilled and stilted lightning. Just touching it made him shiver.

The two of them stared at it. Then Sophie turned her head to the ground again and said very quietly: You shouldn't have won.

At school he never got angry. Some kids could get away with it, but he'd learned that for him it only, ever, made things worse. But he was suddenly very angry.

Who wants to lose? he sneered.

Sophie shrank away from him but recovered. She wrapped her arms around herself.

No one, she said.

Well?

He thought maybe she would go away. But she said: You should miss on purpose. But make it look like you're trying not to.

That'd be stupid, he said. You're just a girl.

She flinched. He felt bad, even though what he'd said seemed justified. He walked away, then turned back. She was a forlorn heap. He started toward her, and she lifted her head, but the shrill bell suddenly insisted, and they were at the far end of the playground, and he couldn't run with the jar so full; he had to go right now.

That evening he asked his grandmother for another jar. He put half the marbles in it and placed it under the lamp in the living room next to her chair. While she beaded she looked up at the jar, and once her hand went out to touch it. The jar made a silence. Words wanted to go into it. She began to talk to him in a way she never had before. She spoke of her childhood, and her father. She spoke of a place called Wounded Knee and of Hotchkiss cannon. Eddie loved the word, it sounded like butterscotch and chocolate. But she said the Hotchkiss made a killing hail that fell and fell and fell. It poured down from the hill above the people. They couldn't run. They were trapped, and it poured down. She was a baby, but her mother told her. Sometimes at night she hears a sound of thunder when there are no clouds. It is like memory coming from a place before memory. Her mother and father had been at another place, dancing with ghosts. Coming back, they heard the Hotchkiss. Her father rode ahead to help, but this was a new thing. He couldn't comprehend it. He lost the four directions. When he finally remembered where he'd left his wife and daughter, he knew one thing only, to flee. They started north and met another family. On the second day her father and the other man were scouting. The women heard shots. They stopped and waited. A whole day. Finally, afraid, they turned back toward Pine Ridge. They knew.

When his grandmother finished talking, she picked the jar up and held it. She looked into all the colors there. Eddie held the story.

The next day when he went to the chalk circle, no group coalesced around him. Rather than clustering where the playground was paved, the boys were scattered on the gravel and weedy grass. Eddie called. He shook his jar. No one turned his way. He walked to boy after boy, asking if they wanted to play, but they continued with their games of tag as if Eddie had no voice. Finally, he intercepted Bill.

Wanna play marbles?

Bill barreled toward Eddie, chased by It, then dodged the tag. It clumped past him.

Nice try, Bigfoot, Bill sneered. Take off those skis, you could run faster.

He stopped before Eddie.

Time, he called. He put his hands on his knees, then skewed his eyes up at Eddie.

Do I look like I wanna play marbles?

I'll spot you five.

Bill took a long, ragged breath. He spit.

Spot your pants, he said. That game's boring.

Bill watched It jerk and reach, other boys shrinking into themselves, twitching away from It's outstretched arm.

Everyone's sick of it, he said. Play by yourself if you think it's so fun.

Eddie looked into Bill's freckled, lovely face.

He held the canning jar up.

You can have em, he said. All of em.

It wasn't begging or benevolence. He saw the jar held up to Bill, his own hands holding it, and it seemed a thing of beauty, and he went soft inside with giving. He wanted Bill to smile and take the marbles, and then he wanted to win them back, so that Bill would one-by-one return them, his fingers lightly pressing Eddie's palm as Eddie knelt on the warm asphalt. He understood what Sophie Lawrence had said: he could cheat backwards, which wouldn't be cheating at all, and he could maintain the game forever, touching Bill's palm, letting Bill touch his, the exchange of marbles going both ways while he got better and better, no longer knocking marbles from the ring but nicking them, spinning them, missing them by tolerances he determined, bringing them to rest on the chalk line itself, in or out as need be, the game completely his, even its rules and the reasons for playing. Eddie wanted Bill, right now, to reach out and take the jar and lift its satisfying weight and put his arm around Eddie's shoulders and draw him close. He wanted the sound and feel of Bill's panting in his ear.

Greed brightened Bill's eyes. He raised his hand. But a cunning look came to his face.

I don't want your stupid marbles, he said. Figure it out. No one's playing anymore.

Suddenly Eddie was tagged so hard he stumbled, and the marbles rattled up the sides of the jar. He took several steps, crouching low, to keep from falling.

Real graceful, Bill Lipking sneered. Guess you're *It*. Who you gonna catch holding that dumb jar?

All around Eddie kids whirled away from him. But he refused to be *It*, though they howled with betrayal. He walked away. Standing by herself near the school building, Sophie Lawrence watched him, but he didn't go to her.

That afternoon he took the jar of marbles off his desk when he went home. Where the road crossed the marshland along Red Medicine Creek, he spun like a discus thrower, holding the jar far from his body. A crescent of colors sprayed outward, as if he were the center of a rainbow failing even as it formed. He looked at the marsh: grass and water and cattails. All the marbles had disappeared. The earth had swallowed them as easily as it had his grandmother's father. They would never come out again. Eddie cocked his arm to throw the jar, then remembered it was his grandmother's. He returned it to the shelves in the lean-to. The jar of marbles under the lamp he also threw away, and for the first time in his life lied to his grandmother, saying he'd lost a big game. He felt a tiny contempt for her when she believed him. He threw his remaining steelies at crows, missing every one.

Lowell was never able to tell Lorena how the wheels stopped fighting him, and the trailer slid in behind the cab like a skier inside a wake. Terror and ecstasy: the best driving he'd ever done, the culmination of all those miles that stood between him and Lorena, the way she wouldn't kiss him goodbye when he left but always had something to do, vacuuming or dishes, or Abbie in her arms, wouldn't even watch him go, as if she wouldn't give him a place in her eyes anymore that he could empty. Goddamn! What was he supposed to do? Truck stops, Jesus! He'd resisted, but there'd been that evening when he got into the cab to drive all night, buzzing on alcohol and caffeine, cheating on his logs to make the extra buck, for Lorena, goddammit, and that little lot lizard had appeared out of nowhere beneath his window, her tits about bursting from her halter-top, her perky face looking up at him and seeing where his eyes were going, and then that little-girl voice, You wanta feel, you may's well, honey. Won't cost you nothing, and he laughing, saying, Since it's a free country, thinking, *What kinda man wouldn't cop a feel?* and he didn't know what Lorena was doing when he was gone anyway, he'd asked her to come with him on the hauls, but she insisted that house they bought in Colorado Springs needed someone in it, but she liked partying and hadn't given up her old friends when she married him, and if he'd never found any real evidence, still, every time he came home he could imagine other men in the house. So he reached down and shoved his hand right into that halter-top, and the next thing she's climbing into the cab and the rest wasn't free, so he had to drive even longer, until it was just years and truck-stop whores and miles.

But somehow Lorena'd known. The worst evening of his life. She'd accused him, and he'd tried to deny it, thinking she couldn't really know, he'd always waited at least five hundred miles, like the song said. But she'd been like a jackhammer: Just admit it, Lowell! Admit it, you coward! Until he'd shouted, Goddammit, then, yes!

He'd wanted to hurt her—for making him say it, for not pretending it was secret.

Yeah, I've been screwing around! he yelled. Every time I go on the road! I'm like railroad tracks, Lorena! I been laid all over this great, fucking nation. I probably screwed someone in every fucking state a the Union except Alaska and Hawaii, and I'd a screwed there if my rig could fly. But you don't gotta drive to screw, Lorena! You telling me you sit in this house and crochet when I'm gone? Why ain't the walls covered in afghans?

Then they'd been so ashamed, for each other and for themselves, that for a while they'd prowled around the living room like two cats silent and bristling, arched, and somehow they'd circled right into each other, all body, Lorena's nails scratching his back and neck, drawing blood, and her voice whispering in his ear: Goddamn you, goddamn you, and there they were, fucking like he couldn't believe right on top of that new Stainmaster carpet he'd installed.

And then Abbie. Jesus, he really had been sorry then. He really had. Abbie. The cord wrapped around her neck and a breech, so they had to do a cesarean, and they brought her to him while Lorena was still in recovery, and he had a half-hour holding the newborn in his arms, alone in a quiet room in the obstetrics ward. He'd had no idea how much a baby's sleeping could still a person, set a person down in a single place. He hated the nurse who finally entered the room, yet when she held out her arms, he placed Abbie in them. Why hadn't he curled around Abbie and made a cave of his arms, and growled and spat, snapped at the nurse? Abbie was his. But he couldn't resist that smooth, assured, professional, female face. He rose from the chair and shambled obediently after her and watched as Lorena held up her arms, still a bit groggy, and claimed the child. Cradled to herself what had for a half-hour been his entire life. To get Abbie back, he would have to ask, Can I hold her again? Like a little boy.

It turned out he didn't know a damn thing about a baby. How he managed not to kill Abbie in that half-hour was a goddamn mystery. He couldn't do anything right. If he bathed the baby and brought her from her plastic tub all warm and wrapped in a towel, Lorena would find some small, uncleaned spot on her skin. If he brushed her fine, thin hair, Lorena would find a curl still in disarray. Even when he sat with Abbie, Lorena would say, Lowell, her neck. You should have more support there. And, Don't drop her, if he carried her down the steps. Be sure to use baby powder, if he changed her diaper. Those colors are all wrong, if he dressed her. It got so his relationship with Abbie was all correction.

So when those buffalo appeared in his lane on the highway outside of Twisted Tree, South Dakota, and his hands touched that massive rig in utmost gentleness and brought it back from the edge of disaster, he wanted Lorena to know. But it was just a story to her, and she was listening behind it to her own reasons for his telling it.

He looked at the phone he'd just hung up, and he looked at the ugly brown mouth burned into the carpet, lewd lips puckered as if inviting him to bend down and kiss them, moldy breath to suck his breath away, and he remembered the trailer after he let off the brakes gliding smooth as a sailboat behind the cab, the only sound the sound of wind. The buffalo were trotting across the road from right to left. He waited a moment more, an eternity, for the trailer to settle, feeling it in his hands, in his butt and back and neck, and the moment he felt all the wheels aligned, he pulled the steering wheel, and the cab careened toward the left shoulder, his headlights spraying into the hills, dying in the distance of them.

The lead buffalo was almost in the left lane, the other just behind it. He could see a hard, black sphere of eye, and strands of hair gleaming in the peripheral light like phosphorescent ocean parasites. The left wheels crashed onto the gravel shoulder. Lowell let them go until he knew he had half a tire hanging over the borrow pit. He saw the lead buffalo jerk back its head, its full face coming around toward him, its horns shining curves. It looked right at him as if it knew he was behind the wall of light. Eyes like stone. The center of the earth. He thought it was going to charge. Then, before he had time to offer prayers or curses or let his life flash before his eyes in all its petty and ridiculous sorrow, the animal swung its head around and veered away, its tail high, and he fleetingly saw the others follow, and then he was roaring past them, safe.

Until his headlights plucked another mountain out of the night. Right in front of him.

Eddie lifts his head again. Stares at the approaching double moons. Or suns. And that racketing. Machine guns. Or—Hotchkiss cannon. He should escape. But he can't think. He'd been trying to go somewhere. He'd tripped on something and fallen. Puked. That was. That was. What he smelled. He'd been thinking about marbles. Bill Lipking. Way back. And a rainbow. A rainbow? And then—there'd been that time, after he couldn't bareback no more. That IHS doctor said bareback could kill him. His spleen. And Eddie said, What do I do if I can't bareback? And the doctor said, That's up to you.

Eddie laughs. He should've asked, How about drinking?

He'd tried breakaway. An old-guy event. And got kinda good at it. Won a few small buckles. That little white girl. She was just a little thing, but there she was, beating girls way older. But she was too far back in the saddle. Her horse's ears flicked at her on the turns. Telling her: *Get it right.* Eddie could see. Her weight. It was fighting the horse. She came off a race, and he was on the fence. She was leading her horse past, and he said: Hey, nice ride. And she said, Thanks. And he said, Tell you, though, you lean forward. Get more over the withers, hey? Make them turns easier on your horse.

He held up his hand, palm stiff, bent at the wrist, imitating the angle her body ought to be. She looked hard at his hand. Then she understood. Like it'd been bugging her, but she didn't know it. Of course, she said. That's it. She put her thumb up, and he put his thumb up. He watched her race after that. She got it right. Like she was water now. Flowing. But completely still. They won the barrels, her and her horse. Her eyes found him. She thumbs-upped him again.

Then later, when he won the breakaway, they had her give him the buckle. He liked that. She held it out and said, Congratulations.

Thank you, he said. You, too.

She grinned. Thank *you,* she said.

Her eyes shifted. He turned. Shane Valen was watching between the rails of the fence. His great-grandfather had been the one. The one his grandmother said. The shots. It wasn't soldiers. They realized it later — where they were, whose land they were riding over. Shane never bothered Eddie, though.

He's always here, the white girl said.

People had stopped clapping, so they were supposed to leave now. It made Eddie nervous, but he said: That OK with you?

She shrugged. He's our neighbor, she said. Kinda creepy, though.

Then she turned and walked away. Time to go. Eddie walked the other way. He got between Shane's eyes and her. Shane moved his head back and forth, but Eddie moved with him. It was like barebacking. Knowing what the horse was going to do. Staying on the line between the girl and the eyes. But pretending he was just walking. It was better than the buckle.

That was the last thing he ever won, though. Breakaway wasn't barebacking. Maybe if he'd never ridden Later On, those cowboys wouldn't have. That cowboy wouldn't have.

They'd turned him inside-out. Because he'd made a mistake. Oh, man! Eddie laughs. That time! They'd beat the shit out of him. He ended up on the pavement just like this. He rolls his head, remembering. Laughing. Stars roll in the sky like marbles. Craa-zee.

He hears the Hotchkiss racketing. So loud. His grandmother said it was so loud. He knows now: it is.

• • •

85

Lowell's hands jerked the wheel back to the right. He'd never handled a semi so roughly—not even that time, right after he started driving, when that woman was in the wrong lane, and he'd started over to avoid her and then she'd come back and he'd barely missed her. But this time, with these buffalo, if the steering wheel had been Abbie, he would've wrenched her apart. Yet somehow—this was the wonder, this was what he wanted Lorena to know—he controlled it. That wrenching of the wheel was the most violent thing he'd ever done in his life. And the best.

The third buffalo was fifty yards behind the first two and invisible in their shadows, and it snapped into existence when the other two retreated, right there in the center of the road. Right there, and heading toward the left shoulder where in another moment he would be. He didn't think. He just moved. He jerked the whole damn rig out of the near-oblivion of the ditch and back to the right. He felt the trailer loop behind him. He felt it heave and yaw, still moving toward the downslope where, if it went over, it would roll like a thing not meant to roll and take him with it, tumbling over and over, shooting him into eternity.

But somehow it stayed upright. He felt the cab's wheels under his feet skip and judder, barely holding the surface of the road as the inertia of the trailer pushed against the direction he'd forced it into. But the tires held, exploding in the cracks of the asphalt, and the whole rig headed back toward the center of the road, shaking and sliding. Kids playing whiplash. The end of the chain flying off. Then the centerline was under him. He felt the trailer rocking. Back and forth. Rocking, rocking, rockabye. Rockabye, Abbie. It was almost that slow and peaceful and bough-breaking. Like he could sing the whole lullaby, and then just fall down. But not really. He couldn't wait. The highway wasn't wide enough. Couldn't wait for the trailer to settle, for its wheels to flatten into the road. He pulled the steering wheel left, completing the S, veering away from the right-hand ditch. He saw the third buffalo's thin, flickering tail with its brush of hair lift and fall like a bearded snake, and then the animal was gone into the darkness beside him, gone from his mirrors, gone. But he'd magnified the rocking when he turned, and, horrified, he felt the trailer's right wheels find air and lift right off the pavement.

Bareback was like marbles. Like he could *see*. Ahead. He could see *ahead*. To where the horse was going. So by the time the horse got there, he was already there. Waiting. And the next jump, too. And the next. Just waiting. That's what bareback was. Like he was always just waiting. Everything going on, twisting and moving and chaotic. And he in the middle of it, peaceful. Waiting. It was weird, man. Horse had to about turn itself inside-out to buck him off.

And Later On sure tried. When the eight seconds was up and he was pulled off, Later On stopped bucking and looked at him. He could about hear the horse saying, *You are one cocklebur cowboy, man, you are one Velcro Indian.*

But it mighta been better if it hadna happened. Because that cowboy come up afterwards and shook his hand and said, Helluva ride. You always ride like that? Looks at Eddie like that and asks a question like that. Ride like that? What's Eddie supposed to think, the way he says it? But Eddie just says, Sometimes. Grins and says, Sometimes. And that cowboy says, Whyn't you come down to the Horseshoe tonight, me'n some a the others're having a few beers. Guy rides like you'd sure be welcome.

The Horseshoe wasn't an Indian bar. Eddie wouldna never gone there without he was invited. But it went OK, just a bunch of cowboys, didn't matter if one was Indian. Until he got a few too many in him. And made a wrong remark to that cowboy. Just a hint. Right away he grinned. Right away tried to make it like he'd been joking, man. It shoulda been OK.

Except.

Eddie laughs again. Rolls his head and laughs, and the stars

87

go craa-zee. He *hadna* been wrong. *That* was why that cowboy wouldn't let it go. Why Eddie couldn't grin his way out of it. The others started kidding that cowboy, saying, You two got something going? Little private rodeo? Ain't had enough barebacking for one day, that it?

No reason it couldna been just joking and drinking and let it go.

Except that cowboy hadda prove to his friends he wasn't who he was. But he was! Which was why he hadda prove he wasn't!

Oh, *man!* Bad timing. Shoulda waited and let that cowboy bring it up. Eddie'd got the shit beat out of him for bad timing. Too-ooooo funny. Got turned inside-out for bad timing. And never did join the Marines. And hadda take up breakaway. Never did carry a flag in a powwow for his grandmother so she could see it.

Bad timing! Eddie laughs and laughs. Those suns. It sure was getting light out.

The trailer was up on its left wheels, like some movie stunt except it wasn't a goddamn movie, the whole rig was shaking and jangling like Lowell was inside a trap set and the goddamn drummer was on drugs. And then the sonofabitch comes down *wham!* on the other wheels, hard as a goddamn maul against an anvil, he chipped two front teeth, and pops up the other way and *whams* back down again and why the *fuck* it didn't flip over he didn't ever know. Except somehow he got inside the pendulum of it and pushed it at just the right time, the littlest pushes on the wheel at the perfect times, and not braking too hard but just enough, and the thing stayed on the road and didn't roll. And he wanted to say, *Lorena, I've been saved. I don't know why, but it's got something to do with you and Abbie, and I swear* — he didn't know what he'd swear, but it was something more'n he'd put in a new Maytag dishwasher next time he was home.

My hands, Lorena. He wanted to lift them up to her face. *Look*

at these hands. They kept that sonofabitching rig on the road. Goddamn,
Lorena, these hands saved me tonight. Saved them buffalo. Saved us all.
But he never got it said. Because it was the phone, and he
couldn't show her his hands. He could hear her thinking it: *Lowell,*
don't tell me no more stories.

Suns? And those Hotchkiss cannon. So loud. He should get away
from them.

And then, another night, the same highway, his speed back up
after going through Twisted Tree. He thought it was a re-tread
someone'd blown. But lights tell lies. He'd been pushing his log
limits again, and thinking maybe he should just build a whole new
house, maybe if they got out of the old one and moved into a
new one that he'd built himself, things'd change. He was seeing it
almost, floating down the road in front of him, and then the re-
tread rose up out of the haze and the tiredness. The lights were
bouncing up and down, and it was behind a little rise in the road, it
doesn't take much to hide something in the bounce of headlights.
Maybe it was just shadow. Or snakes'd sometimes lie on the road.
That was more daytime, though. You just go right over them. And
jackrabbits, he used to try to avoid them sonsabitches, but that
was sure a waste of concentration, the way they'd buck away from
their own shadows until they sucked themselves right under the
rig. Deer, now, were big enough to do some damage. He was cau-
tious with deer. And a few times he'd seen cattle on the highway.
But never nothing like them buffalo.

Wasn't a snake. Big as it was, hadda be a re-tread.

There were lights all over now, but all they did was show Lowell
what he didn't want to see. It'd taken him a hundred yards to get
the rig stopped, and he was dialing for help even before he had it
stopped, but he knew it didn't matter. Not the dialing or the stop-

ping. Then he was running and yelling into the phone, fiercely out of shape. The moment he knew they had his location he heaved the cell phone — god*dammit* — into the darkness. He'd bought it a couple of months earlier, telling Lorena he'd be able to call her whenever. Yeah, she'd said. That's great, Lowell. Now you can call whenever.

It was just a goddamn good thing he forgot to grab a flashlight, because he'd've turned it on, and even without a moon he thought he was going to puke his stomach out.

He could've taken the other lane. Way back when he first saw something. But there was that rise, and he couldn't tell for sure. And you never expect. Jesus! Then he's over that hump, and right there. Right there.

The local sheriff was looking at him, the perspiration on his face blue and yellow and red.

Tell you right now, the sheriff said. Won't be no charges brought. It ain't too hard to see what happened.

But his hands hadn't moved. They'd moved all by themselves that time with the buffalo. By themselves. And this time —

If the guy'd just lain there, the rig mighta passed right over. Lowell was never gonna forget it. The way that head suddenly rose off the pavement and stared right at him. Another two seconds and the rig woulda been over. Two goddamn seconds. And right then the dumbfucker decides to wake up and look around. Head bounces off the pavement like a goddamn basketball. And Lowell could swear he was grinning.

The sheriff was the one found the head. Fifty yards away. Intact. He'd heard of tornadoes putting straws through fence posts, but — Christ! The bumper musta. Fifty yards, not a scratch. That's what he'd overheard the emergency guys saying.

Kinda thing was bound to happen, the sheriff said. I knew this guy. Do a blood test, no telling what we find. Hadna been you, it'da been someone. Passed out on the damn highway.

He smoothed his thin mustache, looked at the road, the semi, the emergency flares behind it, the rectangular frame outlined in orange lights against the sky.

Helluva bareback rider of a time, he said. Started drinking, and it was all she wrote. Nothing but a bunch a stories then, and none a them likely. Wasn't your fault.

Lowell just wanted to go home. Fall like a baby onto Lorena's breast. Clutch Abbie to him and weep. But he wasn't sure he could start weeping. Maybe if Lorena believed. But believed what? The way he'd been thinking about her and Abbie and that new house where they'd be together? Was that what he wanted her to believe?

His hand had just sat there on the wheel and let the rig go down the lane. But if the dumbshit hadn't —

The sheriff reached out and placed a hand on his shoulder.

Tell you something. Guy had nobody. Even his parents. He was raised by his grandmother, and she died a few years back. Never even had a girlfriend. So — I mean, it ain't like — ah, hell. Nothing you coulda done. No one's fault but his own.

He gripped Lowell's shoulder harder, then dropped his hand to his side. Then he held up his other hand, thumb and forefinger apart, between them a marble with a piece chipped from it, a cat's-eye dizzy with tiny fractures.

Found this in his pocket, the sheriff said. Only thing he had. What I mean, see? Guy finds a goddamn broken marble and keeps it. Not a damn thing you can make a that.

Salt

BY THE TIME Richard Mattingly mentioned the salt cedar bush to Stanley Zimmerman, its roots were already deep. Only later would Richard wonder whether his memory contained the plant's germination, its first shoots and growing. When had he first seen it? — a shade of green or shape of leaf along Red Medicine Creek so minutely different that he hadn't marked or noted it. When he mentioned the bush to Stanley, he didn't think it meant anything. It was a joke, a way to laugh at a neighbor who, in his relentless refusal to be a neighbor, had become for those around him a source of entertainment.

Looks like Shane Valen's getting into shrubbery, Richard said.

He was borrowing a horse trailer, and Stanley was cranking the trailer jack to lift it over the pickup's ball hitch. Richard's son, Clay, was standing near Stanley's house talking to Hayjay Zimmerman. The girl had her hair clasped in her fist, her head tilted, her other hand to her forehead, shading the sun. Clay's head was bent as if talking to the ground. Then he lifted it and met Hayjay's eyes. She nodded, and her hair slipped from her fist. The wind spread it forward, hiding her face, and all four of their hands reached into its tangled wave to control it, and then her face reappeared, and she was receiving her hair from Clay, he smiling but she so sober that his smile faded, and he stuck his hands in his pockets.

Yeah? Stanley asked, still cranking. Richard returned to the conversation.

Yeah, he said. Got this purple-flowered bush growing along the creek. Next thing Shane'll be shingling his house. Raise real estate prices. We'll have Californians moving in.

Stanley stood upright. He'd been distant and preoccupied but was suddenly alert. His blue eyes bored into Richard.

Purple? he demanded. Purple how?

There a how to purple?

Pinkish purple? Lavender? Look a bit like juniper?

Yeah, I guess.

He'd been checking cattle out where Red Medicine Creek formed the border between Shane Valen's land and his own. He'd noticed the bush's purple flowers on Shane's side of the creek and had a vision of Shane gardening, with kneepads on, and a trowel, and the greasy CENEX cap he always wore. Richard had laughed, that's all, and gone on.

Stanley took off his gloves, laid them together, wrapped his finger and thumb around them, and squeezed them into a tight neck of leather.

Sounds like salt cedar, he said.

Salt cedar?

Tamarisk. Christ! That's one I really hoped wouldn't make it here.

If it's on Shane's land, it's Shane's problem, Alysha said.

This stuff could dry up the creek, Richard replied. It's everybody's problem.

Stanley tell you that?

Richard nodded.

Alysha turned back to mincing chives she'd brought in from the herb garden she tended along the house's foundation.

I suppose he'd know, she said.

Richard spoke to her back: He says in New Mexico whole lakes have been dried up by this stuff. One plant'll take two hundred gallons of water a day. And its leaves are salty. When they drop, they poison the soil. Nothing else can grow.

And Stanley thinks you should save us from it.

She chopped with quick *chuk chuk chuks* of her knife, her shoulders moving in tight spasms, the smell of chives gradually filling the kitchen.

He was right about fireweed. And leafy spurge. And he was warning about Canada thistle before anyone even knew of it.

I don't like you on Shane's land.

Asking Shane to do something's a waste of breath. Meanwhile, this thing's flowering.

What do you plan to do?

Burn it.

That'll take care of it?

It'll come back. But it'll keep it from seeding. For now.

Why not just cut it down?

It'll sprout two shoots from the one you cut off.

She turned around, surprise and disbelief on her face.

Richard! You're describing a monster. Is Stanley exaggerating, maybe?

He knows this stuff, Ally. Better'n anyone.

I know he does. It's just—

He says about the only thing worse than salt cedar is giant knotweed. Says it makes Canada thistle and fireweed look like dandelion.

Alysha gazed at Richard soberly. Every summer she spent hours spraying Canada thistle, patches of it like living accordion wire in the draws and fence lines. And fireweed was already growing resistant to herbicides, a tangled mess at the edges of stock dams.

OK, she said. But sometimes I wish Stanley didn't have a name for everything.

A few days later Richard rode the four-wheeler to his west pasture. Cresting a rise, he could see Shane Valen's land to the south and Stanley Zimmerman's north, and the big stock dam on his own land where Clay and Hayjay fished, a narrow triangle of water bright as a mirror in the sun, with cattails ringing it. He dropped down to the creek. A few hundred yards beyond it, Shane's place was backed up against a hill — the barn swaybacked as a hoofshot horse, with a rusted galvanized mounting on top that had once supported a weathervane. The house's paint was molting, and between the house and barn Shane's rattrap of a pickup squatted, sunlight glinting in a crack in the windshield. In one of the house's windows a bare light bulb burned, but Richard assumed Shane was sleeping; it was common knowledge he spent his nights grocery shopping, with a rifle.

Following Stanley's advice, Richard had fenced his cattle away from the creek. The two banks were entirely different, the vegetation lush on his side, chopped and staggered on Shane's. He pushed down the wire and swung his leg over, then jumped the narrow band of water onto the eroded bank Shane's cattle had trampled, where the tamarisk bush had taken root. Richard grasped a group of the blossoms. They were cool and silky in his hand. Stanley had said the thing would put out a half-million almost invisible seeds with tiny hairs that rode wind or water. Richard rubbed the flowers and felt them liquefy, then opened his palm and breathed in the scent.

He unscrewed the cap on the diesel fuel can he'd brought and saturated the plant, then threw the empty can across the creek and lit a match. A curlicue of black smoke rose. Then the flame gained momentum and engulfed the bush. Through the haze of heat, Shane's house seemed to float off the ground. Richard wondered if he'd see the door open and a figure emerge to walk toward him, wavering. Inside the fire, wisps of lavender flower, like another genus of flame, shimmered, then charred and lifted. Escaping moisture gave off a thin whine, which the popping bark syllabified into something akin to speech. Richard waited until the flame died and the bush was a blackened skeleton, then crossed the creek and fence again.

As he neared the house, Clay emerged from the door, something glittering above his head. He reached up, waving his hand in circles. Then he pulled, and the glittering straightened into a vibrating line as he jabbed the hook into the cork handle of his fishing pole and turned the reel handle. Richard parked beside him and killed the ATV's engine.

Me'n Hayjay are going fishing, Clay said. It OK if I take Blueboy?

It's all yours. Think this is the day?

Clay was thirteen, Hayjay fourteen, but when they were nine and ten they'd returned from the big stock dam with a story of hooking a huge bass. They'd maneuvered it into the shallows, but when they tried to bring it to the net it had lurched and snapped the line and churned away, looking back at them with a yellow eye. Richard had smiled when they'd told this story, and Clay had cried indignantly: It *was* yellow, Dad. And it *looked* at us!

Behind him, Hayjay had nodded, and for four years they'd remained loyal to the memory. Now Clay shrugged. Never know, he said.

He put his pole into the pipe Richard had fashioned on Blueboy for that purpose, straddled the engine, and set off.

A little over an hour later, Clay returned. Richard, sharpening a sickle, lifted the angle grinder as Clay drove Blueboy through the open machine shed door. The high scream of the angle grinder's motor wound down and died at the same moment that Clay killed the ATV's engine. The machine shed expanded in the silence. Clay plucked the fishing rod from its holder and headed for the door. Richard pushed his goggles onto his forehead.

You're back soon, he called.

Clay turned just outside the door. Richard was taken aback by his expression.

Something wrong? he asked.

Clay moved his wrist, and the tip of the rod rose a foot, then dropped to the cement. He marked a furrow in the dust.

How're we supposed to fish when there's no water?

His despair puzzled Richard. There's plenty of water in that dam, he said. It takes more than a few dry years to do in Yellow Eye.

Clay's face twisted. That was just a stupid fish, he said.

Richard removed the goggles and flipped them onto the welding table. They clattered. He looked at them tangled around themselves.

I don't get it, he said. You've been after that fish for years. Now you just give up?

Then he saw that Clay was desperate to hold back tears, and he was struck by an overwhelming sense of his son as a person mysterious and absolute unto himself. Richard felt profane before him, seeing through to something he ought not see. He averted his eyes, and they stood for a while.

Then Richard raised his eyes again. Behind Clay's head a cloud of tiny insects hovered, so swollen with the light of the low sun they were bright, minor planets tracking random and impossible orbits against the sky. Then a larger movement coalesced at the corner of Richard's eye, and a pale, blue-gray butterfly took shape as if forming from scraps of cloud. It flew into the gnats, and they shaped and made visible the turbulence of its wings, tumbling in curlicues and funnels. Then the butterfly was gone, and the sun descended another fraction, and the gnats dimmed and turned to gray bits of matter that disappeared against the graying sky.

Clay's face shone. Hay. Hayley Jo. Isn't fishing anymore, he said.

Isn't fishing? Richard asked.

But he knew: Clay was in love, and it was over. It didn't matter that he was only thirteen or that he might not have a name for his feelings. Richard gazed at his son's face and felt flayed.

In high school Richard had been skinny and unathletic, his body a series of disconnected juttings and angles. He clumped around the halls, his heels whumping the ground like announcements: *Klutz coming.* Every time Bill Lipking called him Bigfoot or asked him whether those were boots or skis he was wearing, Richard spent the afternoon in a sullen rage, wishing he could cut his toes off. Only when he was acting, absorbed in a role, did he feel lifted away. On stage he felt free of himself. But always, at the end of a play, even as the audience applauded, he felt the churning uneasiness of the real world and himself within it. He might never have been on a date except that Stanley, even then his best friend, bet him he wouldn't ask Sophie Lawrence out.

In grade school Sophie Lawrence had been so quiet Richard couldn't remember her at all, but when she developed a body she turned sullen and flaunty, her sexuality both taunt and weapon. She fascinated and frightened the boys, and they called her a slut and a whore to cover up their fear. She didn't go to dances or football games, didn't drive up and down the streets with her windows open. There were rumors she'd been seen with married men in Rapid City. The idea of dating her was as alien to Richard as living on a houseboat, but once the idea took root in his mind he couldn't let it go: to have her mascaraed eyes notice him for the moment it took for contempt to form and for her to speak what she would surely speak.

He played it as a role — wrote the lines and memorized them

and went up to her and projected loudly enough for the eaves-droppers slouching near. And he almost accomplished it, almost lost himself in the role as he always did on stage. The mere act of speaking boldly and of having an audience almost made him the person who could speak the way he did. But in the silence after his words, Sophie's feral eyes regarded him, and he felt his coming abasement thicken in his throat and rise in his groin. Her eyes flicked to his snickering friends.

Then magically she turned from a woman, formidable and contemptuous, into a girl. It was as if she folded time back. She reached to her forehead and pushed her hair back and bent her head down, and quietly said: All right. Sure. I'll go out with you.

He had to fumble through arrangements then, without lines, a fool. When he went to pick her up, he parked at the curb with the engine running, and when she didn't come down the sidewalk he almost drove away. But he'd never live his cowardice down, so he went to the door and knocked and endured her mother's flutterings and exclamations while her stepfather slouched in an armchair, holding a longneck beer, sullen eyes staring at Sophie.

You take care a my little girl, he said as Richard turned to the door.

He tipped the bottle back, under hooded eyes. Sophie met his gaze and shifted her weight. The floor creaked. Richard had the feeling that if she opened her mouth the house would erupt.

Then her mother said: Now, Sidney —

But Sophie turned her eyes on her mother, and her mother went silent, and then Richard was being pulled through the door, out of the house's smells of machine oil and asphalt and into the dry smell of fall grasses blowing off the prairie.

The evening was nothing like the horror he'd expected. Sophie was quiet and thoughtful. At the movie he spilled soda, and she dabbed at his shirt with a Kleenex so naturally he was able to laugh at himself. When he took her home, she asked him to park the car a block away, and she leaned toward him and said, Good night, and when he turned to reply she raised her hand to his cheek and brushed her lips against his and said, Next week again? and then opened the door and went, while he sat there electrified.

The next week he was surprised to find her standing at the curb before he reached her house. She waved as if afraid he wouldn't notice her, or as if she were hailing a stranger. He stopped, and as he reached across the seat to open the door, she pulled the handle out of his grasp. He barely had time to straighten before she was inside the car. She was panting slightly, and she pulled the door shut and stared straight ahead through the windshield. The car was suddenly crowded. He'd been thinking about her all week, and now he didn't know what to say. He looked at the smooth plane of her cheek, the shadow under the cheekbone.

Go, she said.

Go?

Put the car in gear. Press the accelerator.

Her tone numbed him. He didn't say a word until they were on the highway. Finally he managed, Is everything —

I don't want to talk.

He stared at the faded, intermittent lines of the highway coming toward him.

What should we —

If you want to talk, talk.

You just want me to —

She reached over and snapped the radio on.

There, she said. OK?

CCR was singing about the rain. Richard felt heat rise through his body. His feet felt like blocks. Last week had been a setup, and now she was going to hurt him, and there was nothing he could do about it. Even if he turned around and took her back, he was already shamed, and sorry he was who he was.

Then she said: Turn here.

They were approaching the gravel road that led to Lostman's Lake.

The lake? he asked.

You don't like water?

We'll be late for the movie.

Well. If you don't want to be late for your movie.

It triggered all that he hated about himself. He jerked the wheel onto the turnoff so violently her head swayed, and he fishtailed up the gravel road and past the lake, and when she again said, Turn here, and pointed, and he saw nothing but the shallow borrow pit and the prairie, he turned anyway, while her finger was still lifted, and saw her head nearly smash against the side window, and he hit the accelerator and the car jolted over the uneven ground, banging and hunching, springs creaking, the headlights spraying the sky, their heads nearly hitting the roof, while the Eagles sang of peaceful, easy feelings.

Then she said, Stop, and he slammed on the brakes and her neck snapped forward and she nearly hit her nose on the dashboard before she caught herself, and then the car was sitting in dust above the lake's steel, moonlit surface.

Well, she said. Aren't you something?

She reached over and turned up the radio and opened her door and got out.

He twisted the key. Silence crashed.

No! she said.

He jumped.

Keep the radio on.

Her tone chilled him. He snapped the key to the accessories position. Music sliced back into the night. He pushed open his door, rose, slammed it. He was so sick of his body, sick of being made fun of. She'd let him feel something for her. He strode toward her, he meant to stop and scream at her, though his hand was raised as if to strike and he could feel tears rising, but before he stopped or opened his mouth, she was on him, he never expected her to move toward him, and her mouth was pressing against his so hard he cut the inside of his lip, and he was crying outright, and shame and brutality and anger and desire became one and all mixed up.

He lay on his back, exhausted. She stood naked above him. He felt he would never be the same. It was only when he said, I love you, and she merely gazed at him the way she might look at the foundation of an old house covered in grass, jutting up from the prairie — it was then that he understood they hadn't traveled or arrived together. But he said it again.

I love you, Sophie.

Yeah, she said. Richard loves Sophie. Carve it in a tree. Put a heart around it.

He stumbled up, his foot catching in the grass, then realized he didn't have his glasses on. They'd been taken off or he'd taken them off, he couldn't remember. The thought of hearing them crunch like bones under his bare foot, and her eyes directed at his clumsy feet — to be cut by the glass, blind and lame and completely at her mercy — it hollowed him out. He managed to stand, frantic, looking around like some featherless bird, feeling more naked without the glasses than he did without his clothes — naked in the helpless way of baby mice discovered, or grubs.

He drew himself up, acting: his sole recourse. He straightened his shoulders and lifted his head and looked directly at her as if he could see the pupils of her eyes and not merely dark shadows, as if he could see the points of her nipples and not merely a gauze of possibility, and her navel and her pubic hair, and the moonlight as a blade instead of a sheen on her clavicles.

I will, he said. If you want me to.

It came out as pitiful and humiliating, and challenging and demanding, and it stayed in the air between them, and she didn't have a response. Then she shook it off.

Jesus, she said.

No, he said. No.

You got what you wanted. You and your friends?

He was trying to hold her eyes, though they were too fuzzy to be held, while also searching for his glasses; he was fractured and bifurcated, if touched he would dissolve into powder and shards. It was more than he could endure, and words rushed out.

You were supposed to say no! he cried. You weren't supposed to be *nice!*

Her eyes, vaguely in his vision, widened, the shadow there softening until he thought he might, even without his glasses, actually see the round definition of her corneas. The shining shape of her body slumped. Then he saw moonlight caught in the edge of a lens and took two steps and snatched his glasses from the car's roof (how had they gotten there?) and slapped them onto his face and pushed them up and found her, defined and desirable, and was afraid that in another moment they would be visibly in different worlds. But he managed to focus on her face: its surprise, its brokenness.

It's not that, she said. That's not what I—

He was too consumed by his own self-consciousness to wonder what she meant.

I just want to get out of here, he said.

I *was* nice. Last week. I really was.

Jesus, he said, in the same tone she'd used.

He saw his underwear by the car and pulled them on, leaning against the trunk so he wouldn't stumble, the touch of cold metal making him shiver. Then the ground's coolness came up through his bare feet and he couldn't stop shivering, could barely button his shirt. When he finally got his clothes on he started the car and turned the radio down and the heater on full blast. He tried not to look at her out there in the moonlight, but he couldn't help it, and when she stooped to pick up her shirt and he saw her breasts swing away from her body, so full of soft weight, and then swing so neatly back when she stood, he felt stabbed by loss, convinced he'd never know a woman again.

Wordless, they rode the car over the jostling prairie to the gravel road. They were going past the lake, past its sedately moving lines of light, when she said: It's not what you think.

What do I think?

That I did this to laugh at you.

He wished he hadn't asked.

So, why don't you tell me what it is, then.

She held her left hand in her right, in her lap, and she shook her head. Then she looked him full in the face, and he thought she was going to speak, he waited and waited, the bright lake beyond her out the window, stars, the smell of water, the flinty complaint of stones beneath the tires. But he had to watch the road. He should have stopped the car, but he didn't think to stop the car, he turned from her to face the world moving toward him.

I was nice, she repeated. I wasn't trying—

He waited. She didn't go on. He waited longer, then long enough.

Can you just shut up? he said. All the way home. Every mile? Every yard?

She bent her head again, then lifted her hand to the radio knob and turned it off, and he briefly stopped to meet the highway. In that silence he heard a constrained, soft suck and catch within her throat. He didn't want to hear the sounds of her body or believe she had some claim to hurt. He snapped the radio back on, full. She flinched, and the Who cried out.

Richard had quarantined the memory. He'd grown into his body, and Ally didn't care that his feet were large. But now, standing before Clay, Richard felt the dismay and amazement of meeting himself on a road he no longer thought he was walking.

Did Hayjay tell you why she's not fishing anymore? he managed to ask.

She didn't even want to go to the dam.

What'd you do?

Just drove. Sat.

What'd she tell you?

Nothing.

She must have told you something.

She said she's too old for fishing.

You're never too old for fishing. And Hayjay's —

And she said she doesn't want to be called Hayjay anymore. Only Hayley Jo.

It had to happen eventually, Alysha said that evening. We never expected him to marry her.

It was a response so pragmatic Richard was taken aback.

I'm more worried about her, Alysha said.

This isn't about fishing, Ally. She dumped him. And they've been friends forever.

Well, why would she do that? I don't think a girl would just do that.

The memory of that night with Sophie Lawrence still in his mind, Richard wanted to ask his wife what a girl would just do. He had never told Ally about that night, and it wasn't mere privacy or discomfort. He was afraid of the words. He was almost sure that in that grappling, in that confusion of breath and body and limbs, Sophie had pulled him down. But he couldn't even recall how his glasses had ended up on the roof of the car. And he'd been so hurt and enraged, so strong. If he put it into words, he was afraid of what the words might reveal.

Kris told me she's spending all her time in her room these days, Alysha said. Or out running, with Laura Morrison.

Richard remembered the serious look on Hayjay's face the

morning he'd borrowed the horse trailer, and how preoccupied Stanley had been.

It's probably just, she's fourteen, Alysha said. But still.

Stanley hasn't said anything to me.

He's got a lot going on. Those buffalo are turning into more work than he bargained for. Especially with their getting out like they did.

That's true. But still.

Hayjay quit barrels.

Quit barrels?

Kris told me Stanley was pretty upset.

I bet he was. All that time he spent with her?

He was awfully proud of her.

He was.

Why'd she quit?

That's what I'm saying.

Three weeks later Richard remembered the salt cedar bush and rode Blueboy up to check on it. A green shoot, a foot tall already, had sprung out of the blackened circle where the bush had flamed and collapsed. He leaned on Blueboy's steering bars and imagined the thick taproot Stanley had described going down twenty or thirty feet, drawing water and salt out of the darkness, turning them into a million seeds: a rising blizzard of salt cedar. He spun Blueboy around so hard the wheels clawed up the shallow-rooted Japanese bromegrass that had invaded this part of the pasture. He drove to the machine shed and grabbed spades and a pickax, then went to the house and found Clay, who had been subdued since the breakup with Hayley Jo.

That salt cedar's back, he told Clay. We're going to dig it out.

Can't you spray it?

It takes a herbicide I don't have. And a lot of applications.

It's not even our bush.

Clay, don't argue.

Mom doesn't like you up there.

Ally and Angela Morrison had gone to Rapid for the day. Richard shrugged and said: She's a little weirded out by Shane. But she's not here, is she?

Clay smiled, pleased with this small male conspiracy. He rose and put on his boots.

The first thing Clay said when they reached the creek was: Shane's home.

Richard glanced at the pickup crouched between the buildings where the creek valley began its rise.

He's sleeping, he said.

How do you know?

He spends all night poaching. He's got to sleep sometime. Anyway, if he sees us, fine.

But we're on his land.

He's our neighbor, Clay.

Me and — we'd see him sometimes, when we were fishing.

Yeah? Well, he's a recluse, but he's still our neighbor. I've lent him equipment. He's always returned it.

Richard handed Clay a shovel. It was satisfying to work with his son, to watch the hole steadily deepen, and find the plant's spreading roots and cut through them, see the white scar, the clean separation. They worked rhythmically, not hurrying, and as Richard's muscles warmed he fell into that state of contentment that physical work always brought him. But two feet down he kicked the spade into a rock, and the impact went up his leg and into the small of his back like a clubbing. When he tried to dig around the rock he found the earth layered with them, packed so closely together they were like a horizontal wall barely mortared by soil. He and Clay pried them out, grunting and scraping. Richard's joints began to hurt, his fingers to bleed.

Three feet down, the dirt in the hole began to darken. Richard was puzzled, then understood: They'd dug below the streambed, and the hole was filling with water. The darkening turned smooth, and the bottom of the hole became a mirror in which he could faintly see his face's components configured among the stones. He tried to dig faster than the soil could leak, but the wet gravel stuck to his spade, and he had to bang it edgewise on the ground to unglue it. He worked even harder, fueled by frustration: a panting rhythm of harsh shocks and strikings, all steel and implacable rock against which he felt he could break. Water soaked his boots and pants cuffs and wicked its way to his knees. He slopped around in wet socks, and his latent arthritis flamed.

Richard didn't realize his fury and the frenzied speed at which he was working until Clay's shovel slipped, and he stumbled and plunged into the water, his kneecap thudding against a stone and mud splashing his face. He grunted but rose without a word and stabbed savagely at the ground again, his jeans ripped, exposing an ugly welt.

You OK? Richard asked, but Clay wouldn't look at him. Richard's anger leaked away, leaving him empty and deflated. His son was trying to keep up, to make him proud, and Richard had been too absorbed in his own emotions to notice. He wanted to bend and attend to the wound but knew better than to make a big deal of it. Instead he worked halfheartedly for a few more moments, then stopped, letting Clay go on for a while.

Then he said: I don't know about you, but I'm beat.

Clay lifted his head. For a tick Richard thought he was going to scream at him. Then gratitude, and pride that he'd outworked his father, rose into his face, and he smiled. Still, above the smile Richard saw his large, starved eyes. Clay looked as if he were made of tissue paper, and the dried mud on his skin were the only thing that structured him, and if Richard were to scrape it off, his son would flake away.

They sat side by side on Blueboy. Richard wanted to reside with Clay in that mutual state when weariness holds time in abeyance and the moment goes on and on. He thought how he'd almost destroyed this good thing without even knowing it was forming, and then had inadvertently rescued it. Now he just wanted to have it, and his gratitude. He wanted to stare, with Clay, at the hole and the wet earth piled around, and he wanted to drink water, pass the jug, receive it back, and know that it felt as good against Clay's throat as against his own.

Finally, though, they had to move again. A foot of water covered the bottom of the hole. The root was still down there; they hadn't reached its end. But Richard didn't see how the plant could survive that long journey back to light. And he couldn't bring himself to care anymore.

Let's bury it, he said.

They began throwing dirt back into the hole, tamping it down hard. They were about half done when Clay stopped working and said: He's coming, Dad.

Shane Valen's pickup was grinding toward them, a grim apparition of neglect: smashed headlights, crazed windshield, Shane's left arm hanging straight down from the open window, flopping when the pickup bounced.

Let him come, Richard said.

Dad!

Richard spoke quietly: What's got into you? We've always lived next to this guy.

I don't like him.

We're going to talk to him and have a nice, neighborly chat. OK? Clay — look at me. OK?

The pickup was snorting in front of them, asthmatic, the valves clacking. Clay nodded. Shane shut off the engine. He sat inside, staring through the cracked star of the windshield, his face a series of shattered pieces, his eyes askew in different quadrants. Then his left arm rose like a pump handle, his wrist curled inward, and his fingers found the outside door latch and lifted. The door swung open. He paused, took his right hand off the steering wheel, and let it rest on the seat, looking down at it. He seemed to be stroking something lying there, too low to see, and his mouth moved, speaking. Then his feet slid to the ground, and the rest of his body poured itself into the shape of his skin until he was standing erect under his green CENEX cap with a crescent of grease swabbed across the bill.

Afternoon, Shane, Richard said.

The bill of the cap dipped an inch. Shane stayed behind the open door.

This side the creek's mine, he said. Suppose you know that, though.

The words came out so slowly he might have been counting them on his fingers.

Ordinarily, Shane, I wouldn't trespass any more than you would, Richard said.

Everyone in the county knew that Shane, in his poaching, trespassed promiscuously, with no more regard for fences or surveys than the animals he hunted.

Richard went on: But I'm doing us both a favor here.

Looks like you're doing me a big hole.

Shane reached into his shirt pocket, retrieved a can of chewing tobacco, tapped the lid, twisted the cap off, transferred cap and can to the same hand, pinched up a gleaming wad dark as a horse's flank, placed it under his lip, replaced the cap, lifted his pocket flap, and stuck the can back. Then he came out from behind the door of his pickup and took a few steps toward them, light-footed, graceful, quiet as an antelope.

He suddenly grinned, brown-toothed, and lopsided and oddly young, the grin of a man who didn't imagine himself as seen by others. His whole face was taken. It cracked like a mask of flour paste that nevertheless held together, without reserve or containment other than that of musculature and bone.

Must be you burying someone, he said in his searching way. Gonna get Ol Greggy up here investigating, am I?

You know how it is, Richard said. A guy hates to bury his mistakes on his own land.

Goddamn. Shane chortled. That is the truth.

He laughed: Uh-huh, uh-huh, uh-huh — a goofy, throat-clearing sound that made Clay laugh, too. Shane glanced at him, then turned back to Richard.

So, he said. What is it you got doing here? That is favorable to us both? Seems I ought need know.

You had a weed up here, Richard said. A bush called salt cedar. Real invasive. Figured the neighborly thing was I'd just dig it out for both of us.

Tamarisk, Shane said.

Richard gaped. You know it?

You like digging tamarisk, hell! I can make you happy till the Vikings win the Super Bowl.

Richard absorbed the meaning of this.

There's more of this stuff? he asked.

South side the county. West. The creek up from the river.

Shane's face went soft and distant.

Makes this country smell some good at night, he said. Come upon it? Wake up under it? Like a garden. All mixed up? With cattails and what-all?

Richard wondered if Shane curled up in the dark like an animal, whenever he was tired, and fell asleep. There were stories to that effect, and Richard almost pursued the question but decided he didn't need to know.

How much of it you found? he asked.

Ain't found. Ain't looking. Just there.

Shane turned to Clay again.

You like digging? he asked. Looks like it don't like you.

Clay glanced down at his knee.

Like fishing, Shane stated.

Clay shook his head, not meeting Shane's eyes. Some, he said.

Shane regarded him with a half-predatory look. Ain't fished for a while, he said.

Nah, Clay said. Not much.

Shane spat. Not much, he said. He looked off at the horizon. Why's that?

Clay lifted a shoulder, tipped his head, his eyes on a salt cedar leaf midway between himself and Shane. From the top of Shane's barn a crow cawed.

No reason, Clay said. Just ain't fishing much.

A grin crept across Shane's face. No reason, he said. Well.

He looked into the sky, and the grin got wider. He was suddenly unaware of Richard and Clay, in his own thoughts entirely.

Hear that? he said to the clouds. No reason.

Then he came back, and his eyes latched on to Clay again.

Seen you fishing with that neighbor girl, he said. Name like a bird? Hay Jay? Father owns Valen land? Might be, you ain't fishing with her anymore, she'd go with me, huh?

Clay gripped his shovel in his hands like a lance, strangling the shaft, the muscles of his forearms knotted under his smooth, boy's skin. You stay away from her, he yelled.

His lips were white, and he looked young and vulnerable, yet danger lay on him like a caul. Shane had started to chuckle but stepped back, though he was several yards from Clay, and held his hands up as if to fend off a blow, his palms dirty, his eyes alarmed.

Clay! Richard said.

He stepped between them. Shane dropped his hands. He gazed at Richard, as if assessing something. Then he smiled briefly, and his mouth began working the tobacco. He spat, driving a grasshopper into the ground. It struggled momentously, as if being birthed from dark froth.

Didn't mean nothing, Shane said. Don't do much fishing. Too much work for what you get. Been watching that girl, though, since about forever.

You've been watching her? Richard asked, alarmed.

Shane stretched out an unhurried foot and stepped on the sodden grasshopper. Who ain't? You seen her ride?

Oh, Richard said. Barrels. Yeah, she's something.

Just stay away from her, Clay repeated. He still held the shovel like a weapon, his eyes grim, though Shane now seemed unperturbed.

Mr. Valen didn't mean anything, Richard said. He was making a joke.

Dad says, Shane said, then stopped.

Rodney? He's—

Dead, Shane said. Been sucking roots a while now.

He glanced up like a child with a secret, then lifted his foot and held it in both hands, twisted toward him at waist level, an enigma of filth and graceful balance. He stared at the crushed grasshopper on the sole of his boot, lost to the world, calm as an egret, and as much contained by his own intensity. The shifting breeze blew his scent to Richard—a knockdown yeastiness, and old blood, creases in his skin harboring communities of fermentation. He let go the boot and dropped it to the ground, scraped his foot backwards. The dismembered corpse of the grasshopper appeared in the bromegrass.

Then he looked at Clay again. You and me's a lot alike, he said.

We got nothing in common.

Richard hardly recognized the focused young man before him.

Let's fill this hole and get off Mr. Valen's land, he said.

Land don't smell like it used to.

This dirt? Richard asked.

Said land, not dirt. Don't smell the same.

He jerked his head at the wilting shoot Clay and Richard had dug out.

This stuff, he said. Spurge. Tansy. Wake up sometimes and hardly know where you're at.

We best fill this in. You won't even know it was here.

Oh, I'll know.

He gazed at the hole as if to memorize its contours.

Guess things're OK, then, he said. He spat, turned around, ambled to his pickup, got in, his eyes in their different panes perhaps watching them, perhaps not. He looked at the seat beside him, and his hand reached down, and his elbow and shoulder moved as if he were stroking the upholstery. He spoke some words. He turned the key.

Richard turned to Clay.

What were you thinking?

He can't talk that way about her.

You were going to fight him? He would've knocked your head off.

I would've hit him with my shovel.

He wouldn't have cared about your shovel. Don't start fights you can't win. Especially when there's no reason to.

I had to do something, Dad. He can't just talk about her like that.

Men talk like that. It's just stupid. Stupid and ugly and not funny at all. But it's just talk. If you can't distinguish between talk and action you're going to make trouble your whole life. For yourself and everybody else.

His words swirled Richard back to that night with Sophie Lawrence. It sank into him that he hadn't known talk from action then and had missed something vital that was so far gone it was beyond salvaging or recognition, like something swept off a boat and seen later, far away on the water, unrecognizable except as something left behind, that had been an object with a name and use but was now only a shape to be guessed at, in a vastness, in a space.

Richard was held suspended in that vastness. Then he returned to the world and was awfully sorry. Because he saw Clay's fallen face. And he knew Clay wasn't a troublemaker but would all his life be the opposite, someone trying to keep others from trouble, and that it was a burden hard to bear. He saw his son's life as a whole suddenly, saw Clay as an old man, and it seemed — that life Richard saw — a dignified and sad and noble endeavor never accomplished. Looking back as he was from the end of his son's life, Richard saw the people Clay had tried to keep from trouble as peeping birds blown by irresistible winds against the hard, invisible panes of their lives, and stunned, always stunned, and crying out, on green lawns bloodied, on sidewalks dusty and bloodied. He saw the old man Clay was lift his hand in a final, useless blessing, and around him a great grieving for a goodness gone. Richard was filled with a sense of the myriad disappointments of that life yet to come — and he knew it was already too late to raise his son to be hard, and it filled him with pride and sorrow.

You're not a troublemaker, he said. Jesus, Clay. The last thing you are is a troublemaker.

He saw Clay fighting tears again. He had this moment to wonder whether Clay would let them fall — observing his son in a crystalline, distant space that was both intimate and aloof, like a single prayer offered in an empty church. And he had the clear, complete thought that if Clay were a daughter he would not be fighting his tears, they would be making clean pathways down the dirt on his face, and Richard would go to her, that daughter, and take those tears onto his fingertips and enclose her in his muddy arms, and they'd stand mudded together, until something had passed.

Wakings

One

He wakes to the stars rampant, reeling: hammered, pointed, painted, printed—and through them satellites jerking, light intermittent and doubtful, storms in the stratosphere, currents of shearing air. He stirs. The earth is comfortable here, this small depression just outside the cemetery fence near the corner, among the prairie dog holes, a sinking of the soil like a bed barely too small, the ground rising at his neck like a pillow, and the grass a mattress. He rises, yellow with pollen, into the stars, yellow as the moon, a golden coin of a man who finds his Thermos, twists the cap, pours, squats, two stumps a choice for backrests, immense old cottonwoods that once thrust into the air above this shallow depression, now jagged, splintered, tornado-twisted, unscrewed from the ground, leverage of leaves and limbs, torsion of fiber, until the trunks erupted crystalline, spiking, the severed trees turned into mindless, blowsy birds. He's found them both, bone white, nesting in the grass a half-mile and a mile away, spit out from the wall of wind.

Two

He wakes to the ceiling of a bedroom in the old house, the house whose very mention brought acid to his grandfather's voice, like the smell of the powder coating a battery terminal. A dark crack splits the white ceiling, dark lightning in a dirty white sky. He has scraped away the swallow and raccoon shit to lie in the center of the floor and sleep in the house's sighing, its residual, constant cracking. He can hear it decay, hear it sway slowly back to the ground. He can hear the buffalo herd in the night, as if the night is softly grunting, the air muttering dark to the grass. *I'd burn that house,* his grandfather said, or he thinks he remembers his grandfather said. *I'd burn it I'd burn it I'd burn it, if I hadn't sold it I'd burn it.* And that old, old woman, ancient, rocking in her chair, mother of his grandfather, that old woman with the dark, lightning-like scar on her face, nodding and whispering *burn it burn it burn it,* rocking to burn it, fire of lightning in her face striking outward to burn it. There is a rocking chair in another room, covered in dried dung and dust. It blows in the wind when the east wind blows. He won't go near that chair, it is like her chair, the one in his house upstairs, in the room she lived in, that he won't go into either.

In another room in this house — a room with window intact and a door he keeps closed to lock out the swallows and coons — is a child's bed and a nightstand he dusts with his sleeve, and on it a brush with fine hairs caught in its bristles. They move in the room's small currents. He has poured the fuel, stood in its reek, lit the match, and then held it, hearing *burn it burn it burn it.* But the fine hairs move, as if the girl is alive on the bed, breathing small, regular breaths, and the night outside grunting softly. He lets the match burn down to his fingers, then escapes like a fox through a window. He folds himself into lightning and leaps away from the words.

Three

He wakes to the sound of an owl's wings, which he can't have possibly heard, yet he sees it mooncast on the leaves above him, stalker of air, clawer of wind, nightmare of mole and mouse, dread of snake and weasel. A weasel's nightmare, he thinks, and stumbles to his feet with his rifle already aimed, at nothing. He is lost in the smell of salt cedar blooming: dislocated, ajar. He steadies himself with the Dipper, the sweep of its hand on the sky, the North Star's jeweled axle. He goes to the river. He has tunnels through the tamarisk, and he stoops like a bear in a labyrinth to the edge of the engineered water, a dam he's never seen scribing the flow. He thrusts his head under, thinks *breathe, breathe, breathe*. But his body itself seems against it. He sits on the stones and remembers his mother reading in a chair by the side of his bed. He remembers how he came home with a pheasant in hand to show her, and she wasn't there, she was gone. His wet hair drips on his knees and wets the backs of his hands. *Dick*, he thinks, *Jane*, he thinks, *Sally and Spot*, and the back of the wind somewhere. Aloud he says, Mom, and then says it again.

Four

He wakes inside the herd. He has coated himself in their droppings. He wants to know like they know, wants to suck in the wind and discover with a huff of surprise that his humanness stinks. He wants to know in the smell of their shit comfort, security, care, and other scents as concern. The rumbling of their guts in the night seduced him to sleep: a lullaby of fermentation, digestion, rumination. He couldn't go any further. Through the fence in the dark, quietly clipped, and chin to the ground like a snake toward the sounds of their guts, their lungs, the popping of tendons in joints, the compression of cartilage. Sounds massive and ultimate and quiet. He couldn't keep his eyes open. He wakes to find they've moved closer. They'd mistook him for shit and lie monumental around him. He can't see but hears them, their breathing now, the slide of integument, the music of gas. He lifts his smeared face. He feels like weeping and does, silently, so as not to alarm them, with his face to the ground to withhold the smell of his tears. Antelope are older. Only their bones, their muscles and stride and their eyes looking backwards, remember the dire wolf, the short-faced bear. A predatory world, harder, faster, better. This is as close as he'll get. He drags himself forward among them. But shit doesn't move, so — the logic of beasts — they ignore it. He passes by them so closely he feels their breath on his neck, sees their horns against the sky, is tickled once by a beard. Is this true? He passes. On the other side of the herd he stands. Raises his arms, stomps the ground. He doesn't know what will happen. They may doze on till morning, may trample him, or stampede away. Nothing at first. Then he calls. Shit doesn't speak: they ignore him. He calls again and again and again. Shoo, he says, you're free, he says, goddamn you sonsabitches, get your bisonasses off the ground and move, he says. Human language comes only from humans. The logic of beasts: he hears the herd rising awful and grand, moving away, toward the gap he has cut in the fence.

Five

He wakes to that old lightning-faced woman. She kneels near one of the crosses, thin boards stuck in the ground. Some have fallen. There are names on the cross boards. He can't read them. They were carved too lightly to last. Weather has muddled them, made them in moonlight illegible. He's tried to read them with his fingers. There is an E, a J, an M, a P. First initials. But the smaller letters escape him. His fingers, caterpillars, crawl over them. The starlight flares down. It's no longer his land. His grandfather sold it. To a Damish, who sold to the buffalo rancher, his neighbor, the one with the daughter he saw born and who leans her horse around the barrels and is weightless. But her father has no right to this place.

His grandfather should never have sold it. He lived upstairs with his mother. Each in a room. She rocked. Her lightning struck forward then back and forward again and then back. While the floor creaked. It was his job to take up her meals. Up the stairs with a plate almost too heavy to carry, and through the doorway, after a knock. She made him sit while she ate. Told him stories. Warned him of things. He can't remember the warnings. She knows the names here. She came here in secret, alone, dug the holes, placed them in it, he knows, each in a sheet, and with a knife carved the names. This place can't be seen from the old house. It is covered with buffalo berry and cedar. The old man who gave her that lightning wouldn't have known she was down here. She hid the graves well. He found them fleeing a failure to burn down the house. He ran, hearing *burn it burn it* behind him. He hid under cedar. When he woke he saw them: the crosses. Four of them, next to each other. He raised the fallen ones up. When he sleeps here, sometimes she comes. She lays her clean cheek on the ground, the lightning cheek to the sky. She kisses the graves. It is always while he is waking. When he knows he's awake she is gone.

Six

He wakes in a culvert. The sound of a car stopping wakes him. The tight, ribbed, galvanized sky. Voices coming down into it. This is what death is: the sky close, and voices coming from somewhere. Maybe, he thinks. Maybe. He digs in his elbows, crawls forward dragging his feet, wriggling for purchase, the *O* of the world before him enlarging. What if it didn't? What if he crawled like this toward it, but the burrow just lengthened, the *O* stayed the same size: a circle of light reducing itself, adjusting forever to his movement? He almost wishes it so, these ribs of steel like the bones of the earth close around him, and he thumping within it forever. But the light does enlarge, both wider and more, and the voices, one calm, one almost the cries of an animal, get louder, and then he's emerging headfirst, blinking, quiet as slither, onto the borrow ditch bottom. He hears another car coming, hears it stop, hears a door open and shut, footsteps, a question within the animal cries: Should I go for help? Stay here. He slides up the borrow ditch, peeks over. They're not looking his way. They're looking at what he is: a blood-red girlchild held up to the light, and bawling, a new voice in the morning.

Seven

He wakes among bones. Yards of bones going down, he feels them, the earth a matrix of bones here, the earth crazed with bones. Above him the butte, straight-edged, blocks out all stars to the east. All is dark. All hidden. He nestles deeper and dozes. He dreams of the herds as massive rain falling down, over the edge of the cliff, to cries: hailing down darkly, tumbling, their hooves upside down running in air, their horns like moons curving earthward, their spindle legs which will break upon impact. A blizzard of blood and of flesh piling up. And the predatory men plying spears, cocking their arms, while the women, holding stone knives, wait for the dying to end.

Eight

He woke only once here, to nothing. No movement or sound. But he tasted blood in the air. He thought as he came out of sleep that he had swallowed a knife. He thought he was choking on blood. The stars were serene, the moon distant, indifferent. He coughed into his hand, looked at his palm, expecting a gestalt of darkness. None appeared. He wasn't, then, dying. But the scent of blood grew. As if he had brought down a pronghorn, had opened it, was kneeling beside it. But greater. And not an antelope's blood. He knew. The air or the ground here: one or the other was bloody. Or both. He left. He never returned. The place was inviting, two depressions, with soft grass, far from the old house, from anything. So far that the moon seemed as close as the earth. But the air there was red. Something didn't want him there, sleeping.

Draw

ANGELA MORRISON WAS six years younger than Brock, and only twenty years old, when she married him. She'd visited the ranch before, but settling there, living there — she'd had no idea. It felt like the ends of the earth. There wasn't even enough noise to mark time's passage. She had to keep a radio or TV on. She missed everything about Sioux Falls: traffic, the Empire Mall, restaurants, the muddy Big Sioux River. And green lawns. She spent hours, while Brock was off doing whatever he did with cattle and machinery, watering the grass and flower beds. The garden hose spewed musty-smelling water pumped from the stock dam. She was holding it, watching the arc and splash, when she saw her first rattlesnake, sunning itself on a rock in the bottom of a deep, steep-sided ravine that curved away from the house.

It was so far away, seventy or eighty yards, that at first she squinted, wondering at the rock's weird mottling. Then something in her perception shifted, and the snake's contours leapt into clarity, so defined it seemed to jump off the rock and float in the air between her and the ravine. She dropped the hose with a little cry and ran into the house. When Brock came home for supper, he found the hose running and gullies eroded into the dirt between clumps of grass, and small lakes gathered in wheel ruts. He stepped into the house intending to explain to his new wife that they had enough water in the dam for the lawn and flowers, but there wasn't much sense in letting the hose run once you had the job done, it wasn't like water was a nuisance out here with so much of it around. But when he saw Angela's face, he changed his mind.

Something happen? he asked instead.

When I was watering the lawn, I saw a snake.

What'd it look like?

It was big. It had these dark blotches.

Sounds like a bull snake or a rattler.

A rattlesnake? I saw a *rattle*snake?

How close were you?

She nodded toward the living room window. It was in that ravine, she said.

That's probably what you saw, then. There're rattlesnakes in that draw. You got some eyes if you spotted one from the yard.

You never told me there were rattlesnakes here.

He paused, puzzled at the accusation in her voice.

Didn't tell you there was wind either, Ang.

I *knew* it was windy. You never *told* me there were rattlesnakes.

Brock had jacked his boots off before coming into the house, and now he stared at his stockings. Maybe he hadn't ever mentioned rattlesnakes to her. They were like dry weather or the occasional tornado. You lived with them. He'd bought her a pair of boots, but maybe he hadn't told her all the good reasons to wear them. Still, he thought it best to apologize.

Guess it never came up, he said. Sorry. Now you know.

I want you to get rid of them.

Brock glanced at her just in time to understand she was serious, and he cut off the smile that almost made it to his face.

That'd be a fine thing, Ang, he said. So would getting rid a grasshoppers. Or having enough rain.

Good, then, she said — and rose and kissed him.

He was so surprised he kissed her back. But when he accepted the kiss instead of pulling back and putting out his hands and saying, *Wait a sec. Let's get clear what I'm saying,* he found himself complicit in a promise he'd never made.

Four months before the wedding, while making plans with her mother, Angela had wondered whether she should even get married. She couldn't give reasons. She just wondered, Was it really what she wanted?

Honey, her mother said. It's kind of late for doubts. We've already ordered the cake.

Angela bent, blinded by dismissal, to the wedding magazine in her lap.

Now, the bouquet, her mother said. Carnations or mums? Or maybe roses?

Angela couldn't think. She didn't care about the flowers. She didn't want a thing to do with them.

You decide, she said. It doesn't matter to me.

She was determined after that not to give space to any doubt or uncertainty. She would simply insist that it would all be good, and it would be. Except for a single unanticipated moment, it mostly worked. Right before the vows she handed her bouquet to her bridesmaid, and as she saw it float away in the bridesmaid's hands, she realized she wouldn't have chosen carnations or mums or roses, any of them. A feeling of being out of control of her own life, of being sacrificed to something she couldn't name, bucked into her chest and throat, and with it the added desperation that she couldn't let it show. She jerked her head away from the bouquet to Brock's face and smiled. He saw the glistening in her eyes and was overcome himself.

In those hours alone in the house after seeing that first snake, even before she knew it was a rattlesnake, Angela allowed herself to wonder out loud if she'd made a mistake. Two things kept returning to her mind. The first was the way the snake had suddenly and irreversibly become what it was: the way it had been just a rock with puzzling markings, and then instantly had changed, and she couldn't get the rock back. The second was flowers. There were all sorts of flowers. There were calla lilies, gladioluses. Why not sprays of white and purple lilacs, plucked minutes before the ceremony? Or bouquets of wildflowers, profusions beyond naming? Or why even a bouquet? How about a single flower, a garden tulip, a yellow one, with deep purple striations? Her mother might have been horrified, but it could have been.

When Brock kissed her, she felt better—better, almost, than if she'd never seen the snake. He'd do this for her. But a year went by, and he never went to the draw. Occasionally she would be startled to be looking out the living room window and realize she was seeing a snake out there on the rocks. She'd shut the drapes, and they'd stay shut until Brock opened them with a comment about light.

Brock began hinting at having children. They'd both assumed they would, and Angela didn't understand her resentment when he brought it up. She deflected the discussion. She said she wasn't ready yet. Brock didn't pressure her. He agreed that there was time, and she was the one doing the hard part. But after a while his patience got on her nerves. It felt like prediction—as if he knew she'd come around and do what was expected. It made her more adamant in her refusal. She wanted to have a full-blown fight over it. But she never got beyond irritation. Every time, just when she was ready to get angry, he'd nod and say: OK. It ain't me having em. But think about it, huh?

In spite of her fear, Angela was determined not to be trapped in the house. She had to do *something* on those long afternoons when time ticked in the clocks and the soap operas droned on. Brock suggested she learn to drive a tractor or ride an ATV or horse. He said he could use the help. But she couldn't even imagine herself doing those things. She walked. Nothing moved — maybe a jet lazing city to city, or a bird, or a jackrabbit erratic and pogo-sticking. A faraway coyote once, maybe. *She* moved, but she could hardly tell. It wasn't like she went blocks, something she could mark and count. Wasn't like she went past houses or parks, or even had somewhere to actually go. It was all just land.

But her second encounter with a rattlesnake was close-up, and when she heard its electric buzz coming, seemingly, from the ground right at her feet, like a thousand cicadas gathered into a tight, resonant ball, she was jolted into a stillness so profound the earth's basalt and granite seemed to shift between her heartbeats. When she came out of that stillness, through no conscious choice, she saw the snake ten feet away, mottled brown in the brown grass: the muscular coiling, the glittering points of its eyes, the thin tongue raking the air: a singular thing, distinct, but an evocation of the world, too: almost just grass, but starkly and awfully not. She stood there, stood there, stood there, until the snake finally seeped away like liquid coiled into a shape that lost that shape and was gone, soaked into the ground. Even then she stood for long minutes before finally backing up, keeping her eyes on the place the snake had been, then finally fleeing. On that run back to the house she distrusted every footfall. Once inside, she locked the door. But light leaking under it betrayed a thin crack.

It was worsened because she'd been daydreaming. She'd let her mind go. She'd been imagining finding an old toy of Brock's lying in the grass—a tiny metal car with flaking paint, a plastic horse bleached by sun, a marble so scuffed it had turned opaque: her own hands picking up what his small ones had once dropped. She imagined holding it, bringing it home and putting it under the bed where, when they made love, she could let her hand drop down to touch it.

The snake's rattle ruptured the dream, then compressed the space the dream had expanded. It was suffocating, claustrophobic, insisting she pay attention only to where she was: her next step, the shadow there, right there. Don't think, don't lose yourself. When Brock came home he jiggled the doorknob. She let him call out several times before she rose from the couch and went to the door, a pillow clutched to her chest.

What's this, Ang? Locking doors? This ain't the city.

He swept her into his arms, pillow and all, laughing, but she was so rigid he released her.

I almost stepped on a rattlesnake today.

Before Brock could ask what *almost* meant, Angela cried out: How could you be a child out here? Running around with snakes like that?

He didn't hear the real question, the implication, the future.

You got me on that one, Ang, he said, laughing. I'm sorry. I won't do it again, I swear.

You promised.

It took him a moment to realize the conversation's shift. He spoke softly and urgently.

Where'd you see this snake?

Down by the stock pond.

There's no way a snake by the stock pond came from the draw past the house, Ang. They're a half mile apart. And that draw's the only thing we ever talked about. And I never said I'd clean em out. You just thought I did. That draw's too steep for cattle, so they ain't a problem there, and they ain't coming out of it up to the house. I can't get rid a every snake on this ranch. They're part a the place. Always have been. Wear those boots I got for you when you go walking, and keep your eyes open. That's how you deal with snakes.

She'd never heard him this impatient with her. She felt exultation. He was barely holding his anger in. She pushed harder, eager now.

I'm not going walking anymore.

Brock stared at her. But instead of arguing, he lifted his hands and took a half step back.

Fine, he said. That's a solution, too.

She watched him turn away to wash for supper. She found herself alone in the living room, with her arms crossed, and nothing more to say.

After that she began to take regular trips to Twisted Tree. Brock thought it a good sign. She was getting out, doing something. He didn't realize she was following through—leaving the ranch to walk asphalt streets in town and the gravel pathway along Red Medicine Creek.

She became one of a small number who took regular walks along the creek. The young Catholic priest, Father Caleb, was another. When they passed each other one day, they spoke a few words. She'd always gone to church but had never really talked to a priest, and it was a novelty to stand near the creek like that and speak of ordinary things. She liked the way he listened to the simple pleasantries she spoke, about the weather and the light, as if they mattered. She liked how he waited for her to finish her sentences. The rhythms were right, of speech, of pauses, and of considerations and continuations. A few days later she saw him again, in front of her, going the same direction. She liked to walk fast, to feel the blood pumping in her temples. She debated: slow down to stay behind him, or catch up?

He turned when he heard her footsteps.

Angela again, he said. Hello!

Angela Again? she asked. Are you renaming me?

He laughed: Part of my job.

He opened the pathway to her with a sweep of his hand.

You're moving faster than I am, he said.

I'm finished.

They fell into step with each other.

The creek gurgled beside them, and from somewhere in town came the steady sound of hammering, drumlike, on a roof. Between them, silence: just their steps in unison. They were passing a small wetland near the footbridge that led over the creek to the school. Angela was about to comment on a redwing blackbird swaying sideways on a cattail, when she saw something so startling she stumbled and bumped into the priest, and he stumbled, too, and they clung to each other.

Look at that, she said. Look at that.

On the flat bottom below them, a crow, iridescently black, one wing smoothed into its body, the other ragged, half-out, was pecking at something in the grass. It lifted its head as if to show them. In the black beak was a marble, a tiny globe. As the bird brought it up the sun struck it in such a way that the marble turned to pure light, hardened and brilliant, a moment of angles and coincidence that turned them breathless and grasping each other: great bird and held sun with, deep inside it, an encased helix of green light.

Then the crow sprang into the air. They realized they were still holding each other and stepped back. They looked at their own hands, then at the empty place the crow had been.

That was pretty amazing, he said.

The way the light?

Yes. The light.

It was just a marble?

Their eyes met.

Just a marble? he asked.

They fell into step again, closer than before, a small, warm space between them.

Red Medicine Creek ran at an angle through town, so that streets and alleys dead-ended at it. She had parked at one of these dead ends. As she approached her car, a sudden silence broached her daydreaming. The hammering that had been a metronome in the background had stopped. She looked up and saw a man standing on a half-shingled roof, watching her. He was middle-aged, bare-backed, muscular, thin-waisted, shining with sweat, his arms hanging loosely, one hand holding a hammer. He balanced on the roof like a ship's captain on a deck.

Hey, he called down to her.

Hey, she said back.

Been walking?

She looked at the pathway she'd just left and shrugged.

You like that?

It's exercise.

He placed the hammer in the wire loop at his belt without taking his eyes off her. Don't mind exercise myself, he said.

I don't think we've met. I'm Angela Morrison. Brock Morrison's wife.

Oh, hell, I know. Ol Brock.

She opened her car door.

Figured I'd meet you sometime. Didn't know you were as pretty as they said.

She shut the door, but his voice, laughing, came through the closed windows: Don't mind it myself, Angela. You think about it.

Over supper she told Brock about it, without going into detail. He stopped eating.

What'd he say specifically? he asked.

He made a pass at me, she said.

What'd he say?

He made a pass.

Brock waited. Then he picked up his fork. Shingling, he said. Hadda be Sid Ervin. He's married himself. Got a stepdaughter, even. Always was a jerk. All mouth, though. You don't need a worry about him. But I'm sorry it happened.

Yeah, she said. Me, too.

So, Angela Again, why do you drive ten miles just to walk?

I'm a city girl, she said.

Twisted Tree's certainly a city.

She heard something in his voice—a desire to be elsewhere, maybe. He was making a joke, but not only. It made her honest, or as honest as she could be.

Out there—she lifted her chin in the general direction of the ranch—kind of scares me.

Scares you? Why would it scare you?

Specifically? Rattlesnakes.

And unspecifically?

The question disconcerted her. But he nodded as if her silence were an answer. Brock doesn't understand, he said.

That shook her. He'd leapt through barriers she'd not even known she'd erected.

I didn't say that.

Sorry.

No. You're right. Brock was raised here. He hardly notices them.

I grew up on a ranch myself. Out toward Lone Tree.

You were raised on a ranch?

That surprise you?

Maybe.

She took two steps, then said, Yes, it does.

It was exciting to be precise in that small, quiet way.

Why's it surprise you?

You're not like Brock.

It was so simple, and so simply said. She liked the way she kept accusation out of her voice, the way she just answered the question, gave the bare reason for surprise.

He laughed.

Why are you laughing?

The idea that being raised the same way would make people the same.

Are you OK with snakes?

I wear boots.

That silenced her.

He told you to wear boots, didn't he?

She nodded.

He laughed again. The man is right, he said.

She turned her head down, smiling. Without thinking she grabbed his hand.

They were both silent. Three steps. A cottonwood seed floating by: that long.

She let go.

It's OK, he said.

But she didn't want to be dishonest now. She wanted all gaps closed.

No, she said. It's probably not.

More than three steps, then.

A crow flew over.

You think that's the same crow? she asked.

I can't tell one from another.

What do you think he did with that marble?

You didn't know crows played marbles?

She bowed her head, laughing.

No, she said. I didn't know that.

From a distance his straw-colored hair gleamed in the fall sun. He stood stock-still near the creek, his arms crossed. She stopped beside him.

What are you looking at? she asked.

That branch.

A fully leaved willow limb, with two main branches, had fallen into the creek, and the water had twisted it so that one of the branches was dipping into the creek in a regular rhythm. The current caught it and pushed it away, and it snapped up, reached the end of its arc, sprang back down, dipped again, was pushed away, snapped up, rebounded, dipped back down, on and on and on, the whole limb sympathetic to the water, the leaves way at the end of the other fork shaking in a consistent rhythm that she could almost, as she watched, feel in her body.

What about it?

It's a strange attractor.

She heard *strange tractor*. Her mind flashed to the Case IH rumbling out of the shed in the morning. Strange indeed: like a big insect that Brock, invisible inside the cab, controlled.

It never *doesn't* dip back into the water, Caleb went on, as she tried to catch up to him. Completely regular. The creek flows straight, but the branch keeps returning. That's called a strange attractor. The equation for it is. According to chaos theory.

You read chaos theory?

He smiled: It's not prohibited.

They turned together. She looked over her shoulder. The branch dipped, rose, dipped.

The church needs a secretary, he said after a while.

I had two years of accounting.

You've told me.

She glanced back at the branch again. It was still shimmering, light coming off it in discrete green packets, millions of them shaken.

Once you start seeing them, they're all over, he said.

Them?

Strange attractors. Wind shaking a stop sign, even.

Once the days shortened, it would sometimes be dark before she left the church. One night she turned off the highway onto the gravel county road that ran, in a long series of roller-coaster risings and fallings, to the ranch she couldn't call home. She hadn't gone two hundred yards when she braked so hard the car fishtailed on the gravel, her headlights swinging into the distance as if they held the car to the stars and some far force was whipping her around. Then she pushed the accelerator too hard, and stones banged the undercarriage. She stared into the rearview mirror. In it a man was watching her. He held a knife. He stood in a cloud of rising steam. The steam came from a large animal prostrate at his feet, from its opened interior, from the blood her lights had brightened into redness and that, for a moment, as her brake lights had fishtailed around, had reddened even more. Within the steam the man was a dark silhouette. She couldn't believe that so much steam could rise from a body, could be contained there in such volume and then released: an outpouring. The man had looked right into her headlights. He had seemed about to duck, as if he could roll into a ball and bowl himself into the dark space of the opened animal, which lay with its Cervidaean head lolled back and the hose of its slashed windpipe breathlessly white. Then he straightened and relaxed and merely stared at her: lithe, young, poised on the balls of his feet, neither threatening nor cowed, merely waiting to see whether she would pass or stop. Then, in the mirror, he had bent to his task again: calm, uncompromising, guiltless.

She had pressed the brake so hard and nearly lost control of the car because he had looked right into her eyes, as if he could see through the glare of her headlights and knew precisely what she was doing.

Hadda be Shane Valen, Brock said. That's like seeing a whooping crane. You go to Ruination with that story, you wouldn't pay for a drink all night. You actually caught him.

Caught him?

Shane lives with his dad. They raise a few head, but mainly he poaches. Always out there somewhere. He'll fall asleep, and sometimes don't wake up till morning. People've flushed him out of his naps. But catching him with an animal, Ang—ain't no one done that, far as I know.

Flushed him out of his naps?

Think you got a deer getting up ahead of you, and instead it's Shane getting outta bed.

Where have people seen him?

Wherever. Shane don't know what a fence or a season is.

Has he been on our ranch?

A few times I've wondered why a mulie just dropped its guts in a draw and flew away.

That's horrible.

Shane's a spooky guy. But he don't have a thing to do with people. Just does his grocery shopping a little closer to the source.

You don't care that he's on our land? At night? Without our permission?

Not enough to lose sleep over it. Which is what it'd take to prevent it.

He saw me. He knows who I am.

Brock looked at her, puzzled—and realized she was dead serious about something he regarded as humorous.

Hey, he said gently. It's OK. He'd poached a mulie and was dressing it out, and you happened along. That's all.

I don't see how you can joke about it.

I'm not saying it's right. Just saying, it's not you. Nothing to do with you.

He put his arms around her.

But she shuddered.

Brock felt it and stepped back. He picked a magazine off the end table, collapsed on the couch, opened the magazine, and stared at the page.

People can't see through headlights, Ang, he said. You're making threats where there ain't none. Anyone else here'd brag if they caught Shane. What's going on with you?

Four years into their marriage, still childless and starting to believe he always would be, Brock walked into the house one afternoon and heard the telephone buzzing. He called out for Angela but got no answer, then looked in the garage to see if the car was gone. He stared at its solid presence, wondering why he would think the phone off the hook had something to do with the car. Then he realized he'd imagined it gone for good. He'd never considered Ang would just pick up and leave, but there the thought was, as if it came out of the garage itself or out of the angry, insistent buzzing of the phone: a vision of the car gone and the house empty, and he staring into the drawer where they kept the can opener, figuring out the business of supper.

The vision, brief as it was, frightened him. He tried to shake it from his mind as he walked through the entryway. He went to the kitchen, saw the phone hanging from its coiled cord, and replaced it in the cradle. When the buzzing stopped the house was completely silent. He thought he might hear her breathing somewhere. He walked into the living room and was startled to find her staring out the window, her back to him. She didn't turn around.

She's telling me she's leaving, he thought. They stood in the colloidal silence.

• • •

Speaking in a monotone to the window, Angela said: Roberta called. Mom had an aneurysm. She's gone. Just like that.

Oh — my God, Ang.

That pause: He'd almost said *thank* God.

It wasn't supposed to happen, she said. I can't believe it.

He saw her shake her head, as if trying to dislodge other words. He stepped across the room. He thought she'd turn to him, but she didn't, so he put his arms around her from behind, put his head over her shoulder, his cheek against her hair. In the window's faint reflection their hair blended together so that he couldn't tell hers from his.

Her body didn't change under his touch. It wasn't a time for disappointment, but Brock was disappointed. He wanted his body, right now, to mean something to her. To have at least the power of comfort.

I'll call Stanley Zimmerman to do chores, he said. We can leave in the morning.

If she had turned and folded herself into him, if her limbs had loosened, the conformations of her body changed against him, he might have said things less pragmatic, less tuned to action and solution.

Her shoulder blades stiffened even more.

Look at those snakes on that rock, she said.

Her mother had just died — and here she was, with this old argument. Brock couldn't see anything on the rocks, and as far as he knew, his eyesight was good. He opened his arms and stepped back.

Actually, the Zimmermans just had that baby girl, he said. You give birth in a car, you oughta get a break from doing chores. I'll call Richard Mattingly.

On the way to Sioux Falls the next morning, when Brock saw the small wayside rest along the two-lane road they were taking east, he pulled over. He didn't need a restroom. He just needed to be alone. He didn't understand the depth of the silence in the car. He pulled up to the unmowed lawn that bordered the area, parked parallel to it, and got out, stumbling over a rock hidden in the crabgrass and nearly touching the bottom of the door frame. He left the door open and made his way to the cinder-block restroom. In the stale semidarkness, he leaned against the concrete wall and looked at himself in the mirror over the enamel sink. It was an old mirror, wavy and water-spotted, and it made his face saggy.

The night before, he'd gone out after supper to make sure things were in place for Richard Mattingly. When he returned to the house he found Angela sitting on the couch, her eyes swollen, her face red. He had a guilty, uneasy feeling that her grief was out of proportion: he got along with her mother better than she did. But it wasn't fair to judge someone else's grieving, and he sure couldn't ask her why her mother's death bothered her so much.

Ang, he said gently, you packed yet?

He went to her, held out his hand.

You got to pack, he said.

She let him pull her off the couch, and he took her to the bedroom. She sat on the edge of the bed while he pulled things from the closet, and if she nodded, he put them in a suitcase.

When they'd both returned from the restroom he asked if she could drive. He wanted to escape her silence. If he stayed awake, it would wear him down, or he'd have to probe it, and that would wear him down, too. He crawled into the back seat and fell almost instantly asleep.

Angela stared into the low, rising sun. Dozens of times last night, while Brock was outside, she'd tried to call Caleb. When she'd heard Brock open the door she'd burst into tears, then gone to the couch and tried to compose herself. Again this morning she'd tried, then remembered Caleb was in Rapid City, out of touch.

The astonishing fact of it left her numb. Events were sweeping her along, way, way beyond her control, and the one person she had to talk to she couldn't.

Ten miles down the road she felt a touch of low breeze on her foot. She shifted her leg away from it, but in a few moments the touch came again, harder, sensuous. She unlocked her eyes from the light before her and leaned over and peered through the steering wheel at her feet. For a moment she could see nothing, could only feel, not even a touch — a pressure — on her ankle. Then the sunlight still blinding her faded out of her eyes like a surface breaking up, and the dim floor of the car took shape underneath it. Her breath was jerked from her chest. A rattlesnake thick as her forearm lay under the clutch and brake pedal, its blunt, triangular head touching her ankle softly as air.

She tried to speak, but her throat closed around Brock's name. The snake moved. It flowed past her feet, long and easy in the dim light near the floor, its body looping against her. The muscles were like waves of stiffened water, the scales smooth and cool. It could have been silk. It could have been nothing. It eased itself under the brake pedal and paused, loosely stretched out, its head upon her sandal, its tongue flickering. She heard a faraway moaning, growing until it penetrated the blanket of horror that enveloped her: a semi's air horn. The greater danger pulled her eyes up, the horn devastatingly loud. She was in the left lane, a great, blunt square of chrome and painted metal fifty yards away. She jerked the wheel to the right, her foot still frozen to the accelerator, as if the top and bottom of her body were disconnected. The car yawed into the right lane, bouncing on its shocks, just as the semi's left wheel crossed the centerline, moving to avoid her. She could see the driver's startled eyes as he pulled back, a young man her own age, wearing a baseball cap, and then they were sliding by each other, a foot away, the trailer flickering as sunlight careened off it.

And then the trailer, in the mirror, swaying and diminishing, its brake lights glaring red—but she was going, she was nonstop, alone, the empty road. In the back seat Brock stirred but didn't wake. The snake's tongue and the underlying fangs, folded back, were inches from her foot. If she moved or spoke, she was sure it would strike. But she had to see Brock, had to know she wasn't alone. Brock had once told her to move slowly around animals. She remembered that and let her hand drift off the steering wheel, as if the air were lifting it, to the mirror. She slowly rotated it down until she could see his face in its oblong circumference—his closed eyes, his mouth that seemed to be half smiling though his face was vacant, the white tips of his teeth. She touched his face within the mirror, as if to wake him there. Then she let her hand return to the steering wheel and willed her own paralysis.

The snake's tongue probed the air. It curved along the floor of the car, its scales scraping the plastic mat, its head moving away from her foot. Then it doubled back on itself, relapsed into stillness as if removing itself from the world. Miles and wind and light pouring down. Then movement again, complete and at once, and its chiseled face returning. She was wearing shorts, and she knew what the snake was about to do.

And though she prayed that it would not, it did. Though she prayed to God to kill it, it remained alive. Its head moved forward. Its tongue, light as an insect, brushed her bare ankle. Then it raised its head. It lay the bony underpart of its jaw on her instep, rested there a moment, then glided up onto her, the flex of its body pushing against her bare skin. She could feel the muscles working beneath the scales, and for a moment the animal was staring into her face through the spokes of the steering wheel. Its mouth, under the heat-sensing concavities in its face, was slightly open. The white fangs were curled back against the roof.

It moved, farther up: the scales cool, pushing. It came onto her lap, hung its head over the air toward the door. The thickness of the thing gripped her skin.

The car pounded down the road. Even her prayers had stopped. She had never been so isolate: all calling out contained, her skin a border defining her in opposition to the world.

Brock stirred. In the mirror his eyes remained shut, his face calm and glowing, ardently oblivious, the face of a stranger in another realm.

The snake curled its head back toward her, hesitated, then laid it on her thigh. She felt the loops of its body tighten momentarily, and then the muscles under the scales relaxed and went still. The lidless eyes remained open, but she knew: it had gone to sleep.

It had put an infant's claim on her. Had curled up on her lap and gone to sleep. It had made of her stillness a stillness of care.

Brock stirred again. He struggled, as if trying to remain asleep, then sat slowly up. His foot bumped her seatback.

She could no longer feel the snake against her legs. It had borrowed her warmth, her skin its skin.

Where are we? Brock mumbled. How far we come?

She couldn't answer. She glanced in the mirror to find him, moving only her eyes, but she'd turned the mirror down and his face was gone from it, nothing there but an empty pillow with a depression in the center.

Ang? C'mon, now. You gotta start talking. I'm just asking where we're at.

Then he sensed a new depth in her silence and pulled himself forward.

Ang? You sleeping at the wheel?

She could feel his breath in her hair, could smell the tang of sleep in it, and the sweat on his skin. Then he put his head over the seat, and his breathing stopped.

Jeeee-suss Christ, he whispered.

All those *s*'s moving in her hair, meeting her ear: not just sound but touch: a tiny, connective thread, words that were barely words, coming to her far under the louder sounds of tires and road seams.

She felt the seat move backwards as Brock slowly pulled himself forward. She knew he was peering sideways into her face, though she didn't turn her head to him, didn't do anything that would wake the sleeping creature in her lap. Brock's breath came out in a long sigh. She wanted to lean into it, and she wanted to jerk away from it, but she did neither, and for a moment her stillness protected everything.

Then in a movement so swift Angela was never able to re-create it, Brock's right hand shot around the seatback under her arm and clamped onto the snake just behind its head. It erupted to life, writhing in the air as he jerked it up and hauled it out, its coils striking her shoulders and chest. Its rattle went off, filling the car. She felt that rattle for a moment vibrating, hot as a brand, against her bare thigh. The mouth in front of Brock's fist opened wide with curving teeth.

Stop the car, he yelled.

The snake thrashed. Its tail looped around her right shoulder and arm, clinging, the rattle near her ear like delirium, like light, a bright thing in her brain, and for a moment she couldn't see the road. She might have blacked out. Then the highway was unwinding before her again, and the snake was gone, the rattle shrilling behind her, and over it Brock yelling at her to stop.

But she couldn't stop. She was paralyzed and fleeing both, and in the rearview mirror she saw the pillow, and on it the snake's wizened head, and accusing eyes: it had slept on her skin. In time she would speak to Brock of this, but he would shake his head and tell her it was just being a snake, all along just being a snake, just confused by the vibrations and heat of the car, it couldn't even distinguish her. That's all that had happened. Nothing more. She even probably could have called to wake him, snakes can't hear, it would've been just another vibration added to the chaos.

The air pressure inside the car changed as Brock opened the rear window.

No, Brock, she cried.

Except she didn't. The words would have given him pause, but she never spoke them.

In the side mirror the snake twisted in the car's false wind, awkward and out of its element, an antithesis of bird, a deformity of wing. It hit the road. It rolled like a hose. But its rattle still filled the car. Then she realized her scream had replaced it, language degraded into anarchy, blanketing the words she'd held inside. She felt Brock's hands on her — in her hair, against her shoulders, rubbing hard into her, and she heard his calm voice in her ear.

You can stop now, Ang. Just go ahead and lift your foot. You know how to do that. Go ahead and lift your foot.

But her feet were rigid and far away, her body was far away, and she was fleeing it.

Then Brock, still rubbing her shoulders, still moving his hands against her, still in the same soft, melodious chant, but lighter, almost laughing, said: No need to hurry like this, Ang. Your ma won't be any deader if we get there a few minutes late.

It got through to her. She lifted her foot and let Brock pull her from the car, and she went limp in his arms as he held her by the side of the road. Two days later, in her old bedroom, after her mother's funeral, with dark falling and the lights of Sioux Falls shining dimly and without force through the gauze of curtains, and Roberta and her husband and children somewhere in other rooms, all of them aware of her mother's absence, she left her diaphragm out.

You sure, Ang? Brock asked. You really sure?

She murmured and raised her arms to him.

Because she'd learned she could be cruel. She could throw off what laid a claim to her. She could be as hard as she had to be, and as still, and as silent. What had happened never should have happened. But it had. She'd thought she was swimming in a sea of honesty, and that it was her natural state. It was a lie. She and Caleb should have been less honest from the start.

After they returned from Sioux Falls, Brock went out to the draw with a pickax, shovel, and shotgun. She sat in a lawn chair, sipping water, listening to the clang of metal against rock, the sounds, from the distance she watched, disconnected from the movements that produced them. She saw him run to one side, then another, jabbing with the shovel. Three times he stooped for the shotgun, pointed it below the horizontal, the dust the pellets made marking the perimeter of a circle the snakes could not escape. From where she sat it looked manic and comic and awful.

She thought how unnecessary it was. But she let him have his guilt. And when he returned to the house, blood-spotted, behind him the black smoke of a diesel fire rising, she said: Burn your clothes, too.

In the wind the stench of burning flesh. He'd nodded mutely. She'd risen from the chair. She thought of how much a mother could protect a child. *Not entirely,* she thought. *But some.*

She let that thought sink in, its small, redemptive hope. She pulled her eyes away from the curling smoke. Then she walked into the house to be with her husband. Within two years the snakes in the draw returned. One day she came across the boots Brock had bought for her. She took them from the closet and pulled them on.

Looking Out

ALL MY LIFE I've had a memory of movement, and of opening and shutting doors. Riding subways in strange cities, I will sometimes be convinced, as the doors hiss shut and the car lurches, that I've been on this same train before. Getting in and out of taxis will create the same sensation. For most of my life I thought it was just a mild quirk of my brain.

At ninety-two, my mother takes almost any death in stride, so I thought the news of Eddie Little Feather dying on the highway would be little more than an item to help me pass an afternoon with her. But she was visibly upset, and when I asked her what was wrong, she asked: You don't remember?

What am I supposed to remember? I replied.

Eddie's grandmother coming out when we owned the Valen place, she said. You were maybe five. She wanted to look for her father's grave. We didn't believe those stories, but what could we do? Your father took her out, and you went along. The three of you spent all day driving that ranch. By the end, you were sitting on her lap. You had sandwiches together, out near the buffalo jump.

You never found the graves. But after that your father was always looking for them. Cecelia Little Feather convinced him. I'm surprised you don't remember. You kept asking when that woman was coming back. *I like that looking,* you said.

I had a flash of a long finger lifted into a patch of light, and a voice, very low, saying, *Here,* and a sense of jolting, strange arms holding me, the sound of doors shutting. It was all there at once, sensation more than memory, as if the past had drifted forward to surround me. I recognized it as the original of what I felt in subways.

Maybe I do remember, I said.

Your father really wanted to find those graves.

I doubt they exist, I said. Bea Conway doesn't think they do.

Bea Conway doesn't know everything about events. She only thinks she does.

She's spent a lot of time researching, Mom.

Because a grave isn't marked doesn't mean it isn't there.

I know that.

It may mean it's more there, even.

More there?

Without moving her hand, she lifted her index finger off the chair arm and held it raised, watching it, then set it slowly back down. Then she met my eyes.

I've never told you something, she said. Your father left a grave unmarked himself.

Dad?

Cassie Janisch's grave, she said.

The daughter of the man he hired? You've told me that a dozen times.

Never the whole story. It has to do with you.

Cassie Janisch died before I was born.

Audrey, my memory's fine.

I took my glasses off and let the whole room blur. I held the glasses to my mouth and breathed on them to moisten them, then wiped them clean, replaced them, and found my mother's eyes again.

All right, I said. I'm listening.

It doesn't have to do with you so much as with your absence. You know about that, how we couldn't have children. But when the doctor told us? I walked out of his office thinking: *We have only each other now.* And, Audrey, I didn't know if we were enough for each other. We found a little soda fountain and sat at a table and dipped our spoons and hardly spoke. We were barren together. I felt it. But I didn't know how to speak of it.

She had my full attention now. I'd heard about the miracle of my birth a hundred times, but never in this tone or with that word, *barren.*

We never did speak of it, she went on. When the Valen ranch came up for sale, he bought it. It filled the emptiness for him. I knew it, even if he never said. Or maybe didn't know himself. He'd spend all day out there. Sometimes, when I was alone in the house, I'd reach out with my hands — and here she reached into the air in front of her to shape a round, pantomimed nothing — and feel it. Right here. With me. Walking around the house. Not nothing, Audrey. *A* nothing. They're different.

Yes, I said. I suppose they are.

I'd always thought my father bought the Valen ranch out of simple pragmatism. I never thought my own absence drove that buying, never imagined the work he did out there to be a charcoal pencil shaping shadows, filling in what wasn't. After my mother gave me the whole story I drove out there. No one had lived in the house since the Janisch family left. I had this idea I'd walk through its rooms and feel some emanation of Cassie there, now that I understood what she'd meant. But after Dad died, Mom sold the ranch to the Zimmermans, and Stanley was raising buffalo on it. The herd was spread around the house, which perched over a draw choked with cedar, so close to the edge it looked like it could topple in during the next hard rain. I stayed on the road and imagined Cassie living there with her parents, and my father walking through that door. I could imagine it, but felt nothing of Cassie herself. The house gazed back at me with the indifference of all old houses that refuse to crumble in spite of storms and years.

I was about to leave when I became aware of a figure sitting on the hillside above the herd. I reached for the binoculars I carry in my car, for birds and animals, but the moment I had them focused I turned away and laid them on the seat. It was Stanley Zimmerman. In the brief moment before I averted my eyes, I saw his bowed head, his face like something wind had worked on. I'd heard that he and Kris were having trouble with their marriage. And here he was, sitting alone, buffalo his only company. I felt obscene, to have broken his privacy and barged in on his sorrow. I stared at the door handle of the car to curtail my gaze.

Here we were again. I'd been present when Hayley Jo was born. I'd been driving to Lone Tree to teach and saw the Zimmermans' car parked along the shoulder of the road with the emergency flashers going and someone leaning into the back seat, only his legs showing. I knew it was serious. People don't put their flashers on out here. They just flag you down. I was barely out of my car when I realized that Kris was giving birth. Her moans came from the car, muffled by his body. There was something frantic in his voice as he talked to her, but something utterly calm and in control — and a sense that this was hers to do. I stood stock-still near the trunk of their car.

Should I go for help? I asked.

No, he said. Stay here.

Though I'd asked the question, the fact that he responded stunned me — that he'd notice me and make a decision about my presence, and still attend to her. But why did he want me to stay? What was I supposed to do?

She screamed and gasped, and then he pushed up from the seat with his elbows, struggling, then gave up and went to his knees on the road and flopped backwards and sat down. The reason he couldn't use his hands to rise was because they held a child slick with blood. He leaned back against the opened door and held it up.

Well, Audrey Damish, he cried out. Would you look at this?

I guess that's what I was there for. I looked and looked: a child held like a chalice, as if to cup the world and pour it out again. Then he rose, from cross-legged to standing in one unencumbered movement, flowing upward. He leaned into the car and said, Here you go, Love. Here's what you did.

I heard Kris cooing and the baby crying, but his body muffled the sounds. I felt as if the three of them were self-contained, and I was in a different world.

I'll go get help now? I asked again.

Be a waste a time, he said, standing upright. There and back. I can just drive her in.

Of course. You get behind the wheel, start the engine, go. But how could he think so practically? He seemed unaware that I might attend to Kris. Though I'd never given birth, I felt some right, as another woman, to at least ask her if she was OK. If he had tried to prevent me, I could have insisted. But his innocence concerning any right I felt was overwhelming, and complete. It shut me out. I didn't even have the connection of opposition.

I've got a blanket, I said.

He looked at the back seat, then replied: That'd be really useful.

So I was allowed that: to help lift Kris and the baby off the blood-stained seat and place a blanket under them and follow them to the hospital. I didn't understand why the needlessness of it should sting the way it did.

Now here I was, on his land that had been mine, seeking family from my past — and finding him at the other end of where I'd found him years ago. What was I to do? Walk through that herd of buffalo and climb that hill, no more needed than I was before, and sit down next to him and say, *I've got another blanket. I've got a rug to sit on?*

My father used to run his fingers through my hair when he put me to bed. *Sleep like a pea,* he'd tell me. But when I tried to sleep I'd think of how the peas we picked swelled inside their pods. The covers of my bed would tighten like something green around me. At the moment of dropping off I'd gasp and wake. But I could never bring myself to ask him not to say those words. And now that my mother's spoken, I know that while I lay awake, he twirled a coffee cup at the kitchen table beneath me, watching the handle circle. I'd always wondered why the varnish was worn off the table in that single spot.

When the work on the Valen ranch became too much for him alone, he hired Alvin Janisch and put him up with his wife, Felicia, and daughter, Cassie, in the house out there. He began to spend more and more time with them, even taking noon meals in their kitchen. Mom didn't consider Felicia a threat. Though she sensed something different in my father, she dismissed it. As she put it, *It's hard to recognize betrayals a language hasn't named.* Of course it is — though I wonder whether betrayals that original are betrayals at all. In any case, she didn't notice that their shared barrenness was becoming hers alone. *I never thought he could become a father,* she said, *without another woman.*

She told me the only words she had that might locate Cassie's grave were *between those two big trees.* I thought it was enough, and after leaving the Valen house, I drove to the cemetery. But my father hadn't even named the kind of trees — as if burying Cassie stopped time, and nothing would grow or change to modify his meaning. Even if I could have been certain which trees he meant, I realized that *between* is meaningless, with a million gradations. I needed a map, so many steps from here to there, or three points to form a precise triangulation. With those few, unspecific words, all I really had was the hope that the earth itself might reveal her presence: the green of grass minutely different, or a spot of soil collapsed into a child-size depression.

I wandered around, looking, and found myself before Hayley Jo Zimmerman's stone. It had nothing but her names on it, HAYLEY JO, and HAYJAY, and the dates of birth and death. That's all. I stood before it. Those names told everything: all her relationships; people who knew her only by the given name, others by the nickname, formal length and intimate reduction; all the times those names were spoken by friends and family and acquaintances, in tenderness or anger or concern. It was all contained there. I felt it echoing around me.

After she was killed a group of women came out from Minneapolis. They circled her grave and set up candles. They made speeches about solidarity and martyrdom. But they didn't last long. The wind blew the candles out, and they hadn't considered how little shade there was. They wilted and left not long after the TV cameras did. When Angela Morrison heard about it, she said: What bullshit. Just let us mourn, why don't they? What right do they have to make claims to meaning?

But what else can we do? So much seemed revealed, so much possible to claim, from those two names. For Cassie Janisch, I had no rock or reading—nothing but Mom's words, and so many of them uncertain and secondhand, out of which to create the day she was feverish and my father demanded that Alvin go for the doctor. Alvin and Felicia had plans for a trip to the Bighorn Mountains, a little cabin there, in the lull between calving and haying. They couldn't allow themselves to interpret the flush on Cassie's cheeks as danger. When Alvin didn't show up for work that day, my father went to the house and found him putting on his boots with a casual look set hard on his face. If it hadn't been for Felicia my father might have suspected nothing. But she was a chaos of flesh. And then, surely, he must have noticed Cassie's absence from the kitchen.

What's going on? he might have asked.

Cassie has a cold, Alvin probably replied. It's nothing.

But Felicia's eyes must have denied it, and my father went down the hall to Cassie's bedroom, knocked and entered, and found her flushed in bed, the sound of paper in her lungs, her neck pulse beating, and a scythe of reflected light growing and diminishing with it on her skin.

A fever, Alvin said behind my father. She'll get over it.

The room must have been claustrophobic with the three of them in it, and Felicia in the doorway.

You need to get a doctor, my father said.

We got work to do.

Either you get him or I do.

This is when it is all birthed: the cusp where the relationships writhed and then swelled into being, when all that was conceived when my parents couldn't conceive sprang forth, and my father became a father.

Imagine Alvin staring back, a thick log of stubbornness. This was his house. Cassie was his daughter. He must have dimly sensed the shape and meaning of the argument and weighed it against the fact of his employment. But Felicia preempted him. My father's presence allowed her to override Alvin's authority.

Alvin, she said. Go.

It had to be something like that. And so my father waited with Felicia while Cassie passed in and out of sleep. He heard her moans. He watched her thrash. His eyes met Felicia's eyes. When the doctor arrived, he was there, and when the word *pneumonia* was pronounced, he was the one who asked: How bad is it?

Not good, the doctor said. But with sulfa she should recover.

She did. She improved as though she were swimming upward through murky water, and there she was again, appreciative for the chicken soup Felicia brought and for my father's face above her bed. If her breathing was still like dry leaves on dry ground, nevertheless it was clear she would get well. Alvin and Felicia remembered their vacation.

At this point in the story Mom shook her head and stopped talking. An old man with a walker shuffled by between us and the window. The low sun turned his few white hairs a flaming orange, and the shadow of those filaments wavered on Mom's face. She watched his fragile progress. Then she said:

They wanted to go. They asked if Cassie could stay with us.

We had arrived at what, from the beginning, she meant to tell me.

And? I asked.

We said no.

You said no, I repeated.

He did.

A pronoun's change.

Why?

She was in a halfway world, living as much as telling the story.

I didn't want her, she said. Maybe he knew. Maybe he refused for me.

I understood she was accepting all the blame, and placing it all on my father: a thing doubled in weight, or negated entirely, that still equaled itself. I let the realization fill me before I asked: Why didn't you want her?

A borrowed child?

It took me a while to understand.

It would be hard, I said. To pretend for a week.

She lifted her hands off the chair arms and for a moment held them like she had before when she shaped a sphere of emptiness, but this time it was as if they held the words she needed. When she spoke she went on looking into the space her fingers shaped.

I'd finally understood he loved her, she said. Her illness had freed him to talk about her. Every day it was Cassie this, Cassie that. If it had been another woman, his silence would have betrayed him. But with her it was constant stories. I'll admit it, Audrey: I was jealous. I'd have had to watch him in our house with her, and not be part of it. I would have been the stranger there. And it would only have confirmed what I knew: I was the childless one in our marriage.

But they never spoke of it. It was as if they each tried to protect the other. I'm left not even knowing which of the pronouns she used, *we* or *he,* is the correct one. Maybe in another language more attuned to relations there are a dozen pronouns for the nuances by which married men and women decide things, like Arctic names for snows that contain the winds that laid them.

Maybe he refused for reasons Mom never suspected: he'd wanted the trip for Cassie and now her parents wanted to go without her, or a realization that as long as he lifted her into his arms in those rooms where Alvin commanded, he could sustain the knowledge of his unfatherhood — but if she came into his house and he kissed her to sleep at night as she rolled over and shut her eyes, he might forget she wasn't his.

Whatever the reasons, Alvin and Felicia decided she was healthy enough and took her to the mountains. She touched summer snow. Mom gave me a black-and-white photograph of her there, taken with an ancient camera.

Here, she said, rummaging through a drawer, after I'd taken her back to her room.

She handed it to me.

I found it with his things, she said.

It must be one of the last photos ever taken of Cassie — maybe the only one. It's so blurry and scratched it's like a template by which to build a picture rather than the picture itself. I've thought of showing it to Bea Conway, but she'd want to make it public and say something about it that would diminish or twist its truth. The truth is in what the photo doesn't show, its black-and-white modulations leaving out the flush on Cassie's cheeks, which, if it showed, would suggest health and vitality but would really be its opposite, the signature of coming death. And the snowball in her hand, even as she holds it cocked behind her head, is melting — I'm sure it is — too quickly.

But who would notice that? Who would recognize fever in a snowball's small diminishment? I think I see a glint of water on her wrist, but only because I know the end. Alvin, behind the lens, could not have. Or Felicia, watching. And even if they noticed, who would recognize the proper rate of melt for snow held in a young girl's hand?

She has dark hair, light eyes, some Indian features — clearly mixed blood, though I know nothing about either Alvin's or Felicia's heritage. She looks nothing like me at all. But what do those distinctions matter? My father loved her. She died in part because he did.

She might have died anyway. One can always guess at such excuses. But circumstantial guilt can stain a life more deeply than intention will, ground in as it is with questioning and doubt. Alvin and Felicia brought her home and my father helped bury her in a small, private funeral ceremony. Mom stayed behind to cook.

It wasn't your fault, I told her.

I could have said yes.

She might still have died.

She did die.

She was Alvin's and Felicia's daughter.

I'm too old to be chasing myself down alleys, she said.

You never visited her grave?

You came.

I laid my palm upon my father's gravestone, its rough circumference warmed by sun. I'd searched from fence to fence. Sometimes out here we'll see people walking with their heads down in barren places, looking for fossils or agates: dull stone they've learned to see as something else. What I'm looking for, and now know I have been since I was five, I'm not sure I'd recognize if I came upon it.

Alvin and Felicia trudged onward with their lives. That's not a moral failing, but I can't help but feel they should have stayed, tethered to Cassie's grave up here, offering it littered mementos like the other children's graves I find: flowers, stuffed animals, plastic dolls staring blankly, their painted eyes washed by rain. But we're the ones who stayed.

So much may be real and so much made up out of what my mother told me. I think myself right out of fact. But atoms themselves are more force than matter, mostly hollowness and collapse. Yet they cling to form the breathing bodies we name friends and lovers. The universe itself is a void so vast the stars are tiny things, and the planets only guessed at by the deviations they create, the anomalies of orbit. And maybe we're all anomalies in each other's lives, circling stars that may not be of our own choosing, sending codes into the bigness that we hope someone will decipher, to redeem us from coincidence.

So I can imagine my father stole that photograph. He was helping Alvin and Felicia pack, and found it and held it up and stared at it, then put it in his shirt pocket. And because he did, Cassie's unfamilial eyes can now meet mine when I eat, the snowball in her hand ready to be thrown, as I place my own cup on the spot on the table he twirled bare.

When they were packed and leaving to go wherever they went, Alvin, already in the car, shook his hand and asked him to take care of the grave, letting his eyes drift in this direction. My father murmured reassurances: he wouldn't let her grave remain unmarked.

Yet he did. I'm trying to understand the integument that holds us together in whatever proper ways, and I measure his love for her by his failure to follow through. He could bury her. He had to. But he couldn't complete the loss. A grave that isn't marked is more there than one that isn't.

And so I have no way to find my older sister. Nothing here helps me regain her — no off-color in the grass to suggest an extra grave, no out-of-place smoothness or unevenness in the ground. I've walked up and down these rows of stone, fence to fence to fence to fence, tree to standing tree. There's nothing. Yet she's here. The elm leaves clatter. It could be speech. It could be filling lungs.

Delayed Flight

STANLEY GREW WEARY of the smell of grief. He smelled it when he entered the bedroom at night, having waited, doing other things, until he knew Kris was asleep or pretending to be. It was as if she'd breathed in her own tears until they'd salted the inside of her lungs. Even after a shower there was on her skin a musty and bitter-almond scent that blamed him. She didn't blame him. But her grieving did. The smell of the bedroom did. The way he'd come into the kitchen and realize she'd been crying by the way she stood at the counter with her back to him, her hands doing nothing.

The smell of the herd was something else entirely. Within its aura of dung and humid air he didn't have to remember all those events he wasn't there to see: his daughter getting into the car, the long ride she took, the fat stranger sitting next to her, the knife, and everything else that could be reconstituted from the evidence—and so much could be reconstituted, including her need for him, the strength in his arms that could heave a fence post fifty feet or grip a neck if it had to and crush a windpipe just like that.

The bison shit and stand and eat. They give birth. They flow up and down the hills like a slow brown current, like water moving in another edition of time.

On their little wheels jets rolled out of the snow, and the snow reclaimed and engulfed them. All flights out of O'Hare were canceled. For the third time the announcement came, and Stanley still sat, watching through the plate glass windows the remaining planes arriving like immense animals lost in the weather and dazed by their former speed. He would have to call Kris, and she would tell him he should have come home yesterday, the weatherman had warned them, and now there was nothing he could do.

Nothing he could do. Stanley rose from his chair. Outside the window the storm seemed to thicken precipitously. Then it coalesced into the shape of a jet, so close he backed away.

He thought of this weather sweeping over the old Valen house, the utter isolation there, and the buffalo calm and unconcerned, turning their heads into the wind and letting the snow collect on their coats, and then beginning to drift, the whole herd moving with the lead cow toward the source of the storm. They would come, before they reached it, to the fence he'd built, and there they would gather, baffled but untroubled, everything in the world as it was, and only he, imagining them, desiring the fence gone so they could continue onward toward high pressure twenty or thirty or fifty miles away. Lightless night and snow and the black animals within it. How much they fit.

He wouldn't get back to them today. Or, if this storm kept up, tomorrow. They were as indifferent to his care as to the weather, but he thought how good it would be to see them. Not to be among them, they didn't allow that. But to stand at a distance which they defined and watch.

The first four motels he called were full. When the fifth had a room, he took it, though it was spendier than he cared for. The taxi driver, an immigrant from some African or Caribbean country, drove as if he'd never seen snow, skidding and spinning and keeping up a cheerful, broken-English commentary while the wipers chugged and the heater blasted air. Hey, tanks, mon, he said when Stanley handed him two twenties for the twenty-eight-dollar fare. Stanley had been going to ask for six dollars back, but the man was so pleased that Stanley said, You're welcome, and stepped into the swirling cold.

A bellman ducked out to hold the door, and then Stanley was inside the warmth and enclosed light of the lobby, and everything was calm and ready, and he went up the brass-doored elevator to the eighteenth floor and a room like a tiny kingdom. He dropped his bags and flopped onto the bed. A little refrigerator hummed, and air moved through metal vents, and the bed creaked gently with his breathing. He shut his eyes and let despair leak out of him.

Ever since his daughter's death the sense of something imminent had plagued him — the sense that outrage lay just under the crust of normal order and could erupt at any moment, and no structure he had built around himself could withstand its force. But the snow outside, striking quietly against the windowpanes and piling up, suppressed the possibility of happening, of event. He let the expanse of the feeling take him.

The sound of loud snow woke him — hard snow striking the window with a strange insistence. The room had gone dark except for the illuminated switches on the wall, and a pale strand of light where the drapes were slightly parted. The scratching continued, and Stanley thought he saw — it seemed like a dream he was so barely awake — a shadow transit that narrow strand.

He rose softly from the bed, reminding himself he was eighteen stories up in the middle of a blizzard. Even so he approached the window sideways. The scratching came again. For a moment he felt the unreason of fear before he calmed it and knew: it was pigeons. He pushed the drapes carefully apart.

And stepped back from what he saw. A falcon was perched on the window ledge, pressed against the glass, snow resting on its shoulders as carelessly as a cloak. Beyond it, the storm resided, so thick that across the street another motel was nothing but a pile of obscure lights. Snow falling, and the bird. Its hard, startling eye. He didn't know if it had seen him or not. He hadn't turned the room light on. He stood a foot from the window, and it stood a foot from him, and snow came down and lay weightless on its feathers, and he knew somehow it was female and young. He closed the drapes to protect it from his eyes.

When he bought the place he'd removed all the rundown, rotting fences the Valens had built and gathered them into a tangled pile of rust and barbs and dry-rotted posts. He'd scraped a hole in the earth with his front-end loader, pushed the pile into it, and covered it. He drove the tractor back and forth to pack the dirt down, wondering how many centuries it would take for the wire to rust away and turn the soil red.

Then he built the buffalo fence around the boundary of the ranch—eight feet high, posts as thick as railroad ties, and wire strung so tightly it sang on touch. The interior of the ranch he left completely open. The herd had its own definition of space and allowance, but he gave them what he could.

He didn't remember how he got there, that night he found out. The miles were erased from his mind. He could remember the first words of the argument that would come to define their lives: Kris, coming back from the bathroom looking like a ragged, half-deflated balloon moved by random currents of air, saying: We should have known. We must have known.

We didn't know, he said. You can't let yourself go there.

Already they were fossilizing, already locking in to the views each of them needed, and useless to each other.

She quit rodeo, Kris said. Way back then. It must have started way back then.

He felt his head like an iron weight swinging, torsioned on refusal.

No, he said. If you didn't see it then, you can't remember it now.

Greggy Longwell had told them their daughter was targeted because she was anorexic. She'd hidden it from them, or they'd let her hide it. Once they heard the term they understood some things — but that didn't mean they knew before.

Other people came, the Mattinglys and Morrisons and Thompsons, and Stanley had gone outside and had kept walking, to his pickup, but there were no miles in his memory, he was just, suddenly, in a deeper darkness, hearing the herd shuffling, waiting to see if he was going to betray the distance between them. He realized he'd been walking toward them, and he stopped, and their smell rammed into his lungs. He sat down in the grass. The herd didn't move away.

Stanley stood in the motel shower for a long time, at the edge of scalding, the water pulsing like needles. By the time he shut the water off, he felt formless and spongy. The bathroom was a contained cloud, his body in the fogged-up mirror a pink slab. It helped: he felt hungry. He dressed and was about to leave the room when he turned and went back to the window and parted the curtain. The peregrine slept, its head under its wing. Snow swept in long lines through the window's light. If a wind surged down the canyon of the city's towers strong enough to blow the falcon off the ledge, it would wake from whatever dreams it dreamed to nothing under it — and, element of air, calmly unfold its wings.

He was studying the menu when a waitress appeared at his elbow. She had dark brown hair, cut short, a wide, full mouth, a young and open face, green iridescent eye shadow. Jade blue-green earrings, carved like small alligators or crocodiles, with tiny jewels for eyes, hung from her lobes. They reminded Stanley of the Mayan art he'd seen the day before at the Field Museum of Natural History. She smiled. He realized he was staring at her.

Bet you're stuck here, she said cheerfully.

Her words came out in clear little syllables that seemed to define a private space and to enclose the moment: he was here, now. Inside a storm that wouldn't let him go. He had a little menu thing to decide, and that was all.

It was so small. He experienced a spurt of lightness — a feeling he hadn't known for a year and a half — and with it, gratitude.

The waitress's name, pinned to her black uniform above her left breast, was TRACE. He stared at that name, then, with a little start, said: Yes. The airport's shut.

Bummer, huh? I bet you could use a drink.

I could. A whiskey sour.

Got it.

No. Make it Scotch.

He always ordered whiskey sours. But the feeling of being cut off from everything had overtaken him, the sense that he could free himself, for this little time, from himself, even from his own tastes and preferences.

Neat?

He stared.

Or on the rocks?

Oh. On the rocks.

Got a brand?

He knew the names of Scotches and could have supplied one, but he hadn't expected this question either. He just wanted to be someone different, a man who drank Scotch instead of whiskey sours. He hadn't thought to be a man who drank a particular kind of Scotch.

Surprise me, he said.

She strolled unhurriedly away between the tables, swinging her hips to miss them. In a few minutes she returned, bringing the Scotch on a tray, amber and dewy, reflecting in its deep interior the candles in their red glass bulbs. Her smile as she came toward him seemed half-devotional, as if the glass were a sacred object, and she bent to a ritual. She set it down, leaning close. He smelled skin and musk perfume. A stone crocodile or alligator swung toward him as she rose, almost nipped his cheek, then swung back and snapped at her smooth jaw line.

Ready to order? she asked.

He felt so unburdened even speech seemed new: the way her *r*'s rolled off her tongue like a foreign language.

My name's Stan, he said. It's good to meet you.

He wanted an introduction to mark this little time. He'd always been two-syllable Stanley, and he almost said the second syllable. He felt his tongue touch the inside of his mouth above his teeth for the *L*, but he stopped and let it fall, and with it so much.

Stan, she said. Her tongue, he noticed, didn't even seek the *L*. It was gone completely.

I've never met anyone named Trace, he told her.

She looked down at the nametag, then looked back up, jubilant.

You still haven't, Stan, she said. It's Tray-see.

Oh. Tray-see. I see.

She laughed at the rhyme, and Stanley, hearing it then, laughed with her.

They make us wear these stupid nametags, Trace said.

Then she leaned forward and spoke in a mock-conspiratorial tone.

Want to know a secret? Even Tray-see's not my real name. They make you wear a nametag. But it doesn't have to be your real name. All they care about's the tag.

She stood again, triumphant, crocodiles' jeweled blue eyes winking in the various lights.

So, what is your real name, then?

She wrinkled her nose pleasingly. In here, she said, Tray-*see*'s as real as it gets.

Wind blew against the window a few feet from the table. Stanley flashed to the falcon high up somewhere — he couldn't locate the direction of his room — plummeting, and its unperturbed waking.

But Trace's quiet, meaningless conversation brought him back.

What brings you to Chicago?

A convention.

Where you from?

Rapid City. That's where I fly back to.

He wanted to avoid this infringement of fact but couldn't think fast enough to steer the conversation away, or to make up a different answer. The truth was just there, saying itself. But the effect of the truth was like the lie he wished he'd told — as if he'd named a place exotic and impossible.

Rapid City? she exclaimed. I've always wanted to see Mount Rushmore.

It's pretty grand. It's —

But you're just flying to there. Where are you really from?

Twisted Tree. It's a little —

What a great name. Twisted Tree.

Her lips wrapped around the syllables as if they were physical things she shaped. But Stanley didn't want to remember Twisted Tree. He suddenly saw the town as he imagined she would, with its graveled side streets and single café and stoplight, the hulks of reservation racers on cement blocks in dusty front yards, and the stone-pitted ranch pickups banging down the highway.

There's nothing there, really, he said.

Then the magnitude of its meaning ripped through him. Nothing.

You OK? the waitress asked.

Stanley picked up the glass. He'd forgotten he'd ordered Scotch, and the raw whiskey made his eyes water, but the effort to keep from coughing, to deal with his body's reaction, settled him.

I'm fine, he said.

He looked into the girl's face and felt grateful for her presence. How about Chicago? he said. Isn't it exciting?

She shrugged her shoulders. The alligators—alligators would be Mayan—looped and raged. She held a pen, and she lifted it like a conductor's baton to indicate the restaurant.

Right here's it, she said. Trace's life. Exciting as it gets.

She regarded the room with such resignation that Stanley couldn't even protest.

I raise buffalo, he said, to shift the conversation. That was the convention I was at.

Buffalo? You actually raise them?

I do, he said.

Wow! I've never even seen one.

For a moment Stanley was baffled. She'd never seen a buffalo? It seemed an unaccountable deprivation, like a private extinction.

If you ever get to Twisted Tree, I'll show you, he said.

I'll remember that, Stan. I'll hold you to it.

You do that.

But I better take your order. My manager'll be after me.

What's good?

She shrugged a dozen ways at once.

Depends on what you like.

How's the salmon?

He usually ordered beef, or buffalo if a restaurant had it, but he thought he'd order something else here.

It's good, she said. But your breath will smell like fish.

He was just going back to his room to sleep, but she was smiling so delightfully, it was all light and good again, and he played along.

I sure wouldn't want that, he said. I guess I'll have a T-bone.

She recommended a bottle of wine. He'd have only himself to confront in the morning, and it was pleasant to drink the wine and eat slowly and feel the immensity of the stopped world. Trace refilled his glass when it got low. He enjoyed how her wrist arched when she tipped the bottle. Then she tipped the bottle vertically, and a last drop of red liquid thickened on its lip and fell shimmering into its own small waves.

She brought the ticket in its little black folder and set it near his elbow.

So, you going back tomorrow?

If the airport's open.

They never close an airport long. People have to leave.

In the morning time would resume — all the schedules and itineraries, the implied commitments and promises engaged, the clock hands meaningful. A nostalgia for this evening, fueled by the wine, overcame him.

This was nice, he said. The meal. All of it.

I'm glad, she said.

Remember, now, if you decide to see Rushmore —

I'll stop in Twisted Tree and ask for Stan.

For a moment he let himself believe it, that she'd show up and he'd take her out to see the herd and enjoy her wonder at this good thing he could show her.

She gave the folder a little push.

Whenever you're ready.

He looked at the folder. It was time to go.

I'll take care of it right now, he said. Save you a trip.

Tripping's what I do. But OK.

She left with his credit card and quickly returned.

You're set, she said.

Thanks, Trace, he said. You—

We'll see you, Stan.

Then she was gone. Slowed by the alcohol, it took him a while to figure a twenty-percent tip. But after he'd written it and signed the receipt, it didn't seem enough. He wanted her to know how much he'd appreciated her. He reached into his wallet to give her another twenty, but looking at the money there, he had the sudden urge to empty himself—of something. He pulled all the bills out, he didn't even know how much money it was, he didn't feel like knowing, he just wanted to be profligate in riddance, without counting or comparing. He had more money in his suitcase, it wasn't sacrifice he sought—just momentary lightness, the doing without consideration. He dropped the money onto the opened folder and closed it and stood. He looked into his empty wallet. It contained a plastic tab to hold two quarters, and long ago he'd put two quarters in it and forgotten them because bills had always covered them up. He dug the quarters out and laid them on the table, too, then placed his wallet in his pocket. He liked the way it felt, so thin. He stumbled, then carefully made his way to the elevators. The doors closed with their conclusive click and reconstituted him, wavy and boxed, within their brassy blur.

In his room he carefully pulled aside the drapes. There was no city—only a closing veil and a far-off suggestion of lights, and on his window ledge a bird of snow. In the morning the falcon would wake as if shattering itself and leap from its own brittle form and raise warm wings and fall off the building and rise. The privacy of the bird was so intense it almost hurt to see it. Stanley closed the drapes.

He stripped to a T-shirt and underwear and crawled into bed.

He dreamed of buffalo jumps. There was one on the Valen ranch, a pile of bones under a steep drop from a bluff. In his dream he saw the carnage of it, a kind of hideous flying, the immense beasts tipping in the air, splayed in all manner of wrongness, falling on top of each other, their bones shattering and ripping through their hides with awful cracking sounds, like white and bloody sticks, tree limbs twisted out of flesh, fertilized in blood. When he woke he didn't know he'd left the dream. The sharp cracking of bones continued, until he realized it was a knocking on his door. He panicked, thinking there was a fire, and threw back the covers. The red numbers on the clock said 11:47. He looked around wildly, trying to remember where he'd left his pants.

Hey, Stan. It's me.

The voice froze him. He stared. Then he saw his pants on the back of a chair. Still drunk, he stumbled to them and, holding them in front of him, went to the door. Through the peephole he could see Trace in the hallway, so close one of the alligators swung up and grew immense, its jeweled eye flashing light, before falling back again.

I know you're looking at me. You gonna open up?

Her voice was very low, her forehead probably touching the door.

He turned. The movement sent him reeling. He looked at the window.

What are you doing here? he asked.

You don't know, Stan?

His mind cleared. The tip: of course. She thought he'd made a mistake, and she had his name, so she'd gotten his room number and was returning the money. He pulled on his pants, then fumbled with the chain, freed it, and snapped the bolt open. Just as he turned the knob he realized his naiveté. What if she was out there with a tattooed boyfriend tucked against the wall? But it was too late. He could only raise his elbow against the door being kicked against his face. But it swung slowly open, and there she was, alone.

Hi, Stan. Told you I'd see you.

Just like that she was past him. He watched her recede into the room, toward her own reflection in the mirror on the far wall. Her eyes in that mirror met his, then flicked around the room: his unzipped suitcase, his reading glasses with one bow folded on the nightstand, his copy of the convention's program lying on the second bed. She reached the space between the two beds and turned.

So, Stan, she said.

Stanley. Really. Everybody calls me Stanley.

Guess I'm not everybody.

She brought the smells of the restaurant into the room — smoke and grease and spices, and her own smell, the perfume he'd noticed earlier, shampoo and perspiration — various and alive, and it made the room feel cramped, as if she'd brought a multitude with her.

You were a great waitress, he said. I mean, if you're here — the tip wasn't a mistake.

The tip? she said. One-thirty-four-fifty plus twenty percent? A mistake? That extra fifty cents was good, Stan.

He was disappointed to hear the actual figure: that it had a number at all, which made it something that could be restored instead of something purely gone.

Trace walked to the window. Panic seized him. He didn't want her frightening the falcon. He didn't want her even seeing it. He thought she might open the drapes, and to stop her, he said, too loudly: Why are you here, then?

She turned from the window, her eyebrows raised, then sat down in a chair and crossed her legs. The black skirt stretched tight over her thighs.

God, it feels good to sit down, she said. That damn restaurant, Stan. You wouldn't believe what it does to a girl's legs. And they sure make it hard to get to the rooms. If they knew I was up here—whew.

He looked at her legs and the dark triangle of shadow they formed.

Cowboys make that kind of money, huh? she asked.

It took him a moment to realize he was the cowboy, and she was referring to the tip.

I'm a rancher, he said.

She reached up and fiddled with the drape cord. His hand involuntarily rose from his side, to restrain her from pulling it. But she merely rolled it between her thumb and finger.

Right, she said. A *rancher* wouldn't want a tip like that to show up on a credit card.

She shifted her legs. The black skirt rode higher, the little cave of shadow lightened.

Raising buffalo, she said. Hundred-fifty-dollar tips. You like doing good, don't you?

He'd started out raising buffalo believing in a natural order, but after Hayley Jo's murder, he just *needed* them, to know they were there, in all kinds of weather, living in their patient, impervious way.

I just wanted my wallet empty, he said.

It was the closest thing to the deep truth he'd said all evening. Her hand quit rolling the cord. She clearly hadn't expected the answer. She stared at him, and a doorway opened, a chance to tell the whole story. The desire to do so overwhelmed him: to unburden himself of it. But he would break down if he so much as spoke his daughter's name. He jerked his head downward, away from Trace's eyes, and slapped his palm against the wall to steady himself. He was watching the floor heave when she spoke:

You're out of money, Stan?

No. I've got. I meant I wanted—

I didn't think so. You want to be empty, you got a ways to go yet. A hundred-fifty more, say—that get you closer? It'd sure do me some good.

He was still fighting off the nearness of what he'd almost tried to say and couldn't comprehend what she meant. A hundred-fifty more? he mumbled. For a tip?

He lifted his head and tried to come back to the present. She was smiling at him, and the alligators danced and swayed asynchronously.

Call it a tip, it's a tip.

He couldn't shake off the swaddling of memory. Something about her smell filling the room confused him. Then he knew: it wasn't grief. She smelled like someone just living, going through life, collecting its scents.

Under his stare, her smile faded. Her mouth closed and tightened, and the confidence that had been there dissolved into doubt. She dropped her hand from the cord.

Ah, hell, she said softly. Guess I misjudged.

She rose and adjusted her skirt. She'd loosened one of her shoes when she sat down, and she worked her foot back into it. Then she started toward him, her eyes on the door.

Wait, he said.

If she walked out she'd pull her smell with her, and he'd be alone with his memories so almost-voiced. He knew what was going on, but he was dulled enough by drink and memory to believe he wasn't sure.

If you need money, he said. A hundred-fifty dollars. I give that much to charities all the time. At least I know you.

She burst into laughter.

Right, Stan, she said. She reached out and touched his chest with her fingertips. You know me. It's not like I'm some starving Somalian you never get to see eating your rice.

Her smell was like a drug. He brushed past her to the bed. An alligator, calm against her neck, winked at him as he went by.

He rummaged in his suitcase for his cash, found three fifties, and turned to her. She reached out, took the bills, fanned them in the air, pushing a hundred scents or a single one against his face, then lifted her skirt and put the bills into a little pocket sewn inside. He caught a glimpse of black silk.

Can I ask? he said. The money? What you need it for?

We can do that. You like education?

You're going to college? That's good.

Jesus, Stan. I don't mind playing your game. But I don't have all night. You want me to say a poem or something?

A poem?

I don't know if I know any poems. I could say you a song.

Her hands lifted her skirt again, and then black silk slid down her legs like shining skin. She lifted one knee, then the other. Black silk hung for a moment off the end of her index finger, before she dropped it.

How's that for a poem?

He looked at the window, the closed drapes. She touched his chest and lightly pushed. He gave way and fell backwards onto the bed.

He was in Washington, DC, the next year when Kris called to tell him she had talked to a lawyer.

Who? he asked.

What do you mean, who?

Orley Morgan?

Not Orley Morgan. My God, Stanley, I don't want Orley involved. I went to Rapid City.

Good. Good, then.

I can't live here anymore, she said.

I know.

He did know. They'd been through it so many times, but her announcement finally freed him to understand, because he could do nothing to keep them together.

The divorce wasn't because of Trace. Kris didn't even suspect. That was just part of everything else: the way Kris ate her meals without seeming to taste them; the way they never had sex because he couldn't bear the small humiliation of asking; the way, in spite of himself, that he felt she was right, that food should never taste and sex should not delight. It was the way she couldn't understand his devotion to the buffalo herd, and the way he couldn't speak his daughter's name and the way she spoke it every day, and the way he couldn't attend the trial, and the way she had to.

The day after Kris called, Stanley skipped his meetings and went to the Mall. He sat on the steps of the Lincoln Memorial for a long time, watching people form clusters and patterns. When he finally rose, he found himself behind a couple holding hands. He crossed the street behind them, not paying attention to where he was going. Then he looked to his left and saw the black wedge of the Vietnam Veterans Memorial rising from the ground right next to him, the names of the dead already growing up around him. Shocked that he hadn't noticed, he thought: *That's how it is. You're into things before you even know it. And people are dying already.*

He walked forward under the rising names until he felt buried in them. He saw himself reflected in the black stone, behind those names. His daughter was there, too, but in such a different way. He touched a name. His hand within the stone came forward to touch the obverse name. It was cool, but the next name so hot he withdrew his hand. Within the black granite his mirrored self wept. Then he saw how, where the monument angled, it reflected itself and the reflections it contained, so that the future hazed away. Within the double reflection, everything was fuzzy and of a peculiar beauty, and shapes could be other shapes. It could be his green shirt up there in those trees that floated in the stone, or it could be someone else's.

People moved slowly past him, and in front of him, doubled and hazy, they massed, moving too. He thought of his herd grown to immense proportions, swelling through the fence he'd built, trampling to dust the old Valen house, stampeding over the cemetery where Hayley Jo lay buried, knocking down gravestones, planing irregularities, their hooves cutting into the earth, erasing all marks but the marks of their own passing, and then allowing even those marks to be gone with rain and wind and the flow of time. He had a vision of the world returned to a time before his daughter stepped into that car, before the possibility of his daughter stepping into that car, before Joseph Valen ever saw land he thought was good, before cavalry and cannon had made possible that goodness. Stanley stood in the black mirrors, looking out and in, ahead and back, and saw it all erased.

When he returned home, Kris had already gone to stay with her sister in Rapid City. Stanley walked through the empty house. He came to his daughter's room and paused, then pushed open the door. Kris had cleaned it out: the posters, the bedspread, the knick-knacks, the jewelry, the books, the bridle. Even the championship rodeo belt, Hayley Jo's proudest possession, was gone. It was just a bare and ugly mattress inside four bare walls. He couldn't believe it. He knew it wasn't cruel, and that's what made it awful. Kris didn't believe he'd want any of it. He sank to the floor inside the doorjamb. He had no idea how to ask for any of it back.

When he rose he went in a great numbness to his pickup and drove out to the herd. They were at some far end of the old Valen ranch, and he stood before the house alone. Those empty rooms there, too. He walked inside. Dust and dung. Tracks of trespassing boots. A cleared space on the floor. An old rocking chair. A closed door, and behind it an empty bed, in an empty room, strangely free of dust. A hairbrush on a nightstand. Voices: the whisper of wind, the crackle of lumber.

He struck a match, held it, let it drop.

Everywhere he went he visited memorials and monuments: the Custer battlefield, Wounded Knee, Sand Creek, Gettysburg. From them all he came away unsatisfied, though he had no idea what he sought. A few years after Kris left, he was in New York City for another convention and took the subway to the World Trade Center. He emerged onto the street turned around and wandered in the wrong direction until, at a street crossing, as he stared at his map, a young black man with fierce tattoos asked him where he was going and pointed him in the right direction.

He walked until he realized that the hollow square to his right, where nothing shaped a space, was what he was looking for, an architectural negative formed against the surrounding towers. At Liberty Street he was finally able to look into the hole. Gray concrete. Orange flags. A gull flying through. That's all. It had a prison camp look.

At the interpretive center he rented an audio tour. The tape instructed him to imagine the size of the towers by doubling the height of the skyscraper across the way, and for a moment he had a vision of what was gone. But he couldn't sustain it. A woman spoke of running down the stairs and, twenty stories from the ground, meeting firemen running up and knowing for the first time that the ground was attainable. Stanley thought of the firemen going up until *up* came down with them in its fierce grip. The scene played in his head: hope passing hopelessness on a particular step, a single moment, and each life going on to its future. And which future was better? He stared out the window. An immense machine drilled holes for foundation casings.

He returned the tape and entered the exhibits at the interpretive center but felt no connection to any of it. When he came up the steps from the basement, he entered a room with walls papered with photographs. A square of metal benches in the middle of the room allowed people to sit. It was all just jumbled faces, and Stanley almost walked on. But he felt some duty of reverence to the place and sat.

When he lifted his head, he was gazing directly at the photograph of a young girl, joyous in the camera's lens, luminous and delighted to be seen, in some moment of her life when delight and attention were so clearly called for. She seemed to stare back at him, yet in her face there was no knowledge of the future, including this wall or the aluminized light on these benches, or strangers' eyes gazing at her.

Stanley jerked his head away but couldn't get the image from his mind. He stumbled out the door, blinded, to the subway and the refuge of his motel room. But even there he kept seeing those dark eyes staring from the wall, seeming to look back at him — and yet not: not at all. For some reason he thought of Trace. The moment he remembered her, he knew there was something she could tell him. He called and rearranged his flight back home so that he had a four-hour layover in Chicago.

At O'Hare the next day he left the secure area and walked outside into a heat wave. The taxi driver ran the air conditioner full blast and, intent on traffic, delivered Stanley wordlessly to the motel. It was early afternoon, the restaurant nearly empty.

One? the hostess asked.

He drew his breath in a staccato stutter.

I'm looking for a waitress who works here, he said. Her name is Trace.

Tracie? I'm pretty new. I can ask the manager.

She walked across the restaurant and in a few minutes returned with a thin, unsmiling man who had a look of permanent irritation on his face.

You're looking for a waitress named Tracie?

Yes. I—

Don't recall her.

It was a few years ago.

Waitresses don't stay long. His tone suggested injury. Spend all my time training them, and then they leave.

His voice turned hopeful: She in trouble?

No. Nothing like that.

Just looking for her, huh?

Stanley had prepared reasons for asking after Trace: she was his niece, or he was a teacher and she a former student. But he couldn't say them.

It's not important.

You sure you got the right restaurant?

Stanley suddenly remembered that Trace wasn't her real name, and his heart raced.

I was stuck here in a snowstorm a few years ago, he said, controlling his voice. She said if I was ever back to stop and say hi. But I don't know her real name. Trace was her nametag name.

They think that's so cute, the manager said.

She spelled it like *trace*. Like copying?

Stanley moved his finger as if holding a pencil.

T-R-A-C-E? he said.

Wait, the manager said. Yeah. I remember. Good-looking one? Might've fired her. Always getting sick and leaving in the middle of a shift.

The words seeped into Stanley's mind.

You OK? the manager asked.

I'm fine. The heat. I ate at the airport, and—

Airport restaurants.

Suddenly the manager turned and yelled: Ivy!

A middle-aged waitress was setting tables. She walked without hurry across the room.

This guy's looking for that waitress nametagged Tray-see.

Spelled it cute, though. *T-R-A-C-E.* You know what happened to her? What was her real name?

Ivy's own nametag, pinned to her drooping uniform, faced the floor, unreadable. She stared at Stanley for a full second. Finally she pushed a strand of graying hair off her forehead and turned her gaze back to the manager.

She left. Lucky girl.

Yeah, you got it hard, the manager said. We want to know how to find her.

Stanley lifted his hand to dissociate himself from the manager's *we.*

It's not important, he said. She waited on me once. I was stuck during a snowstorm.

Ivy's eyes were drill bits, that pointed and hard.

I don't remember her name, she said. I don't know where she went.

It was a lie. Complete and brazen and without apology. Stanley realized she was protecting Trace from him. His knees went weak. She didn't know anything about him. And he couldn't tell her. Anything. The things he couldn't tell were enlarging. They were growing. They were expanding beyond his control.

Prize Money

IN HERE, BUYERS FLAUNT their cheapness, demanding deals, or else they're hushed and furtive, pretending they can't be seen. They want to believe what they buy's a bargain, only that, and not what someone else couldn't afford to keep. And sellers, ticket holders? They come to salvage what they can from their delusions. They want to pretend this place is a museum where their ruined dreams will be preserved forever. I make my living in the gap, keeping the two apart. It's what the markup's for. I know what things are really worth. Things are things, dreams are dreams. I pay only for the thing, and the thing is what I sell.

The other day this kid comes in looking for a car stereo. He's maybe twenty, got his hair spiked, got an earring, got a tattoo slinking off his neck underneath his collar. Got a shorter friend looks just like him. These two come in, smelling of their parents' money but going to try to talk me down. Come in smiling. Like they own the place. Not smiling at me. Hell, they hardly see me. Just smiling.

Gotanee car stereos? the tall one says.

Says it just like that. He's hardly in the door, got his hands in his back pockets, not a hello or a how-are-you, just *Gotanee car stereos?* like he's talking to the stuff on the walls. I nod at the glass case. Fourteen car stereos there. It's not like they're invisible.

I go back to watching one of the TVs I got in. They find the case, and they're bending over the speakers and amps when this woman walks in the door. It's awful hot out, this damn drought we've been in, the sun like bubbling oil, and I keep it dim in here, bad light on used things is worth ten percent, but I got a bright light on the counter I can turn on when I buy. Sellers'll try all sorts of tricks. One time a big Indian tried to sell me a clock radio that didn't work, figured I wouldn't plug it in. Anyway, everyone stands still when they come in, getting used to the dark. This woman does that, too. I mark her for a seller, the way she looks lost, then finds me and kind of solidifies. Buyers look at the merchandise hung up, sellers look at me. Who do they got to talk to's their only question. I pretend I'm watching TV, don't want to make eye contact, disorientation's in my favor. But I manage to look her over. She's not bad in the store's light — not great-looking, but not bad. Her mouth's a bit big, and maybe she's a bit overweight but who isn't these days? She's not carrying anything, so whatever she's selling's small, or so big she needs help hauling it in.

I've seen people bolt. They come in, take a look, go right back out. So when I see she's kind of adjusted to being in the door, I catch her eye to pin her down. She nods at me. Then her face, it's kind of like leaves falling inside it, it settles into something bare and determined, and she comes across the floor. She's got on flat, soft-soled shoes, and she makes no sound. Some women, you wonder how they learn to move like they do. She's like a lot of rain gathered on a street and the flow so heavy it's gone smooth and curved, and still more coming, and you can't take your eyes off it, all you can do is think, *Look at it go.*

I got to remind myself this is a deal coming toward me. I put my hands on the counter to brace myself. Over at the case the two earrings have pulled out a couple of systems. The short one lifts up a price tag and grins, and they shake their heads. You ever see someone in a retail place behave that way? That's where the pricing's dishonest, except when they have a sale and get the price even close to what it ought to be. The regular system rips people off as standard practice. Tells lies as business, buys and sells dreams all the time, preys on people's insecurities, convinces them garbage is value and brands are religion — and people suck it up. And here, where prices are pinned to what things are actually worth, everyone assumes it's crooked. I have yet to read where a Chamber of Commerce has named a pawnshop Business of the Year. It's because we don't lie. We pick up where the lie ends and the dream disintegrates, and what's left is what's really there.

Then she's in front of me, her hand in her purse. I want to sell this, she says.

If it came out any faster it'd be one word. OK — she wants to get it over. Women are always fumbling in their purses, got them stuffed so full they can never find a thing. But she finally brings it out, and I think, *Damn, it had to be.* She lays a ring case on the counter.

They always save their ring cases. Like they expect someday they're going to have to put the rings back in and take them somewhere. I reach out and open the case, this is the worst kind of dealing there is, and I'm looking at a set, engagement and wedding, all polished and taken care of. She doesn't say anything, she's just watching me.

Say!

The tall earring's holding up an amp and a set of speakers.

You think maybe we could install this Pioneer? See if it really works in the car?

Excuse me, I say to the woman.

I keep my finger and thumb on the ring box and look at the kid. I don't answer right away. I want him to think he's putting me out. And he is, that *see if it really works* crap, as if I'd sell something that doesn't. But once he gets that system installed he won't want to remove it. I make fifteen percent by saying yes — maybe more, if he thinks he's skinning my nose some by putting it in.

It works just fine, I say.

We wanta be sure.

You got my word.

Yeah, well, but, you know. We wanta know how it *sounds*.

The shorter earring's nodding, like maybe he's got a clapper inside his head gonging against his skull.

How it sounds, I say.

Yeah. You know. In the car.

I stare down at the counter like I'm trying to see around some trick they're pulling on me, get them feeling like they're just on the edge of being sleazeballs and I'm trying to see just when they're going to fall over into it. Finally I say: I guess I can let you do that.

You got some tools?

I got thirteen socket sets, I got a bushel and a half of screwdrivers, I got two Rubbermaid tubs of adjustable wrenches and one of open/box-ends, I got a five-gallon paint pail of various kinds of pliers, I got fourteen cordless drills, twelve to twenty-four volts, three of them DeWalts, and one of *them* a lithium-ion some moron bought to hang pictures with and then couldn't afford the pictures, I got —

Look around, I say. And whatever you use goes back where you got it. You hold em where I can see em going out the door. And I'm telling you right now, that system works. So if it don't after you're done with it, you get to purchase it. OK?

Gong, gong, gong, a couple of Bobbleheads — which is one

thing I won't buy, though people've tried to sell them to me — nodding away.

I turn back to the woman. So, I say.

So, she says.

We both stare at the rings. Even in the dim light they glitter. But that's what rings are made to do.

What will you give me? she asks.

No chitchat. Just plow ahead and get it done. I don't even have to ask if she's pawning or selling. Pretty obvious she's here to get something over and hopeful that what I'll give is close to what she wants. Almost never is. Dreams and things hardly ever match. I pluck the wedding band out of the box, flick on the lamp, put on reading glasses. Inside the band I can see LORRAINE AND BILL. FOREVER. 7/7/83.

So: Lorraine's forever was twenty years long. These days, that's not a bad forever. I push the ring back into its slit. I've always liked that little friction, the way those cases hug the rings. Fourteen-carat gold, the engagement ring has a twenty-five-point diamond. Good stuff, but not worth much on resale. Jewelers get to charge for the dream. This set'd probably go two thousand retail. But I can't buy the dream back any more'n I can sell it. People don't come to pawnshops for symbols of forever. Maybe they should — get a dose of reality along with the romance. For me, it's a puddle of gold. A bright stone at the end of a tweezers.

I put it on the scale. The wedding comes to three grams. I get out my wholesale book. I know what it's worth, but the drama helps, shows there's a standard, it's not just me picking a number out of my head. People have faith in the book, they feel better if I look up what I already know. She doesn't even fidget while I turn the pages, making a show of peering through my glasses. I go past the right page on purpose a couple of times, don't want to seem too sure, then pretend to finally find what I'm looking for. I lay the book down, take off the glasses.

It's three grams of gold, I say. It's a twenty-five-point diamond. Four a gram for the gold, six a point for the diamond. I'll up it to two hundred dollars.

She looks at me. Usually there'll be a flicker of eyes, calculating going on, doing the math. But her eyes just hold me. The light reflects off the glass countertop up into her face, makes her look stark. She was prettier back by the door. But those eyes—they're great, light brown, almost the color of brick. And I remember that walk, and I'm thinking, *Eyes like that and a walk like that? What the hell'd Bill find better?*

Four *dollars?* she finally says. Six *dollars?* But that's—

I know, I say. But that's what they're worth. Really. You need to think, you go ahead, I've got to check on something.

The Bobbleheads are bobbling out the door with my tools and car stereo, and if I push too hard, she'll get proud and walk. Not that I'd care. It's not like I need to campaign for more divorce because I'm short on used ring sets. But you can't do business unless you do business, so I leave her to think and amble out the door after them. The sun whams into me. This heat. It's just unending. Sure enough, they're heading for a black Camaro. Why'm I not surprised? I note the license number.

When I come back in, she hasn't moved. I go around the counter and stop, facing her.

I want seven hundred and fifty dollars, she says.

She's one of those. My little show of looking in the book, all that stuff—useful as casters on a crutch.

Six a point and four a gram's standard, I say. You want, I'll show you.

I want seven hundred and fifty.

Look, maybe three hundred, but that's a stretch. I know these mean a lot to you, but—

No, you don't.

She sounds like she's stopping a child who's about to throw a toy.

You don't know anything, she says. Maybe these don't mean much to me at all. Maybe a great-aunt I never even liked willed them to me.

I don't say anything, but I have my doubts — unless Great-Aunt Lorraine got married in 1983 to a real romantic Geezer Bill.

I need seven hundred and fifty, she says.

Needs now. Like I'm a bank? Or a mission? Like I got a sign on my door saying my job is helping out? I feel like telling her, *You know who buys used jewelry? No one. Except once in a while some geezer or great-aunt, and then only because they never got out of the Depression and they're still stocking up, or else it's cheap decoration while they go to Deadwood to gamble their great-niece's inheritance away. Either way they won't pay for your story.*

But I don't owe her an argument. She needs a dozen stores with the same answer.

You'll have to try somewhere else, I say.

She shakes her head, like she's the one refusing. No, she says. No, that's no good.

What's *good* got to do with it? We trying to end starvation here? She thinks I'm begging to buy her stuff? Like right beneath us, under the counter's glass, I don't have enough old rings I haven't sent to the refinery yet — class and engagement and wedding and just plain showoff rings — that you'd have to measure in square feet? And every single one of them is someone's castoff past or pride or loyalty or love. How many forevers? She thinks I need hers, too?

Her hand floats over the counter, and I think she's going to pick the rings up and pout out of here, too bad, Mister Pawnshopman, you missed your chance. But her hand hangs over them, pale and light-veined, a leaf that started to fall but stopped in midair.

Fifteen hundred dollars, she says. That's what he paid. I don't know how many times he told me. Bragging about it. Like I was supposed to be grateful I was worth that much. Every time we had an argument, I'd learn how much these rings were worth.

I knew I wouldn't avoid it. Put it in a book somewhere, maybe it's worth something.

I want half, she goes on. That's all. Seven hundred and fifty.

Got a Phillips screwdriver?

The short earring, in the door, sweaty. Looks like a dog wandered in.

One or two, I say. I'll get one for you.

An opportunity to get away from the sob story. I walk around the counter to the tool section. The earring trails me. We stand over the Rubbermaid full of screwdrivers.

What size? I ask.

Oh, maybe two, three inches long.

What, he thinks I'm talking about his dong? The number, I say. The screw head size.

They have sizes?

He acts genuinely surprised and kind of pleased, like he'd like to hear more, could I maybe give a lecture on how Phillips screws came to have sizes, and who was Phillips anyway?

I reach into the bin. Here, I say. There's a One and a Two.

Hey! That's great! Thanks, man!

He grins like I gave him a Christmas present and heads for the door. I wait behind the shelves a bit, hoping she'll take the opportunity to leave. But no. She's standing where I left her. OK, then — time to get her out of the store. I don't need to hear more about Bill and her sad little troubles. I go behind the counter and take the cash box and pull up six fifties. It pisses me off that I'm going this far, but it's the limit I'd set.

There's three hundred. It's a gift. I'll be lucky to get that back.

The sight of cash usually does the trick. But she doesn't even look at it.

He started playing golf, she says.

Now there's a futile dream. I got two sets of clubs gathering dust. It was widows brought them in, and I thought I could turn them over. But golf clubs aren't like power tools. You don't expect a drill to make you a better driller. But golf clubs — who wants to buy them if they failed at turning someone else into Tiger Woods?

He met someone, she goes on. Who golfed, too. Drinks at the clubhouse, I suppose.

I nudge the money. But she's going now. I'm bound to get the whole sorry story.

What do golfers talk about? she asks. A year ago he left on a business trip. He had a round-trip ticket. He only used half of it. You think he was the only one on that plane did that?

I push the money against her hand.

That's three hundred, I point out. It's more'n you'll get anywhere else.

I suppose.

OK, then.

I take my fingers from the bills and reach for the ring case.

I need seven-fifty.

I hate it when I'm too sure to close a deal. There I am, with my hand hanging over those rings like one of those claws in those glass-cased games that rip off little kids. I drop it to the counter, trying to make it just a hand again.

He called me two days ago, she says. From Tucson. Told me he made a mistake. He wants to get back together. What do you think of that?

I'm supposed to have an opinion? What I think is, she's one of those people thinks other people care about her story enough to think about it.

She answers her own question.

I think she got sick of him, she says. He wasn't up to par. Not enough *foreplay.* Not nearly. So he thinks he'll just come back to me. An easy lie. A hole in one. Who invented golf language anyway?

I damn near smile. I damn near say, *Musta been that screwy Phillips.* But I keep my mind on what's at hand. She lifts a shoulder.

He told me he'd wrap things up and come home, she says. We'll work things out. You know what I told him?

She's here with the rings.

To go to hell, I say.

Kind of, she says. I said, Sure, come back, you know where the house is.

I'm not following. But I remind myself that I don't have to.

A reunion, I say. How nice.

That's why I need the seven-fifty. A first-class ticket from here to Tucson is seven-forty. It all works out. If he can wrap things up in two weeks, so can I. I've been wrapped up since he left. So, I find out when he's leaving Tucson, and I take a plane so I pass him in the air. Or as close as I can. What do you think?

She keeps asking me that. This time it's the tall earring who interrupts. I guess they got a tag team going. He sticks his head in the door. Say, he calls. It doesn't work.

I thought they might try something like that: *Now we got it in the car, since it doesn't work anyway, how about we just leave it there?* You got to get up a hell of a lot earlier than that to put one over on me.

It works, I tell him. A minute. I'll be out.

But now she has a head of steam. It's like the kid and I are in some other universe, and she's still going on: Once I realized a ticket was half the price of this ring set — that can't be coincidence, can it? I mean, it *means* something. There's even a word for it.

There's coach, I say.

He splurged on this ring set. I've got to honor that. Serendipity. I've read about it. Things are connected, and they'll just — they connect.

I stare at the rings under the glass, the diamonds, the rubies, the Black Hills gold, the big old class ring for Spearfish High School right under my nose.

Lorraine, I say, you're doing some mean math to get to serendipity. But OK. It all works out. Bill comes back and Lorraine's not there. Lorraine's where Bill's been, flying on a wedding band. Cute. I'll give you that.

When I look up, her eyes are wide.

How do you know our names? she asks. Her voice is breathy with surprise.

I act dumb: You must have told me.

No. I didn't. Did I?

I shrug. She lets it go.

So, she says. When he comes back, guess what? I won't be at the airport waiting to pick him up. How he's going to get home, I don't know. But when he does, the door'll be open. And on the table, what? A receipt for my airline ticket. With the destination cut out. And the price circled. And a receipt for these two rings. With that price circled, too, and then multiplied by two. And I'll leave him a ten-dollar bill for the difference. He only owes me the flight.

Lorraine, I say, I'm impressed. Only, serendipity's not worth much in here. There's coach. Bill'll get the message.

The message is for me.

Her voice is hard, like I have some kind of obligation to understand.

I don't buy symbols, I tell her.

Seven-fifty.

We've got nothing to talk about.

All right, then.

All right.

But she doesn't move. She tips her chin up and to the side and gives a little sniff, but that's all. OK. Let her pose if it makes her feel better.

I've got to check on those kids, I say. Sorry I couldn't help you.

And I actually am, a little. But I'm not in business to help every nut case who walks through my door. I scoop the money back up, lock the cash box inside the case. When I go outside, my tools are scattered all over the sidewalk. It's near closing time, but it's still hot. The earrings have crossed some wires. They can't even match colors. By the time I get out from under their dash, the back of my shirt is soaked. I turn the ignition on. They've got a CD in already, and it starts up, someone screaming something. I turn the volume down.

It works, I say.

They're grinning, bobbling their heads like they think there's a rhythm somewhere in that noise, matches the clappers in their brains.

How about we drive it around some, the tall one says. Could we? See how it sounds moving? You know, with the windows open and all?

That's the stupidest thing I ever heard, but Lorraine must've weakened my defenses, because I say, OK. But I've got your license number. I close in half an hour. You're not back, I call the cops. And pick those tools up first.

Back in the shop, I can't believe it, she's still standing there. Hasn't moved. Doesn't move when I go around the counter. Doesn't even turn her head. When I come right in front of her, her eyes catch mine, but barely. That's all.

You're still here, I say.

I've got my toe on the floor alarm button.

You changed your mind, then? You want the three hundred?

I open the case, get out the cash box, lay the bills on the counter.

There, I say, and push the cash toward her. I pick up the rings and put them on the shelf behind me, but I don't completely turn my back. You read it in the paper all the time, it's the quiet ones who end up going postal.

But she doesn't move a muscle. I turn, tap the money with my index finger.

Go ahead, Lorraine. Take it. It's worth more to you than the rings.

You'd think she'd had a stroke.

I'm closing soon. Cash or merchandise, one or the other.

Her mouth sets hard.

Cute, I say. Except I don't see the humor. You're not out of here when I close, I call the cops. How's that for cute?

It doesn't faze her. It's like she's turning into stone in front of me, except for her eyes. They're brighter all the time, brick-colored but nothing like stone about them. I put both hands on the counter and lean toward her.

Come on, Lorraine, I say quietly. You don't want the cops to haul you out. Take the three hundred. I can't go higher. That's the limit. Really. I'll give you a receipt for the seven-fifty. Bill won't know the difference.

She doesn't say a word, but I already know what she's thinking: *I'll know the difference.* It occurs to me that I might sound just like Bill, bullying first, then pleading—even if in either case I'm the reasonable one. I throw up my hands and spin away from her.

You want to get arrested, fine! I yell. Just don't blame me. It's my store, Lorraine. My place! My money!

I go to the window. The light's so bright out there it hurts, but I stare into it wide-eyed until it doesn't anymore. A couple of Chinese women from the air base, married to American guys, are leaving the little spice store across the street. Or maybe they're Filipino or Korean or Vietnamese, or hell, I don't know, Cambodian, Thai, what else is there? Their mouths are open, their teeth are white, they're laughing.

And then I turn around to this dark thing. Standing there. I've been looking out the window so long, and it's so dim by the counter, I can hardly make her out. She looks like some statue I got in, some mistake in judgment, cast in concrete and painted black, that I'll never unload. Like a bad dream of dealing. Like something that if I bulldozed the place, knocked the whole building down, would still be standing there when the dust settled, like an old stone chimney in the middle of nowhere where a house once stood.

I've never cheated on my wife. I give to CARE and March of Dimes and I walk in Relay for Life and I call the cops if someone tries to sell me stuff I think is stolen. Everyone comes in here *wants* to think they're getting cheated—because by God, if I'm cheating them, that's proof they're innocent and pure. All I do is buy and sell and pawn. Stuff doesn't get mucked up with meaning here. It's just stuff. My house doesn't have a million rooms and I don't drive a Hummer just so I can send a message: *I got it and you don't, and to hell with anything else.* My son never got a girl pregnant and dumped her, and my daughter never neither. They both worked down here and knew a thing was a thing. I didn't have to give them a Game Cube or an iPod—which I got a few of here—to let them know they meant something to me.

So what right's Lorraine got to make me feel like nothing counts for me but money? I get so sick of people using this place to prove how good they are. They may've got themselves so addicted to drugs or gambling or some other demon that they need to unload everything they own to keep the addiction going, or they may've lost all their dreams some other way—but by God at least they're not that cheap sonofabitch who buys and sells the things. I've never bought or sold a dream, or a demon for that matter, in my life, and it's a hell of a lot more moral to make a gram of gold a gram of gold than it is to make it forever or some such goddamn nonsense.

I walk back to the counter, banging my heels on the floor so the whole place shakes and echoes, and I grab the phone off the hook.

I'm calling the police, I growl. It's past closing. You're trespassing.

That gets her, I can see it. Probably never even had a speeding ticket. But she holds her ground. I don't use 9-1-1, it's not a real emergency, and the last thing I need is the police not responding to a real emergency because I've given them fake ones. I punch the numbers in, then hold the phone away from my ear so she can hear it ringing.

Police.

I've been watching her, and all of a sudden there's this voice in my ear wanting to know what I want, and I'm staring at those frightened eyes of hers — and I can't do it.

Sorry, I say. Wrong number. Sorry.

I slam the receiver down and spin away from the phone and bang my hands on the counter. Light jangles off every shivering point and edge of ring and jewel under the glass.

All right! I yell. I'll give you your seven-fifty. Because I don't care about it, Lorraine. You understand? I don't *care* about that money. And I sure as hell don't care about your serendipity. It's bullshit, what you're doing, making these rings into —

I wave my hands, I can't even finish that sentence. It's pathetic is what it is, me giving in to this. But I don't care.

I grab the cash box off the counter and open it so hard I bend the hinges. I lift it three feet off the countertop and tip the whole box upside down. Coins roll and clatter, landing at her feet and mine, and rubber-banded wads of cash thump and flop, and loose bills float and settle, on the counter and the floor and around her thin hands unmoving as tree roots on the glass.

There! That's all the cash I got. Take it all if it means so goddamn much to you. Fly to New Zealand, first class and one way. Just get out of my store.

Her whole face softens and breaks apart, like the life in her eyes is melting out into the stone. Then she shuts her eyes and holds them shut. I stand there with the cash box upside down in my hands, the bent lid hanging. And I realize how hurt she is. It's seeping out of her, now that her face is softening. I can't move. It's like I'm seeing her for the first time, like that statue I thought was concrete, I'm seeing through the dust and grease of it to some lost piece of art and am just starting to comprehend what's being offered.

Then she sighs, and her eyes open, and they're bright and not angry, and I realize by the way they're looking at me that they're not seeing angry either. It's all gone. From both of us. It's just us, looking at each other.

Thank you, she says.

Which, after all this, is as crazy as anything else she's said.

Her hand floats over the bills but then pauses and just hangs there. Now she's undecided. Happens all the time. The deal done, and then the doubt. I could say, *Forgive him, Lorraine. Maybe he's changed. How do you know unless you find out?*

But I made the deal. I'm a pawnshop owner, not a counselor.

She goes through with it, but not so easy. She finds seven hundreds and two twenties, but then her hands shuffle through the bills like she can't focus. I bend down and pick up a ten that's on the floor by my feet and hold it out to her. It's limp, moving a little from the air conditioner's flow. She looks at it for a while, then finally reaches out and takes it.

Then, before I can drop my hand, she grabs it and squeezes. She's holding the ten, so it's a paper squeeze, but even through the crumpled money it feels real.

I don't know your name, she says.

Ed. Ed's Pawn?

Of course.

She squeezes again, the ten crushed between us, then lets go.

Ed, she says — and it's funny to hear, no one ever says my name in here — what happens?

She's looking at her rings — my rings — on the counter.

Yeah, I say. Well, sometimes I'll get a young couple in here, you know, without a lot of money but, you know, in love, and —

She reaches out and touches the back of my hand.

It's OK, she says. That's a lie. You're sweet.

What can I say to that? I tell the truth in here all the time, and no one ever tells me I'm sweet.

I better go, she says.

Aren't you forgetting something?

She stares at me, then it hits her. The receipt! she says.

I find a pen and hunch over the counter with it.

Last name? I ask.

Lipking — no, Durant. It was — I mean, Lipking's his name. But mine's Durant.

Lorraine Durant, I say aloud, writing it.

I concentrate on the letters and numbers, making sure they're legible and pressed hard so her copy will be clear. I circle the $750.00 for her, then pull the receipt out of the box and tear it off. I separate my copy and hand her the yellow one. She fumbles around in her purse, putting it under some flap, then puts her hand out. It's so thin in mine I'm almost afraid I'll break it.

Lorraine, tell me something. Would you've let the cops haul you out? Really?

She hesitates, then says: I would have.

I look at her, debating.

I'm glad to hear that, I say. But why here? Why me?

I cook Chinese, she says. So, you know, that store over there. I'd see your sign. It's hard to find Chinese spices in Twisted Tree.

Twisted Tree! Where that girl was from.

Yeah. I know the family. She used to run. She and her best friend would run by my house.

197

She was in here.

In here?

Brought in a rodeo buckle. I told her, Keep it. Someday you're going to want to show that to your kids. But she insisted. Had this air. Like she knew exactly what she was doing. Then three weeks later I see her picture in the paper.

What happened to it?

The buckle? Guy bought it. Some collector. I kinda hid it, figured she might come back for it, but he nosed it out and then there wasn't nothing to do but sell it.

That's too bad.

Yeah? Maybe it is.

I gotta go.

Wave to Bill for me up there when you pass him.

She smiles, sort of: her lips smile, her face looks sad, and her eyes — they look like they're already gazing down, and the world's going by.

I watch her out the door, then pick up the fallen money. I'm turning the OPEN sign around in the window when I hear drums and screaming coming around the corner. The Camaro sways into a parking spot. Fifteen minutes past closing. They hop out and march through the door. Before they can say anything, I do.

You're late. I gave you guys a break. Could've had you in hand-cuffs by now.

Sorry, the tall one says. We lost track of time.

I let them shuffle. Finally he says, The system's OK, I guess.

That's bullshit. You don't lose track of time with an OK stereo system. But I just wait.

Will you take a hundred and fifty for it?

That's fifty less than what I got it marked, and they're feeling guilty. Can't, I say. That one's already clearance. Blue-light special. Low as I can go.

They look at each other.

Well—it's too much.

I've got them over a barrel. I could say, *If you think so, take it out. You know where the tools are.* It's tempting. But hell—I can get my price and make them feel good besides. Why crucify them? They're just kids.

Look, I say. The deal's good. You won't get a system like that anywhere for that price. You already got it installed. You can use it tonight. Impress the girls. Who knows?

They grin. The shorter one lifts up on his heels and drops back down, and the tall one looks at the floor and then says, Well, OK. Two hundred. With a three-month guarantee.

Surprises me. Got more in reserve than I thought. Good for him. But I never give guarantees. This is used stuff. I don't take in junk, but it's buyer beware here. But I think of Lorraine, probably the first time she's ever flown, lifting up to some other life. What the hell.

Two months, I say. I'll guarantee it two.

They look at each other, debating.

But they're already there. I clinch it. I wait a moment more, then say: With a system good as that one is, two's as good as forever.

Traces

WE ALL KNEW the crazy sonofabitch was out there. Don't know how many times people told me of waking at night to the sound of his rifle. Hell of a way to be jerked out of dreaming. Shane Valen was a weird sonofabitch from a long line of weird sonsabitches. Not that anyone ever caught him in their headlights bending over an antelope or mulie. Nothing like that. Just guts the next day stinking and shining in a cloud of flies. We all knew who'd done it. *Goddammit, Greggy,* they'd say to me. *Can't you do something about that goofy bastard?*

Tried once. Turned on my rack and pulled the sonofabitch over for a friendly chat. This was the middle of the afternoon, after he was leaving the rodeo — about the only thing that got him off his ranch during the day. He'd show up, stand at the fence a couple hours, then leave. Never cheer, never clap. Just stand, looking through the fence at the barrel racing. I pulled him over at the edge of town as he was heading home.

Shane, I said when I got to his window.

He jerked his head, I guess he was responding.

Enjoy the rodeo?

It against the law? he asked.

Hell no, Shane, I said. You watch all the rodeo you want. Reason I stopped you is, I been getting complaints you're driving at night without headlights. Reports you're trespassing all over the county. Thought we should talk about it.

He stared out his windshield. Stared so long I damn near wondered if I'd really spoke. Finally he said, Anyone cut me?

Cut you? I asked.

Trespassin? Anyone cut me trespassin?

Hell, wasn't nobody in the goddamn county hadn't come across Shane's pickup parked along some back road at night with Shane behind the wheel and his rifle across his chest. Maybe you're coming home from Ruination or from a wedding dance, weaving a bit on the gravel, and then up from the night that rusted hulk of a pickup rises. Crazy bastard'd stare right into your headlights, so your lights'd bounce up and down on washboards, say, and his eyes'd be going on and off red. Spooky as hell. And you know damn well he was creeping along, poaching, and saw your headlights from miles away, so he pulled off the road like that. A piece a the darkness. You know damn well, too, if you'd go over the next hill and cut your own lights and come back, you'd find that sonofabitch moving along slow, feeling the edges of the road in the dark like a goddamn snake.

Well, Shane, I said. They ain't so much caught you, but—

You cut me?

No, I ain't caught you either. Point is, though, you got neighbors, and—

Neighbors on Valen land. You catch me, we kin speak again. I'm goin now.

And he did. Put his pickup in gear and left me standing there, the only person ever did that. And I let'm go. I hadn't cut Shane doing anything. Couldn't even catch the sonofabitch actually driving at night without headlights. He always saw me first.

Two camels short of a caravan. Crazy as a bag of drywall screws. Thinks just because Old Joe Valen owned a chunk of land back when men were men and sheep were nervous, he's got a right to go wherever he goddamn pleases. That time Stanley Zimmerman's buffalo got out on the highway I know damn well he was the sonofabitch cut the fence. Thinks it's still his land. Shoulda locked him up just for the way he smells and thrown the key in the river.

Everyone figured his father, Rodney, would end the Valen line. How the hell Rodney managed to find a wife's beyond anyone. He's forty years old, living with his father, Ralph, and his grandmother, Emma, Old Joe's wife, in that house out by Mattinglys'. Damn near the same day his old man died, Ralph sold the original land, with that house Old Joe was so damn proud of. Stories are Emma fought that move, but what's she going to do, sit out there on that place so far from anyone she had to keep her own tomcat, and chew the air? Why she'd want to stay out there is anyone's guess. She finally gave in and moved to the new place with Ralph and his wife, who stuck it out till Rodney was twenty-five, then decided she'd had enough of the good life and left. So there the three of them are, Emma and Ralph and Rodney, the lot hootier than a trunkful of owls. What kind of woman would marry into a deal like that?

Story is, Rodney traded a couple of horses for a car and started driving and didn't know how to stop. Ended up in Minnesota, comes back telling of a woman he met in a bar. Dream on, broomstick cowboy. But two weeks later this woman shows up, Sarah Cornwall, asking directions to the Valen ranch. Once people get straight she's asking for the present Valen ranch and not the old one, they send her out and, no one could believe it, she up and marries Rodney.

Ralph and the old woman moved upstairs, leaving Rodney and his bride all that privacy — but even so. And even when the old woman hit ninety and got forgetful enough she couldn't remember she was too damn stubborn to die, that house couldn't've been too roomy, especially with Shane now born. Sarah finally wakes up and looks around and realizes what everyone else knew all along and gets in her car and returns to Minnesota, leaving seven-year-old Shane to his father's and grandfather's care. In other words, not much care at all, and even less when Ralph died a couple years later.

I was a few years older than Shane, but what I remember most about him is how little there is to remember. Never knew if he was going to be in school or not, it was all haphazard with him, so I remember him more by his absence than his presence. Even then he was out prowling. Spent more time with animals than with people, slept outside more than he slept in. Not too surprising he'd grow up and decide on a career in poaching, even if we can't prove that's what he did, since no one ever *cut* him at it. But his letter writing—no one knew a goddamn thing about that until Sarah returned and the whole business burst out of that ramshackle house into the light of day. Crazy thing. You think you know every weird screw that puts a guy together and what his secrets are, but it turns out he's got secrets beneath the secrets, and the ones you know are just keeping you from thinking he's got others. Like a black hole. So goddamn invisible it's gone right through to being visible again. To where everything is pointing to it, things warping around it, deforming. But unless you got a notion of what a black hole is, a theory of why, you just think, *Hell, ain't that an odd region a space.*

Shane always had his pickup lights off and his house lights on. You could see the damn thing, lit up every room, off the Red Medicine Creek Road right before you got to Mattinglys' and Zimmermans'. Didn't matter what time a night. Didn't matter if Shane's pickup was there or not. Lights were always on. So what the hell was the crazy sonofabitch doing?

She brought the letters back with her. I found them inside her car, seven thick packs of them tied up with satin ribbons. Trying to figure it out, you don't know how far back to go. Maybe to when

Sarah up and left. Or maybe to whatever the hell appealed to her in Rodney that got her out here. Or maybe you got to go clear back down the Valen line, to when Old Joe managed to wrest that land away from the Indians and the government and build that house out there like some prairie palace. There's a sonofabitch! He's still being talked about. Story is he once whipped his wife with barb-wire for not having a meal ready on time. Bea Conway, of course, who's the expert, and if you don't believe that, just ask her, don't put much stock in stories like that. *Where's the documentation?* is her favorite question. But if you look at the records she's got in her own damn book, it's goddamn odd how many kids in Old Joe's family died young: *Cause unknown.* Unknown by who? Must be kids buried all over that Valen ranch. Little bundles of baby planted. You go out there, you wonder what you're stepping on.

Then there was Eddie Little Feather's story, before he got run over, about his great-grandfather being shot by Old Joe when he was trying to get someplace safe after Wounded Knee. Not that Eddie had the kind of authority that made people take his word for things. As Bea would say, there's no proof — and who the hell'd want to find it if there was? Point is, with Shane, it wasn't just himself spooked people. Wasn't just those red eyes behind that windshield. Was his whole family history. It ain't pretty imagining a woman whipped with wire — and she had the face to prove it, unless the face started the story. People claim sometimes to see her parading by with children following, none a them speaking a word. Course I can't afford to put no more stock in stories like that than Bea does, or I'd be off on wild goose chases every goddamn night. That's in the past. Had nothing to do with Shane. Just ghosts. Bleeding mothers and dead children and an old man who finally got his hot meal, and some Indians who disappeared a damn long time ago. Cause unknown. All I've really got to make sense of anything are the letters — that is, what I've got of them.

• • •

Here's the first one:

july 15 1963

der mom
how are you. i ben fine. dad to. thank you for the birthde card. and
the mony. i bout shotgun shels. i got a grows. there harder then
fezzant.

shane

A few things could intrigue you about that letter. For instance,
the year. Shane was only eight years old when he wrote it—his
first birthday after she left. She sends him money. She can't even
imagine something he'd like.

And then the month: grouse season don't open till October.
No sense waiting till you're grown to get started on your career, I
guess.

But what gets me is how, even way back then, he's got that
dad to.

On Shane's seventh birthday Rodney handed him a loaded twelve-
gauge and his mother left. Rodney wasn't what you'd call elo-
quent, but he had a couple of guys he used to drink with, so we
got these bits of quadruple-drunk story: Rodney drunk when he
told it, his friends drunk when they heard, then drunk again when
they retold it to a bunch of drunks. So, Rodney gave Shane that
twelve-gauge, and you can imagine Sarah watching from the window, though that detail's not supplied. Been watching for eight
years. All that hope she stuffed into her car in Minneapolis when
she first came out here is about to crumble into dust. The last
straw's about to get loaded onto that goddamn, overworked cam-
el's back. She sees her son lift that shotgun, taller than he is, while
her husband points to the pump, crooks and uncrooks his elbow,
imitating how it works. Points to the bead on the end a the barrel.
The trigger. Then stands back, looks around, shrugs his shoul-

ders, opens his hands. I can just see it: *Whatever the hell you can find, son.*

Shane's skinny arm bends and straightens, works the pump. She's watching. Her little boy. Then the gun swings up and the barrel sweeps toward her, there's that sickening moment when its black dot is winking right at her and she's not sure what he's finding to shoot at, doesn't even know if he knows she's behind the window, and then it's gone up and by and then *boom!* She jumps and crams her fist into her mouth to tamp her scream back down, she's afraid if she lets it out she'll never stop, she'll become the kind of thing they put on display at Wall Drug for tourists to see, the Screaming Woman, right next to the piano-playing gorilla with the grody knuckles, him playing and her screaming, a real duet. The weathervane on top a the barn, one a them old rooster things, half-rusted out and been pointing the same way for as long as she's been Rodney's wife, don't matter how strong a different wind's blowing, she sees it rise off the roof. For just a moment it looks like that metal rooster's going to up and fly away. But then it tumbles and falls and clanks down the shingles on the other side, where I found the damn thing in a patch of leafy spurge grown up around it forty-odd years later.

There she is, her fist in her mouth, she sees her little boy knocked back by the kick of the gun. He's wounded, something's broken. His shoulder's twisted, his eyes are astonished he's hurt so bad, she's never seen that look on his face before. It unparalyzes her, she pulls her fist from her mouth, he needs her, she cries at the windowpane, Shaney! and starts to go to him.

But before she can turn her head from the window she sees his grin, perverse as a goddamn zipper opening in the middle of his mouth and spreading both ways. And then Rodney's voice, you can just hear it rumbling through the windowpane: *Good shootin, son. Now you know how, you shoot that gun anytime you want. Shells're in the broom closet.*

She leaves that afternoon. What's the point of being a mother? Just gets in her car and leaves. Shane's prowling the pastures looking for nonmetal birds to shoot, and Rodney's she doesn't know where. She throws a suitcase of clothes in her car. Takes nothing with her that wasn't hers when she came, including her son.

Here's the two that got me thinking:

July 15, 1976

Dear Mom,
Thank you for the money. Yeah, I turned 21. It ain't a big difference to me, though. I been doing pretty much what I want for kind of forever anyway. It ain't like 21 and there you are like I hear with college kids. Dads doing fine. Cattle prices been OK.

Shane

July 17, 1977

Dear Mom,
Thank you for the money. My birthday was real good this year. Cattle prices was better than maybe ever least what I can remember. Dad said we ought to celebrate so we drove down to Rapid had dinner at the Howard Johnsons. I dont know if you was ever there but its good food let me tell you. Dad makes about the best pies ever but that Howard maybe has him beat. The waitress kept flirting with him and he was joking all night maybe I shouldnt be telling you that kind of stuff. Even people at the next table was laughing at Dads jokes wondering if he was a professional comedian come to do a show at that Civic Center they just built in Rapid. Anyway Dads doing real good and my birthday was real good and the money you sent Ill get something real nice with it dont know what yet but itll be nice. Something youd like and Dad too.

Shane

Look at them letters. I was leafing through them in my patrol car about a week after the whole thing happened, passing time while I kept an eye on the radar, and wondering what I should do with the things, when I come on those two, one after the other like that. I can see how Sarah, getting them a year apart, might not have noticed anything. But me, I'm reading along, and I got thirteen letters where Shane hardly says a damn thing, and then all of a sudden, in 1977, Rodney's all over the place—taking Shane to Rapid, flirting with the waitress, telling jokes, making pies. Where the hell'd this come from? Wasn't the Rodney Valen I knew.

Maybe I shouldn't have been reading them letters at all. There was nothing to investigate and no one to indict if there was. At the time I thought the whole thing was as obvious as when Eddie Little Feather passed out on the highway and that Colorado Springs truck driver hit him. Same sort of thing: hell of a mess but once you get it cleaned up, it's over and done with. Legally, those letters might've been private, not mine to read at all unless I was pursuing a case, which I wasn't. On the other hand, there was no one to protest or care. So I'm passing time with them and trying to get my head around Rodney Valen making pies when it hits me: he died in 1976. Collapsed on the sawdust of the Ruination Bar. Middle of a sentence. No one ever did find out what he had to say, which was maybe for the best. But he'd just refilled his glass, so it was a waste of beer. And he was running a tab. Miller Freeman says he's seen all sorts of ways to get out of paying for beer, but Rodney Valen's method topped them all.

Hadn't of been she opened her car door we might still not know about it. Richard Mattingly's out spraying herbicide on that damn salt cedar's infesting Red Medicine Creek between his ranch and the Valen land. That salt cedar, now's, a battle, and he's out there two days in a row and sees that car sitting there outside that molting house. Told me it just didn't feel right. Not a car he recognized, first of all. And then the door open like some broken wing. And Shane's pickup there, not moving. It was that last bit that convinced me. The thing about weird sonsabitches is they stick to their weird. You can trust them. Normal people keep their weird hid, so if it ever gets out you have no idea where it'll go. But Shane Valen—I knew if he wasn't crawling around the county in his pickup, with his lights off, poaching, something was serious wrong.

I got out there and parked behind her car, which at the time I didn't know was her car. Wasn't a sound out there, and that house with the blank windows waiting. I opened my door, called out, Shane! It's Greggy Longwell!

Wasn't even an echo. Was like that house was so moldy and soft it absorbed my voice.

I didn't think Shane'd actually shoot me, but no one I knew'd ever drove up to his house and tested his paranoia. So I got out of the car low, but not so low I'd look like I was sneaking. In other words, I looked damn precisely like I *was* sneaking and made myself a good target besides, which shows the value of compromise.

Shane, I'm coming up to the house, I called.

Not a sound. But there wasn't nothing to do now but do it, so I shut my car door and started walking forward real slow, up past her car. And then, Jesus!

I'm standing by that open car door, looking at this old lady, and she's got a big hole in her chest, and there's blood spattered all over the far window and a big smear of fingers through that blood like she reached up to grab the window and then gave up and just slid back down to the seat. She's laying horizontal, her legs in the driver's seat, her shoulders in the passenger's. The shotgun blast must have lifted her right up and knocked her over. Her eyes're staring at the velour of the car roof, blank and blue as marbles. But I can handle that. Even the two-day stink I can handle. What froze me were the goddamn snakes.

I know snakes will crawl into open cars for warmth. Brock Morrison still talks about that time twenty years ago it happened to his wife and she drove fifty miles with the damn thing on her lap, afraid to move. But that was just one of the sonsabitches. I was looking at snakes everywhere, twisted around like some puzzle that wouldn't never unravel. Snakes on the floorboards, the dash, slung over the backs of the seats. And that wasn't the worst of it. There were snakes all over her body, twisted in figure eights around her almost-nothing breasts, snakelaces wrapped around her withered, rotting neck and snakelets around her bony ankles and wrists. Snakes in her hair, vined around her feet. Crowned and booted with snakes.

Wasn't a soul in the county knew Shane well enough to confirm he actually had rattlesnakes living with him, though talk was he let them curl around his feet while he drank his evening coffee before he went out poaching. But who the hell'd believe that kind of shit? Sure as hell not me. I got enough to do sorting out the bizarre from the just plain strange without adding in the implausible. But shit! Now I had to wonder just what was in that house. When I was finally able to move I went toward it real slow, watching every goddamn grass blade and every goddamn shadow under every goddamn grass blade.

I stood on the cinder blocks Shane used for steps, wondering if there were snakes curled up inside them. I moved to the side of the door and turned the knob and pushed. The door swung in, but nothing happened. Now I had me a hell of a fix. If I walked in slow, the crazy bastard might shoot me standing up, and if I barged in rolling on the floor like on some goddamn TV show, I might be rolling into a dozen rattlers. I eased away from the door and ducked under the kitchen window, then peered in sideways through it. It was so grimy and streaked and covered with dirt I couldn't see a thing, and I didn't want to get too close, so I'm peering and peeking at an angle trying to see through that dirty glass, when my eyes adjust and instead of seeing past the glass I look right at it, and them smears ain't dirt blocking my view, they're blood spatters turned dirt-brown, and specks of dried-out tissue and little slivers of bone.

Shane! I called. You stupid sonofabitch, Shane! You get your ass out here, hear?

Nothing. Just a constant, swishing sound I'd been hearing a while already, which just then I realized what it was. It was snake-skin moving against itself, so goddamn many of them sonsabitches in that house it sounded like wind in a forest in there.

Goddammit, Shane! If you don't get your ass out here, I'll —

But I didn't have no idea what I'd do. I looked at that dried blood on the windowpane and thought: *There's someone dead in there, and there ain't but two vehicles, and one's hers and the other's Shane's, so it don't take no Dick Tracy to figure out whose blood's on the window.*

But I had a helluva time steeling myself to walk into that dim kitchen where Shane Valen was perched on a ladder-back chair without his face, a short-barrel twelve-gauge on the floor next to him, and the back of his head blown against the far wall and that window, and the biggest goddamn rattler I'd ever seen coiled in his lap, shaking its tail when I walked through the door.

May 23, 1991

Dear Mom,

I been well, Dad too. He bought another section of land in order he's raising more horses. People said to him you aint never going to make a go of it raising arabians here but Dad said what its less rain here than in arabia? If you can raise arabians in arabia why cant you raise them in south dakota? Maybe we need to import some sand is that it? And I guess he proved right. We got people from places like france and new york come out to buy dads horses. Them colts sure is cute. Long skinny legs cant hardly stand but you ought to see them run. You wouldnt hardly beleive it. Aint nothing more peaceful of a evening than watching them mares and colts and the sun setting and the grass so green and some of Dads cof-fee and pie. He added onto the house maybe I told you that already last year or before and sometimes people will stay with us buying horses and all and Dad will just invite them to stay overnight so well sit on the deck and watch the sun go down and its about the finest thing they ever seen they say. And Dads been everywhere buying horses and he talks about them places and its something to hear him talk. Anyways thanks and I hope your well.

Shane

Check the date on that letter. First, Shane's writing more often, ain't just waiting for his birthday thank-you note in July. Second, Rodney's been dead fifteen years—and look at him, by God, still making pies but now traveling around the country, too, raising horses, entertaining guests, adding onto his goddamn house. He sure as hell started to live the good life after he died. And every single letter's like that—Rodney rescuing people stranded in snowstorms and speaking up at public meetings. Mother Teresa and Winston Churchill rolled into one. Shit, in one letter he even learns to speak some goddamn Japanese.

Ralph must've built that house right next to a rattlesnake den. He was in such a hurry to get away from the memories of his old man he didn't even bother to look where he was going. I suppose for a long time they battled the sonsabitches and kept them down, but somewhere in there that started to seem like a lot of work. So the snakes eventually come back to their old den and by God they see it's been added on to, so how about that?

It was a mess getting her out of that car, with them damn snakes everywhere. We opened the doors and poked at them with sticks. Noisy as hell, all them rattles going off. But we finally got them out. It was me, I'd have had guys with shovels smacking the damn things, but news of Shane and Sarah had made it to Rapid, and the county commissioners was afraid the *Rapid City Journal* or the AP'd show up and report a rattlesnake massacre. And then, who the hell knows what'd happen? Get them goddamn PETA freaks out here holding up signs and telling us rattlesnakes have rights, too. So I had orders: No bad press, just get them sonsabitches out of the car and get this whole mess over with.

Which is what I would've done hadna been for them letters. Once we got her body out we started going through her stuff, a single suitcase was all she brought, and there at the bottom were them packets tied with ribbon. By now I've got her ID'd and have figured out Shane murdered his own mother. But them letters — they're all in the original envelopes — all neatly slit open — all addressed to her, with Shane's return address. I throw them in an evidence bag, but I ain't thinking I'm going to have to produce them for any trial, since I didn't know then that Shane was bringing people back from the dead and might could resurrect himself.

The whole thing's at first so goddamn clear. Not a shred of doubt what happened. She comes, he shoots her, shoots himself. And since there wasn't going to be a trial, there didn't have to be a motive. And there wouldna been if I'd left them letters alone. But once Rodney come back to life, I couldn't quit. Shane's bragging about Rodney started to piss me off, just like when any dumbshit brags, Bill Lipking, say, bragging about his golf score, though Bill's been doing less bragging since he come back from Tucson and found Lorraine gone to who knows where. In fact, the last time Bill bragged about golf was at Ruination when he made a big deal about shooting a 68 and Miller Freeman had just plain heard enough and leaned over and asked him whether that impressed Lorraine. Of course Bill's still alive and Rodney was dead, so the comparison ain't quite accurate, and I maybe should've ignored Shane's bragging on Rodney's accomplishments. But Rodney Valen, dead or alive, raising Arabian horses? Japanese businessmen sitting on his deck — a deck he didn't even have? It was too much. I kept reading to find out what other bullshit Shane would invent, the sorry sonofabitch.

But then I read myself right into wondering about her coming back. I mean, twist this thing around and look at it from her view.

She mighta believed every one a them letters. Years of bullshit piling up, but she don't know it. Her memory of Rodney's not strong enough to fight off the Rodney Shane's inventing. So when she comes back to visit, who's she coming to see? Hell! Her little Shaney and her breeder-of-Arabian-horses-and-pie-making husband. A goddamn dream, that's what. A goddamn world that ain't and a person who never was.

And when she gets here? Shane looks just like his father. Both got that stare like their old ancestor's, you can see it in Bea Conway's county history. There the old guy is, staring out, dressed in his best clothes, surrounded by his wife and the kids that lived — Ralph and a couple sisters who married far away — Old Joe in black and the family in white like they're froth floating up on the surface of something dark. Of course, like I say, Bea doesn't say anything about him whipping his wife to shreds or the kids who ain't in the picture. Bea claims she's a careful historian, and them are the kinds of things she's careful to ignore. But all I'm getting at is Rodney and Shane both got that Valen look, you could mistake one for the other if you forgot one was forty years older.

And them letters of Shane's could make you forget. If anything, Rodney keeps getting younger after he dies. More and more the man Sarah must've wanted him to be in the first place. Like time stopped for her. She looked in the mirror every day and saw, sure enough, she was getting older. But them damn letters were making Rodney younger. Like a goddamn fairy tale, near unbelievable — except people believe in fairy tales all the time as long as they ain't written down and called that. So what's she thinking when she pulls up to that dry-rot house out there?

It ain't nothing like the horse ranch she's been imagining. Worse than when she left. But Rodney himself steps out the door — and time just crushes itself, and what the house looks like don't matter. Because he looks like she remembers. Maybe dirtier, but he's a working man — all them Arabian horses to take care of. There, by God, he is. All these years she's been half-guilty and wondering what would have happened if she'd stayed. Wondering if Rodney would have been the man she first drove out here for, the man them letters made him into. And now here he is, walking out of the house, holding a twelve-gauge.

Wasn't till I had to figure out who the place belonged to that I started to make sense of it all. End of the Valen line, so where's the land go now? How deep do I have to dig to find the uncles or cousins who got as far from their past as they could but who still had rights to the place? I knew something was up the moment I went in to see Orley Morgan. It ain't like some high-class lawyer is going to come to Twisted Tree to advance his career, but Orley got even shiftier than usual when I asked him about the Valen estate. Didn't know a damn thing. Shit no! Jesus! That was so long ago when Rodney died, how the hell could Orley remember?

I ain't said a word about Rodney, I pointed out.

That shut Orley up long enough for me to say: I ain't testing your memory. Just check your records. You keep records, I suppose?

Orley started babbling then. He'd been in charge of the Valen estate when Rodney died. And Rodney and Sarah hadn't never got around to divorcing. One a them things just never got done, like cleaning behind the refrigerator. So they were still legally married when Rodney up and spilled that beer in the Ruination bar. And who do you suppose estate law gives damn near the entire estate to? The surviving spouse, that's who.

Orley explains this to Shane. And ain't it odd how every goddamn letter Orley writes to Sarah Cornwall Valen comes back addressee unknown? *She musta moved agin,* is what Shane tells Orley. *Goddamn movingest mother I ever had.* And then, shit, seems Sarah Cornwall Valen spends half her time out of the country. *She's in Europe. She likes that kinda thing.* Orley couldn't keep track of all the places Sarah traveled. Every phone call he made, the number was disconnected or someone else answered the phone. *Moved agin. Even the goddamn phone company can't keep up with her.* And Orley, of course, is just lazy enough to want to believe it all. He ain't going to buy much Glenlivet off what he'll make handling the Valen estate anyway.

Jesus Christ, Orley, I said. You never got suspicious he was handing you a line?

Dammit, Greggy, he named cities in Europe. Named buildings. Described them, even. Described what she said was in*side* them. Named people she was seeing. With foreign names.

Guess those are the same people who came to visit Rodney later, I said.

He ignored that, too much for him to process. He picked up this paperweight on his desk, one a them water and fake-snow things that are supposed to make you think there's a whole world in there. He looks at it like maybe there actually is, then gives it a shake.

It's just, he said, Shane didn't have that kind of imagination. Did he?

Well, ain't that the question right there? Shane never once let on he didn't want Orley to find his mother. Just the reverse. Gave Orley so much help he wore him out. Had him writing letters all the time and all over the place, till Orley's the one arguing why don't they just wait. And pretty soon the Valen file gets covered up with other files, and then one day I suppose Orley come across it and just kind of put it in a cabinet to keep from being reminded, telling himself he'll get back to it when Sarah settles down, and congratulates himself for that decision with a drink. And Shane rents out enough of the ranch to pay the taxes on the whole, and there you are: he gets to live out there and no one around here likely to go out and ask him how that works.

Seems Shane had more imagination than about anyone here, and enough left over to keep us thinking he didn't have none. And once he discovered he had it, he couldn't put an end to it. He's worried someone's going to figure out what he done, and he gets more paranoid every year, imagining his mother out there somewhere, antennae up to sense Rodney's dying so she can come and snatch that land away, which is all he's got. Without that land, he's nothing. Hell, he's still bothered his grandfather sold land before he was even born, so what's it doing to his head to think about his mother taking away what he's living on? He imagines her so goddamn hard he resuscitates his father and imagines *him,* a counter-imagination to keep his imagined mother at bay. Jesus Christ! And all that time alone, sitting in that pickup or taking his naps somewhere, and no one to bring him back to reality, tell him, *Shane, the garbage is starting to stink.* He mighta started to believe his own bullshit, mighta half thought his father was actually alive. Except it gets even weirder than that.

For one thing, there's missing letters. Can't prove it, of course — like proving there ain't space aliens or intelligent Democrats. But like I said, weird has its ways. So when Shane writes letters for thirty-four years, faithful as a grandfather clock chiming on his birthday and three or four more a year besides and then in 1997 don't write for damn near a year and then starts up again, something's going on. I can't imagine a guy as goofy as Shane, once he got going with something like that, stopping, and then starting again. It ain't like someone deciding to take up cross-stitch and then getting too busy for a while. So, if he wrote them, there's a year of letters she didn't bring back, who knows why. Not much you can make of evidence that ain't there, so I'm not going to waste a lot of time trying. But it does make a guy curious, wondering what was in them letters or, if he quit writing, why.

But even that ain't the strangest. It's the direction them letters took once he started writing them again. Course I might not a noticed the gap if Rodney'd just kept his mouth shut — stayed at least that dead. But when the sonofabitch started talking again, in 1998, it kind of made me sit up straight and listen.

Here's maybe my favorite from before Rodney found his voice:

May 19, 1995

Dear Mom,

How are you? Were fine. Its spring like I suppose its spring where you are too aint a lot of difference between here and there far as springs concerned I guess. The colts is wobbling around following there mothers like colts do and the meadowlarks is singing how they do I aint never been sure whether its a bell or a whistle they got in there throats. And the swallows and the hawks is flying. National park service people been out talking to Dad about the black-footed ferret I think I told you about that once. Dad got to studying about them ferrets and by god if he didnt up and make himself a expert on them critters. He convinced them national park guys they ought to put some ferrets on our land and you oughta see how Dad watches and mothers them things. They was having trouble with some they put in the badlands so they come out and talked to Dad to see what they was doing wrong. So Dads been gone some this spring off in the badlands with them national park guys keeping them ferrets alive. Ferrets eat prairie dogs maybe you know that and prairie dogs sure make a mess of the grass aint hardly none left for cattle. Theres some people think prairie dogs is endangered now what sense does that make? Like rats should be endangered. Anyway, Dad likes them ferrets so much he says thats how we should be controlling prairie dogs not with poison. But poison now that stuff kills them. Theres times Dads ideas go a bit screwy far as Im concerned but maybe hes right you get enough ferrets they could handle the job. But that manyd be as bad as prairie dogs.

Shane

Ain't that something else? It's not just Rodney's a goddamn expert on ferrets, and it's not just Shane's making up letters he didn't goddamn write—he never once before so much as mentioned ferrets, so he's making stuff up about making stuff up and packing twice the bullshit in per sentence—but now he's even inventing what Rodney *thinks* and then, Jesus Christ, *arguing* with him! It's just layers and layers of bullshit. And Sarah's getting this stuff year after year, and she couldn't have been all that much in touch with reality if she married Rodney in the first place. And she's guilty about leaving little Shaney, she'd never imagine her little boy could lie. So hell, yes, she believes this stuff, maybe she even gets so mixed up she starts thinking she actually remembers Rodney being the kind of guy Shane's bullshit's making him into. So she ties those letters up and forgets what's in them, except not really—she remembers it as memory. *Remembers it as memory:* that's the kind of mumbo jumbo Shane's got me talking. All I'm trying to get at is, Sarah maybe got to where she couldn't tell the difference between what she remembered and what she read.

And like I said, to come out here and marry Rodney in the first place, after meeting him in a bar—if Rodney was telling the truth about that—she had to be one of them women believes love's a goddamn abracadabra that whooshes the past away to some never-been and leaves only the goddamn shining future, unattached, like some Santa Claus gift. And who the hell's going to tell her she's stepping onto pockmarked land and a family strange as a three-dollar bill? Love's a magic act, all right, but that kind of thing don't fingersnap away. It's like the elephant that disappears. Only an idiot actually believes it went anywhere.

So one day her son blasts a weathervane rooster off the barn, and she sees eight years of elephant dung she's been refusing to notice. *Poof!* She's gone. But that don't erase anything any more'n love did. Elephant just goes on eating and crapping, whether you see it or not. And then, in Shane's letters, by God! the Rodney she came out here to marry shows up, the cowboy who'd take her away from whatever she didn't like about her life or herself and give her everything pure, green grass and big skies and horse rides in the sunset. It ain't like Shane creates someone new for her. He justifies her falling in love with Rodney in the first place.

And then, like I said, this starts:

September 7, 1998

Dear Sarah,
I hope you have been well. It has been far too many years since I wrote. Our son tells me he keeps you informed about our lives here. I dont hold nothing against you I hope you will believe that. I know you always liked the city life and when you went back it didnt surprise me. Its a hard life here even if weve done right well. I fear our son may paint a better picture then it always is. But its right for us like where your ats right for you. Im writing not for anything in particular. Just times gone by. I know when our son writes he tells you things I dont know about. And thats all right. But you cant believe everything he tells you. Hes a good boy but sometimes he dreams things and then wakes up and forgets it was a dream. Im glad hes been writing to you and all, but things arent exactly like he always says. Anyway I hope your well.

Love,
Rodney.

Love, Rodney — ain't that sweet! And that *our son* stuff. And that oh-so-subtle convincing her to stay in Minneapolis. But the best is how he damn near tells her it's all a bunch of bullshit. Maybe them missing letters had gone too far, and he had to figure a way to pull things back, and the only way he could think of was to let Rodney argue the other side. Or maybe he said something so outrageous about Rodney even she knew it was bullshit, so she threw them away, and it was only when Rodney himself woke up to make the correction that she decided there was enough truth to start keep-ing them again. It just twists your head around thinking about it. After thàt, it's sometimes Shane and sometimes Rodney writing, and half the time they're arguing with each other, and neither one of them telling the goddamn truth. He had her spinning so fast she thought she was seeing straight.

I found dozens of them stick pens all over the house. Empty, not a drop of ink in them. Scattered around. Husks of dreams ripened into letters. I can see it — Shane rolling in at two or three in the morning, no headlights, been up all night, rolling in by feel with some new-dressed deer or antelope in the back of his pickup, and pulling into that shed on his place that I can't figure out how it manages to stand, and hoisting that animal out of that pickup with the come-along he had hooked to the rafters, and then walking out of that shed with those dead eyes swiveling behind him, groundward-facing, the come-along creaking in the beams. But Shane's already gone, he's been inventing his father for his invented mother the whole goddamn night, the whole thing has grown beyond his control, it was just a way to keep his mother away from the land and it turned into something bigger than he knows, and now he walks into the light leaking out of that shot-through house, carpeted with snakes, stepping between them, his clothes all bloodstained from his work, sits down at that kitchen table, the varnish worn off for years, and picks up one of them stick pens and licks the end and grips that sonofabitch like it was a chisel and starts to dig words into a notebook, so hard in some a them letters I can see imprints of the previous one in the paper, and who knows, maybe the one previous to that. Maybe the last letter has the whole goddamn thing pressed into it, and you could get the entire story out of that one page if you took an impression with dust or ash and could decipher the words cutting across all the other words, the maze of the whole thing put together. Somewhere in there, maybe, you could even find the missing letters and figure out what was in them and fill in that gap, and maybe that'd help make sense of it or maybe it'd just make it more bizarre.

I don't know. Could be I'm bullshitting myself and all that really happened is Shane was a paranoid sonofabitch and anyone shows up at his place, he blasts away without asking questions. I could be a bigger bullshitter than Shane. But I keep seeing him in that house, snakes sleeping around him or hunting in the walls where mice claws are clicking, and he's inventing Rodney's life. For her. For himself. Memory and bullshit and loneliness so mixed up that years back and years now are the same thing, and little things like time and dying just don't matter.

Here's the last one:

October 16, 2003

Dear Sarah,

It has been some remarkible events out here as you may know if you watch the TV. I believe our son has written to you about our neighbor girl, name of Hay Lee Jo Zimmerman. She moved to Rapid City and got killed it was in the news. We dont hardly know what to do. You should have seen her ride the way shed tip her horse and stay so strait on it it was great just watching her. We know every time she won a race and kept track of it. She used to fish to. Theres a big stock pond on another neighbors place and shed go fishing there I think our son has told you about that how shed fish and all. It aint right having her gone like she is. Whod do a thing like that? I suppose maybe it shouldnt be such a big deal but we knew her from the moment she was born and its hard to say things right. Anyways the horses is whinnying and I have to get up now and take care of them so I hope your well.

Love,
Rodney.

Of all the people to be bothered by that murder, Shane Valen's the last person anyone'd pick. Knew her from the moment she was born? Jesus Christ. So lost in his own world he don't know up from down, but he's feeling all peaceful because she's fishing? Then she gets killed and the poor sonofabitch is heartbroken. And the only person he can tell is his mother. But he can't tell his *mother*, for

Christ's sake. But Dad can. And she comes back, feeling his loneliness like a real thing coming through all the bullshit, I don't know. Or maybe it was just she wanted to see her family again before it was too late. In any case, she was the only person ever Shane didn't see coming. His letters were making too much light around him, he couldn't see past them. She doesn't call, she wants to surprise them maybe. She pulls into that driveway after a day of driving, and it sure ain't no Arabian horse ranch where foreigners sit on the deck and drink bourbon. This is her real memory trying to get back inside her head. But she ain't got room for it, her head's so full of Shane's imaginings.

And then, like I said, before she can even get out of the car, who's she see walking out of the house but Rodney. Hasn't aged a bit. Walking out of the house with a shotgun in his hands, squinting through the glare off the windshield, trying to figure out what this car is doing in his yard. She's not seeing the blades of grass moving all around him. Christ, it gives me the willies. Here he comes, she's got her window open, she thinks she's hearing wind.

Rodney? she says. You can just hear her saying it. She almost recognizes something's wrong, but she can't unlock it. *Rodney? It's me. Sarah.*

She opens her door. Then she sees his eyes widen. But what her husband says doesn't make any sense.

Mom? he says.

And even as the shotgun's sweeping up, everything's collapsing, all those lives, the real and the dreamed, falling around her, winds are blowing them over, and she's a rusted weathervane that in spite a those winds ain't never pointed anywhere but where she's at right now. She's knocked backwards by the blast, lifted clear off the seat and knocked into the passenger side. Time ain't never passed, she's right back in the moment she left, her baby swinging that gun up, the black hole of the barrel turned to her, and then stopped forever.

Shane turns back to the house and goes in and sits in that chair and pumps the action of the shotgun, and the spent shell goes somersaulting through the air and clucks onto the floor against the baseboard where I found it, and he knocks the pump forward and sticks the barrel against his eye and the stock on the floor and leans for the trigger. He's been cut, cut bad. Far as he knows she finally saw through it all and had come back to claim the land. What could he do? Then there's nothing in that house but rattle and alarm and hazard, the singing of a hundred snakes in a concert you'd never want to hear.

I looked all through that house for those letters but couldn't find a thing. Just junk, a bed so grungy I didn't want to touch it, and a freezer full of meat, and a kitchen table and that chair he shot himself in, and an old rocking chair in an upstairs room and a single fishing rod and reel, and his various rifles and shotguns. On the wall he had a bunch of dates written down, who knows what the hell they were. I wish to hell I had Sarah's side of it, but he wasn't near as careful as she was. Just thinking of those snakes out there in that house, the only company and family Shane had that wasn't in his head, I'm tempted to go out and burn it down. Snakes sprawled on the floors at night, coiled by day waiting for mice to wander by or slithering out under the doors or through various cracks. He might've actually felt something for them, but I know goddamn well they didn't feel a thing for him.

I'm tempted — go out and burn it down and throw that damn pack of letters in and walk away. But they got a grip on me. I can't stop reading them. I'm afraid some night I'll be looking into my headlights and the Valen women will parade in front of me, one cut and with children clinging, and the other with a hole in her chest and snakes twisting up and down her, and she looking at her empty hands, trying to read those letters, still all tangled up in them, but not knowing where they've gone.

Reflectors

WE LEFT THE CHURCH in a warm rain and processed out to the cemetery. It wasn't many, and even fewer who got out of their cars to stand beside the grave — all men except for Sophie Lawrence and Audrey Damish. I'd forgotten rain gear, and Audrey caught up to me and brought me under her umbrella. She made the usual comments about it being good to see me, and funerals bringing people together, then asked me if I'd ever noticed anything that looked like unmarked graves up here. I had no idea how to take the question. When I said no, she replied: I thought maybe — you used to come here — you know — a lot. Before I could find out what she was after, we reached the grave, and the conversation ended. Beside us, Sophie Lawrence pushed her stepfather, Sid Ervin, so close to the open hole I feared his caster wheels were going over the edge. The rain wetted his knees, and the knuckles of his good hand went white on the chair arm. I had this vision of the soaked ground collapsing and Sidney tumbling down, twisting sideways as that one hand gripped the chair. I touched Sophie on the shoulder to suggest she back him off, but she looked at me with that smile that could convince the prophet Jeremiah everything's just fine, and I let it go. We stood—Richard Mattingly, Stanley Zimmerman, Brock Morrison, myself, and a few of Shane's relatives—while the women watched through windshields, the wipers purring and clunking. Father Obermann pronounced the words as carefully as if it were a saint or loyal banker he was committing, and the day a sunny one.

I'm not sure how it fell to him. Most of us couldn't imagine Shane Valen in church even in a casket. I suppose the relatives felt they owed some ceremony to the man whose death had opened an inheritance. They made the most of their time: funeral on Wednesday, land auction on Thursday, back to their lives on Friday. I'd like to think the town's ministers got together at the Coyote Café and threw dice, the loser taking on the sermon, but Shane must have been baptized Catholic, though I have no memory of a Valen ever darkening the doors. Maybe Bea Conway produced a record, and Father Obermann interpreted it in the broadest possible way, as I would have myself. He was wise enough to keep the sermon short and not invent Shane's goodness but to simply speak of loneliness and how we can't completely know another human being.

With the graveside service over, I walked under Audrey's umbrella back toward our cars. Stanley Zimmerman intercepted us. Haven't seen you in a while, Caleb, he said.

I've been scarce, I replied. Been a busy season.

Audrey shifted the umbrella. I thought she wanted to leave.

Thanks for the dry, I told her. I'm OK now. I've got a hat.

She hesitated, then started off.

Good seeing you, Audrey, Stanley said.

She turned with some alacrity, as if she was pleased he'd noticed her.

You, too, Stanley, she said warmly. How are you?

I'm good, he said, then turned back to me: Come for supper. We'll catch up.

It wasn't really rude, just quick—yet past Stanley's shoulder I saw Audrey bow her head, and the umbrella wavered, and rain pearled her white hair. She was disappointed. I almost told him so. But Audrey's a bit odd, and I decided whatever business she had with Stanley, she'd get around to it eventually.

It was a disquieting meal. Stanley talked of nothing but his buffalo. On the face of it, that's fine, but his talk, for all its effusiveness, ran down a dissonant rail, as if he feared stopping would let something else — and it was obvious what — emerge. Kris asked me polite, innocuous questions with an indifference palpable enough to be disturbing. They used to get along so well, and here I felt like I'd been invited to fill for an evening a dead zone between them.

It used to be I would have come right out and asked how they were holding up together. It would have been my job. But when you do such things professionally and then stop, you get uncertain. I noticed at their front door a pair of running shoes, with dried mud on the soles. How long had they been there? I let Stanley talk. I've seen it before: fervency can be a fence to hide inside or to hold the world away. After a while Kris got up and left the room. The stairs creaked as she ascended them.

It was dark when I left, and the rain had started up again. I'd taken my boots off at the door and when I put them on found myself staring at those running shoes, and so drove from their place remembering how I used to sometimes come upon Hayley Jo and Laura running together at night, the reflectors on their shoes moving elliptically and disconnected, an alien movement like some dance of UFOs on the horizon — not quite real, a spinning, as their heels struck down and rounded back up, circling outward from their knees in the way of girls. Next, my lights would reflect back from Laura's hair, a hazy glowing, and then the two girls themselves took shape, nylon-suited, moving side by side along the shoulder of the road, in a world of their own making. I wanted to turn and stare back at them, to see in Laura's face her mother's, but I restrained myself, and by the time I could pick them up in the mirror they were invisible again. It was maybe four or five times I saw them, when I was on those roads after dark, and then they weren't there anymore. Laura had quit running, and Hayley Jo took it to the track in town, doing loop after loop, in a dogged, relentless circling. I missed them — or missed the pang of seeing them: that brief excitement of those strange, circling lights, as if the universe were occupied by beings more wonderful than we knew. And then to see that indeed it was, and they were running through the darkness.

I was five miles toward home when I came over a hill and saw police car lights ticking on and off, scattered by a million drops. I pulled my foot off the accelerator and let the pickup coast against the engine drag. The lights puddled in the water on the windshield, and the wipers swept them away, and they gathered again. As I descended, the black crest of the hill in front of me rose over them, and then it was just my own lights on the road. I considered stopping, turning around, and sneaking away. I could go back two miles and pick up the Red Medicine Creek Road, past where I'd just come from, and take gravel home. But that would take me past the Morrisons', and in spite of the years, I was still avoiding memory. More practically, in this rain those gumbo clay roads would ball up on my tires, and with a two-wheel-drive pickup I might as well take my hands off the steering wheel for all the good they'd do.

I watched the double yellow lines thread under the pickup's grille. *I'm just a rancher,* I told myself. *Whatever's going on down there, it doesn't have a thing to do with me.* I put my foot back on the accelerator, and the engine grunted, and the headlights swept into the rain up the hill. I topped it and as suddenly as if they'd been clicked on, the distant lights were stabbing into the cab again. I thought I might avert my eyes and go by. But would anyone do that? People want to know what's happening. They stop just to know the story even if they can't do anything to change it. At least that's the way it seemed to me. Even after all these years I find myself wondering how ordinary people would ordinarily behave.

It did occur to me that it wasn't just an accident but another young girl's body found. The man had been caught, but things like that haunt. We expect bodies to turn up yet: the residue of acts done and finished still surfacing, gruesome discoveries on routine days. My foot hovered over the accelerator. I considered letting it all diminish in my mirrors while I went on alone. But I touched the brake and pulled onto the shoulder and shut the engine off. The lights cut slow swaths through the air, but when they hit the cab they were hard as a punch and all-at-once, then lazy out there again in the wet vegetation, barely lighting the sage. I opened the door. I expected noise and confusion, but silence sat out there like a waiting dog.

In the ditch across the road three men squatted under a low tarp with someone lying between them. A car lay upside down inside a ruined barbwire fence that was going to need fixing or there'd be cattle on the road. The car was twisted toward me. It looked like a giant, helpless turtle on its back — wheels like stout legs, big headlight eyes. It had no windshield, just a dark, compressed oblong where the windshield'd been, and a pile of shattered glass beneath. I pulled the seat of my pickup forward to get rain gear, then remembered I hadn't stowed it.

I let the pickup seat bang back. *I won't be here long,* I thought. I stood at the edge of the pavement, feeling the rain against my neck. Beyond the ditch a small hill appeared and disappeared, grayly blue and red in the circling lights. One of the men turned his face to me, smooth with rain, a repository of changing light.

Greggy, I said. What's going on?

He shielded his eyes with his hands.

Caleb? That you? Stand in the lights, I can't see your face. You bid Shane farewell?

Yeah. Stayed a while. Heading home.

Some strange deal there. Tell you what I found in that car sometime. Anyway, the antelope are celebrating. Lot a people there?

Some. What's going on here?

Accident.

Anything I—?

I stopped myself. But Greggy shook his head.

We got her stabilized. Ambulance's coming from Lone Tree. Nothing to do but wait.

I couldn't see who it was. Just some cloth, an old white coat not moving. Greggy's shoulder hid the face. If it was someone I knew, he'd say. One of the patrolmen with him turned to me, a young face looking awed. A drop of water sparked bright blue and fell from his chin.

I'll be going then, I said.

They all looked up, like I'd said something significant. It was like a bunch of statues'd turned to stare at me, three faces shining, and behind them the hill going on and off, amber and red and blue and nothing. I shivered, stuck my hands in my pockets.

Sure, Greggy said. We don't need help waiting. We got that practiced.

The older patrolman chuckled, a strange, dry sound in all that murmur of water.

Although, Greggy went on, this one looks like the type upon a time you coulda done some good for.

I stopped in mid-turnaround and shut my eyes. The lights filtered through my lids, reddening the darkness. When I turned back to the ditch, Greggy was grinning at me like an obscene shepherd from a perverted Christmas crèche, and the patrolmen looked as puzzled as any wise men ever.

She's Indian, Greggy said.

What's that got to do with anything? I asked.

I sometimes drink coffee with Greggy at the truck stop in Lone Tree. He'll talk of easy wrongs and quick solutions: crossing double yellows, running stop signs, ninety-in-a-sixty-five, all balanced out with fines and time.

Indian, Catholic, sinner? he said. All about the same. You two know any difference?

He looked at the patrolmen. The older one grinned, his teeth sparking in the roving lights, bright as cheap jewels plastered to his face.

Be damned if I do, he said. Now you mention it.

Someone was in a lot of hurt down there. I turned to go back to my pickup.

Don't you guys get wet, I said.

A stone skittered from my boot, bounced against the asphalt, through the slick glaze of puddles there, then shushed into the grass on the opposite side of the road. Water sprayed from my boot tips in an arc, like thrown claws caught in the lights. My boot heels made the only sound against the rain.

Then Greggy's voice came, explaining to the patrolmen: He used to be a priest.

The words reached out from the ditch and stopped me in my tracks just a few feet from my pickup. Just words, and I should have been able to walk away from them, out of their range and back to the present, but I stood eavesdropping on the rumors of my own past as if they might reveal some secret about me I didn't know.

He give it up years ago, Greggy went on. Me, I didn't know you could do that. Went back to ranching, which he grew up doing. Out toward Lone Tree. So now he's just a rancher.

Was it he wanted to ranch or didn't want to preach?

He don't talk about it.

A priest. Huh. Never woulda figured.

A priest?

It was a new voice, wavering, drawing out the word, reedy through the rain. It froze me, like a voice in the night coming out of someone else's dream. It was a woman's voice with something deeper in it than a woman's voice, a huffing, like a blacksmith's bellows being used to make a grass blade sing. I had my hand on the door of the pickup. I shivered again and bumped against the mirror.

I need a priest, the voice said. Those drawn-out *e*'s rising at the end.

Silence then, except for the rain. Then Greggy's voice, low to the patrolmen: He left yet?

Then, shouted: Caleb? You still here?

Then, muttered: Well, I'll be damned. Call me a prophet.

They hunched themselves over, and I squatted down. She lay on her back, her hair streaked black and grayish white. Rain had blown against one side of her face and smoothed it, but the other side was wrinkled, the skin parched. She wore a dirty white coat with fur trim, way too big for her—looked to be drowning in it. Dark brown eyes, large for her face, gazing widely at me.

A priest? she asked. Her voice was a whisper but with that huffing resonance I'd heard across the highway, as if her breathing were too big for her chest. Maybe the accident had hurt her lungs. Our touching shoulders held her voice within a circle, magnifying it even more.

I shook my head. No priest, I said. An ambulance will be here soon.

She held her fists on her stomach. She curled one of her wrists and bent her elbow the way a pregnant cow lifts her back foot from the earth, careful and slow. She did the same thing with her other arm. I thought she was drifting off. Then her eyes suddenly blazed so hot and immediate I jerked, my foot slipped on the grass, and I had to grab Greggy's shoulder.

I *heard!* she hissed.

I gained my balance.

You did, I said. Just, they were wrong. Greggy — you have to keep those lights going?

Rules.

They're driving me nuts. How bad's she hurt?

Not sure. Got thrown from the car. Make my job a lot more pleasant if people'd just put their damn seat belts on. Hasn't moved her legs.

I took off my hat and stared at a blond hair, stuck there, glinting blue and red. When I lifted my face to replace the hat, my eyes went to the knoll. For a brief moment the lights seemed to open a door in space, and a white animal was standing there, patient in the rain. A Charolais heifer, maybe. I didn't see it long enough, and when the lights swung back it was gone.

I turned to the woman. The afterimage of whatever animal it had been hovered between us. I could hardly tell which one I was seeing and which my eyes created. Then she emerged from the afterimage. Her nostrils flared.

Why are you here? she demanded.

For someone hurt she was pretty pushy.

Just happened by, I said. That's all. I best be going.

I stood. Rain smacked against the tarp and shattered. The lights swung over us, fierce in their coming, lazy in their leaving. The knoll appeared and went away. Then that damn Greggy.

He ain't a priest, really, spite a what I said. He *used* to be. But not anymore, see?

Her hand shot out and attached itself to my pants cuff, so tight it looked hard and solid as a hoof. I stood looking down at it, the rain coming in under my tipped-up hat brim and running down my neck. Then I squatted back down on my heels. Greggy seemed mighty interested in the furred fringe of the woman's coat. The wet side of her face had gone smooth as something molded, shining, her eyes darkly radiant.

Then you *are*, she said.

Used to be. Like Greggy said.

Yeah. Like I said.

But nothing changed in her face, and I knew what she was thinking. She let go my pants cuff and shook her head slowly, as if it were way more massive than it was and her neck barely had strength to move it. She reached up and put her hand on mine, resting on my knee. Hers seemed hard as rock, but then warmed and softened.

Once a priest, she said, always a priest.

Greggy coughed, then stood and went through the rain up the road ditch. The two patrolmen looked at the woman, then me. The younger one said, Gotta stretch my legs, and the older one agreed, and they drifted off.

I was just driving by, I said, more to myself than her.

You stopped.

Anyone'd stop.

You are a priest. Nothing changes that.

I shook my head, but I knew what was coming next.

You have to hear my confession.

I slid my hand out from under hers and smelled tobacco on it, and something else, soil and mold, as if her hands were soaked with the smell of grass and ground. I looked up at the knoll. The white animal was suddenly there again, barely visible, shaped by the lights, seeming out of space. I shut my eyes so tightly my eyeballs hurt. When I opened them it was gone.

I can't, I said. I'm sorry.

You must.

It sounded like a tired argument — an am-not/are-too argument she would stubbornly chant against me until the rain ended and the world dried up. But I had only to resist until the ambulance came, and it was arriving already, somewhere. I felt sorry for her, but there was nothing I could do. Nothing I had to do, nothing I was meant to do. I was supposed to be on an empty road.

But then she said: Your belief doesn't matter here. Mine does.

I thought at first it was the kind of arrogant, militant religious stuff that lets suicide bombers and murderers feel holy. But she said it and went still, and her meaning sank into me. It wasn't arrogance. It was humility, or something like — an admission of helplessness, or emptiness, or need. And because of it, her belief had precedence: if she believed I was a priest, then, for the sake of her urgency, I was.

The lights circled and the rain dripped off the edges of the tarp and rolled down the grass blades to the ground. She pulled her arms into her chest and wrapped the ragged coat tight. She withdrew into it. She closed her eyes. Under the coat her thin body heaved. I thought to call Greggy, not sure she was all right. But the lights mesmerized me, and I just squatted on my heels and watched them illuminate her face and color the gray-white coat. After a while she quit struggling and went completely still. Her movements had been frail and small, but now, as if stillness had mass, she seemed to fill the coat. I thought she'd gone to sleep and that, after all, the issues that confronted me would be lifted into dream, and I would wait a few moments and rise, relieved, and walk through the rain and nod to Greggy and climb into my pickup.

But when I shifted, readying to go, her hand unfolded on her stomach, and her fingers lifted and moved back and forth in a slow rhythm, like grass moving in a quiet wind. It held me.

You can't just walk away from yourself, she whispered.

I thought I knew what she meant and opened my mouth to reply, but before I could she continued: Who was she?

It was as if the grass asked the question, the wet grass and wet land and invisible herds of animals on invisible hills rising and falling into distances all around us. I absorbed the question as if it were soaking into me with the rain, inarticulate and meaningful as water filling pores in rock, creating reservoirs. I didn't even wonder how she knew to ask—as if the entrancement of the lights and the rain drumming against the world had merged all memory, mine with hers, and I wasn't answering her but, unsurprised, was answering myself.

Her name? I asked.

She nodded.

Angela. A parishioner. Married.

She nodded again, as if merely confirming what she knew.

It shouldn't have happened, I said.

But it did.

No. That's too easy. Not just happened. I wanted it.

And she?

I think so. Yes.

Was it sudden?

It was sudden when it was sudden, I said.

We were talking so quietly under the rain that I wondered how we heard each other. Greggy and the two patrolmen stood near their cars like sentinels, the night just cold enough that their combined breathing formed a little cloud above their heads that the lights cutting through filled with changing color.

What happened then? she asked.

They had a child. That ended it. But it had to end anyway. Somehow.

You couldn't go back to what you were?

It wasn't there to go back to.

Brock and I are pregnant, she had said. *He's always wanted children. He deserves them. This has to end.*

This was on the phone. The words had the chiseled, precise sound of words memorized. I felt as if she were cutting ropes and I was falling and she was watching me.

236

What am I supposed to do? I'd asked her. She'd had no answer. And neither did the church and all my learning. I couldn't understand her sudden hardness, her ability to extricate herself, to lift herself up wholly and away and speak to me as if she were on some ledge beyond my reach. Yet I was the one who should have been telling her to do what she was doing. When I hung up the phone I had no world.

It was there.

She was speaking again, this woman with grass reeds in her voice.

It's always there, she said. You just couldn't find it anymore.

I saw no use in arguing. All right, I said. I couldn't.

So we're here.

We're here.

I believed she meant the impasse between us. But she was silent, and as I watched her I wondered if she meant something else, some resonance in the world, as if what I'd done twenty years ago had sent a wave through time that nudged her off the road so I could come and kneel now wetly by her side.

It is indelible, she said.

I assumed I knew what she meant: how the soul is marked by sacraments, and nothing can erase the mark, no omission or commission, no thought or word or deed, and the power I'd been given remained, regardless of belief.

Greggy and the patrolmen murmured. I felt how wet I was. My hand on my knee seemed apart from me, veins gleaming in the blue light snapping by. She lifted her own hand and slowly reached inside the fringe of her coat, struggling as if its weight alone resisted her attenuated strength. When her hand came out, her palm was down.

When we ask a holy man for a ceremony, she said, we give tobacco.

A spasm passed across her face. A strand of white hair blew

across her eyes and tangled, and something wild came into her pupils. Then it passed, and she turned her hand over and revealed a leather pouch decorated with glass beads. I recognized the diamond pattern in red and yellow and blue and green: triangles reflected, tepees standing by still water.

She raised the pouch to me, but I couldn't do what she wanted. It would be an empty act. I hadn't felt holy for over twenty years, and I knew too well the old lessons of sacred objects that required, for their touching, consecrated hands. So I only looked at what she held.

She shook her ponderous head.

What do I have to do to get you to take a gift? she asked.

It occurred to me to say: *Make me worthy of it.* But it sounded like self-pity or false humility. Before I could think of a way to phrase it, she said: I saw my grandmother tonight. She died years ago. I've seen her before, alongside the road. But tonight she wasn't on the shoulder. She was right in front of the car.

The rain had thinned, I didn't know when, to barely more than the smell of itself.

That's never happened before, she said. I reached for the rosary on my mirror. And this.

She moved the pouch. The beads caught light.

Her lips twitched in the briefest smile.

Of course, she said, that took both hands.

She rolled her head away from me and looked into the night. Then she turned back and pressed the pouch against the back of my hand, the spent blood of my veins under the skin.

This was hers, she said. It goes back to before Wounded Knee.

I felt the leather against my hands, this old, old thing touching me, having been touched by others, caressed and used, and having come from an animal that, if one believes it, offered its life to align itself with purposes greater than existence and was transformed by prayer and ritual, and then handed down through feuding generations to this moment of our meeting. It was too deep, too old. I turned my hand palm upward.

Memory overwhelmed me. I thought again of Hayley Jo Zimmerman: her baptism the last sacrament I'd ever performed. Even as I'd poured the water and pressed the Sign of the Cross into her forehead, I'd already betrayed my vows and allowed a married woman to betray hers. But I'd told myself — I had to — that grace cannot be weakened by anything a human being does or disbelieves. It runs on, a pure thing, in spite of, as well as because of, us. And if grace exists at all, what I'd told myself was true.

I looked at the tobacco pouch. Its earthy smell rose through the damp air. Maybe merely accepting it made me worthy of it. Hayley Jo Zimmerman had carried my baptism into her death. How small human acts — a few words and signs — and how little we know of their consequences. The next baptism in that church was Laura Morrison's. I couldn't have stood before Angela and heard her say what name she gave her child. Those two girls had run together, their heels in my headlights elliptical and wonderful, so familiar and so alien. Daughters and friends. Someone else's. I'd drive on by and resist the urge to look back into their faces.

And now this stranger and this object in my hand: I bowed my head. We began the old, familiar words, and she told me the things she felt she had to tell, to the God she believed worked through me. I let myself be the ears of her belief, and if I lied in so being, I lied myself into a kind of truth. When she was done I assigned a penance. She was in pain enough already — but suffering has got to be given order. Otherwise it's just chance, just randomness and happening. So I gave her a penance, and she accepted it. Then I forgave and blessed her.

Pilamaya, she said when I finished.

I knew to reply, *Ohan.*

I opened the tobacco pouch and took a pinch. I held it to the compass points, then the sky, the earth, then the seventh direction, inward between us. I didn't know if there were proper words. I said what seemed appropriate, then took a pinch and with my thumb and forefinger broke it in half and held it out to her. She raised her hand. I placed a pinch between her thumb and first two fingers, then placed what remained between my lips and gum. She did the same. We shared the taste of tobacco, its holy rush in our blood. There should be smoke, or there should be bread, to drift away or to be swallowed. We did what circumstance allowed.

In the distance a scatter of erratic lights appeared through the nearer, stronger ones.

The ambulance, I said.

She nodded, slow as a great, standing animal dozing. Behind us now the lights of the ambulance increased the chaos with their steady order, and a door opened and shut, and then another. She raised her hand toward me. The furred cuff of the coat didn't slide down her wrist. Her hand was closed, her fingers pressed into her palm so tightly they seemed to be growing into it. She made a little circle with that closed hand.

Bless you, she said.

I rose, hearing the steps of the EMTs in the ditch behind me. She shut her eyes and began a chant that seemed to roll out of the land around us in a language I didn't understand. It seemed all huffs and grunts and multitude. Then the EMTs appeared around me, moving with great precision and grace, communicating in gestures and throaty murmurs, seeming everywhere at once. I walked up the ditch slope and stood on the road with Greggy and the patrolmen while the EMTs, faceless, their heads enlarged by rain hoods, their shoulders humped, strapped her onto the backboard, grunting with effort, and carried her up the road ditch, their heads turned earthward. I tried to catch a glimpse of her face as they put her through the door, but all I could see was the coat, the shaggy trim moved by wind, looking empty.

Well, I said, watching the wet road between our boots deepen with light. I better get back.

I looked up. The ambulance was gone. I hadn't heard the door shut or the tires hiss as it pulled away. I thought I might see the reflection of its lights in the low clouds, but time had passed without my knowing, and the only light I saw was a bluish star on the horizon, underneath the leaving rain.

Yeah, Greggy said. We'll get a wrecker out here, then tack that fence back up.

She told me she crashed because her grandmother was standing in the middle of the road.

I felt their palpable stares.

Her grandmother?

Died years ago, I said.

The older patrolman broke into a grin. Yeah? he said. What bottle'd she come out of?

But Greggy lifted his hand. He was looking into the lights, or looking at the dark land invisible behind them, like he was expecting some immense thing to emerge from it.

These women, he said. They keep coming out of nowhere.

Postings

HE LIMPS THROUGH corridors of concrete and steel, calm. From him worlds flare into being. His worlds: hoarded, unshared. But he's patient.

He regrets losing the buckle. It fell from his trunk. And then suddenly he was lighted. He didn't pick it up. But they would have reduced it to evidence, as they have his clippings and mosaics. Such limited vision. They can't see the creation: whole lives made of postings.

He loved all his Anas. They all understood that. They revealed their lives. They spoke their intimate secrets. They told him their fears. In postings all over the Web, he's created their portraits and stories. The right links can put them together. He has faith. Artists have always leaned on the future. Someday they'll discover his work. His genius will be revealed.

Only the last Ana's portrait remains incomplete, the final postings not made. He thinks of it often: How the cattails broke before her. How she hummed. How the earth seemed to jump from itself.

A shape rising, she told him, and she, falling backwards, the cattails swaying and breaking, the redwing blackbirds disturbed. A cloud of cattail seeds, and a shadow behind them, with voice.

I saw you.

She dropped her fishing pole, crawled away. Splashing. Mud in her eyes.

The voice: Hay. Jay. I was there.

A hand on her ankle.

She twisted, blinded by mud, screaming and kicking, and the voice: I been watching, I have to tell you, I saw you, don't *scream,* I just want to tell you I saw.

A hand on her mouth. She can't see who it is.

Then the hand gone. The water, she's under it, in a green blindness, until the need in her lungs is stronger than terror. She shoots to the surface and whatever awaits. Silence and emptiness. Still water, with hills rising. She's breathing, and nothing is out there. Already she's not sure what happened. She's planted in doubt. Already she's memorizing silence.

She can't even name it. She's not sure *who,* to say nothing of *what.* Her father might do something violent, her mother be more hurt than she was.

Is she hurt? She's not sure of that. She's afraid. But protective. And maybe not innocent. She snuck from the house.

A tiny adventure. But secret. She'd risen in the dark. She thought she might catch that big fish. Hold it up to her boyfriend's awed eyes.

She treads the green water, ringed by cattails. Near shore a cloud of seeds scatters. Is someone watching? Is that where she was?

I have to tell you.

Everyone has something to tell. Everyone is waiting. Sleeping and dreaming and waiting to wake to someone, who understands.

Alexander Stoughton. Alexander Stoughton understands.

Quitting the Game

NEAR THE END of two-a-days his senior year in college, Clay Mattingly stopped at the coach's office after morning practice.

You wanted to see me, Coach?

The coach waved at a chair. Clay sat down, his hands on his knees. The coach stared at him as if considering what to do with him.

You've been practicing well this week, he said. Working hard. Hitting hard.

Thanks, Clay said. He knew there was a *but* coming: *But it's about winning, and our sophomore, Janeway, has really come on. I'm going to need you in a backup role.*

Clay didn't even mind, much. He'd been a solid high school player, but he didn't take from the game the kind of violent joy some of his teammates did. When his father had asked him why he was going out for college football, he couldn't give an answer. He still couldn't. At this point, it was just finishing what he'd started.

Janeway's coming on, the coach said. I'm going to be watching both of you. He's quick, but you've got more focus. I like that. You stay awake, and the spot's yours.

Clay pretended he'd expected this.

I'll stay awake, he said.

I don't want you overcelebrating, now.

I won't. I'll —

He saw the coach was smiling.

You got some work ethic, Mattingly, he said. But have some fun. It ever occur to you this is a game?

I don't get it, Clay told his roommate.

Why's that?

Janeway's brutal. He hits harder than me. Runs faster. Everyone knows it.

Clay couldn't figure Janeway out. Janeway was never serious except on the field. But there he went beyond serious to some kind of dark. Other players had methods to fire themselves up — but not Janeway. He'd be laughing and joking all the way to the field, and he'd step off the bus and turn instantly ugly. No chants, no ceremonies or rituals of rage. It was just there for him. Even in practices, against his own teammates, he'd cut people low, elbow, use fists underneath. He seemed to love to hurt people. Or seemed unable to not hurt them. But later he wouldn't remember it. Like he got nothing long-term out of it. Like it was just his body doing what it did, and his mind retained no mark or memory.

What the *fuck* were you doing out there today? the halfback once asked him. Jesus Christ, Janeway, I'm on *your* team.

This was after practice, during dinner. Janeway had taken his tray and sat down right next to the halfback, just as if there were no reason not to. Now he looked at the halfback in surprise and then grinned and reached up and put his arm around his shoulder and hugged him.

I love you, man, he said. What'd I do out there?

The halfback stared at his food, pressed up against Janeway's shoulder like a kid.

Nothing, he said. It's OK.

Now Clay's roommate said: I'll tell you why you're starting. It's because you don't care.

What's that supposed to mean?

About being hit. You don't know what getting stopped is. Janeway does.

I don't know. Janeway's got — whatever it is. I'm not even sure why I play the game.

Tell you, the roommate said. Janeway don't believe he can be stopped. So when he is — the roommate puffed out air — he thinks the play's over. Thinks he's it. But you get stopped, you're still playing. Janeway likes to hit. But you don't give a shit if you *are* hit.

Huh.

That tackle you made on Woolford today? You were stopped three times. I watched it all. Stopped cold. Three times. *Bam. Bam. Bam.* And you know what? Your eyes never left the ball. You're still going after it.

Yeah?

There was something to it, maybe. He'd tried to cultivate Janeway's rage but couldn't get amped up that way. But there was a weird, satisfying indifference to being hit — now that the roommate had said it.

That old saying? the roommate went on. About the hammer and the anvil? Most people think the anvil's getting the worst of it, getting beat on. But it's the hammer that breaks. You're anvil, Mattingly. Janeway's hammer. Got a fiberglass handle. But it's still the hammer breaks.

The fourth game of the season, it was like the roommate had said. Too much like. The opposing fullback came out of the line, head down. Moving, if anything, too fast. Janeway would've side-stepped, come back in, hit the halfback, who was following, so hard he would've seen lights. But the other way to do it was to take the hit yourself.

In the instant before the fullback crashed into him, Clay knew: this was why he was out here. To be hit just this hard and to feel this cool, pure indifference. Like he was watching himself, the way he might look at photographs of suffering somewhere and think he ought to feel sympathy but couldn't: it was just images. He moved, at the last split second, directly into the fullback's path. There was that moment of hearing the collision rattling up into his helmet, his pads popping with compression, his own expelled air. These noises from inside and outside his body. Even his ribs popping, cartilage and ligaments stretching and snapping. But it was just noise. He didn't feel anything. Or he did, but it was a feeling of not-feeling. Like a slow-motion, muted action scene in a movie: a loud silence, a slow speeding. All noise and concussion and jarring—but nothing. Later he couldn't remember feeling anything at all.

And he might have seen—or maybe only imagined, because he knew it had to be—the fullback's body slink into itself. Like, for the barest moment, the fullback could actually tuck his head into his shoulders and turn inside out, and wouldn't that be a trick, wouldn't that be a move no one had seen before? The fullback's head moving downward into his shoulders when he hit Clay, and Clay not feeling anything, and the fullback's head like a turtle's, except so quick Clay couldn't be sure he'd really seen it. Then the halfback, trailing. That second concussion, insulated. That feeling of being on one side, the anvil, and the light hammer speeding in its arc out of the air. And, what his roommate forgot, the piece of soft metal between them.

Earlier in that year that Hayley Jo was killed, Laura Morrison had come to Clay. No e-mail or phone call or text message—she was

just there, and his roommate, who'd answered the door, was saying: Mattingly, hot one for you.

Clay pushed back his dorm chair and went to the door, and
there she was in the hallway.

Laura, he said. What are you doing here?

You got some time?

He lifted the calculator in his hand and looked at the graph he'd
forced it to produce.

I got a test tomorrow, he said. How much time you talking
about?

I don't know. Time.

It important?

I'm here.

She went to college on the other side of the state, four hundred
miles away.

She was dazzling, and her sadness made her even more so. She'd
been attractive in high school, but—could a few months do this?
Did a place lay some dimming dust on its girls that got washed
away when they left? It made him feel rich just sitting across from
her in the restaurant.

She's not going to listen to me, he said.

This isn't a time to be hurt, she said.

It brought him up short.

I was only thirteen, he said. We weren't even going out.

That's not how she saw it.

She broke it off.

So then? There must have been something to break off.

Before he could respond, she said: She felt right with you.

Then she must've liked feeling wrong.

This silenced them both. He adjusted his silverware. She aligned
the salt and pepper shakers' hexagonal sides.

I think she loved you, Clay, she said quietly, watching her out-stretched hand, her eyes hidden by a sheath of hair.

Don't lay that on me, Laura. I was thirteen. We fished.

You're still angry.

Disappointed. Every boyfriend she had was some kind of no-body. She wouldn't go to college. Even her barrel racing she quit.

She's killing herself.

He met her eyes. They were blue and serious.

She's anorexic. I think she has been for years. Back when we both took up running. Maybe before. I thought it was cool at first, running together. But it was something way more serious for her. I could never go far enough. I think she wanted me to quit, so she could be alone. Finally I just let her. But now — it scares me. She'll hardly even talk to me anymore. She tells me I'm interfering in her life.

Have you talked to her parents?

Her parents?

Well, yeah.

I suppose I could. But it's — she told me her dad was really upset when she quit rodeo. I'm not sure they get along that well.

Upset? Geez, Laura. Do you know how many hours he spent with her? Helping her train? Taking her all over to compete? Of course he was upset. Who wouldn't be? I was upset. She was beyond just good. And then she just quits? Come on.

I think she moved to Rapid to get away from them.

Of course, if she's trying to hide it. That's why you should tell them.

I'm telling you.

He reached out and twirled his cup, watching the dark liquid ripple and the overhead light shatter in it. After a while he said: Did she ever tell you why she broke up with me? If she felt — like you say?

When she'd told him she didn't want to fish anymore, he'd been hurt and angry, and in the face of it she'd gone silent. He remembered how silent—how she hadn't said a word more, had just climbed onto the ATV and waited for him. She had her hands on her knees. He'd gotten on and turned the ignition. He'd felt her presence behind him, her lips so near his ear she could have whispered and he would have heard her over the noise of the engine. Of everything that had happened that day, what he remembered most was that silence. A sense that she might have said more if he'd waited to respond, if he'd listened differently. She'd sat there, looking at her hands.

She never told me much, Laura said. We were best friends, but even I didn't know she wasn't eating until I got away from her and then saw her again. And I thought, My God.

Then she said: But when she did talk about you, it was always good. That's why I came. I thought maybe if you—you know?— even now?

When the halfback discovered, too late, that the fullback wasn't moving, and churned into him, the fullback's head was doing that little twisting, slinking motion into his shoulders. Had it been slower, much slower, the way memory made it slower, it would have seemed he was turning himself inside out like a mitten. But the halfback's hammer speeded it way up, too much way up, and among the ordinary, indifferent sounds of pads and lungs and ligaments and joints, another sound floated out, like a single bubble quietly breaking the surface of chaotic water. It was strangely soft, this sound: a thin stick under matted, wet leaves, or a beetle under a stepped-on two-by-six.

Then the safety came from the flat full tilt and smacked into them all to finish it, and the whistle blew, and they all rose and looked around out of their face guards, except for the fullback, who, when the halfback reached down to help him rise, simply stared at the hand held out to him as if it were an alien thing float-ing in the air that he had to figure out.

Clay had his hands on his hips. He was standing over the fullback. He'd never talked to Hayjay after Laura left. He thought he was going to. But it was large, being a voice from another time. He feared he would hear about something he'd missed. And after all this time, he wasn't sure he wanted to hear it. The silence had fi-nally earned itself, worn into itself to become what it was. He had this feeling that if he broke it, he'd have to break other things, too, and he didn't know what they were. So he had her number memo-rized but never dialed it.

He and the safety and the halfback formed a triangle around the fullback: the halfback in red and black, with his hand extended down, the safety in white on the other side, and Clay in white at the fullback's head. He was looking through his facemask into the fullback's facemask, the upside-down eyes wide open though in shadow, the three of them forming a small cave of shadow under the high lights, and the noises of the crowd in the distance and the chants of the cheerleaders.

When Hayjay was murdered, Clay had grieved. Of course he had. But he didn't really feel connected. In some ways, even less connected than he would have with a stranger. With a stranger, you could work up a response and at least be horrified. But this news: having known her and established a distance and preserved it, hav-ing honored it, if that's what it was — it made grieving strange. As if he grieved but mistrusted the feeling. Like he was borrowing it, trying it out for a while, to see if it really fit. And it didn't, quite.

The fullback's eyes were placid. No pain — just puzzlement, as if he were wondering what they were doing standing, or what he was doing lying on the ground. Clay had his hands on his hips. He was furious. He'd never felt this way in a ball game before. He al-ways just did his job. But this — it must be what Janeway felt. *Get up*, he was thinking. *You goddamn, fucking sonofabitch, get that stupid-ass shiteating grin off your face and get your fucking ass UP!*

I didn't sign up for this, he said. This isn't what I signed up for.

You signed up for the game, the coach said.

He was a decent man, and he said it gently, but there was rebuke in what he said, too.

This can happen in a game, he went on. He didn't expect it. No one would expect it. But did he sign up for it? Well, in a way, yes, he did.

No, Clay said. No one signs up for that.

It's not your fault. You'll understand that eventually. Just like everyone else does right now. Even he doesn't blame you. I'm sure of it. He hit you, and the halfback hit him. Even if there was fault—and there isn't—it'd be—spread out. It happens. Sometimes.

I don't want to be where it happens.

I'll start Janeway this weekend. But I expect you back. You're going to get over this. I expect you to. We all do.

You're not listening. I don't want to get over it.

Right now you don't think you do. But you do.

You know his name?

His name?

Troy Lucas. That's his name. I had nothing against Troy Lucas. I could've just let Troy Lucas go running up the field. And Troy Lucas would still be running.

It's the game. You can't let him go running up the field. Deep down you know that.

If it's the game and deep down I know that, I don't want the game.

The coach leaned back in his chair and looked at Clay. He wasn't exasperated or impatient. He was a decent man. He understood trauma—or understood there could be such a thing as trauma. He was sick himself over what had happened. But he had to pretend wisdom and calm. This was a young man in front of him. He'd dedicated his life to working with young men. And he had to deal with this. He was trying. He was trying very hard to deal with it.

There's a good chance he might walk again, he said. At least fifty-fifty. That's what I've heard. Let's let the doctors do their work.

Janeway would've tackled the ball.

And he might've missed. That's why you were out there and not him. You stopped the run. That's your role. It doesn't matter how.

Doesn't matter how? Jesus.

I didn't mean it that way, Clay. I didn't mean it that way.

They were both close to tears.

I gotta quit, Clay said. I can't play anymore.

I can't let you quit. That's the worst thing you can do.

If I quit, you're not my coach anymore. You can't stop me if you're not my coach.

Saying that, that they no longer had that relationship, broke them both. Clay wiped his face with the back of his wrist, and the coach sat there with his hands on his desk, letting tears fall, watching this young man whom he'd seen work so hard for four years and finally succeed. He was as convinced Clay had to keep playing as Clay was convinced he had to quit.

You don't quit in the middle of a season, Clay, he said when he could talk — and it was a long time before he could.

What you don't do is break a guy's neck — Troy Lucas's neck. You don't put Troy Lucas in a wheelchair.

You didn't. It happened. What happened, did. Quitting the game won't cure it. What you've got to do is look after yourself. You quit now, you'll never be able to forget it.

I don't want to forget it.

The chants of the cheerleaders had faded out like birdcalls receding, and then the crowd sound had fallen, too, leaking out of the world, a deflation of sound, and then, in a silence palpable and cast, a single cry had hammered down, breaking itself: No! No! No!

A woman's scream. And in the stilled crowd of hundreds, a movement of color, a bright red and yellow ski jacket, moving even before the trainers did, a yellow headband, red mittens, stumbling down the row, jerking down the stadium steps and lurching over the rail and then running awkwardly over the turf, a bumbling, shambling run, almost an antithesis of run, and the police who were supposed to prevent fans from entering the field standing stock-still except for one of them, a young reserve officer who started to sprint after her, a former athlete himself who gained ground on her as if he were devouring it and then as he neared her tapered off, powerless, like a too-light fishing leader cast into a wind folding back on itself, limp, and she came on crying, *Oh God, oh God, oh God.*

The roommate suggested a bar. Clay finished the pitcher and ordered another before the roommate had finished his first glass.

Guess we know who's driving back, the roommate said.

Clay stared out the plate glass window next to the booth.

A few girls had come over and offered consolation. He hadn't been unkind to them, but they withdrew after a while.

I know you've heard it all already, the roommate said. It wasn't your fault and it's a risk anyone takes in the game and you were just playing your position and Martians are green.

Yeah. I've heard it all.

You really quitting?

You see his mother run onto the field?

The roommate nodded. Then he asked: How'd Coach take it?

Clay grunted.

He say you were throwing four years of work away?

You think I am?

The roommate fingered his beer, then lifted it to his mouth, emptied it, set it back down, and for a while watched the foam running slowly down the sides of the glass.

You know what they used to do for fun where I come from? he asked. Way back when? Blow up anvils. Fourth of July, lay an anvil on a bag of gunpowder and see how high they could send it. Pretty damn poor entertainment, huh? Then when the fun was over, pick the thing up and haul it back to the shed and set it up again.

That an answer?

Just a story, man. Ain't no answers.

By the time the bar closed, the roommate was drunk, too, but not so much he didn't know it, so they left the car and walked back, both of them wobbling. In a residential section of town, they passed a lot where a house had been torn down, leaving nothing but a ruined foundation, a big hole, and scraps of lumber and broken concrete. Clay stopped and stared at the mess.

C'mon, man, the roommate said. Just a few more blocks and we're home.

Goddamn, Clay said. Sonofabitch.

He walked off the sidewalk toward the hole.

The roommate caught up to him. C'mon, he said. There's nothing here.

Damn right there's nothing here.

He pushed off the roommate's hands.

Against a sawhorse, in the bluish light of a faraway streetlamp, a sand shovel leaned. He picked it up and hefted it. Goddamn, he said again.

What are you doing, man?

Clay didn't answer. He lifted the shovel over his head and slammed it down on the edge of the concrete block foundation. The handle splintered so loudly it echoed.

Jay-sus, Clay! What the hell are you doing?

Sonofabitch, Clay said. Sonofabitch, sonofabitch, sonofabitch.

In rhythm with his chanting, almost ceremonially, he brought the shovel up and crashed it back down against the concrete, the tough hickory handle splintering with each vicious stroke until, with a final rending crack, it broke, and the head of the shovel flew into the ground, and he was holding the jagged stub of wood.

A dog barked down the street. A light came on.

Let's get outta here.

He let the roommate push him away, out the other side of the lot, stumbling over the chewed ground. When they were four blocks away and still hadn't heard sirens, and the adrenaline and alcohol together had made them giddy and high and exhausted, the roommate let them slow down. They had to cross the football practice field to get to their campus apartment. Sprinklers were pulsing, sending foaming white rainbows of water over the field.

Wait, man, wait, the roommate said, and made them both hold their shoes in the jet of a sprinkler to wash the dirt of the empty lot off. They got soaked in the process and stood in the middle of the practice field laughing their asses off while the sprinkler swung around and nearly knocked them over when it hit them. Finally they trudged up to their apartment and threw themselves, soaked, onto the furniture.

After a while they settled down. They were staring at the walls.

What the fuck'd you do that for? the roommate asked.

I got no fucking idea, Clay replied.

No fucking idea, the roommate said.

He started to chuckle. Clay followed suit.

No fucking idea, they said in unison, laughing so hard they hurt, their ribs hurt, their lungs hurt, their eyes and stomachs, they could hardly bear it, it was so funny. No fucking idea: the punch line to every joke ever told, and every one not told, too.

Running Alone

AFTER GRADUATING FROM college and working in retail for a year, Laura returned to school for her teaching certificate. After receiving it, she accepted a job in Sioux Falls, then returned home for the summer. She started running again. When she and Hay-jay had run at night, Laura had always liked the sound of their footsteps striking the pavement in unison, the enclosing darkness, and the way, when a car passed them, their elongated shadows spidered out in front of them and then swung wildly sideways and twisted together and collapsed. But now Laura found it easier to get up early than stay up late, and she liked the land in the morning, the way the light and shadows textured it.

Sometimes, rather than running straight from the door, she would drive to a new location. She tried to surprise herself — to drive mindlessly, turning without premeditation onto unknown gravel roads. She liked seeing unfamiliar land unfold at the slow pace of a jog. One day she drove especially far, until she had only a general sense of how to get back. She came over a hill and couldn't see a single sign of human beings: no houses or pole sheds or cattle or power lines. She stopped the car and gazed. She'd been raised to know space, but this was a little intimidating—so large, so unmarked. Still, she wanted to run into it. She reasoned with herself: it was safer than running with traffic, and drivers who didn't pay attention or called taunts. Only the emptiness itself was unsettling: the endurance of it, the sense of its long being.

She checked her watch so she'd know when to turn around. Fifteen minutes later she came over a hill and saw them. In the instant of seeing them, she thought they were immense black stones, a monument, arrayed on the grasslands before her, a tableau suggesting meaning so esoteric or particular it touched the edges of awe. Then she realized they were buffalo, and where she was. This was the old Valen place, and the buffalo were Hayjay's father's.

Laura slowed, disturbed. The last thing she had expected was to be reminded, out here in the emptiness, of the way Hayley Jo had detached herself. Seeing the buffalo wasn't like seeing a ghost. She wasn't even brought up short. It was more like a thin net vibrating, through which she could feel the past, distant and dealt with, but suddenly very tangible. The herd even looked netlike, strung out as it was, the massive animals like nodules on invisible filaments that connected them to the others. They wove together the land on which they stood—and her, too. She felt like a smaller nodule.

She jogged on. She noticed a blackened square above a steep ravine halfway up the hill across from her. When she got closer she recognized foundation stones. She'd read Bea Conway's account of Joe Valen building the first frame house in the area, refusing help, hauling stones from the river with an ox sled and ordering lumber brought in by railroad. In spite of Bea's enthusiasm, he'd seemed to Laura a stolid, irrepressible figure—slaving wordlessly away, with only his wife, whom he'd imported also, to help. The next generation of Valens had abandoned the house. Laura didn't know who lived in it after that. Here it was now, a scorched patch of ground.

The herd was a quarter-mile away and grazing away from her. She could see a dirt road curving toward the burn site. When she got to it she turned and jogged down it and through an open gate in a tall wire fence. She slowed to a walk. Except for the driveway itself, so meager it might have been a double game trail, there was nothing suggesting that human beings had ever visited this place. Only the absence of wolves shadowing the herd hinted at history.

She walked into the blackened square, imagining it roomed, divided, the Valen family moving in and out of doorways. She stood at the edge of the foundation, as if there were a window she looked through into the ravine below. She'd heard the stories Bea hadn't included, and she wondered what it had been like for Emma Valen, trapped by distance out here, with a husband impatient with anything not aligned with his will. Laura remembered her father telling her that as a child he'd seen Emma, and her face had given him nightmares of a bear in a rage, great claws reaching for his cheek. Laura touched her face. She saw in the ravine what looked like a faded wooden sign barely visible beneath the cedar. She thought she might climb down to see it. Then she heard a distant engine and turned. A pickup crawled over a hill from the direction of the herd. She walked slowly out of the ashes and waited.

Laura!

She might have just showed up on Stanley Zimmerman's doorstep, a surprise visit after years away, instead of being almost a trespasser, caught. He opened the door of the pickup and stepped to the ground. But in spite of the pleasure in his voice, there was something resistant to surprise, too — as if he was tired of suddenness and had found a way, within himself, to slow it down. He was older, of course, and heavier than she remembered. Not fat, but fleshier, in a way that made him less solid than she recalled, not as hard-edged or defined. Still, he was so familiar, all those nights she'd spent in Hayjay's house doing homework or watching videos, that she felt the meshing of old relationships, the cogwork of memory. It made her feel newly bereft.

I was running, she said. My car's a couple miles up the road.

Running, he said.

There was in his face that quiet, warding-off look.

She felt the need to explain.

Then I saw this. She moved her hand to indicate the foundation. I've been hearing about this house all my life, and—I didn't think you'd be here.

He smiled: Guess I wouldn't leave the gate open if I wasn't here.

Of course, she said, flustered. I didn't think.

They got out once, he said.

I remember.

It's good to see you.

Oh, come on, she thought—and didn't know where the thought came from, or the sudden, astonishing anger.

When she didn't respond, he said, How long has it been?

Since the funeral.

She said it breezily: the factual answer to a question. But she pushed her hair off her ear and lifted her eyes to him, and she saw his face distort briefly, like a movement underwater. She'd surprised him. Good. He couldn't absorb or resist it. He reached his hand back and sideways. For a moment it moved in the air as if he were conducting some whimsical orchestra. Then his fingers found the smooth metal of the pickup, and his palm flattened into it, and the machine's solidity seemed to flow into him.

Of course, he said.

So, she asked. What happened here?

She flicked her left index finger over her shoulder at the house that wasn't there.

He looked over his shoulder at the herd. She looked at them, too. She wondered if they'd changed position at all since she'd first seen them. She couldn't tell.

Fire, he said.

That's too bad.

Is it?

Kind of. It's history.

Yeah. It is.

Lightning? she asked.

A match.

She'd been in control. And suddenly wasn't.

You —?

He nodded.

But.

She looked at the rectangular boundary of stones and the blackened ground within it and the desolate springs of a mattress.

She turned back to him. You just — all of it?

He opened the door to his pickup, reached across to the glove compartment, opened it, brought something out. When he stood upright again, he was holding a mother-of-pearl brush, lustrous and small in his large hand.

I couldn't burn that, he said.

It held her eyes like a flame would.

Whose is it?

Without knowing it, she'd lowered her voice.

No idea, he said. The rest — he swept his other hand like a wing coming up, dismissive.

She felt as if she were breaking up — were being transmitted from a distant place, through turbulent air and ionic storms. If it hadn't been for the touch of the foundation against the back of her knee stabilizing her, she might have turned to snow.

Can I see it? she asked weakly.

He held the brush out to her. It was warm, it felt alive, a hard, alive thing, with bristles, as if it could flex and morph in her hand.

Some girl, she murmured.

Yes. That's why I couldn't.

Her breath caught. She pushed the brush back at him.

Take it, she said.

He replaced it in the glove box. They looked at each other.

I've got nothing of hers, he said. Kris and I — she has it all.

The feeling of breaking up, of barely coalescing: she pressed the back of her knee harder against the foundation and lifted her hand, palm out, near her face to stop him, but he went on.

She had a rodeo buckle, he said. If I could just have that. She was so proud —

He stopped and gathered himself.

So proud of it, he said. I asked Kris — I asked her if — we spent so much time together training, and — but she didn't have it. It's gone. We don't know what she did with it.

She lifted the other hand and held them both out. I don't know. Why would you think I'd know?

I'm sorry. I'm not asking. I'm just — I'm sorry.

Why didn't you — ?

She couldn't finish. Her voice, like her body, lacked coherence.

Didn't I what?

But she could only stare at him.

He nodded, understanding.

You blame me, he said.

She still couldn't speak.

I thought I was a decent father. I don't know what she told you. I thought I wasn't a terrible father, at least. When she was born, I — that morning was —

She wasn't prepared for the sadness of his statement: how small its hope — to not be terrible. Sweat was cooling on her, and she shivered in spite of the sun. The stone against her leg sent a spike of cold through her, but she wouldn't step away from it. She crossed her arms on her chest. The herd moved the net of itself slowly across the land.

You cut your hair, he said. Kris used to always say how different you and Hayjay —

He stopped. He turned his head down. She could see him fighting for control.

Yours was always long and blond, and hers —

I got tired of it long.

It looks good.

I don't need compliments.

I don't suppose. It is good to see you. I wish —

He shrugged. He turned as if to get back into the pickup.

Is that what you want to know? What she said about you?

He turned back. He looked her in the eye.

I couldn't say her name, he said.

Her name?

I couldn't say it. Just now? That's the first time I've said it since — Hayjay. My God.

You haven't said her name?

Hayley Jo.

He reminded her of someone learning a foreign tongue, trying out the sounds. She wrapped her arms tighter around herself.

All right, she said softly. All right.

You're cold, he said. I can give you a ride back to your car.

She shook her head. You weren't a terrible father, she said. I wanted to believe you were.

I didn't even realize. Didn't know.

I don't know why she did it.

Maybe I didn't want to believe.

She liked it.

He gazed at her.

The starving, she said. Maybe not *liked*. But —

263

She gave in to the shivering. Rather than shaking her apart, her body seemed to gel with it, becoming itself again.

I should have told you, she said. She had me believing—

It took him a moment.

Good God, Laura, he said. It wasn't your fault. Of all people.

Everyone says that.

Because it's true.

I've been waiting for someone to tell me what I did wrong. Or what I didn't do. Maybe that's it: I didn't tell you. Is that it?

He made no move to comfort or hold her, and it seemed right to her that he would stand at this small distance and watch and attempt no wisdom.

I mean, if I failed, OK, she said. It'd make some sense. But if I didn't? If I did everything right? Everything I could? Then what good was it? What does all that mean? If you can't help someone even by doing everything right. So, is that what I did wrong? I didn't tell you? Is that how it makes some sense?

Her teeth were chattering.

I've got a blanket in the pickup, he said. It smells like horses, but—

He turned to get it, but she moved into him, pulling him into her, and he slowly brought his arms up and wrapped her in them. He stroked her hair.

It's OK, he said. It's OK.

It wasn't enough, she said.

He was so solid, she felt her own shivering magnified by it, vibrating against that solidity.

I'm not sure that's what it's about, he said.

What what's about?

Whatever we're talking about.

She let herself shiver. He held her. She him. The buffalo grazed.

Heyoka

WE ALL ENDED UP keeping vigil, sitting in our lawn chairs roasting hot dogs on sticks, eating Indian tacos and drinking Budweiser and waiting for Wilbur's wind to blow. It was so cold the lawn chairs squealed, and I said, If it's too cold for a Kmart lawn chair, what are we doing here?

Big-K, Gerald White Wolf said, and after a while of thinking on this, Jake Red Heart said, Huh? and Gerald said, They changed their name. It's Big-K now, not Kmart.

When'd they do that? Jake asked.

Oh, some time now.

Hadn't noticed.

Don't much matter. Write a check to Kmart, they still take it.

I took the last sip from my Bud and set the can down and was reaching for another when a gust of wind, but not Wilbur's, came up, and that can and the others, and Tostitos and paper plates and plastic cups, went whirling out over the frozen lake and toward the Continental. Wilbur White Eagle looked at his watch — the only time in his life Wilbur ever cared about time — and then he looked at his Big Chief tablet where he'd written down all the guesses, and he drew a line with a pencil, then looked across the fire at Myrna Walking Elk. She nodded, accepting it, and gazed out at the lake like she was making sure the car was still there and Wilbur wasn't seeing wrong.

Mighty cold St. Patrick's Day, I said.

Gonna warm up, Wilbur replied.

The sun was a big orange ball on the horizon, hazy through the ground blizzard.

Usually does after the sun sets, I said.

Wilbur just looked into the fire and settled deeper into his Big-K chair.

You'll see, he said. Warm wind gonna come up. One a them Chinooks.

You're thinking the Black Hills, I said. Chinooks don't get way out here.

Big-K, huh? Jake said. They changed the sign and everything?

I had a bad feeling about that Continental from the start, but Leonard Sends For Him didn't listen to me.

Been sitting here for like six months, he said. They got to want to get rid of it, huh?

He opened his door, and chunks of rust from his Citation fell onto the lot of Miner's Good Deal Cars. I'd told him when he bought that Citation, Don't buy no Minnesota car, all that salt on the roads in the winter, humidity in the summer. But Leonard thought cars were better far from home, or maybe he preferred to inherit strangers' problems instead of someone's he knew. When that Citation started to rust like I said it would, he just said, Oh, man, Ian, a Citation's just a lousy car, it ain't where it's from — which, if I hadn't known Leonard, I would have asked why'd he buy it in the first place then.

I been totally researching this one, he said. Chunks of rust crunched under his feet. I come here on Sundays, you know? When the salesmen aren't around. This one's just been sitting here. Losing value, Ian. What you think they'd take for this? What you think?

Leonard always brings me along when he's close to making a deal, just so he can make it no matter what I think. Leonard is a kind of *heyoka* without knowing it, always doing the opposite. Or maybe I'm his *heyoka*. Maybe we're *heyokas* to each other. Anyway, I tell Leonard what not to do, and he always follows my advice partway—he does the *not* part of it.

Them salesmen got no idea I know how long this car's been here, Ian, he said. No idea how much I know. Knowledge is power. Especially when someone else don't know you got it.

I hauled myself out of the Citation, stepping over my own rust puddle, and went over and touched the Continental's hood. It wasn't in bad shape, but as soon as I touched it I got a bad vibe. I took my hand away and rubbed it on my pants.

I wouldn't buy that car, I said.

He grinned, happy. It was just what he wanted from me.

It's in great shape, he said. Not a scratch. Got—he pushed his face against the driver's window, leaving the imprint of his hand and cheek in the dust there—only a hundred-fifty thou. Good tires—he kicked the front one hard like he was trying to punt it out from under the car—and it's dark blue. My lucky color.

I've noticed something. People who got the worst luck got the most lucky things, just like people who got the worst health take the most vitamins. But maybe if they didn't take all them pills they'd up and die yesterday. Which makes me wonder how much bad luck Leonard's lucky things were keeping at bay, considering how much still gets through. He's got so many lucky things he's lucky to keep track of them. Only person I know's got a lucky color. I told him once, You could at least make it light blue, like a sunny sky. Dark blue's storm blue.

Rain's a good thing, Ian, he replied. And anyways, lucky things just are. You don't go choosing them. If you did, they wouldn't be lucky, would they?

I couldn't follow that argument. All I knew was this car was some kind of trouble no matter what color it was, even if I'm not someone who normally has premonitions. But Leonard was convinced it was the steal of the century, and even more convinced by me not being convinced. If I'd said, *Leonard, you won't never find a better deal, we need to go find a salesman in church and pull him away from Communion so we can buy it right now*, Leonard woulda found all sortsa things wrong with that car. Mighta even discovered it wasn't quite the right shade of blue.

But this way he just grinned at me. Ian, he said, whinnying my name like he does when he's kidding me, sounding like a donkey. Eee-ahn, Eee-ahn, Eee-ahn, three times like that, so some white guys over in the other line where the newer cars were parked stared at us, and one took off his cowboy hat and looked inside like he thought maybe he'd find the donkey in there.

Leonard didn't notice. See, that's how it is, he said. Every time I find something I like, you think something's wrong with it. You weren't my buddy, Ian, I'd think you was jealous. But you know what? I know that ain't true. So what is true is, you're just wrong mosta the time.

I looked at the rust underneath his Citation. Sometimes my self-restraint amazes me. All I said was, I still wouldn't buy this car. It don't feel right.

Feel right? What's that mean?

If I knew it'd be more'n just a feeling.

I'd accidentally stumbled onto Leonard's kind of reasoning, and he looked at me real serious. I was making a whole lot of sense to him, and if I'd stopped right there a lot of things might've stopped with me. But instead I decided to give some real reasons, make myself happy rather than keeping the objective in mind.

There's gotta be something wrong with it, I said. A car don't sell, they don't keep it on the lot. They ship it somewhere else. So why's this one been here so long, like you say? Even the car washer guy don't wanta wash it. That's telling you something. Only dusty car on the lot.

We both looked around to check it out. All the hoods were gleaming, all the chrome stabbing the air like a bunch of boxers throwing punches. Almost made me duck. Then we looked back at that Continental, looked like it'd just come off a long drive on a dirt road following a stack mover. The only way you knew it was dark blue was where my hand had touched it — a dark blue, unlucky palm print. I never seen a car so much in need of a wash, and in Twisted Tree kids don't bother to write WASH ME in the dust on cars till it gets so thick they got to use a stick, their fingers ain't enough.

We have a thing we agree on, Leonard said. This car is a dirty car. But a bad look on a good car is a good thing if you're buying it, because it makes the car look bad.

All I said was, It needs a wash.

Which turned out to be truer than I knew.

Myrna Walking Elk was the one eventually found out that car's secret. When David joined the Marines and went to Iraq, she started watching TV news all the time. She had three cheap TVs she picked up from garage sales in Rapid and one junked one she took from the back of a pickup about to make a dump run. Myrna wasn't a collector of old TVs and computers till David turned fifteen or sixteen. Some of his friends started doing alcohol and meth, and then Eddie Little Feather got run over on the highway. Myrna'd known Eddie since when they were both kids, and she took it kind of hard, he was such a sweet guy, she always said. And the Zimmerman girl, too. It was like Myrna figured there were too many things out there that were waiting to get people, and she needed

269

something to keep David focused. Even the white women under-stood. Myrna saw that junk TV in the back of Orville Germaine's pickup, this was when he was alive, and she went to the door and knocked and explained to Marge how, if they were going to throw that TV away anyway, maybe she could find a use for it.

It for David? Marge asked. Everyone knew about him fixing TVs and computers when he was just a kid. Myrna nodded, and Marge called into the house, Orv, it OK if Myrna Walking Elk, she's at the door here, takes that old TV we got going to the dump?

No skin off my nose, Orville called back. Save me the trouble a throwing it off.

Myrna kept David out of trouble through high school, but the last thing any of us expected was he'd join the Marines. Wasn't un-til he re-upped and went into bomb squad training that it made any sense to us. Even if we never thought David was the kind of guy who walked toward things other people ran from, we all agreed if it's got wires in it, there's a better chance of things com-ing out right with David working on it than just about anyone else. That didn't help Myrna any, though. She'd tried to protect David and then ended up feeling she encouraged him to walk to-ward things that explode.

When David got sent to Iraq, Myrna took all four of them TVs and hooked them up in her kitchen. David'd installed a sat-ellite dish — he'd got it out of the dump site, too, and was proba-bly bootlegging signal, who knows? — and Myrna kept all four of them TVs turned to Iraq news, different stations, channel hopping with remotes whenever anything else was on. People got to visit-ing Myrna just to watch her watch all those TVs at once, flicking those different remotes to the four directions around her kitchen and still cooking and talking to visitors. She knew more about Iraq than the CIA, which isn't saying much, but still. Maybe she thought like Leonard that knowledge is power and if she just knew enough she could stay ahead of anything happening to David. Leonard himself, though, said Myrna was just worried, and women plain do weird stuff when they're worried.

Anyways, it was Myrna's watching all them TVs that uncovered that car's history. By the time she figured it out, though, the car had already done some strange things. Right away after Leonard bought it, it took us right into a thunderstorm, which, just having a thunderstorm was pretty strange, we been in a drought for who knows how long. It was one of them nasty, early-summer thunderstorms we could see thirty miles away in the south when we left Rapid, black thunderheads riding way up in the sky and lightning snapping down out of them like cats' claws. The sky east and north was bright and blue, though, and all we had to do was go east out of Rapid and we'd drive right around that storm, then we could turn south and head home. So I'm kind of enjoying watching that storm from a nice, safe distance when I kind of wake up and realize I'm watching it through the front windshield and those thunderheads have gotten so close I can't see their tops no more.

Uh, Leonard, I said. What are you doing?

He looked at me, and right away I saw it, there were storm clouds in his eyes.

Driving home, he said.

It's what you're driving into I'm wondering about.

Right then a lightning bolt slammed into the prairie in front of us. It was daytime, but the air inside the car got brighter, and no waiting for the thunder either, it was more like a bomb; I thought the windows were gonna break. But Leonard didn't even flinch. He was in a daze.

Rain is a good thing, Ian, he said.

I just thought Leonard was being Leonard. But we got in the middle of that storm, rain coming down so hard we couldn't hardly see the road the way it was — and the wipers quit.

Guess we'll have to wait it out, Leonard said.

Some cars, the wipers work even when it's raining, I said.

Leonard pulled to the shoulder, and we sat there with the rain coming down so hard it sounded like we were inside a powwow drum, and the lightning all around, so we're looking through this incandescent river, like blue light pouring down the windshield. I got a little stir-crazy, got the urge to open my door and go screaming out into it, and I had to shut my eyes and think of Bonnie, but Leonard just sat there like he sits anywhere, like wherever he's at is where he's supposed to be. After a while the sun came out. And the windshield wipers started up.

See? Leonard said. The wipers work just fine.

There's a thing about windshield wipers, I said. They can't make up for lost time.

Leonard shrugged. Car's clean, he said. Saved me the trouble a washing it.

If that'd been the end of it, OK. But two weeks later Leonard decides to take a road trip to Sioux Falls. Out south of Mitchell there'd been a big hailstorm, killed hundreds of geese — blues and snows out in the fields eating and this storm comes up, but why would geese worry about rain? They just go on eating. But that storm builds up, more rain and then the wind starts blowing, and then it starts to hail. The hail gets larger, the size of golf balls, and then baseballs, some of it, coming down from twenty thousand feet and blown about horizontal by the wind, all of that comes sweeping down on those flocks of geese out there in the open, like that storm is strafing them. When it's over so much rain's fallen the fields are turned to brown lakes, and dead geese are floating like big dabs of Reddi-Wip.

Snow geese are getting to be real pests, there's so many of them, and hunting's not enough to control them, so there was people said that hail was nature's way of keeping the goose population down. I think it'd take a lot of hailstorms pretty strategically placed to have much effect, and I can't see nature doing that much planning. But what I'm trying to get at here is, Leonard was going to Sioux Falls, and what does he do but detour to go look at them geese? Why would anybody do that? I mean, not even Leonard, on his own, would drive out to see a mess like that.

But he did. My phone rings, and it's Leonard, and he says first thing: Oh, man, Ian, you don't know what stink is.

Leonard, I say. Where are you?

Leonard's no troublemaker, but a comment like that right off the bat, and I'm thinking there's been some misunderstanding and he's sitting in some county jail where the plumbing doesn't work too good.

There's a pause, like he's looking for a name or sign, and then he says: Pat's Wrecking.

Pat's Wrecking where? I ask.

Eventually I find out he's twenty miles south of Mitchell, and he's wondering if maybe I could make it there that afternoon with fifty bucks to pay for the tow so he can get his Continental away from Pat.

I smelled them geese a long time before I saw them. It was like a Great Wall of China of stink. My eyes were watering so bad when I finally got to where the hail'd actually gone through, I couldn't hardly see to drive. All over in the fields there was mud and standing water, and clumps of feathers sticking up, feathers piled on feathers in some places where them geese tried to fly and were knocked down on top of each other. It was like the whole world'd died and was rotting, and I was driving through it.

The first thing I saw when I pulled up to Pat's Wrecking was that Continental, just dripping mud, so much mud I couldn't see any of that lucky color Leonard'd bought it for, stalagmites of mud growing up underneath it, and mud globbed on the hood and roof like the earth had decided to manufacture itself a car but couldn't get the shape quite right and just piled itself up close enough.

Holy cow, Leonard, I said. What happened?

273

I don't know, Ian.

What you mean, you don't know? You fall asleep?

It was very weird. I was driving along, you know? And the stink was so bad, and maybe I shut my eyes or something. Anyways, there I was, going off the road into one a them big puddles in the ditch. All of the sudden there wasn't no road in the windshield, nothing but water.

He was staring at his car like you might stare at a dog that was a good dog but had done something you'd rather it hadn't a done, like eat a loaf of bread you'd left in a grocery bag on the floor when the phone rang, you can't blame the dog for that, but you wish you could, and you do, but really you can't, so it's a real dilemma — that's how Leonard was looking at his car.

Whyn't you just take the freeway? I asked.

I was going to.

His face got even thinner than usual, like it was stretching to help him remember.

Maybe I wanted to see them geese, he said. You think?

When I paid Pat the fifty he bent up a dog-eared corner of the bill and smoothed it out, and then, like I was paying him for his opinion, said, Never seen a car so goddamn stuck. Thought I wasn't gonna getter out. Thought I was gonna hafta getta goddamn semi-towing rig. That mud was suckiner back down every time I gotter hoisted up. Christ! You'd think that goddamn car loved water the way it was rooted down in there. Like a goddamn hog.

Then Myrna, flipping through her channels, trying to protect David or maybe just being worried and weird, came up with that car's history and more or less proved Pat right.

Good as she was at remote-control gymnastics, Myrna couldn't keep every one of them TVs on Iraq all the time. She was bound to come across other news. And what she comes across is this segment about a couple of states, South Dakota was one, trying to figure out who got to execute the I-90 Killer. They caught him here, but his first murder was in Montana, even though that was one of the last bodies found, so there was this argument about who had rights to him. Of course Myrna paid attention when this segment come on. The Zimmerman girl had gone to work in Rapid, and those freeway towns, every kind of person goes through them, all kinds of people getting away from all kinds of things. You live in one of them towns, there's more strangers than locals, in tourist season at least. Anyways, it was national news, so I guess I'm saying what everyone already knows, dead girls, all of them real thin, all of them with broken bones, start showing up in the borrow pits or the pastures off I-90 all the way from Washington to Minnesota, someone mowing the grass finds one, or someone stops with engine trouble and looks up from his radiator and sees what he thinks is some old clothes dumped in the ditch.

It took a long time for the police to put it together, all them states and all that distance, and they didn't really find out till the guy'd been caught how he was locating them girls on the Internet, pretending to be a woman and advising them on how to stay skinny, so by the time he shows up he knows everything about them. The only reason he got caught was because this rancher out to Kadoka'd been drinking enough to forget to turn his headlights on driving home at two in the morning, and he comes over a hill and sees a car along the shoulder and realizes his lights are off and flicks them on and right there, *blam,* is this pudgy guy staring into the windshield, holding a body with blood dripping off the tips of the fingers, and something shining by his feet. He was parked at the top of the hill, thinking he'd see cars coming for miles, never counted on someone driving without lights, and with his head in the trunk and all he couldn't hear the rancher's tires.

Anyways, he tries to correct one wrong mistake with another. He throws the body back in the trunk and takes off after the rancher. Maybe he'd seen *Fargo,* that's what we figured, where that murderer chases down those kids and kills them, and he figured he'd do the same, only he wasn't counting on the rancher having a cell phone and a rifle and knowing how to use them. So the rancher's already called his wife and she's called the police by the time the murderer gets the body back in the trunk, and when the rancher sees those headlights pull onto the highway behind him, he floors his pickup, it's only a six-banger and it can't stay ahead of a dark blue Continental with a good V-8. The rancher sees those head-lights getting bigger and bigger in his mirror, so he stops, grabs his rifle out of the cradle behind him, and hides on the other side of the pickup. When the murderer pulls up and jumps out to Fargo the guy, he discovers he ain't in a movie, and all he gots is a knife while his intended victim has a deer rifle.

Not only that, the murderer leaves his headlights on, so the rancher waits for him to get illuminated nice and pulls the trigger, puts a bullet right through his hip. When Leonard heard that part he said, He couldna been too drunk, shooting like that, and I said, Unless he was aiming at the guy's head, and Leonard allowed how that would be pretty bad shooting, especially with a deer rifle, unless maybe the lights blinded him some instead of helping him out, but even then. Of course it didn't much matter to the murderer whether it was a good or a bad shot, it had pretty much the same effect.

Anyways, I was saying how Myrna sees this segment on these states fighting over rights to this guy, and the news has pictures from way back when it happened, and in the background of one of them pictures is the car the guy used. I suppose it'd been confis-cated as evidence and then auctioned off when the trial ended, and Miner's Good Deal Cars thought it was a pretty good deal. And wouldn't you know that Leonard Sends For Him would be the guy to find it and bring it back to the last place it ought to be.

It's a haunted car, I told Leonard.

I was kind of proud to've picked up on the bad spirits of that car when I first touched it, and I wanted Leonard to admit I was right. But he just said: Cars can't be haunted. Cars move.

So? I asked.

Ghosts like to know where they're at. They don't go visiting. They don't say to each other, *Tell you what, I'll haunt your place tonight and you haunt mine.* They like to stay put. Like it so much they don't even move away when they're dead. You got to have a ceremony to make a ghost move. So a car can't be haunted. All cars do is move. Maybe a car that didn't run, had its wheels off, could be haunted, though.

It was a kind-of point. But maybe what'd happened to them girls was so awful their spirits couldn't leave that car in spite of it moved. Or maybe it was the car itself. They'd found five different kinds of blood in that trunk. Even a car might want to get rid of that.

That car's trying to get clean, I said. It don't care how. It'll drown you, even.

We were outside the Kwiker-Fil, and Leonard had just bought a sixty-four-ounce Dew. I've told him he drinks too much of that stuff, it's going to give him diabetes. He took a big slurp out of the cup and did his donkey imitation, Eee-ahn, Eee-ahn, Eee-ahn, cars ain't cats, they don't clean themselves.

He waved his Dew to emphasize his point and right then he tripped and the entire cup splashed over the trunk and bubbled and fizzed down the paint.

I tripped, he said. That's all.

I looked at the parking lot. New asphalt, laid last summer. Not a crack in it.

Leonard and I knew each other from when we were kids. Even when I got married it didn't put nothing between us, even though Bonnie got tired of him coming around and asking me to do things for him. *With* him, I'd tell her. I'm doing things *with* Leonard, not *for* him. As I saw it, with Leonard and me, the difference between *with* and *for* wasn't any.

It's something when a car can do more to ruin a friendship than a woman can. That car totally unbalanced things. I started finding excuses not to ride in it, and Leonard knew it. It was like he'd found a woman he liked, and I quit coming around because she had a screechy laugh I couldn't stand. The more I avoided that car, the more he latched on to it. We were really *heyoka*-ing each other over it. I shoulda maybe got some cedar and put it in that car, but that mighta made things worse, fooling around with powers I don't know much about.

Then came the fire hydrant. I thought for sure that'd make Leonard see my point. He says he was reaching down for a can of Dew that was rolling around on the floorboards. He always had some explanation, even if they always amounted to he was a lousy driver who didn't pay attention to where he was going or what he was doing, and I'll be the first to agree with that — but he never ran his Citation into a fire hydrant. Anyways, he claims he was reaching for that Dew, and the can rolled away from him, so he leaned further and musta pulled on the steering wheel, and *boom!* He runs right into that fire hydrant out by the abandoned bowling alley.

You'd think between a car and a fire hydrant the hydrant would win, but it just shows how desperate that Continental was. It sheared that hydrant off and was squatting over it like a pig — Pat was right — soaking up water, and the dent the hydrant'd put in the bumper made it look like it was smiling, the headlights like eyes and the bumper crumpled up at the ends and down in the middle. Greggy Longwell gave Leonard a ticket for careless driving and did a Breathalyzer on him, even though Leonard ain't drunk nothing but Dew for seven years and Longwell knows it — but hope springs eternal, as the saying goes.

They got the water shut down eventually, but not before the entire town had come out to see, white kids and Indian kids both in their cutoffs running in and out of the water vaporizing against the car and turning to rainbows over it, and the parents standing around in the sun talking. People even went back home and returned with coolers and lawn chairs, and it turned into a fountain party and a relief from the drought, and people got to wondering why that hydrant was necessary anyway, if the bowling alley burned down how much loss would it be, being's it's been abandoned for who knows how long, might even improve the town if it burned, and be a lot cheaper'n taking a bulldozer to it.

I was the only one made the point maybe the car itself was the problem. Everyone else thought it was just Leonard being Leonard, trying to do two things at once when doing one thing at once stretched his concentration limits. Up to then I hadn't talked to anyone else about my suspicions about that car, but I decided it was time people knew, and maybe if enough of us pressured Leonard he'd get rid of that car before it killed him.

But when word got to Leonard what I was saying, twenty-eight years of friendship went down the tubes. It was kind of like the woman thing again. If you got a friend takes up with a woman you know's bad for him — say you got some down-and-dirty on her — you sure ain't gonna help the situation by telling him what you know. If he believes you he'll be mad at you like you didn't just tell him what you knew but caused it, and if he don't believe you they'll both be mad at you, so you're best just letting him find out the hard way. That's what it was like with Leonard and me and that car. And the more I tried to defend myself, the more it sounded like I was accusing Leonard — like trying to deny you're in denial: it just proves the point.

And then people took sides, like Leonard and me was an old married couple getting a divorce, and for some reason most of them sided with Leonard. At least Bonnie didn't side with him, though she wouldn't agree with me that the car was a hundred percent the problem. I got tired of people cornering me about Leonard's car, like they were Jehovah's Witnesses and had to convert me to their way of seeing. Bonnie and me started going to Wall for groceries instead of Donaldson's Foods just to avoid them. We'd wander around Wall Drug with all those tourists gawking at the piano-playing gorilla and the fake cowboy band and the *Tyrannosaurus rex* that wakes up every few minutes and roars at kids to give them nightmares all the way back to New Jersey. We had some fun sticking our heads through the holes in the covered-wagon scene and having tourists take pictures of us, Bonnie with a sunbonnet on and me with my stern face determined to go out West and settle on some Indian land. We had a laugh with those pictures. Leonard would've laughed so hard he'd have fallen on the floor, giggling like he does, and that woulda made us laugh even harder. I tried to laugh extra hard, but it didn't work so good.

For several months the car laid low, and I thought maybe the fire hydrant'd done the trick. Then Leonard decided to go ice fishing. That's something Norwegians do. When you think of someone sitting on a five-gallon bucket in the middle of a frozen lake staring at a hole in the ice, you think of a white guy in insulated coveralls and snowmobile boots, you don't think of a tall, skinny Indian wearing Nikes and blue jeans and a couple of sweatshirts. It was about funnier than me and Bonnie playing pioneer. But Leonard, when he and I were friends again, claimed it was a natural thing to do. He said once the Bureau of Reclamation dammed Red Medicine Creek to make Lostman's Lake, it was only a matter of time before an Indian started ice fishing there. I didn't see the logic, and I didn't bother to point out that he never actually fished.

He had the idea he could take that Continental onto the ice and drill a hole and open a window and listen to the radio and catch enough fish to live on for a while. So he packed some fishing gear and drove down the boat ramp. That car had him in a sure-enough trance. But once he hit the middle of the lake, the ice shuddered—he could feel it right through the tires, he says—and he was out of that car so fast he claims he was thirty feet away from it before he even knew he'd opened the door.

What I think is, that ice cracked loud enough to break whatever grip that car had on Leonard, and once he got away from it there was no going back, even if he hated to leave it out there with the engine running and gas over three bucks a gallon. As it turned out, the ice was strong enough to hold the car up, but Leonard didn't know that.

It was a long walk back to shore, he told me. You think it's possible for it to be longer one way than the other, Ian? Cause it sure was. I was tiptoeing all the way. You think you weigh less when you tiptoe? Cause that ice kept cracking and making noises, and I was trying not to weigh any more than I had to. I guess I didn't weigh very much, huh? Cause I'm telling you about it, right?

That's how we all came to be roasting hot dogs and sitting in squealing lawn chairs around a fire on the boat ramp. It was Myrna's idea. All those TVs finally got to her. She realized they weren't doing a bit of good, and she couldn't put anything together from them anyway.

I thought I could predict the future with them TVs, she told me later. But I don't guess TVs are any good for that. The more I watched, the less clear things got. So when I heard Leonard's car was sitting on the ice, well, maybe I needed to get my mind off the war.

Leonard drove the Continental onto the lake in January, and then the weather was off-and-on above and below freezing, so it was hard to tell if the ice was getting thicker or thinner. Longwell threatened to fine Leonard if that car fell through, but that wasn't much incentive for Leonard, since he didn't have enough money to pay a fine anyway, and he wasn't sure Longwell had jurisdiction over the lake and maybe the car was actually a boat since it was out there and not on a road. But it was out of anyone's hands by then. Wilbur White Eagle had already started collecting money and writing down dates and times in that old tablet he'd dug out of a drawer, and if Leonard had worked up the courage to get the car off the ice, people would've made him take it back out. There's only so much disappointment people will live with, and Leonard bringing that car in would've been worse than government cheese not arriving on time.

Wilbur gained a lot of authority just by being record keeper. He carried that tablet everywhere, and people would stop and consult him and look at the betting. After a while Wilbur went beyond just showing the bets to commenting on them, offering his own insights, talking about *El Niño* and the *Farmer's Almanac*. Then someone asked him if he knew so much about the weather, what day would he bet on, and he came up with St. Patrick's Day and, once he said it, defended it so confidently people couldn't help but believe he was on to something.

Which is how half the Indians in Twisted Tree came to celebrate St. Patrick's Day sitting on the shore of Lostman's Lake waiting for Leonard's car to fall through the ice. I'd kind of made up with Leonard, since without his car he needed someone to take him places, but it wasn't a real made up, just him needing and me giving. I was allowed to sit around the fire long's I didn't hog a spot and didn't say nothing about it being a good thing the car was finally going to be got rid of.

But then I made the mistake of not believing Wilbur's prediction. Every time he looked at his watch and then at the next bettor who'd lost twenty bucks, I couldn't help but make a comment about how cold it was, which didn't make the person who'd just lost any happier, and it got so people started thinking I was hexing the weather and keeping it cold, even though that made no more sense than a Chinook wind reaching way out here from the Black Hills. I didn't mind rubbing it in, though, that people were guessing wrong, since most of them had sided with Leonard about that Continental.

Wilbur never lost his confidence, though, even when the sun went down and the fire was the only light, reaching out to the various faces around it, and sometimes reflecting off some part of the lake out there, like the ice was burning underneath. He just kept repeating, every time someone gave him a chance: You'll see. A big wind gonna come up. Warm one.

People stayed, based on nothing but that. I never knew Wilbur had them kind of leadership qualities. Right next to the fire we couldn't see the car, so people would stand away from it in twos and threes and watch it, a dark spot sitting out there alone in the middle of all that white, and then they'd come back to the fire to warm up and other people would take their places. And people talked of Red Medicine Creek, and some of the elders told stories about what it was like before it was a lake, and kids fell asleep in their mothers' or fathers' arms, and some people speculated that Leonard's car wouldn't be the first one at the bottom of Lostman's Lake, and Ted Kills Many, who'd come in from his place way out of town and was sitting talking with Norman Walks Alone, neither of them drinking beer, just smiled, and Norman allowed how he'd heard those stories, too, and that was the thing with stories, you never quite knew what to make of them, but you had to make something of them anyway.

Then about midnight the wind started blowing warm. Wilbur sat staring at his tablet and after a while he said real quiet, like he was reading it off the page, Is that a warm wind blowin? Or is it just blowin across the fire at me?

I was sitting across the fire from him, and anyone could've answered, but I knew. I could be proud or I could laugh at myself, and Wilbur was letting me decide.

Must be you, Wilbur, I said. I shivered and pulled my coat

tighter. Feels to me like it's getting colder all the time. Wouldn't surprise me if it started a blizzard up.

I held my hands toward the fire and rubbed them like they were freezing, and people chuckled, and a way opened for me to be right with people again, even if I'd never actually been wrong. I kept it up — the warmer it got and the harder the wind blew, the more I bundled up and asked for more wood on the fire. I started borrowing people's clothes they were taking off, so by early morning when the sun was coming up and the temperature had probably got to the fifties and people had moved back from the fire, I was sitting right next to it, adding wood and shivering and stomping my feet and wearing three stocking caps and two sweatshirts over my coat and three pairs of gloves and two blankets, and complaining how I was freezing to death, and little kids were piling more clothes on me. Wilbur was smiling and quiet. So I ended up playing *heyoka* to everyone that night, and it was a good thing, even if I'm not a real *heyoka*. When Leonard took off his coat and gave it to me and I chattered my teeth and thanked him, we were finally OK again, and even Bonnie smiled when she saw it.

The funny thing is, no one saw the car go down. We watched all night, and it was still there when the sky turned orange and the lake ice with it, glowing like the ice was a muted sun flat on the ground. Since I was tending the fire, I put on water to boil for coffee, and we were all so tired we were punch-drunk, just glad to have people around, and laughing at anything. When the sun came over the hill east of the lake, I added another stocking cap and told Wilbur if he got any worse at predicting the weather he could get a job on TV, and he played along, said, Uh-huh, that car might never go down, and Jake Red Heart said, It's gone.

Then he said it louder: It's gone. When'd it go?

We all looked then, and maybe it was because we were so tired, or maybe it was that car'd been on the lake so long we'd started thinking it was a natural thing. Whatever — when we looked and it wasn't there, for a couple seconds none of us quite knew where we were. It was like the lake was a different lake and we were someplace else. We stared at it, then stared at each other, and asked each other if anyone'd seen it go. No one had, and there'd been no sound, but all that was out where the car'd been was a jagged hole, and sun on the tips of the waves the new wind was making there.

And Wilbur forgot to look at his watch. Careful as he'd been all along to check it, when the actual time came, he forgot. By the time he remembered, no one was sure when the car'd last been seen. Wilbur couldn't tell whether it was closer to the last name he'd crossed off or the first name not crossed off — so they split the pot, each winner getting a quarter of it, and Leonard getting half for providing the car. Then the three of them offered to host next year's party together, so a tradition got started, though I still don't believe in Wilbur's forecasting abilities enough to think it's likely that the party and the car's disappearance are going to be the same again. Finding a junk heap on the rez won't be a problem, though after Leonard's stories about that ice cracking, we might have to find a Norwegian to drive the car onto the lake for us, maybe give him a free chance to bet in exchange, and invite him and his family and friends to the party. Of course, if the EPA ever finds out we're sinking cars in a lake that's supposed to be a creek, we'll have to switch to big stones or something, and just tell each other they're cars.

Me and Bonnie and Leonard went over to Myrna's after it all broke up. Leonard and I didn't say anything to each other, we didn't have to, we knew we were OK again, and Myrna made breakfast for us, and more coffee, and we reviewed the whole night, and Myrna's four TVs sat there shut down, and after a while we got silent, too, and I figured Myrna was thinking of David walking toward an object on a road that everyone else has run away from. No TV will tell you anything about that.

I thought of that car again, a little light down there, fish swimming into the window Leonard left open, lying down along the brake pedal and the accelerator, looking up through the windshield like they got their own fishbowl they can look at the world out of and then swim out again if they want. Everything all quiet. Maybe that car finally got clean of its awfulness. Or maybe not. Maybe something like what happened in that car's so bad you drown yourself trying to get clean of it, and you still ain't clean.

I think I need to sleep, Leonard said.

I looked up, and there we were in Myrna's living room, and just the fact of Leonard mentioning sleep made me suddenly so tired the room was swimming, and Myrna and Leonard wavering and floaty. We all stood up. I was feeling weightless and heavy at the same time. I kind of paddled toward the door, following Leonard out, but just before I got there Leonard stopped and walked over and hugged Myrna. Sometimes Leonard just plain does the right thing, and there's nothing to do but follow his example.

Acknowledgments

I wish to thank the following people for their generosity. Without any single one of them, this book would be less than it is.

Vince King and Amy Fuqua read, with an astonishing attentiveness, every draft I put before them. The whole first chapter stems from their advice, and their insights are so numerous and so woven into the book that I cannot isolate or distinguish them.

Wendy Mendoza shaped and inspired parts of this novel before it realized it was a novel.

Lia Purpura suggested memorials and chaos theory and questioned chapters no one else did. Her advice sharpened the language, deepened the ending, and clarified the structure. She also said, "Salt."

Judith Kitchen's rock-solid insights into character, relationships, and architecture, into what really mattered in the story and why, anchored and aligned me through two years of work. Her enthusiasm for the novel allowed me to believe in it. And she laughed at the right, dark things.

Bill Kamowski spent an afternoon on a mountainside with me

discussing this book. His exploration of possibilities at a critical time allowed me to restructure and continue.

Al Masarik encouraged me in the earliest stages of the novel. His appreciation for the third chapter, in particular, kept me writing.

Deaver Traywick said, "I want to hear more from the killer."

Ryan Bush said, "Maybe Hayley Jo comes into the pawnshop."

Karl Lehman said, "Audrey's the reader. That putting the binoculars down."

Christine Cremean talked with me about motels and bartending, and trauma, and the spiritual components of anorexia.

Dave Cremean said, "What about the dinosaur at Frontier Village?"

Elea Carey said, "I don't think Stanley and Laura should meet in a restaurant."

Julie Case recognized the fishing pole.

Peggy Schumacher believed in the whole.

Ahrar Ahmad, Tim Steckline, and Roger Miller helped me understand machine guns and their history.

Jace DeCory helped me with Lakota names.

My copyeditor, Barbara Wood, caught numerous mistakes, and even noticed the colors of characters' eyes. Lisa Glover kept it all straight.

Sam Hurst invited me and an entire class I was teaching to his buffalo ranch, and spent an afternoon with us. Dan O'Brien's writing also contributed to my understanding of buffalo.

Black Hills State University supported me, and the Faculty Research Committee provided travel funds for research.

Noah Lukeman's agenting skills and understanding of both literature and publishing are indispensable to me. He represented the book with his usual verve and passion, understood its value, and made others believe in it — and helped me believe in it myself.

Jenna Johnson insisted, insisted, *insisted* that the book could be more, and she wouldn't let up until it was. She had a vision of the book that opened it up creatively for me. I don't know what more a writer could ask for in an editor.

My family, Zindie and Derek and Lauren and Jordan, supported and believed, and anchored and allowed and made possible.